INCEF

"Brilliantly plotted original story, б··ғ ғ – ᴜ ᴊ
combining the historical with the futuristic. It's a real edge-of-the-seat
read, genuinely hard to put down." – Sue Cook

CARINA

"This is a fabulous thriller that cracks along at a great pace and just
doesn't let up from start to finish." – Discovering Diamonds Reviews

PERFIDITAS

"Alison Morton has built a fascinating, exotic world! Carina's a bright,
sassy detective with a winning dry sense of humour. The plot is pretty
snappy too!" – Simon Scarrow

SUCCESSIO

"I thoroughly enjoyed this classy thriller, the third in Morton's epic
series set in Roma Nova." – Caroline Sanderson in The Bookseller

AURELIA

"AURELIA explores a 1960s that is at once familiar and utterly
different – a brilliant page turner that will keep you gripped from first
page to last. Highly recommended." – Russell Whitfield

INSURRECTIO

"INSURRECTIO – a taut, fast-paced thriller. I enjoyed it enormously.
Rome, guns and rebellion. Darkly gripping stuff." – Conn Iggulden

RETALIO

"RETALIO is a terrific concept engendering passion, love and loyalty. I
actually cheered aloud." – J J Marsh

ROMA NOVA EXTRA

"One of the reasons I am enthralled with the Roma Nova series is the
concept of the whole thing." – Helen Hollick, Vine Voice

THE ROMA NOVA THRILLERS
The Carina Mitela adventures
INCEPTIO
CARINA (novella)
PERFIDITAS
SUCCESSIO

The Aurelia Mitela adventures
AURELIA
NEXUS (novella)
INSURRECTIO
RETALIO

ROMA NOVA EXTRA (Short stories)

———

ABOUT THE AUTHOR

A 'Roman nut' since age 11, Alison Morton has clambered over much of Roman Europe; she continues to be fascinated by that complex, powerful and value driven civilisation.

Armed with an MA in history, six years' military service and a love of thrillers, she explores via her Roma Nova novels the 'what if' idea of a modern Roman society run by strong women.

Alison lives in France with her husband, cultivates a Roman herb garden and drinks wine.

Find out more at alison-morton.com, follow her on Twitter @alison_morton and Facebook (AlisonMortonAuthor)

·INCEPTIO·

ALISON MORTON

To Lorraine,

Best wishes,

Alison Morton

PULCHERIA
PRESS

This is a work of fiction. Names, characters, places, incidents are either products of the author's imagination or used fictitiously. Any resemblance to actual events, locales or persons living or dead is entirely coincidental.

ISBN 9791097310134

DRAMATIS PERSONAE

New York
Karen Brown – New York advertising agency employee
Hayden Black – CEO of Bornes, Black, advertising agency
Conradus Tellus – 'Conrad', a messenger from Roma Nova
Sextilius Gavro – An inventor
Jeffrey Renschman – EUS covert security services 'fixer'
Lev Palicek – EUS citizen of East European extraction

Legation in Washington, Eastern United States
Claudia Cornelia – *Nuncia* (Ambassador)
Favonius Cotta – Chief of staff, a power-broker
Aelia Pasella – His daughter, a typical adolescent
Gaia Memmia – Protocol officer, nervous but nice
Sergia – Political officer, serious but sour
Grattius Duso – Cultural officer and teacher
Galla and Maro – PGSF Guards

Families and household
Aurelia Mitela – Karen's grandmother, head of Mitela family
Quintus Tellus – Conrad's uncle, Roma Nova imperial chancellor
Helena Mitela – Karen's fashionable cousin
Junia – Steward of Domus Mitelarum

Palace
Silvia Apulia – Imperatrix, ruler of Roma Nova

Department of Justice
Aemilia Fulvia – Minister of Justice
Inspector Cornelius Lurio – Special assistant to Fulvia
Sentius, Senior Justiciar – Organised Crime Division

Pulcheria Foundation
Apollodorus – Career criminal, head of the organisation
Flavius 'Flav' – Criminal strategist
Philippus – Their armourer
Justus – Informer and intelligence gatherer
Hermina – Administrator and organiser of people
Pollius – Doctor
Dolcius – Technical wizard

Military – Praetorian Guard Special Forces (PGSF)
Lucius Punellus – Adjutant, Conrad's comrade-in-arms
Daniel Stern – Lieutenant, on secondment
Julia Sella – Training major
Robbia – Lieutenant
Paula Servla – Sergeant
Somna – Captain, Interrogation Service (IS)
Murria – Lieutenant, Interrogation Service (IS)
Livius and Atria – Other 'Victis' team members

Other
Felix – A leader, training bootcamp
Dania – A friendly bar owner
Martina – *Goldlights* club manager

PART I

DEPARTURE

1

The boy lay in the dirt in the centre of New York's Kew Park, blood flowing out of both his nostrils, his fine blond hair thrown out in little strands around his head. I stared at my own hand, still bunched, pain rushing to gather at the reddening knuckles. I hadn't knocked anybody down since junior high, when Albie Jolak had tried to put his hand up my sobbing cousin's skirt. I started to tremble. But not with fear – I was so angry.

One of the boy's friends inched forward with a square of white cloth. He dabbed it over the fallen boy's face, missing most of the blood. Only preppy boys carried white handkerchiefs. Aged around eighteen, nineteen, all three wore blazers and grey pants, but their eyes were bright, boiling with light, cheeks flushed. And their movements were a little too fluid. They were high. I dropped my left hand to grab my radio and called it in. Passive now, the second boy knelt by the one I'd knocked down. The third one sat on the grass and grinned like an idiot while we waited. If they attacked me again, I had my spray.

Keeping my eyes fixed on them, I circled around to the slumped figure lying a few steps away on the grass. Their victim. I laid two fingers on his neck and thankfully found a pulse. After a glance back at his tormentors I bent my face sideways and felt his breath on my cheek. He groaned and his body tensed as he tried to move. A battered brown felt hat lay upside down by the side of his head of long silver and black hair stiff like wire. He opened his eyes. Dull with sweat and grime, the red-brown skin stretched over high cheekbones showed he had to be an Indigenous. Well, damn. What was he doing this far east, away from the protected territories?

Path gravel crunched as Steff appeared through the cherry blossom cloud, driving his keeper's buggy with Tubs as shotgun.

'Karen?'

'One with a bloody nose, and all three for banning. Tell Chip I'll do the report as soon as I finish here.'

They herded the three delinquents onto the buggy. Before they left, I helped myself to dressings and swabs from the emergency kit in the buggy trunk. I had to see to their victim. He sat up and put his hand to his head. He shrank back, his eyes full of fear. when he saw me. Maybe it was my green uniform, with its park logo and 'Autonomous City of New York' stamped on the shoulder.

My hand started to throb, but I managed to unscrew the top of my water bottle and gave it to him.

'C'mon, old guy, drink this.'

He lifted his face, grabbed the bottle and drank it in one go. His Adam's apple bounced above a grimy line on his neck around the level of his disintegrating shirt collar. And he stank. But, right now, he needed my swabs and Band-Aids. Under a diagonal cut on his forehead, a bruise was blooming around his eye to match the one on his jaw. His hand was grazed, with bubbles of blood starting to clot. I cleaned his wounds, speaking calming words to him as I bandaged him up.

'Okay, let's get you to the nearest hospital,' I said, but, as I lifted my radio again, he seized my wrist.

'No,' he said.

'It's okay, there's a free one, the other side of the park in Kew Road West.' Which was just as well, as he plainly couldn't pay private.

'No. Thank you. I'm well. I can go now.'

The anxious look in his dark eyes swung between my face and the safety of the tall trees. I'd have to call in for the Indigenous New York Bureau number. As I spoke to Chip, I looked over the lake at the old wood boathouse on the far side. Beyond the trees behind it, the windows in the red-brick Dutch highhouses along Verhulst Street threw the full sun back. When I turned around at the end of my call, the old man had disappeared.

'You did okay, Karen,' Chip said later in his office. 'Little shits. They've been processed and taken to the south gate. I checked with the Indigenous Bureau for reported wanderers, but they had none listed.' He grinned at me. 'Jeez, the woman there was so prickly and made me feel like Butcher Sherman.'

Every kid knew from school the Indigenous had been more or less protected until the British finally left in 1867, but that, almost as the door shut, a rogue officer in the new American army ordered the massacre of Sioux and Cheyenne on an industrial scale. A hundred and fifty years on, the Indigenous Nations Council in the Western Territories still reacted like it was yesterday. I was more than pleased I hadn't had to make that call.

I filed my report among the pile of paper in Chip's in-basket and thought nothing more of it until, after a tedious week shut in my office at my regular job, I was back on duty in the park the next weekend.

That Saturday morning, I changed into my green pants and tee in the locker room and pinned on my team leader badge. The May sunshine would bring out people in droves. I picked up my volunteer's folder from the wall rack. Hopefully, I was back on meet-and-greet supervising, instead of patrol. I could walk all day in the fresh air, greeting visitors, giving directions, answering park-related questions, laughing with the sassy kids, and helping the lost and crying ones find their parents. I knew every corner of the park from north to south, the history back to Vaux and Olmstead, who'd founded it with a huge grant from the Royal Kew in England.

I hummed a little tune and anticipated the sun on my skin. But all there was inside the folder was a note to report to the park director. What was that about? I'd met him twice before when I'd been awarded commendations, but never seen him around the park itself. Not weekends.

The sour expression on his face told me I wasn't here for an award. Chip stood with his back tight into the far corner, no sign of his usual jokey grin. I was not invited to sit on the green-padded chair this side of the director's desk.

'Miss Brown.' The director frowned at the sheet of paper in his hand. He looked up. 'Show me your right hand.' He spoke in a hard, closed tone.

He took hold of my hand and twisted it over, not caring that I winced. He glanced at the purple and yellow skin around my knuckles, grunted and let go.

'You are dismissed from the Conservancy Corps, with immediate effect. Hand your uniform, ID and any other park property to your supervisor and leave within the next thirty minutes. You have become an embarrassment to the Autonomous City of New York. We cannot stop you as a member of the public entering the park, but you will be watched. That is all.'

I stared back at him and grasped the back of the chair.

'But why are you kicking me out? What have I done?'

'Assaulting a respectable member of the public as he and his friends were quietly enjoying a walk is completely unacceptable. Even more so when drunk.'

'Drunk? How dare you!' I was hot as hell with fury. 'They were all high as kites and attacking a defenceless old Indigenous.' I took some deep breaths. 'I did what the training said. I remonstrated with them. I attempted to mediate. I placed myself between them and their victim. It's all in my report.' I threw an urgent look over at Chip, desperate for his support. He looked away.

'Have you quite finished?' The director looked at his watch.

'No, I haven't! The lead one took a swing at me. I ducked. He went for me again, so I hit him on the nose. You know I'm within my rights to defend myself.' But this was the first time I'd ever had to do it all the years I'd volunteered here. Unlike others, both volunteer and regular, I'd chosen not to carry a nightstick when I was assigned patrol.

'This interview is finished.' He nodded to Chip who stepped forward, took me by the arm and ushered me out with a murmured, 'C'mon, Karen.'

'What the hell happened there? How can he do that? And I wasn't drunk. Ask Steff and Tubs. It was eleven in the morning, for

Chrissakes!' I threw my folder on his desk. 'If it wasn't so stupid, I'd kill myself laughing.'

Chip shifted his weight from one foot to the other, no grin, his easy fidgeting gone. 'You bloodied the nose of External Affairs Secretary Hartenwyck's son. He's fuming. And Mrs Hartenwyck's not only on the board of trustees, she's a major patron of the park.'

I sucked my breath in. Hartenwyck, the second most powerful person in the country. My heart pounded with fear. I closed my eyes and shook my head. He was from one of the old Dutch families, a privileged class who still called the shots even two hundred years after their last governor had sailed out of the harbour in 1813. Even though the British had stepped up from number two position and taken everything over for the next fifty years, the 'Dutch mafia' still ran everything today. And I had a British name. I didn't have a chance.

'Then they should make sure Junior doesn't take drugs,' I said. 'Or beat up old Indigenous in a public place. The Indigenous Nations Council would wipe the floor with him.'

'But you can't produce the old man to testify.'

'Steff and Tubs saw him.'

'They've been told to shut their mouths if they want to keep their jobs.' He looked at me, almost pleading. 'They've both got families, Karen.'

I walked back and forth in front of his desk, waving my arms around, but I sensed it was no use. The decision had been made and Chip was stuck with executing it.

'So, my four years' volunteer service and two commendations aren't worth jack-shit?'

He fixed his gaze on the scuffed door panel directly over my shoulder. 'I'm so sorry.'

Heat prickled in my eyes, but I was not going to cry. I wouldn't give him the satisfaction. I walked out, shut the heavy oak door with supreme control, changed back into my jeans and tee in the locker room and left the staff building, my head up. I threw the green park uniform and ID in a public trashcan. Childish, but satisfying.

2

Back at my apartment, I made a cup of tea and sat at the tiny table by the window for three hours. A whole slice of my life had been cut out in a few minutes by some rich-kid druggie. I'd loved the openness of the park, the stunning trees, kids playing naturally, the illusion of being in the country. Not the Nebraska of my teens, but New Hampshire with Dad before he died. Those weekends when we hiked and camped, surrounded by the fresh, warm air, the two of us alone. Then the day came when he lay in the hospital bed, skinny thin with his face shrunken like an old man, struggling to whisper my name. As I left the hospital that evening, when he'd fallen into his last sleep, it had rained and the air was sullen. I felt my throat tighten. The pain of losing him was as raw today as it had been all those years ago. I bit my fingernails, gulped, dropped my head in my hands and burst into sobs.

It had to be a mistake. I swallowed my pride, gathered up my grit, like Dad used to say, and spent most of Sunday drafting a respectful mail to the director asking to be reconsidered.

I blinked when a reply hit my inbox within forty minutes.

From the desk of the Director

Madam,

In reference to your recent communication, the Director finds the contents unacceptable and untrue. All allegations or claims against the Constituency of New York and all permissions and privileges are hereby rejected. Your record of attendance has been deleted.

The consequences of harassing municipal and public employees are severe and constitute a Class E Non-Violent Felony (CNY Penal Code S180).

You are advised that, on advice from the Department of Internal Security, your name has been placed on a national security watch list because of your antisocial behaviour and foreign parentage.

I stared at the screen. I felt like I'd been struck in the face. This couldn't be happening. I wasn't a terrorist or criminal. Sure, my mother had been born abroad in Europe, but she'd been dead for twenty-one years. My father was born in England but had been a naturalised American for nearly two-thirds of his life, even decorated for war service in North Africa. That kid being pissed at me couldn't have gone this far, could it?

I started shaking.

God. What else could these people do to me?

The next morning, at my regular job, I drooped over my desk and shuffled papers in folders, but I didn't know what I was doing. I worked Monday to Friday at Bornes & Black, a Connaught Avenue advertising agency handling niche inventor accounts. Pretty mundane in the two years I'd been here, but it nearly paid the bills and gave me – no – *had* given me precious free weekends in the park.

Damn.

'Hey, Karen.' A paper ball landed on the back of my right hand. I looked up. Across from me, Amanda, the other assistant account executive in our team, grinned and tipped her chin up at me.

'What's up? Eat a lemon, or did you get a tax bill?'

'No, nothing.'

She rolled her large brown eyes, but before she could open her mouth to start an interrogation, the boss's assistant materialised in front of me. This god-like being had never before looked at me, let alone smiled at me. Maybe calling it a smile was stretching it. I was to report to the boss 'at my earliest convenience' to talk about a special project. The immaculate figure turned about in a swirl of dark blue, the tail of a green and yellow silk scarf dripping down her curved, swaying back.

Amanda and I both stared.

I pushed my hair behind my ears, brushed the front of my skirt to ease the creases out, grabbed my notebook and scuttled after her. What could the boss want from me? I was nobody. With no college degree, I had watched with second-hand pleasure, but a twinge of envy, as others overtook me. But it hadn't seemed so important; I had lived for the park. Maybe I needed to change that now.

I stumbled out of the boss's office an hour later, head whirling. After nearly two years, they'd pulled me out of the herd and given me my chance. I was to make the pitch presentation to new, and important, foreign clients. Back at my desk, I stared at my notes, terrified at the responsibility, but thrilled to be chosen.

I slogged away researching, drafting and reworking my material over the following four days. I practised in front of the mirror to get it word-perfect. I worked on it over the weekend; I had nothing else to do.

Now the day of the meeting had arrived. I glanced again at my watch, checked my face again, happy that my hair was still in the elegant chignon I had persuaded it into this morning. I knew my new blue linen suit was right – the vendor in Nicholson's had said so.

Unable to bear waiting any longer, I got up from my desk. Amanda squeezed my hand and said, 'Go, girl.'

I had made the long walk into the conference room but my hands wouldn't stop trying to rearrange the neat stack of paper in front of me. I gulped some water to relieve my parched throat. Hayden, the boss, glanced over at me, one eyebrow raised. He was English. Proper English, not one of the 1860s left-behinds. His old-fashioned sports jacket and pants made him look like a crusty old guy from a black and white movie, but he gave me a human-enough smile.

The new clients came from Roma Nova, where my mother had been born. I couldn't remember too much from the Saturday class my dad had insisted on, so I was curious about what they'd be like. Checking off 'Latin (elementary)' in the language ability section on my application had seemed so irrelevant two years ago. Now it was my springboard.

A buzz on the intercom, and the door of the glass-walled conference room opened. Hayden and I rose to meet them. A short, brown-haired man walked past Hayden and held his thin hand out to me. Hayden nodded at me, nursing a half-smile, and made the introductions. This was our inventor.

'*Salve*, Sextilius Gavro,' which was about as much Latin as I could muster at that precise moment.

'My interpreter, Conradus Tellus,' he said in a sing-song tone.

His colleague was more than striking – blond hair long enough to slick back behind his ears. And tall. Several inches taller than me, even. Above a smiling mouth and a straight nose marred by a scar, his eyes were tilted slightly upwards, red-brown near the pupil, green at the edges. He fixed his gaze on me like he was measuring me up, assessing me. I refused to break, but felt warmth creeping up my neck into my face as he widened his smile. A little flustered, I eventually looked down at his outstretched hand but hesitated. I gave myself a mental shake, threw myself into businesswoman mode and stretched out my own hand to meet his.

Over the next two hours, the interpreter's gaze tracked me as I moved to the screen on the back wall and around the table, giving out mock-ups and sales projections. He asked me to pause now and again so he could interpret, but when he had finished each time, he flashed me a half-smile. Sextilius Gavro scribbled notes ceaselessly, his fingers twitching with nervous energy. He kept looking up from his papers and fixing me with a stare. Although I described market segmentation, platforms and the importance of usability in full detail, they still asked so many questions. I was a prisoner under interrogation.

I only realised hours had passed when my stomach bubbled; it was running on empty. I stopped talking. I had nothing else to say.

After they'd left, I sank back into my seat and shut my eyes for a few moments. My pulse was still pushing adrenalin around my body.

'Your research was excellent, Karen,' Hayden said, his face serious. 'More importantly, the Roma Novans were impressed by your ideas.'

I flushed. 'I was just concentrating on getting my pitch right.'

I sipped my dose of coffee. I glanced over at the papers strewn over the large, gleaming table like so much ticker tape left after a parade. That was all it came down to after days of solid work.

I rode along more familiar ground that afternoon, briefing the art director and marketing team. I needed to have the draft campaign plan ready for approval for the next client encounter in two weeks, so I settled down and attacked my keyboard.

A while later, my stomach growled. It would be home-time soon. Amanda had gone a while ago. I glanced at the clock. How could it be past seven? I was alone in the open-plan office – except for the IT engineer in the corner, and he was a geek. I had gotten lost in my so-called boring job. I smiled and admitted it felt good.

I treated myself to a gnocchi marinara and a glass of red at Frankie's on my way home. I didn't run into anybody I knew. I didn't really expect to: New York was a city of isolated strangers, smiling outwardly but all intent on their individual universes. I was savouring the fruit-laden tang of the wine when the interpreter invaded my head. Sure, his English was excellent, British-sounding, but just a little too perfect. He wasn't an interpreter; that was way too ordinary. Self-assured, nonchalant even, he had watched everything and missed nothing.

Next morning, I was immersed in developing the implementation outline when the harsh ring from my desk phone broke through. I grabbed the handset and struggled with untwisting the cord.

'I hope you don't mind me calling you at work, but I wondered if you'd like to meet for a drink or some dinner on Saturday.'

The interpreter.

'I'm sorry, but I don't date clients on principle.'

'I didn't mean a date; simply as colleagues.'

I heard an undertone of laughter in his voice.

'No, I don't think so,' I said.

'Out of your comfort zone?'

I gasped. What was that supposed to mean?

'Sorry,' he said before I could slam the handset down. 'That was rude of me. But will you still come?'

I hadn't been asked out to dinner in six months. Why the hell not?

3

Renschman was more used to the dull thud of a silencer than the ping announcing a new message. Yawning, he detached his hand from under his chin, stretched out and tapped the screen to open the message. From External Affairs. He began skimming the words of the cover sheet, his eyes half-closed with boredom.

Opening the attachment, he saw the name 'Karen Brown, father William Brown' on the first page. He jerked his head forward, breathing suspended. He read the message and the file through again. Twice. He didn't notice his other hand snap his pen, the red ink spreading over the desk.

Anger flushed through him at the memory of his last meeting with William Brown. The man was gone, but his daughter would do.

He reached for his frameless glasses. The father's blond smugness was as Renschman remembered, but the mother's immigration photo showed red-brown hair and a soft face, with light eyes like a frightened rabbit.

His task was to watch the girl and report back; she was flagged up as a Category 3 risk. What the hell had she done? She was a weekend volunteer park attendant. But it came direct from Hartenwyck's office. The stills showed her coming out of the advertising agency where she worked during the week: a tall strawberry blonde, chin jutting out, her body caught in a long stride.

She must have pissed somebody off really badly. He started

scrolling through his resource file, selecting the four grunts he'd need to cover her.

But they had to know her connections, didn't they? He smiled. If they hadn't realised who she was, he'd be happy to spell it out for them.

Very happy.

4

That Saturday evening, I'd hesitated as I put my hand into the closet to pull out my usual pants and silk shirt. Damn it. I'd wear the new dress I'd been saving for the park awards ceremony next month.

By seven, I'd been date-perfect for an hour. Not that this was a date. On the fourth look in the bathroom mirror, I told myself to stop checking. There was no room to pace about my apartment; I was lucky to have a two-window living room. I perched on my love seat, wriggling my toes to ease the stiffness of my new shoes and flicking through a magazine to pass the time.

A story about a celebrity who'd married a European but come back home, divorced, a year later caught my attention: A pouting face on a perfect body posing on a white leather couch. She complained that if she'd known how different and foreign it was in Prussia, she would never have left the Eastern United States of America. What had she expected? I threw the magazine on the table.

But did I know any more about Roma Nova? Dad made sure I knew where it was – squashed in between Italy and New Austria – but that was about it. Maybe I'd find out more tonight. A beep from my calendar clock sounded. Crap! It was twenty-five after seven. I grabbed my coat and purse, and ran for the elevator.

Through the lobby door, I could see Conradus Tellus leaning against the cab, arms crossed, one knee bent with his foot behind his other leg, toe on the sidewalk. Totally relaxed, but he scanned the street like he was a cop. He was wearing a light blue-grey casual suit and open-neck blue shirt. A deep breath to steady myself; then I stepped out of my building. He held the cab door open for me. His smile should have been listed as forbidden under the Vienna Conventions. But it didn't spread up his face into his eyes.

The taxi stopped outside a double-fronted restaurant with a dark green awning curving over like a protective hood. Soft yellow lights shone through tinted glass. Inside, it was subdued, intimate and rich. Light music played and couples danced. I'd never been in such a place before.

He helped me off with my coat, his hand lightly brushing my shoulder as he did so. He waved the server back, held my chair and made sure I was seated comfortably before sitting down opposite me. The hard-eyed observer at the client meeting had been replaced by a polite socialite out of a 1950s film.

'So how long are you in New York, Conradus?' I asked.

'Please call me Conrad, if it's easier.' He smiled almost to himself. 'It depends. Now that Sextilius has got his project started, he'll need a few days to see a lawyer about patents and permits then he'll want to go home. He'll send one of the English-speaking legation commercial people along to your next meeting and only come back when the prototypes have been developed in two to three months' time.'

'Oh.'

His long fingers, tapering from square knuckles, played with a heavy gold signet ring on his right hand. 'I might stay on and look around a bit now I'm here. I've never been to New York before and I've got some leave to use up.'

I grinned at him. 'If you have about a year and a half, you might see around a tenth of what's on offer.'

'Could you give me a few pointers?'

'If you want to be a real tourist, you could take a trip around the harbour,' I said. 'You know, Fort Amsterdam, Hudson statue, Franklin Island. Or a comedy club or a show. Maybe Jonas Bronck's zoo or a walk around the old Dutch Quarter in Manhattan, or the Georgian lanes.' I didn't mention the park.

We ordered and I continued my tourist guide presentation as we ate. I felt mildly foolish as I chattered on, compelled to keep up a stream of conversation. I so wanted him to find me interesting. He seemed content to watch and listen. After the waiter had cleared the dessert dishes, I caught my breath and looked away as I lifted my glass to finish my wine. I glanced back and saw his irises contract, light brown fighting it out with green as the pupils expanded. Tiny tight lines appeared at the far edges of his lips. What was he thinking?

In an abrupt switch, he smiled at me and stretched out his hand. 'Dance?'

He held me firmly, but didn't attempt to pull me in. He talked lightly, making semi-cynical, jokey remarks. Glancing over his shoulder at the room and the other guests in between his banter, I saw a man with wavy black hair sitting at the bar, studying us. Not in that half-amused, half-superior way other diners do as part of their evening's entertainment, but purposefully. It was creepy the way he stared at us as we moved around the floor.

The music stopped moments later, and Conrad led me back to my seat. As the waiter brought new drinks over, I noticed the man at the bar had disappeared, his full glass abandoned on the counter. A few minutes later, I looked over and somebody else was sitting there, drinking out of the same twisted-stem glass. That was beyond odd, like they'd changed shifts.

I glanced at my wristwatch. I thought I'd been discreet, but Conrad gave me a half-smile. He called for the check and we made our way out onto the sidewalk to find a cab. At my building, Conrad made sure I was safely inside. He raised my hand to his lips, kissed the back and said goodnight. I was too surprised to say anything – it was such a foreign gesture, like in an old movie. I caught a smile on his face as he turned and left. From behind the glass entrance door, I watched until the rear lights of his cab merged into the pattern of the night.

5

Next morning, I went jogging in the park. I refused to stop going there on principle. They'd watched me at first but hadn't bothered in a while. Tubs waved to me once, but dropped his hand and hurried off like he'd remembered he shouldn't. But, this morning, two joggers I hadn't seen before in our Sunday morning group seemed to be playing tag with me. When one wasn't close behind me, the other was. When three others of my group split off to go up the hill rather than round it, I struggled after them. My legs were on empty, but I got there. And so did my two followers. I headed home, uncomfortable at being stalked.

Opening my apartment door and desperate for a cooling shower, I almost missed the card lying on the mat: Conrad had invited me to meet at South Street Seaport and take a harbour cruise with him that day. As I showered, I debated whether I should ignore the invitation; I had plenty of chores to do. But despite, or maybe because of, his detachment, he was an immensely attractive man. As common in my life as a blue moon.

It was sunny and warm, typical May weather, perfect for being outdoors. I waved as I spotted his figure by the pier. I gave him my hand, but he laughed, bent down and kissed my cheek.

Jesus.

As we sailed back past Hudson's Statue, enjoying the breeze and sunshine, his left arm settled against my right. His polo shirt sleeve revealed a muscled arm, covered in fine golden hair. I glanced sideways at him, but he carried on talking as casually as before.

After the boat docked at South Street, we grabbed some lunch nearby. We talked and walked. Sitting on a bench by the old Fort Amsterdam rampart, looking toward Upper Bay, we were still talking two hours later. His face warmed with enthusiasm for the mountains, grapes, olives, even the cold weather perfect for skiing, as he described his home in Roma Nova. He'd been raised on a small farm by his uncle after his mother died, but visited now and then with his cousin Sextilius who'd always made models and invented things, even as a kid. Sextilius's mother was a professor of control mechanics, and an old university friend as well as cousin of Conrad's mother, Constantia. A shadow crossed his face at her name, but I learned why he had a distinctly un-Latin name.

'My father was Austrian. He was on holiday in the south, met my mother halfway up a mountain. She invited him to stay with her. They'd been together for over three years when—' He stopped and looked down. He wouldn't say any more. But I guessed it also explained the blond hair.

As he listened in turn to my memories of growing up in New Hampshire with Dad, and the not so happy time living with his cousins later, it struck me he really *was* interested, asking me questions and drawing out detail from me. How often did any man pay attention like that? At the end of early dinner by the harbour, he brushed the back of my hand with his fingertips. My fingers fell away from the stem of the glass and he took my hand in his.

'I've enjoyed every minute of today,' he said, his hazel eyes warm at last.

I invited him back to my apartment.

Nothing happened. He drank his coffee and, as he went out of the apartment door, he kissed my cheek with a light touch. Maybe he was being a gentleman, or just plain clever.

I watched him from my window as he moved down the street, graceful as a big cat. As he passed the third building down, two men emerged from the doorway opposite. One in a black fleece hoodie and jeans set off after Conrad. The second made a call on his cell phone.

After he finished, he pocketed it, then swung his head upward to my apartment window. He locked his gaze on to my face.

I flicked the drape across to shield myself and took a step back from the window. Who were they? And why were they following Conrad? Was this what the email meant when they said I'd been put on a security watch list? Maybe I should call the cops. Or maybe they were the cops. I reached for the phone. When I turned back to look out of the window, the watcher had vanished.

6

I played the incident outside my apartment over and over in my head. Even my favourite songs blasting from my headphones as I got ready for bed couldn't stop the nagging. I should have made the call. What could I have said? It was too late.

Back at my desk the next morning, I made myself focus on putting Sextilius's campaign together. Bornes & Black was small but niche to the scientific sector, so provided the full service: strategic planning, creative development, production, media planning, media buying, sales promotion, direct selling, design and branding. I was loving planning the strategy side, like a general matching wits against the world. I only looked up at the ping from an email arriving or when Amanda plunked a coffee down on my desk.

After three days, I stopped watching for a flashing light on my answering machine when I got home. Over bagel, lox and cream cheese I'd brought in for us – partly to kill the guilt I felt toward Amanda for ignoring her and partly for comfort eating – Amanda told me to write it off; he wasn't going to show. She had four brothers and God knows how many male cousins, so I guessed she knew all there was to know about how men behaved. And was it as important as my job now?

Sunday evening, I was in my pyjamas in front of the TV and on the point of going to bed, when the door phone rang. I glanced at the clock on the display screen – only nine thirty.

'Yes?'

'It's Conrad. I want to explain.'

'Make an appointment,' I said and pressed the off button.

Inevitably, it rang again.

'What?'

'Give me ten minutes. Please.'

'Why?'

'It's about blood, survival and money. Mostly yours.'

That was original, at least. I hesitated for a few moments, caught between curiosity and peevishness. In the end, I pressed the release button. I grabbed my robe and pulled a comb through my hair.

'I didn't mean to interrupt you like this,' he said as I ushered him in, 'but I wanted to talk to you as soon as I could. I've been in Washington for a few days.'

'There's an invention called the telephone, you know.'

'Don't be angry. Please.' He came over to me, took both my hands in his and pulled me down onto the couch.

'There's something I must ask you. It's why I was in Washington. What do you know about your family? I mean, your mother's family.'

'What's that to you? Do you know them?'

'Bear with me. It's important.'

'No, you explain first.'

'I'm sorry,' he said. 'I don't mean to be rude, but I need to know.'

I looked at him, searching for clues in his face, but his expression was bland and, despite the eye colours seeming to shift, his gaze was steady but not cold. I shrugged. 'Mom came from Roma Nova, like you. My father told me they met when he was in Europe on business. She came here to the EUS, they married, she had me and then drove herself off a cliff when I was three.' I heard the bitterness in my voice. 'I never knew what made her leave like that, and Dad never discussed it.'

He pressed my hand as if to comfort me. After a few moments, he said, 'I can't answer that, but I can fill in some other gaps for you. Do you have any family documents or old photos?'

'Why?'

'Do you always challenge everything?'

'Yes, especially when I'm not told the reason.'

'I *will* tell you, but can you get the papers first?'

Why would I? He was a stranger. An exciting, beautiful one that I found deeply attractive. But he was a foreigner who looked like he was under surveillance. Maybe I needed to check with the cops or the FBI first. I hesitated. I could imagine how stupid it would sound to them – I'd file a complaint and he'd turn out to be an old family friend. Would they take any notice of me anyway? I was already on their security watch list.

The hell with it.

I decided to show him the photographs to start with. In my bedroom, I pulled out the box stashed on the top shelf of my closet: my parents' wedding; them with me as a toddler; my father alone; my foster parents, the Browns; high school friends. In the end, it was easier to hand him the whole box. He picked out the ones of my mother looking like any other American housewife and mom, and discarded the rest. I had to dig around in my file box for the certificates and passports. I kept them bundled on my lap, but showed him her old passport, the corner clipped off.

'Have you ever been in contact with any of your mother's relations?'

'I had a letter now and again from my mother's mother, but nothing since I came to New York. When he was alive, my father insisted that I wrote back. I remember going to see her once when I was a kid. After my father died, I went to live in Nebraska with his cousins. This grandmother kept inviting me for a visit, but they wouldn't let me go. It was too expensive, they said, and Uncle Brown didn't like foreigners.'

'What? There was plenty of money for that sort of expense. Were they that narrow-minded?'

'Hey! They gave me a home when my father passed on.' I defended them, instinctively, out of duty. I always had sufficient to eat and was adequately clothed. I hadn't been Cinderella, but I was firmly outside the core family circle. Maybe, despite all his efforts, they'd never forgiven my father his Englishness. Although the withdrawal by the British in the 1860s had been amicable on the surface, resentment endured, especially in the rural areas where they'd been big landowners, and still were.

I came back to the present with a jolt.

'What do you mean – "plenty of money"?'

'Your mother left you her personal portfolio, and your father's electronics business will be yours when you're twenty-five. You've got income from both held in trust.'

'You have to be kidding.'

'Haven't you had any of it?' His eyes widened in surprise. 'At all?'

'Since I've been in New York, Brown Industries has sent me three thousand dollars every quarter from New Hampshire. I try to save most of it, but I have to use some of it for my rent.'

'Your grandmother, Aurelia, set up a portfolio for her daughter when she went to live in America. Naturally, it came to you on her death. Your father and your grandmother formed a trust for you so you could be comfortable, go to college, do whatever you wanted.'

I heard the words. I saw his lips forming them. I ran them through my head again. I sat completely still, numbed. The only sound in the apartment was the refrigerator humming in the kitchen.

Uncle and Aunt Brown must have known about the money. I'd wept angry tears of frustration when Uncle Brown forbade to me have any thoughts of going to college. I knew Ivy League had been way out of my reach, but the state university should have been possible. How *could* they have done that to me?

'And just how do you know all this?' I had recovered speech, but couldn't keep the steel out of my voice.

'From your grandmother. Your father wanted you to grow up like any other American girl, but left instructions in his testament that you should be told everything at eighteen. That obviously didn't happen.' Conrad handed the photographs and passport back to me, his face grave. 'He probably never imagined these cousins would keep it from you.'

My fingers fretted and tumbled over each other as I squared the pile of photos so they would fit back in the pressed paper box.

I looked up at him. 'So what's your part in this?'

'I'm the messenger. I'd already promised to help Sextilius. I spent some time in England when I was younger, so my English is reasonably fluent.'

It was beyond fluent; he sounded like the real thing.

'Aurelia asked me to find you while I was here. You've changed job a few times, and Karen Brown isn't an uncommon name,' he continued. 'I tracked you down to Bornes & Black. But I didn't know it would be you handling Sextilius's account until we walked into your meeting room.'

His matter-of-fact voice and the hint of calculation in his eyes proved he'd only been pleasant and flirty so he could deliver his message. And I'd fallen for it. For months, years, I didn't meet anybody interesting, let alone compelling. When I did, he turned out to be a messenger boy from my foreign relations. And another thing; just how did he find out where I worked? It was too much of a coincidence that his inventor cousin came to Bornes & Black rather than another agency. And he was being followed by somebody with resources: cops, FBI, who knew?

I stood up and pulled the belt of my robe tight around me. 'Look, Conrad, I'm really tired and I have to get some sleep.'

'Did I say something wrong?'

'No…not really.' I stalled. 'It's getting late.' I couldn't look at him; I didn't want him to see my disappointment. 'You'll have to let me have the practical details for the bank.' I smiled and held my hand out in dismissal.

'Are you trying to get rid of me?'

I said nothing.

'Very well. Get some rest. I'll be in contact very soon.'

As I shut the door behind him, I was determined to make a few enquiries of my own.

7

Hand clamped on bag against purse snatchers, I wound my way through the mass of people hurrying to work next morning. I was still processing everything Conrad had said. If any of it was true, how could all that have been hidden from me for so long?

About a hundred yards before my station, I sensed something was wrong. Out on the edges of my consciousness, I knew somebody was watching me. Acting like James Bond, but feeling ten times more foolish, I stopped to look in a shop window, so I could glimpse back. Thankfully, it was full of shoes, so it was a reasonable thing to do. Up the street was the same man with the cell phone whose stare had pierced the glass of my window the previous Sunday.

When I looked again, he'd vanished; I didn't see him for the rest of my journey. At the office, I shut my mind, pushing it away. I settled down to my work, talking through a couple of points with Hayden. Now I had caught the attention of the boss, I was determined to stay in his sights.

After putting it off a few times, I eventually grasped the telephone and called the commercial section at the Roma Nova legation on the pretext of getting biographical details for Sextilius Gavro. When I slipped in some questions about Conrad, I knew I sounded ditzy, but he checked out as Gavro's interpreter. As I replaced the handset, it struck me that the commercial officer had stonewalled me, giving me nothing else about Conrad but that one fact.

I buckled down and produced outlines, plans and graphs, irritating a bored Amanda by grunting in reply to her needling. But, by late afternoon, I'd finished most of it and sat back, sipping a well-earned coffee. My browser was still open and I couldn't resist searching the Internet about Roma Nova; meeting Conrad had thrown some type of switch inside me.

The images showed mountains and forests, a lot like the Helvetian Confederation, and a big river, cute stone buildings with curled tile roofs, and old monuments. On one site, the writer conceded Roma Nova's high-tech and financial services economy gave them a standard of living exceeding most Western economies, but criticised them as 'hidden and discreet'. He didn't think much of them staying neutral during the Great War.

I leaned back in my chair. Who wouldn't have sat out that ten-year savagery if they could have? Although it ended in 1935, it had taken most countries until the sixties to recover. But the writer admitted that the rebellion and civil war twenty-three years ago in Roma Nova had torn the country apart. I counted that through in my head; that horror happened after my mom had come to the Eastern United States.

I scrolled down, fascinated, not sensing the time sneak up on me. Interpedia gave the usual historical stuff: the Western Roman Empire had fallen, and Roma Novans had retreated to cold, fortified villages in the mountains north of Italy. Protected by political truces and economic links with their Byzantine cousins, they had fought to recover the lower-lying parts of Roma Nova, holding against all comers, even after the Eastern Empire was overcome by the Ottomans. The key had been knowing more secrets, having more money and striking back hard when attacked. Now they sat on the precarious frontier between the eastern Reds and the free West.

I sat back and stared at the screen. Who were these tough people? Could I really be related to them?

As they traded their silver, financial acumen and knowledge across Europe and the rest of the world, they spread their philosophy of female leadership. I knew foreign countries like Louisiane and Québec had elected female presidents and, I thought, some European ones. Our own president was on her second term; now she was supporting her husband's campaign to get into the Presidential Mansion. Would it have been any different, then, without Roma Nova?

· · ·

A little before six, I stepped out of the elevator into the lobby and found Conrad waiting for me. Before I could stop him, he'd bent down and kissed my cheek casually, like a friend. He took my arm and pulled me out into the noise of Connaught Avenue. I looked both ways to gauge the traffic. I couldn't believe it but twenty yards to my left was the same man as this morning, seeming to get a paper. This was becoming creepy.

'You've spotted yours, have you?' Conrad said. 'I know it's very tempting, but please don't turn round again and look at him.'

In movies, the character who turned around when told not to instantly regretted it. But we weren't in a movie. Surely, they weren't spending that many tax dollars tailing me? We found a booth in a bar peopled by suits of both sexes. It was noisy but clean, and the food smelled good.

'Okay, explain, please. Just what the hell is going on?'

'Irritating, aren't they? Ignore them.'

'I can't ignore being stalked. There's a law against it.'

'Yes, but what if it's the law that's stalking you?' He fixed me with those strange copper-green eyes. 'It's me they're targeting. They think I'm up to something. Now I've contacted you, they're sure I am.'

My head whirled, and not with the din. I raised an eyebrow and looked straight at Conrad, challenging him to come up with something logical.

'I work for the Roma Nova government,' he said, his face bare of any emotion. 'But I'm on leave, and my visit is for private reasons: to help Sextilius and to find you. I have a diplomatic passport – it makes things easier.' He flicked some crumbs off the table. 'Unfortunately, the EUS administration is a bit paranoid about Roma Nova. They don't understand who and what we are. They're frightened of our technology, but they can't buy us and we don't toe their line. The politicos on both sides smile at each other but conceal their bared teeth behind closed lips.' He shrugged. 'That's what my uncle says, anyway.'

The waitress approached. Conrad touched my hand and narrowed his eyes. After getting some beers, I ordered a salad and, like a tourist, he went for the cardiac-arrest-inducing house special burger and fries. He saw my look of disapproval and laughed.

Half-slouching in his seat and relaxed as if we were discussing the latest gossip, he explained. 'Your father's company is of immense strategic importance to the EUS. A lot of their specialist technology is designed and manufactured at Brown Industries. All the time it's owned by a loyal American, even a naturalised one like your father, they only keep a watching brief. But the smallest whiff of "foreign influence" would set alarms ringing. I'd refuse the bet that didn't say you were in the diary for a security interview in the next few weeks.'

The normal clinking of crockery and cutlery, the swish of drinks filling glasses, and the laughter and talking in the busy bar acted like a reality barrier. Listening to Conrad, I wondered if I'd crossed into a parallel dimension. This was getting worse by the day. I was too embarrassed to tell him I was already under scrutiny.

'Why...why would I be interviewed?'

'Your twenty-fifth birthday is in a few weeks' time. You'll get complete control of BI on that day. They'll want to press on you the necessity of keeping the company one hundred per cent American. Basically, they're going to put the frighteners on you.' His smile was so cynical, I was repelled.

Fortunately, the waitress brought our food at that point.

'They can't do that!' I hissed at him. He might come from some tinpot little country, but this was the land of the free. I was a good American; Uncle Brown had insisted we took part in every national event, Franklin Day, Memorial Day, everything.

'Look, I don't know about Roma Nova but that type of thing doesn't happen here. Every citizen is free to do as they please, as long as it's not illegal. That includes businesses. The government can't force them into anything.'

Then I realised what I'd said. God, it was ironic. When I floored Junior Hartenwyck, I'd become a victim of that same government. But I wasn't going to back down now, not in front of a foreigner and certainly not in front of Conrad.

'Okay, Karen, have it your way.' He looked at me with a long stare, almost like a teacher working out how to explain a complex point to an ignorant child. I found it unnerving.

'Humour me about the watchers, though.' His eyes narrowed and seemed to tilt up at the outside edges. 'Keep a note of when they're near. If you get worried, you contact me immediately, okay?'

He handed me a card with his name and cell phone number – and nothing else.

This was getting too deep. Maybe it was true, maybe it was a scam. I didn't want to get into any more trouble. Taking my time, I drew my knife and fork together on my plate, pushed it away and stood up.

'I'm going to leave now and go home. What you've told me, it's like something out of a bad movie.' I looked straight at him. 'I need time to think.'

I weighed up what he'd told me as I rode back in the cab. I reassured myself I'd done the right thing. I'd had one run-in with the establishment and lost. Badly. I shivered when I thought about that. Now I'd begun to succeed in my normal job, I wanted to hold on to it, to keep my life regular and safe.

8

I peeked round Hayden's office door next morning. 'Just to let you know, everything's commissioned. I don't expect much back until Monday.'

'Morning, Karen. Come in a moment, would you, and shut the door.' Hayden always kept his door open. Right now, his face was solemn, like at a funeral.

'What is it? Did I miss something?'

'No, nothing at all. You're making excellent progress on the Sextilius account.' He put his fingertips together. 'I feel rather embarrassed to ask you, but have you been up to anything you shouldn't have?'

'What are you saying?'

'I had a visit last night, at home, from a couple of government people. One was from the FBI and the other from something called the Economy Security Department.' He pushed two business cards across the dark oak table.

I picked up the cards and read the details. The names meant nothing to me, but the government logos in dark solid colours looked all too real.

'What did they want?'

'They warned me about the penalties for my employees infringing EUS government rules on dealing with foreign countries. I would be held responsible as well as the employee. I should carry out a thorough check on my employees to ensure I complied. The one from the ESD said that withholding any useful information wouldn't be in my best interests, and so on.' He looked around the office, settling his gaze on his Addy Awards in the bookcase, lingering on the slim gold crossed 'A's. 'They were perfectly polite, but I got the distinct feeling I was being threatened.'

Fear pulsed through me. Not here, please.

'Surely some kind of mix-up?' I managed.

'That's what I hope,' he said, picking up his silver pen and twirling it through his fingers like some majorette. 'The only overseas contract we have open at present is Sextilius. Does anything occur to you?'

My heart hammered.

'No, nothing. Roma Nova's not on any trade list, is it?'

'No. I know you will have done it, but I checked again with the Treasury. Roma Nova continues to enjoy "normal trade relations" status. They've recovered from the débâcle twenty years odd ago when Roma Nova embargoed all American goods after the expulsion of a dozen so-called "EUS diplomats". In my experience, the Roma Novans are frighteningly well-educated and clever, like Sextilius, a bit eccentric, but never any trouble unless you attack them first. They tend to react robustly.' He waved his fingers in a shallow arc. 'Every schoolboy knows the original Romans were world-class engineers. These descendants seem to have embraced the digital revolution with the same relentlessness they once used to conquer the world.'

'Did these men say anything else or name any names?' I swallowed with some effort.

'No, but I'm sure they were serious.' He released the pen and turned to me, a look of enquiry on his face.

I was desperate not to disappoint him, but I had nothing to say.

'Well, I won't hold you up any longer,' he said after a full minute's silence. He returned to playing with the silver pen and looked away.

'Sure, anytime.'

9

Clyde, Renschman's supervisor, had congratulated him on his research. Not only had Renschman filled out Karen Brown's background but he had also pointed out that her approaching birthday on August tenth would give her full legal possession of BI.

Brown Industries was a closed company and had refused to be drawn into the Washington network. It couldn't be bought politically either. The administration had sought for years for a way to reverse its dependency on the company. Now a chance had presented itself.

Clyde glanced at the other man. His talents as a fixer would be perfect for the job and he seemed motivated.

'I suggest we frighten her a little, sir,' Renschman said. 'To get her to sign BI over, of course. After my visit, I think we could pressure her employer some more.'

'Whatever you need, Jeffrey. We can't let this opportunity pass.'

Back at his desk, Renschman lit a cigarette and sat back, inhaling the smoke. Relaxed, he mapped out every next step. He smiled as he crushed the stub. It flew from his fingers in an exact trajectory and landed in the centre of the paper bin. He wouldn't touch another until he had ended this.

10

I left work a little earlier than usual. The sun's powerful light pouring in through the office window drew me outside. I would take a detour through the park and find a tree; stretching out under fresh spring leaves, my back supported against the warm trunk, and my eyes closed, I would rebalance. I had no doubt Hayden's visitors meant me. Maybe I should resign and move away now. I could start over somewhere else where nobody knew me.

More than a little depressed at that thought, I trudged on in the increasing heat. Only three more blocks to the park. I had crossed at the second intersection and reached the far sidewalk almost without realising it when I sensed somebody directly behind me. I heard the rustle of their clothes. I was too frightened to turn around, so I made a sharp left and hurried along a street of row houses.

A hand grasped my arm and I cried out. 'Get off, get off, I don't have any money!'

How stupid was that? The cops always say you should hand your purse over and run.

'I don't want your money, you silly girl,' Conrad Tellus said in an exasperated tone. He was gripping my elbow so tightly it pinched.

'You!' I couldn't put more loathing into my voice. 'Let go of me.' I cast around, desperately looking for a cop. Or anybody. The street was deserted except for two older people in the distance wrapped up in their conversation.

'Calm down. I'm not attacking you. If you stop trying to pull away, it won't hurt.'

He was right, damn him.

'What do you want?' I used the coldest voice I could.

'Let's get back to your apartment and I'll tell you.'

I glared up at him, but all I gained was a bland smile and the hard eyes. He was perfectly capable of forcing me, so I strode along, ignoring him. Irritatingly, he fell into perfect step with me. As we approached, he pulled me round to the parallel street and we entered my building via the service door at the back.

'What the hell are you doing?' I struggled against his grip.

'Later,' he said and released me once we were in the elevator.

I stomped along the hallway, unlocked my door and pushed it so hard it rebounded on the doorstop.

'Okay, you have five minutes then I'm calling the—'

'Could you make us some coffee?' he interrupted, placing his finger on my lips. I was too surprised to resist as he nudged me into the kitchen and set the kettle on. He left the faucet running, then made a circuit around the apartment with some hand-held device. He picked up a newspaper from the recycling pile and scribbled *Keep talking. Please* on the blank edge.

'Black or white?' I said, but glared at him. 'Sugar?'

'White. Sugar, please.'

I ground coffee along with my teeth and filled the press pot, keeping up a stream of trivialities in between noises. I turned the faucet off. I couldn't afford to waste money like that. Or maybe I could now, with my mother's money. I closed my eyes and shook my head.

A few minutes later, he dropped down on the couch and breathed out forcibly. 'You're clean.' He gestured with the electronic device.

'What do you mean?' Then I got it. 'You thought somebody had planted listening devices in my apartment? Are you crazy?'

He stood up, pulled me over to the window and drew the drape back a fraction. 'Look down there,' he said. 'That's why we came in through the basement.' In the street were two men, the same ones as before.

Well, crap.

I took a deep breath. 'Okay, now you have some explaining to do. I don't know whether the money's real or if my grandmother's still alive or anything. And those people following us could be protecting me. Against you.'

'Yes, I heard about your phone call to the legation. You're right to be careful, of course.' He glanced at me. 'My government work is in the security field.'

'You're a spy? Like those people following me?'

'I wouldn't put it quite like that.' He rose to his feet and looked around. 'Can I log on here?'

'Why?'

'You want proof, don't you?'

I fired up my laptop and left him to it while I cleared the cups and made noises in the kitchen. I wanted to keep busy.

A few moments later, he came to the kitchen door. 'Come and have a look at this – perhaps it'll help.'

On the screen was a sequence of messages in Latin between him and Aurelia, my grandmother. I right-clicked to get them up in English. Reading through the stilted automated translations, her concern that I was safe and well, that I knew about my mother's money and that I was happy shone through.

'You could message her live, or talk on video if you wanted.'

I'd only ever seen her once, the summer after my mom died. Clutching my father's hand, I had crossed a long hallway lined with statues into an enormous room. An older lady had crouched down to speak to me. She had smelled like cookies. Her face had been sad, but she'd smiled at me.

I nodded at Conrad.

He tapped a sequence on the keyboard then made a call on a tiny cell phone the size of a powder compact while software was downloading and installing. I had never seen a phone so small or slim.

What was I supposed to say to this grandmother? Panic grabbed hold of me. I almost told him to cut the connection, but it answered too quickly. Below a mass of grey hair, a strong, sculptured face with fine lines and my blue eyes looked out of the screen. The cookie lady. Conrad greeted her in Latin then beckoned me forward and switched to English.

'Aurelia, may I present your granddaughter Karen Brown?'

'Er, hi,' I stumbled. 'I'm...I'm very pleased to see you again. I'm sorry, I can't remember much from when I visited.'

She laughed – a funny, friendly laugh. 'I'm not surprised! You were only four and it must have seemed so strange to you. I hope we can remedy it soon, though.' Her tone was melodic, but her words clipped and British-sounding. I didn't have any intention of visiting at present, but it never hurt to be polite.

'Sure, that would be great, Gran, er, Grandmother...Oh! What shall I call you?'

'The traditional Latin is "Nonna". I think the Italians also use it, but we won't mind that!'

I smiled at her semi-disparaging tone. I rubbed my fingertips along my jaw. 'Look, I'm finding this all a little weird. Do you know why these people are following me? I'm not being dumb, but I can't see the threat.'

She looked steadily at me and waited a second or two before answering. 'Has Conradus explained about Brown Industries?'

'Yes, he thinks there may be a problem with our government, but I told him that type of thing doesn't happen here.'

She glanced up at Conrad. 'I wouldn't want to be the one to disillusion you, Karen,' she said briskly, 'but I agree with him. We've liaised discreetly with BI through the years to protect your interest. We've made damned sure it's been compliant in every way. I didn't want to give them the least excuse to take it from you.' The lines on her face deepened as she frowned. 'We know the American departments of Trade and Security have been trying to monitor our contact, especially recently. Your father was an honourable man. I hope his adopted country respects that, for his daughter's sake.'

Good grief. I wouldn't care to get on her wrong side.

'I wish I was there to help you, but Conradus is perfectly capable of doing everything necessary. You can ask him to do anything. He has my full confidence and my instructions.'

On the way to my desk next morning, I grabbed a coffee from the machine and took another ten minutes to mull over Hayden's visitors in the light of what Conrad and my grandmother had said. She'd been so concerned for me, but not in a soppy way. Direct and 'no-nonsense' fitted her perfectly, but her smile had been warm. I couldn't help speculating how it would have been to grow up with her instead of the Browns.

I started tapping the keys, surfing for Roma Nova while I was drinking and thinking. I couldn't leave it alone. My grandmother's name shot out at me. Fascinated, I loaded the English translation. The screen displayed a list of her business interests. Sketchy on detail, it gave some personal stuff at the end; head of the influential Mitela family, senator and government advisor, cousin to the current imperatrix. She really was a big hitter.

I took her advice and had Conrad arrange an appointment at the bank holding my trust accounts. The alien world of the vice-president's leather and polished teak office and his smooth condescension were intimidating, but so were the amounts.

'This is real?' I asked as I studied the series of zeros on the account statements.

The banker looked offended for a second, but put his full-teeth smile back on and nodded.

'When can I draw on this?'

'Immediately,' he said. 'These figures represent the dividends and interest payments net of tax from your mother's portfolio into your checking account. We had instructions to transfer any balances unused after three months into high-interest accounts and bonds. Nothing has been withdrawn since the arrangements were set up. The trustees made provision for you to have limited access at age sixteen and full rights at eighteen.'

He looked at me speculatively, but I was far too annoyed to say anything. This money would have set me free from Aunt and Uncle Brown.

So what was I going to do? I wouldn't leave Hayden in the lurch, but I thought my days at Bornes & Black were numbered. I could study at some truly snooty school like Cambridge Vassar or Smith Watt, and afterward start my own business. I could travel, certainly visit my grandmother for a few weeks each year, or longer, even. I could have a *good* seat at the theatre, not have to stretch my neck from behind the pillar. I could buy a house back in New Hampshire. The possibilities chased each other around in my head.

While I tried to unscramble all this, I decided to leave the portfolio at the bank for now. I drew out two thousand dollars, feeling both daring and guilty at such a large amount. I asked the vice president to set up Internet access and send me a debit card. He promised card and codes would be couriered to me within the next forty-eight hours.

As we descended the bank steps into the street, I glanced up at Conrad and smiled to myself. Now I had Nonna's support, I would enjoy having him run around after me, and not tell me what to do. I insisted we went for a celebratory lunch with a good champagne. The waiter nearly had heart failure when I laughed and counted out the hundred-dollar bills on the table. I had a vague memory of getting home, supported by a strong arm. But through my light and airy connection to reality, I knew I needed to tell Conrad something very important, but the more I tried to remember, the quicker it faded away until it was gone completely.

11

A goblin was hammering in my head when I woke next morning. I heard a voice shouting on the telephone, the sound echoing around the living room. Conrad. How the hell had he got into my apartment? I closed my eyes. Of course – he was a spook. He could probably burglarise the Presidential Mansion if he wanted. I groaned; then heard his laugh. A few minutes later, he appeared with a steaming cup.

'Here, drink this – you'll feel better quite quickly.'

Sure I would. But, out of politeness, I took a sip. The spicy warmth rolled down my throat. It smelled like ginger and malt.

'What *is* this?' I croaked.

'It works as a post-alcoholic pick-me-up. I imagined you might find it helpful this morning.' He didn't laugh out loud at me, but for a few seconds his lips were pressed together a little firmer than was natural, under very liquid eyes.

Then I remembered. 'Hayden's visitors. My purse.'

I'd memorised the details on the cards left by Hayden's government visitors and written them in my journal. *That* was the important thing I needed to tell Conrad.

'Hayden was really unhappy about the way they threatened him. But he looked more upset at the thought that anybody in Bornes & Black could have been careless or disloyal.'

Conrad scanned the notes, muttered a word under his breath and snapped the journal shut. His mouth tightened into a ruler-straight line. He pulled his cell phone from his pocket and stabbed at it. I finished the wonder drink and made for the bathroom. He was still talking harshly and rapidly after ten minutes. He glanced at me, then finished his call. His face was calmer, but set like a concrete mask.

'I have to go to Washington, but I'll be back in a couple of days, Saturday evening at the latest.' His gaze flittered back and forth across my face like he was searching for something. 'Listen to me. Do everything as normal, but be careful. If anybody new pops up in your life, or somebody you know changes their behaviour or their attitude to you, treat them with caution. Promise me.'

His seriousness frightened me. Cold goose bumps spread all over me. I nodded but couldn't say anything. He touched my shoulder, gave me a tight smile and was gone.

Headache and thirst vanished, I rushed to work. With no time to make a sandwich, I decided to get lunch out at the grill down the street where they could process you in just under the half-hour. Besides, I wanted to be among normal people. Waiting in line, I sensed the brush of somebody's clothing against my back. I took a half-step forward, shifting my body a little sideways at the same time.

'You want to keep away from foreigners. If you don't, we'll destroy you.'

At first, I didn't register the voice was aimed at me. By the time I did, nobody was there. I searched up and down, pushing past people as I tried to find the invisible speaker. I seized the server's arm and demanded to know if she'd seen him. I cast around frantically, but only saw normal people waiting for their lunch, looking away from me. The threatening words penetrated my brain, and I started to shake. I stumbled back to my office, not caring who I pushed against. I fell into my chair and stared at my blank screen for a full five minutes. I let out a long breath. This was unreal. Who the hell were they? How dared they scare me like that?

I went home that evening by yellow cab. Lucky to get one at that time, I hesitated on the sidewalk before I pulled the rear door open. Suppose the driver was one of them? A woman hovered by my side, ready to cut in, so I blocked her and jumped in. The driver's bored eyes were impassive as I told him my destination, so I figured he was safe. All the same, I was relieved to reach the 7-Eleven in the block before mine. I paid, leapt out and hurried home where I ran around the apartment locking and bolting every window as well as the door. I checked the latch at least three times. It wasn't the best night's rest ever.

I had to go shopping Saturday morning for food, but scrutinised each face I encountered. Despite being scared of every human being around me, I became fascinated by the variety in the size and set of noses and mouths. And the shape and colour of eyes – narrow, large, mean, pale, warm, uncaring. And the contrast of a neat Asian teenager and her impatient blond counterpart in need of a diet doctor, and an older man slouching in the line. I hadn't ever thought about how different people were. And any one of them could be a danger for me.

Safely back behind the doors of my apartment building, I checked my mailbox and, along with my movie periodical, found an envelope with my name but no return address. Setting my shopping down in the small lobby, I opened the envelope, handling the sheet inside by the edges. I'd seen CSI shows. I no longer cared if people thought I was crazy.

BETRAY YOUR COUNTRY AND YOU'LL GET 20 YEARS OF FEDERAL HOSPITALITY.

I stared at it. I couldn't believe it. I read it again. After a while, I squashed it back in the envelope, gathered up my shopping and went up to my apartment. The envelope quivered in my hand until I dropped it on the table. One of my shopping bags fell over on the table, spilling the contents and a glass jar rolled over the edge. I gulped as my floor was covered in a large red star of tomato and olive pasta sauce and glittering shards.

I left the chaos, closed the drapes, changed into my pyjamas and retreated to my bed, pulling the comforter over my head. I lay there, shaking, frightened into my soul.

Thumping at my apartment door jolted me awake. Instantly. Somebody rattling the handle. They'd come for me.

'Karen?' A voice shouted.

Conrad! I ran to the door and looked through the spyhole. It was him. I gulped with relief, unlocked the chain and pulled the door open.

'What's happened? Why are you in your pyjamas at two in the afternoon?'

I told him about the restaurant line and the letter. As he fetched it from the kitchen, I heard him mutter, 'Bastards'. Despite my earlier doubts about him, it was annoying to admit he'd been proved right on all counts.

'Are you up to going out?' he said. 'I need to meet up with somebody, so we could eat at the same time.'

By the time I'd showered, and dressed in tee and jeans, Conrad had cleared up the mess on my kitchen floor and made me a cup of tea.

'Before we go anywhere,' I said, standing in the living room 'I have something else to tell you.' I studied the print on the opposite wall of old New York in 1837 – the Governor-General's loyal address on Victoria coming to the throne – my father's favourite. 'Maybe I should have mentioned it sooner, but I have a problem of my own.' I told him about the encounter with Junior Hartenwyck, getting thrown out the Conservancy Corps, being placed on the national watch list, everything.

'Why didn't you tell me anything of this before?'

'I was too embarrassed, okay?' I dared him to say anything.

He looked angry as all hell. He rubbed the first two fingers of his right hand on the hairline at his temple. 'That explains why they knew you and reacted so quickly when I contacted you.'

12

He didn't go an inch beyond meticulously polite and only spoke to me when absolutely necessary during our journey. We took the subway to the Bouwerie and walked west into a side street off Kenmare Street to a bar oozing Italian nostalgia. Green and red horizontal stripes circled the whole dining room accompanied by photos of famous Italian Americans and prints of old Venezia with gondolas and extravagant buildings. To complete the kitsch, out came an Italian poppa, apron round his waist, black curled-up moustache, big grin.

'Conrado!' He kissed Conrad on both cheeks and pumped his hand. Jeez, it was like something out of a bad movie.

'Gianni, can I introduce my friend, Carina?'

Carina? I glanced at Conrad, but he didn't say any more.

Above his wide and brilliant smile, Gianni's eyes scanned me like a photocopier reader.

'Please, come up and see Mamma – she'll be thrilled to see you!'

Laughing and talking, Gianni led the way upstairs. '*Ciao*, Mamma,' he said, as we entered the first room on the right. He shut the door behind us. If Mamma existed, she wasn't in this room. Small and untidy, a faded red carpet, daylight barely penetrating through windows unwashed for years, and posters of Italy hanging half-heartedly on the papered walls. A small Virgin Mary blessed the television in the corner.

'Okay, Tellus, how can I help?' The smile on Gianni's face

dissolved, his eyes sharpening, his full attention on Conrad. Even his accent changed from broad Italian-American to a clipped but still accented English.

Conrad glanced at his watch. 'You'll be getting a party in to dine in about an hour and a half. One of them is going to ask for the bathroom but come up here.'

Gianni nodded.

'Can I use your commsline while we're waiting?'

Gianni went to his cluttered desk, selected a stick from several in a dusty plastic cup and handed it to Conrad, who inserted it into a slim silver laptop. A bunch of vacation photos came up on the screen with toothsome children and wholesome mom and pop. Conrad selected one of two laughing children on a beach, zoomed in to pixel level, copied a line of them and then the photo disappeared. He pasted the pixels into the password box and dialled.

Waiting for the encrypted connection, he said, presumably to me but looking at the computer screen, 'You're safe here. We're going to find out who these people are and what we have to do to protect you. Go and sit down near the window, but don't let yourself be seen.'

Gianni brought warm panini, a jug of water and glasses, then left us to it. After we'd eaten, Conrad hunched in front of the screen again, sometimes talking to somebody, sometimes tapping on the keyboard but saying nothing. I figured he was still miffed with me. I ignored him and flicked through the Italian computer magazines stacked up by the desk, pretending I could understand them. I closed my eyes and pretended to doze.

An hour later, a redhead wearing a dull purple coat, and with black plastic spectacles masking her face, stood in the doorway. I heard voices filtering up the stairs along with the smell of cooking. She closed them out as she shut the door.

'Tellus.'

'Sergia.'

She looked at Conrad as if he was nothing but trouble, glanced in my direction then ignored me. She took a step towards Conrad and started talking at him in fast Latin. From her tight, hard face and aggressive tone, I could see she was sounding off about something. Conrad answered her as robustly. I caught the odd word, but I couldn't follow what they were saying. He must have seen my puzzlement and switched into English.

'I understand your frustration at being hauled back from Mexico so suddenly, but this is more important.'

'You're out of your mind.' After a short pause, she said, 'Declined,' with a sour tone of finality that sounded like a ten-foot thick bank safe door shutting. 'I don't know what you're doing here anyway – you're not active.'

'You can't refuse.'

'Oh, really? You supply the paperwork; then I'll consider it.' She made her way to the door, but Conrad got there first and blocked her.

'Enough! I'm only going through you out of courtesy. It's an executive order. Your role is to organise it.'

She hung in there. 'I'm not risking my career on the word of some jumped-up imperial playboy!'

He paled but kept his voice steady. 'Perhaps you'll accept the instruction from the chancellor, or shall we go right to the top? You might like to explain to the imperatrix, and Countess Mitela, exactly what your reasons are for refusing your assistance. I wouldn't like to be in your sandals when you do.'

He dialled again. As the LEDs flashed, she stared down at the monitor, her mouth turned down and a scowl on her face. I wasn't sure what was happening here, but it sounded like a turf war.

The screen changed, revealing a woman in a business suit.

'Good evening. Conradus Tellus for Quintus Tellus, please.'

'Hello, Conradus, what can I do for you?' A genial, bearded face with oak-brown eyes appeared. He looked anywhere between fifty and seventy.

Conrad beckoned me over. 'Firstly, may I present Karen Brown? Karen, this is my uncle, Quintus Tellus. He's the imperial chancellor, similar to the American president's chief of staff.'

I swallowed. 'Hello, Quintus Tellus.'

'Good evening, Karen Brown. A pleasure to speak to you. I look forward to seeing you in person.'

I glanced at Conrad and he nodded. I gabbled something polite then retreated to my seat by the window to let Conrad get on with it. Sergia's gaze swivelled around to me. She stared at me so intensely a red flush spread up my neck to my cheeks, but I refused to drop my eyes.

'I believe Antonia Sergia would like to speak to you, Chancellor.' Conrad turned from the screen, bowed ironically to her and extended his arm, inviting her to take the seat in front of the computer.

'What the hell was all that about?' I whispered as they talked behind us in Latin.

'Sergia getting her feathers ruffled. She's good at what she does, but takes herself far too seriously.'

She logged off, stared at the blank screen for a few moments and then squared her shoulders. She gave Conrad a curt nod then stomped back downstairs. Gianni brought us up some coffee, rich and dark, while we waited an hour to let Sergia get clear.

We went through the farewell motions, including kissing and handshakes, a bottle of wine from Gianni and cries of 'Come back soon'. Despite the overt friendliness, I wasn't too sure I wanted to.

13

'*Merda!* They're boxing us.'

'What?'

'The watchers. See those two ahead of us? The one in jeans, next to the one wearing the black fleece? With the two behind, they make a box to contain us.'

My throat tightened. I stared at the men ahead: the first, wavy brown hair, chunky build, and the second, a slim black guy. Both looked fit and alert.

'There'll be a car somewhere.'

He linked my arm with his and smiled down at me. He scanned the street of neighbourhood stores and restaurants without moving his head while we strolled along, seemingly happy and relaxed. The tables, chairs and plant troughs sprawling over the sidewalk made it difficult to navigate though.

'I think they're going to jump us,' he whispered. 'When I say run, go like the Furies. Aim for one of the side alleys.'

'But we haven't done anything wrong. Why should we run?'

'Just do what I say. Please.'

The two men ahead of us slowed their pace. We would catch up with them within moments. Conrad stopped suddenly. Shielded by a tall menu board with a grinning caricature of a waiter, he thrust me through the door of a 24/7 store. Behind the counter, the clerk looked up with bored eyes.

'Can we use your restroom?' Conrad asked, injecting urgency into his voice.

'No public restrooms,' the clerk replied in a monotone, and turned back to the magazine she was reading.

'But my wife's pregnant,' Conrad said, throwing me a stern look as my jaw dropped in surprise, 'and she's about to throw up. We need a restroom. Right now!'

The clerk's eyes widened in alarm. I could see her thinking of the cleaning she'd have to do. I coughed hard like I was heaving. She leapt up, darted between the lines of canned food and flung open a door to the storage area. She jabbed her finger at the back corner and retreated. We pushed through the plastic-wrapped pallets and boxes. Left of the restroom door, we found the half-hidden fire door. Conrad threw the trash bags to one side, seized the horizontal bar and rammed it open. We raced out into the alleyway.

At the corner, where it intersected the main street, he pressed me back, side by side with him, against the rough brick wall. My breath came in snatches and I tried to swallow the dryness in my throat. No sound of footsteps behind us, nobody running toward us. In the street in front of us were regular people doing regular things on a regular Saturday. Glancing back once, Conrad laid his arm across my shoulder, his hand gripping the top of my arm, forcing me to slow down to a sauntering pace as we crossed the street.

Three stores further up, we pulled the same trick, emerging near a subway entrance. We ran down the metal-edged steps, plunged into a side passage, and waited ten long minutes behind a vending machine.

'I think we've lost them, but they'll pick us up at your flat. How do you feel about a hotel for tonight?'

My head was thumping with tension, and my body was drained. I'd been threatened with jail, denounced as a traitor and chased by security agents. A fortune had landed on me, along with a new family. And then there was Conrad…

'I want to go somewhere quiet. I know it sounds lame, but I just want this to stop.'

It was dark. A police siren screamed out. I sat up, panicked. But nothing was moving except the drapes in the warm breeze through the half-open window. The siren faded, its discordant note changing tone as it moved away. The soft swish of a bus door opening and closing took its place. I glanced at my watch. Twenty after five. I stretched my hand out for my glass of water but found nothing. I wasn't in my own bed. God! It had all been real.

My clothes were folded on a chair and I was buck naked. And alone. The other side of the bed was untouched. A note in black rounded handwriting told me Conrad had gone out to find breakfast. This wasn't the kind of hotel that did room service. I had to go to the bathroom, so I showered as well and wrapped myself in the robe I was surprised to find hanging there. I fixed myself a cup of coffee from the tray and huddled on the bed, trying not to think about the past twenty-four hours.

I was still there by the time daylight had bleached out the street lighting. Where the hell was Conrad? I called his cell. No answer. I scrambled into my clothes and pulled my comb through my hair. To cover the silence, I switched on the television. Still no sign of Conrad.

I rang his cell again but, instead of no answer, heard the unobtainable tone. I texted. The message couldn't be delivered. My second-hand phone bought in a street sale might have been chunky but it was reliable enough to send texts. Over at the window, I peeked out to see if any watchers were there. None that I could see. I sat down on the edge of the bed, without a clue what to do.

Somebody knocked on the door, hard enough for the inside panel to shiver at the blow. I flinched. I stood up. I had to run, to save myself, but my feet were welded to the floor. I heard a shout: 'Ten minutes.' They wouldn't give a warning like that. I took a deep breath and opened the door a few inches. The desk clerk from the night before. His face was framed by the gap.

'Yes?'

'Ten minutes,' he said, pointing at his plastic strap watch. 'Your client paid last night. Time's up.' He jerked his thumb away from the door. 'Unless you want to earn an extension.' He leered at me.

I slammed the door in his face.

Where could I go? I wanted to go home but I couldn't take that chance. They would be watching my building. I threw out the idea of going to Amanda for help; I couldn't endanger her. I couldn't go to the cops. The precinct sergeant would take one look at me, uncaring, only thinking about his lunch or getting home in time to watch the ball game, and throw me out as a crazy. Or run my name, have me put in a holding cell and call the FBI. And one of Hayden's threatening visitors had been FBI. I knew I hadn't done anything wrong but I was thinking like a criminal already.

I had to go somewhere crowded, where they couldn't touch me. Where did people congregate on Sundays? A church! I would maybe get two hours' breathing room if the preacher was inspired.

I left the hotel, careful to avoid CCTV cameras as much as possible. But they clung on every building, inquisitive little eyes roosting on every corner. Like a fugitive in my own country, I looked up and down each street I crossed, as if scanning supermarket shelves. After ten minutes, I was sweating. Where were all the good people and their churches?

Fifteen minutes later, I crouched behind a dumpster in a narrow alleyway, watching people filing into the neighbourhood church opposite in ones and twos, their faces composed, ready for a re-injection of goodness. After ten minutes, no one else appeared. I drew myself up and ran my hands down the front of my jeans, attempting to smooth away creases. My heart thumping, I forced myself to walk across the street at normal pace. But I remembered Conrad's words about being ready to run.

I looked up and down. Nothing. I put my foot on the first grey stone step. Only four more and I was safe. I heard singing behind the now-closed door. As I grasped the handle, I released a breath I didn't know I was holding. I was easing the door open so I could slip in as quietly as possible when two pairs of arms grabbed me and dragged me back down.

'So you see, Miss Brown, you are in a fragile situation.'

I'd stumbled as a woman and man in suits pulled me back down the steps. She'd flashed a gold badge and declared herself as Special Agent O'Keefe. One of the people who had visited Hayden. Still gripping my arm, she'd put her hand on my head and pushed me down into the back of a plain grey car that had whirled from around the corner and braked hard in front of the church. It stank of stale junk food. I'd flung myself at the far door but it was locked.

'How dare you? Let me out this minute.'

'Sit down and keep still. I don't want to have to cuff you,' she'd said as the car pulled away from the kerb.

I gave up arguing after ten minutes of her ignoring me. Shortly after, she tapped the driver on the shoulder, and we stopped in a deserted street of warehouses.

'I'm going to give you a friendly warning.' She looked straight ahead, focusing through the windshield glass on the end of the street. 'You need to keep away from dangerous people like Mr Tellus.'

'You can't tell me who I can and can't see. This is a free country.'

Her laugh didn't sound mean, just cynical. She swivelled around to face me. 'You may like to think about this. Firstly, for whatever reason, you're on the national watch list, where they put subversives and potential terrorists. Secondly, sure your father became a good American. He even reconnected with his cousins in Nebraska. But your mother stayed a foreign national. Maybe there was something irregular in her paperwork. Could be that you don't have right of residence here, after all. You couldn't work then, without a social security card.'

Bluff. She was bluffing. Besides, I had my mother's money.

'Your bank accounts would be frozen, of course, pending investigation, which could take years.'

'You can't threaten me like this.'

'I'm not threatening; just showing you what could happen if you were unwise. Surviving on the street is very hard. Especially for a naive young woman used to comfort and decent behaviour.'

'You…you shit!'

She shrugged. 'If you keep away from Tellus, your happy and safe little life will settle back to normal, and your listing might get cancelled. You have a fine future. In a few weeks, you'll inherit a prosperous business, with a raft of secure government contracts. It would upset me to learn you'd thrown it away on a whim.' O'Keefe fixed her light grey gaze on me. 'We'll take you back to your apartment now. But we'll be keeping an eye on you for a little while longer, for your own safety.'

Outside my apartment building, O'Keefe got out and unlocked my door, opening it like she was a parking valet. I couldn't scramble out fast enough.

'Do I have your undertaking, Miss Brown?'

'What do you think?' I said. I turned my back on her and fled inside.

14

Renschman jammed his lips together and exhaled in one heavy pulse through his nose. Exasperation was an alien emotion. He'd been forced to accept the help of O'Keefe's First Bunch of Idiots, but they couldn't keep hold of a sandwich box if it was welded to them. With skin buffed clean of any emotion and a tight smile ending one millimetre above her top lip, O'Keefe had seemed perfect. The last time he'd seen such a hard face was the madam in the projects he'd been forced to live in when his mother had drunk them into debt.

O'Keefe had been lucky picking up the girl again – but to have fallen for the pregnant switch? Twice?

Jesus!

He longed to get hold of the girl. He'd enjoy scaring her half to death. He'd have her roughed up first; then an overnight stay on a filthy mattress in a cold, unlit room and she'd sign anything. He slid the inside of his hands against each other, slowly, crossways as if they were caressing each other. Just a little pressure on her soft white neck and it would all be over.

15

Upstairs, I let myself in. My hand shook, making the drapes flutter when I pulled them aside to peer down into the street. O'Keefe's car had vanished.

Where was Conrad? Had they taken him? Maybe I was dumb to have tried calling him. These people were probably intercepting my phone and my mail. Maybe they had deported him already. Or worse.

Despite the danger and anxiety of the last few days, he had made me feel excited to be alive. More than anyone else, ever. But, just as important, he was the key to me learning who I really was.

Next morning, I woke early with my stomach in knots and my head heavy with the sleeping tablets I'd made myself take. After I called in sick to the office, citing a cold with fever, I dressed in jeans, tee and sneakers, and stuffed money and cards into my purse. I planned to go find a public phone and try call Conrad again. If I didn't get through, I'd contact their legation or go back to Gianni's.

Looking sideways through the drapes, I couldn't see any watchers. I thought I knew now how to spot them. But who was I kidding?

I was stretching out my hand to grab the door handle, when somebody knocked. Catching my breath at the interruption, I peered through the spy hole and saw a distorted figure in a brown uniform. I hesitated. They knocked again. I decided to open the door.

'Sign here, please.' He thrust a padded envelope at me. I signed and he hurried off. My hands trembled as I opened the envelope. Inside was a tall, narrow book: *The Complete Illustrated Map and Guidebook to New York Kew Park*. It opened naturally at the first map page. Running down its length, an eighth-inch-wide ribbon of paper was jammed up against the gutter. I nearly missed it. I eased it out, dreading tearing it. Tiny black marks turned out to be handwriting:

P. 109 A fine spot to take pictures 11.30, Tues. Destroy this note. C .

He was still here. Alive.

The rest of Monday went by in a cross between nightmare and hallucination. I tried to focus on mechanical tasks like laundry. I even attempted to read a book, but the letters ebbed and flowed in front of my eyes without making any sense. After going to bed early, I was up just after six, unrefreshed and overwrought. I called and spoke to Hayden's PA, saying I couldn't get in but that Amanda could follow my projects through. I hated loading it onto her; she was my friend as well as my colleague.

On Tuesday morning, I gritted my teeth and dawdled up the path in the park. I made myself recite the details of each shrub and flower individually in order to stay slow; I knew the name of every one. The elaborate techniques practised in spy films didn't seem so stupid now.

At eleven twenty-five, I sat down by the pool at the north end. The soft, quiet retreat, reminiscent of original woodland, was so calm. I lay back on the grassy bank, watching sunshine dribble in between the willows, listening to the sound of ducks splashing. I shut my eyes.

'Darling, here you are.'

I sat up so quickly my head swam.

Conrad. A fake cheery smile plastered on his face. He knelt down and kissed my cheek. 'Smile,' he whispered. 'Relax your shoulders.' He narrowed his eyes, searching over my shoulder for anybody watching us. 'Difficult, I know, but we have to appear ordinary and casual.'

I couldn't see a single person anywhere, but I knew we had to be careful. I'd already crossed into a shadow world. This was merely a part of it. He pulled a cloth out of a picnic basket, followed by acrylic glasses, a bottle of wine, plates and food. He sat down on the grass close beside me so we looked like any other couple.

'Thank the gods you're not hurt. I'm sorry if you thought I'd deserted you. They took me when I was buying breakfast. I had to get the legation to spring me.'

I told him about O'Keefe.

'They're really piling on the pressure now.' He looked down and played with a blade of grass. 'One of those who visited your boss, a brutal bastard called Renschman, warned me that if I came within a hundred yards of you, or contacted you in any way, he'd arrange a fatal accident.' He snorted. 'He can't terminate me; he knows the legation is aware and we'd retaliate hard.' He turned to me. 'But you're not safe. He said he'd put you away, and I think he could.'

After that frightening business with O'Keefe, I had no doubt.

'The safest thing would be if I kept away from you.' He looked across the pool. His Adam's apple bounced hard.

'Would they keep their word?'

He shrugged. 'Who knows?'

'No.'

'Karen—'

'No. Nonna would send somebody else. It wouldn't change a thing.'

He stretched his arm up to stroke my hair, and his polo shirt lifted to show a huge bruise.

'What the hell is that?'

'A little souvenir from Renschman. Diplomatic immunity isn't part of his personal vocabulary, it seems.'

'Jesus. Who is this guy?'

'Probably black ops, CIA or similar. But whatever he is, he's a nasty piece of work. I don't want him anywhere near you.' He looked into the distance. The back of his fingers caressed my cheek as he brought his gaze back on me. A ripple of warmth crept over my face in response. I closed my eyes to savour the feeling.

'If I don't leave, he'll keep after you.' Conrad's voice broke into the moment. I opened my eyes and searched his face. Anger, I thought along with fear. 'But I can't abandon you without any protection.' He stood up and walked to the pool edge, crossed his arms and stared down at the water. He didn't move or say anything for several minutes. The cords in his neck were taut, highlighted by the shadows forced by the bright sun.

'There's another choice. You'd be completely safe, they couldn't get near you, let alone touch you, but it would be the most disruptive thing that's ever happened to you.' His voice was low, sad, as if regretting the passing of something. The soft gurgling of the water and staccato of chirruping birds continued, but my world stopped as if we were held in stasis.

I was so absorbed with trying to figure out what Conrad meant that I was totally unaware of anybody approaching us. Too late, Conrad twisted round. A man jabbed a gun barrel right under his jawline.

'On the ground, hands behind you.'

A second man drove his fist into Conrad's stomach and slammed him down, another kneeling on him, handcuffing his hands behind him. I recognised the third one: he was one of the watchers. No. Not again.

He seized my arm and forced me up. I kicked him hard in the shins. His grip eased; I flailed him with my fists, aiming at his eyes and the bridge of his nose. I landed a punch on his cheekbone and nearly succeeded in pulling away, but another man lunged at me, crushing our picnic underfoot, and grabbed my other arm, twisting it up behind my back and forcing me to bend over. They dragged us through the trees, out through the Kew Road West entrance, and thrust me into the back of a waiting car. They opened the trunk, flung Conrad in and slammed it down.

'No! No!' I cried and launched myself at the rear door. 'What are you doing? You'll kill him.'

The dark-haired one snorted, but didn't say anything. He shoved me back on the seat. Again. It was happening again. Both big men, they sat legs apart, clamping me between them. We drove at normal speed, through small streets. After a few minutes, the car stopped. As the dark-haired one looked out of the window, shifting his lock on me, I wriggled around between my captors. Through the rear window, I saw them haul Conrad out of the trunk. One released the handcuffs then threw him onto the sidewalk and kicked him several times. He didn't move. He lay there as if in a deep sleep. Or dead.

'Let me out. Now!' I fought and scratched to get to the door but was yanked back by my hair. I lunged out and my nails made contact with flesh. I dragged them across the man's face. I heard a string of obscenities. He slapped my face. Hard. My neck was wrenched and I was sure my head was going to fall off. Tears rolled down my face as the blood and pain flowed back into my right cheek. I shivered as cold metal slid over my wrists and snapped to.

16

The car dove down into a garage under an abandoned building. They dragged me into an elevator lined with cracked brown plastic panels. It was intimidating to be crushed into such a small, dirty space with these brutal and silent men. The elevator clanked up, hissing when it braked two floors up.

They pulled me along a white-painted corridor and into a plain room. A nondescript man with frameless glasses was sitting on a chair behind a plastic-topped table, his fingers playing with an unlit cigarette. My purse was emptied out, the contents strewn over the table, like for a match of Kim's Game. One of my captors forced me down onto a chair opposite the man. They left, except for the one I'd attacked in the car. I was pleased to see blood oozing out of the scratches I'd made on his face. My heart was pumping hard. I was frightened, but I was more angry.

'Oh dear, Miss Brown, you do look a little out of sorts.'

I instinctively disliked Mr Frameless. He gave me a creepy feeling. 'Who the hell are you?'

He smiled like a tax official, but said nothing.

'You can't kidnap me like this – it's against the law.'

'I *am* the law.'

'So read me my rights.'

He laughed. Not like some movie villain, just normally, but I didn't like it.

'You're becoming tiresome, Miss Brown. We've tried to warn you but, as you weren't taking the hint, I thought we needed to have a little heart-to-heart.' He sounded like a high school principal admonishing a wayward student.

'You can't be the law. They don't brutalise people like this.'

'When it comes to traitors, we have to be a little robust.'

'Who are you calling a traitor?'

'Oh, I think consorting with foreign intelligence operatives and conspiring to hand over vital strategic assets to a non-treaty-bound foreign power would put you in the frame.'

I stared, open-mouthed, at him.

'Personally, I don't care who you fuck, but I will not allow Brown Industries to go out of our control,' he said. 'You'll go down for twenty years unless you sign it over to a government nominee. And I'll make sure it'll be a very uncomfortable twenty years.'

Jesus. This was one vindictive son of a bitch.

'My father was loyal to his adopted country – he fought in Somalia Dawn.'

'Ah, yes, William Brown, the great patriot. Was he trying just a little too hard to show us all just what a good EUS citizen he had become? Strange how he went running off after glory a little over two years after your mother drove herself off that cliff.'

'Don't you sneer at them. My father built up his business with his own money and effort. He didn't owe you anything. Neither do I. You can go screw yourself.'

'Bravo! I do like to see some spirit.'

Patronising jerk.

'I think some time out will help concentrate your mind. We'll continue our talk later.' He nodded at the man whose skin I'd ripped. 'Put her in one of the cells.'

The watcher yanked me up from the chair. He pushed me down the hallway to another door, which opened outwards. He shoved me in and slammed the door shut. In the cell was a mattress, a bucket in the corner and a small barred window high up. Dirty white tiles, some missing, lined the cold cell.

Where the hell was I? Who were these frightening people? Was Conrad still alive?

'Let me out. Let me out of here!' I banged on the door with my shackled fists. Silence. I banged again, but nothing. I caught the outer edge of my hand on a raised stud. I stared at the blood welling from the broken skin. My teeth started to chatter. I was so tired. My nerves were beyond shredded. I lay down on the mattress and cried myself to sleep.

The loud clanking of the door woke me. I shivered with cold. I was so stiff I could hardly move. I wiped over my eyes with my palms, hoping that, when I opened them again, it would all be gone. It didn't work. A different watcher came in and pulled me to my feet. I guessed it was time for the 'further talk'. What were they going to do to me? I knew one thing. If – no – *when* I got out of here, I was never going to let myself be this vulnerable again. Ever. Whatever it took.

The watcher pushed me into the same room as before. But this time Mr Frameless was standing away from the table. Another man, medium height, fair hair, a square, pleasant face showing a solemn expression, stood by the table, his briefcase resting on its top, a bunch of papers in his hand.

'Good evening, Miss Brown. Steven Smith, attorney at law. I've been retained to handle your affairs. You're to be freed this instant.'

I stared at him.

'Furthermore, a restraint notice is being served on the ESD on your behalf. Proceedings for compensation will be filed at the local courthouse tomorrow morning.' He handed the documents to Mr Frameless. 'Remove the handcuffs, please.'

Mr Frameless looked seriously pissed. Frustrated of his prey. Would he go for the lawyer? Nobody moved.

'Now,' said Steven Smith.

A heavy minute passed. Frameless signalled the watcher and my wrists were free. My shoulders fell back, and the binding ache in them eased. Steven Smith turned to Mr Frameless and said in the same deadpan voice, 'Thank you for your cooperation. Open the door, please.'

Mr Frameless turned to me, breaking the unlit cigarette between his fingers. 'Your round, Miss Brown.'

Like it was some suburban tennis match.

'But do not be under any illusion we have finished.'

17

Steven Smith guided me out to the unlit concrete yard where a sedan and two dark-coloured SUVs were waiting, the dazzling white headlight beams focused on the compound entrance. He opened the back door of the sedan and Conrad pulled me in. He was alive. Alive. He said nothing as we drove along, but his arms were stiff and tense around me.

At my apartment building, two people spilled out of the front SUV, one of them punching in my access code. Steven Smith followed, briefcase still in hand. Upstairs, another two were guarding my door. Inside the apartment, Conrad sat me down on the couch and gripped my hands.

'It's all right, you're safe. We'll never let those people touch you again.' He looked murderous as he scrutinised my bruised face.

'God, Conrad, they were terrifying.'

'Let's get you cleaned up.'

'Yes, but first...' I turned to Steven Smith. 'I don't know who you are, but thank you.'

'My pleasure, Miss Brown. I'll call tomorrow at eleven to discuss our next step. I bid you good night.'

I let Conrad lead me into the bathroom where he ran the shower. I peeled my sweaty, dirty clothes off and stepped into the warm flow which cleaned my skin and hair but didn't wash away my hurt or anger. Afterward, Conrad applied arnica cream to my red wrists and bruised face. My neck hurt like hell.

'Your face isn't cut so it should heal without a mark,' he said.

Pain jagged through me as I nodded. 'What about you? Are you okay?'

He shrugged. 'They didn't detain me this time. They took you, the soft target – the bastards.'

I smelled that delicious drink Conrad had given me as a hangover cure. A smile, and then a hand extending a steaming cup.I didn't look up, but gulped it all down.

Shortly after that, the only thing I remembered was my eyes becoming heavy and closing.

A huge dark mass swirled toward me, distended like some ugly growth from which amber eyes glowed at me through frameless glasses. It billowed and towered over me, sucking the air from me. Clawed hands reached out for me. My feet were glued to the ground. I twisted and pulled, but I couldn't move. I fell, and the black engulfed me. I choked, suffocating.

'It's okay, it's okay. You're dreaming.'

I opened my eyes. Sweat ran over me. I wasn't trapped in a B movie, but safe in my own bedroom, soft green surrounding me. Conrad sat on the bed, his warm hand holding my cold one.

'Hi.' He kissed me lightly on my left cheek. 'Are you very sore?'

My wrists and arms ached, my face hurt, my neck was a nightmare.

'Not so bad,' I said. 'What about you?'

'A few bruises. I've had worse.' A narrow bandage was taped across his forehead. Grazed skin on his nose and cheek overlay purple bruising. He handed me a glass of water, and I listened while I drank. He'd recovered consciousness, gotten to a phone and called Gianni, who had picked him up and organised people and cars. I'd been detained in a former station house, scheduled for demolition. He looked away when he explained the minuscule tracker he'd clipped into the lining of my purse.

'I'm sorry if you think it over-protective,' he said. 'Jupiter, I'm a thousand times glad I put it there.'

I let that pass. I was alive after all. 'Who were they?'

'The one who questioned you is that bastard Renschman, from the Economy Security Department. It's not a group we thought we needed to monitor before, so our intel's a bit sketchy.'

'They were so casually brutal,' I said, trying to sound more together than I was. 'When that one smacked my face, he did it so deliberately. How can they be that cold?'

'Agencies here don't beat up their own unindicted nationals unless they have very strong reasons. They can't have much of a legal case. Probably why they tried the persuasive method.'

I was shocked that he said that so calmly, but not as shocked as I would have been a few days before.

'No point offering you money; you've potentially got too much to be bribed. You're young and female, with no close relatives apart from the Browns to protect you. They're unlikely to be of any help pressuring you either, so scaring you is the logical way.'

'They were mean bastards,' I said. 'That son of a bitch called me unpatriotic. If he's the real America, you can screw it!' I hung my head. 'I feel so stupid, lecturing you about how this didn't happen here.'

He tipped my head back up and looked me full in the eye. 'But you knew that it did, after that business in the park.'

That was cruel, but honest.

'Anyway, Steven Smith has stopped them for the time being,' he continued. 'They won't want their activities highlighted in open court – he thinks they'll offer a compromise of some sort.'

'Who is he? He was so composed in front of those creeps. He looked like a stationery salesman.'

Conrad laughed. 'He's one of the sharpest lawyers in New York. He represents your grandmother personally as well as the Mitela family interests here. Aurelia Mitela doesn't have anything cheap or shoddy, including advisors.'

'I need to get up, I guess, if we're expecting such illustrious company. What time is it?'

'Just before nine.'

'What? My boss. He's expecting me to brief him this morning on your cousin's project.'

'No, he isn't. I phoned and explained you'd had an accident and would be laid up for a while. He sent his good wishes for a speedy recovery, but asks if you would call him "at your earliest convenience".'

'I'll call him back right now. You know something, Conrad, thanks, but I can call in sick myself.'

'Not sure you could lie so well, though.'

I shuffled out of my bedroom half an hour later, heading for the kitchen to fix myself some breakfast, and found my apartment full of people. Sleeping bags and backpacks were piled up in the corner, my furniture was all moved around. Conrad was sitting on the displaced couch, half an eye on the TV newscast, half-listening to a man next to him. A dark-haired woman perched on one of my dining chairs, her head forward, intent on the other man's words. Both wore jeans and tees, the woman with a tan leather jacket.

A man with a clean-shaven head and gold earring in his ear, and wearing a cook's apron, pushed through the kitchen door and smiled at me.

'Good morning, Miss Brown. Are you hungry? I have a selection for you, but I expect you'd like a cup of coffee first?'

Who the hell was this? And in my kitchen?

'I'm Marcus. I'm looking after your housekeeping so you can do the important stuff.' He waved his hand toward Conrad and the others. He had a light, melodious accent as if he were speaking opera.

The talking stopped and the others sprang to their feet. Conrad waved the other two back down. He came over and led me to my own thrift shop table, now impeccably polished and set.

'What the hell is going on?' I whispered.

'After yesterday's débâcle, I've arranged some protection for you. There'll be one guard inside, one on the door outside and one in the lobby downstairs. You can't be expected to cater for them, so I've brought Marcus in.'

'And asking me wasn't an option?'

'No.'

'You're damned high-handed.'

He did that annoying shrug thing. 'I will not allow you to be hurt again or put in any kind of danger, ever. I wanted to come into that building and tear that man apart last night. Steven Smith said it would have endangered everything. I respect his judgement. But if I ever meet Renschman again, I will kill him.'

God, he was scary at that moment.

Luckily, a plate of breakfast arrived.

'I ate earlier,' Conrad said when I looked at the gap in front of him, but he took a roll to eat with his coffee. It unnerved me, eating in front of these other people. Marcus seemed approachable. The woman and man nodded politely and kept their distance, but I could see the intense interest in their eyes as they glanced at me.

'If for any reason I'm not here, if you have any questions or want anything, you ask them. They both speak good English. Their names are Galla and Maro,' Conrad said. 'Do you understand?' He talked at me like some junior recruit. I almost saluted, but didn't dare. I was only too glad he was on my side.

18

Renschman scratched at the cloth on the back seat to counteract some of the urge. It would be so easy to stretch his hand out, tap the driver's shoulder and get a cigarette. But he'd promised himself, so he didn't. He looked up at the girl's window. He'd seen one of them in the lobby as they drove past. There had to be at least three upstairs, including that bastard Tellus. He should have beaten the shit out of that pretty boy when he had him. Or waterboarded him. But O'Keefe had grabbed his wrist – no mean feat, for a skirt.

'You can't terminate him. He's diplomatic.'

'He's a damned spook.'

'He's on a CD passport. Leave it.'

But that lawyer. The girl's lawyer. So smug, looking down his nose when he sprang her. Another privileged Harvard weenie. He considered rearranging his body like that Chicago termination four years ago. The patrolman had thrown up when he found that corpse. No, he needed to focus on the girl. Even his supervisor had upgraded the operation to 'all necessary means' to secure Brown Industries. It was past time for scaring.

19

Steven Smith arrived exactly on time, as unruffled and self-contained as in yesterday's nightmare.

'I hope you've recovered from your unhappy experience yesterday,' he said. 'I sent draft papers for proceedings for compensation to Mr Renschman's agency this morning. Unless I have a satisfactory answer by midday, I intend to file them at the local courthouse later today.'

'Thank you, Mr Smith, but I don't want the money. I just want them to leave me alone.'

'You should never despise money, you know,' he said. 'The punitive damages claim is to make him back off, to show we're serious. I really don't see why we should be reasonable in these circumstances.'

His matter-of-fact tone made his words sound so much more ruthless. He looked at Conrad who nodded.

'I discussed the situation before us last night with Conradus Tellus and your grandmother. I think it would be useful to outline your options for the future.'

'My options?'

'You turn twenty-five in August. Because you have two nationalities, this Economy Security Department is concerned that you may take control of Brown Industries abroad with you should you ever decide to exercise your right to go and live in Roma Nova. As of now, they have not quite fifty days to get you to assign the company into their control.'

'Wait a minute, what do you mean: "two nationalities"?'

The lawyer frowned. 'How long have you been in New York, Miss Brown?'

'A little under seven years. Why?'

'The Roma Nova legation in Washington will have sent you a letter when you were eighteen, inviting you to contact the legation to reconfirm your identity as a Roma Novan and discuss your automatic right of residence. It will have gone to your last known address in Nebraska. Didn't you receive it?'

'No, no, I didn't.'

'Or the reminders?'

I shook my head.

'Did you maintain contact with your cousins after you came to New York?'

After their refusal to let me go to college, I'd run off to New York on the interstate bus the day after I graduated from high school, paying the fare with money scrimped from carrying out other students' homework assignments. I couldn't meet his eyes. 'Not very often,' I mumbled. 'We...we fell out.'

'Do they forward mail?'

'One or two letters from school friends at first, but nothing for years.'

I'd gone back once, three years ago; even had a cab drive me between the featureless stubbled fields, through clouds of dust to the farm front door. I'd gazed at the faded paint for five minutes, and then told him to take me back to the railroad station.

'I see,' Steven Smith said, and waited a few moments. 'Well, I think we can conclude that, for whatever reason, these letters did not reach you. Your grandmother inferred that you didn't want to make contact. She was concerned that you should receive your mother's inheritance, even if you didn't want anything to do with your Roma Novan family. Conradus Tellus was sent as a final attempt to find you.'

Damn Aunt and Uncle Brown. No, it was probably him – I knew how much of a bigot he was; he hated 'foreigners'. Could he have been envious, deep down?

'How much do you know about the set-up in Roma Novan families?' Steven Smith asked, interrupting my irritation.

'I know my grandmother heads up the family – that's about it.'

''Well, very simply, extended families form the basic social structure; property and family names descend through the female line. Aurelia Mitela would naturally wish to welcome home not only her granddaughter but also her direct heir.'

'So you're saying that I have a Roma Novan identity, and my grandmother would accept me into her family, even now?'

'I think she would be ecstatic,' he replied with a half-smile.

'Okay, tell me about my options, Mr Smith.'

'If you stay here, Renschman will pursue you by any means possible, including legal or administrative loopholes. A former classmate of mine in the External Affairs Department made some discreet enquiries. Mr Renschman is, let us say, very focused on achieving his goals, to the point of ignoring structures and frameworks. I would do my absolute utmost to protect you legally, but I can't prevent your physical seizure.'

He paused, looking at me, waiting for some reaction, I guessed. I couldn't say anything, but nodded at him to continue.

'Conradus Tellus and his people can't stay and guard you indefinitely; their duties and the cost to the imperial public purse would rule it out. A private security firm is an option, but it could be easily infiltrated by Renschman's people.'

A wave of cold washed through me.

'However, if you chose to make your home with your grandmother in Roma Nova, you would be out of their jurisdiction. No extradition treaty exists at present with the EUS. Apart from belonging to the European Economic Federation, Roma Nova has few treaties with anyone. All you need do is reconfirm your Roma Novan citizenship and renounce your EUS one.'

What was he suggesting? That I emigrate to Roma Nova? Permanently? He couldn't be serious. But there seemed to be no way out of this. He was convinced it would be unsafe for me to walk along the street. That I would be in danger of getting snatched again by a government spook agency and 'disappearing'. I didn't see a trace of humour in his face. A week ago, I would have thought he was insane. Now, he made a macabre kind of sense. The hell of a decision to make.

Strange – my mother had made her choice the other way around, out of love. She hadn't been threatened by maniacs sponsored by her own government.

'And Brown Industries?'

'If you decided to emigrate, I would start filing protection procedures immediately. Ways exist for non-EUS overseas residents to do this which are not open to EUS residents. I'm sorry to be able to give you only one realistic option. But it's your choice, of course.'

'Okay, thanks. That gives me plenty to go on for the present.' I caught myself picking at the fabric on the couch arm.

He understood immediately and got up to leave. I stared at the wall, numb at the immensity of what he had said.

20

I retreated to my bedroom. I needed to collect my thoughts somewhere away from all those people. Until an hour ago, having a nationality wasn't something I'd given much thought to. I was Karen Brown who lived in the Eastern United States of America. Period. So giving up something so formless was weird. My father, but much more so the Browns, had drilled into me how lucky I was to be born in the greatest country in the world, where rights and freedoms were sacred. In the last week, I'd discovered nothing was sacred. I'd seen first-hand what a shovel-load of hypocrisy it was. I wanted to go shout in the street about how I'd been betrayed. I pulled up fistfuls of bedding and wanted to tear them into shreds.

I had an alternative. But, if I took that, there would be no return.

Half an hour later, Conrad put his head around the door and came in with a tray of sandwiches. The warmth in his smile travelled up and filled his eyes. Sure, he'd been the one trying to protect me in all this danger, but what I felt for him wasn't gratitude.

'Not a great set of options, is it?' he said.

'Was this what you meant when we were talking by the pool?'

He nodded.

Disruptive didn't begin to describe it. I would have a family there, I'd be comfortable materially, and I would be able to keep my father's legacy. But every tiny thing would be different.

I'd been forced, sobbing, from my East Coast home after Dad died, and dumped in the Midwest when I was twelve, and survived. I'd escaped that bleakness and settled in New York, and adapted. Hell, given the choice between twenty years shut up in a miserable penitentiary and another move, I knew which I needed to pick. I could do this. I took the sandwiches and smiled back.

After breakfast the next morning, Steven Smith called. I put it on loudspeaker.

'Good morning, Miss Brown, captain. I'm afraid I'm going to have to rearrange our next meeting to tomorrow morning at ten thirty instead of this afternoon. Something has come up which must be done immediately. I apologise for the inconvenience and trust you understand.'

His tone was tense, insistent even. I didn't know we had fixed a definite meeting time. And he'd called Conrad 'captain'. So, was Conrad military? Why hadn't he told me? But, as I replaced the handset and turned to challenge him, my question fled. His face had gone white; his mouth reduced to a thin line as if pulled tight by a thread.

'Galla, Maro, Marcus – in here, stat!' he shouted at the closed kitchen door. The three of them materialised within seconds. 'Emergency evac. Galla, transport.'

She nodded and stabbed a number into a tiny cell phone.

'Marcus, get the domestics arranged, especially that sign on the door.' Next, he turned to me. 'You have exactly fifteen minutes to gather up essential items. Then we're leaving. Everything else will be packed by Marcus and will follow us. We have to get you out.'

I stared at him, dumbfounded.

'I know it's difficult to grasp, but you need to get moving *now*.' Conrad's voice was firm. His eyes bored into mine as if forcing me to move by his willpower alone. 'Give Marcus your Internet access details. He'll stop them hacking your accounts and seizing your money. He can block them but needs the passwords. Please, Karen, believe me on this.' He fished out his tiny cell and started talking without waiting for any reply.

My stupefied brain managed to organise itself. I gave Marcus my cards, accounts and codes. I listened, almost detached, as I heard my voice speak clearly and make perfect sense. That done, I pulled a case out of my closet. I threw in a change of clothes and my box of photos. I seized a frame of my parents. I left the Browns. I grabbed my file box, crammed it into a duffel, picked up my case, a sweater and coat, changed into my toughest sneakers, grabbed my purse and was ready. I did it within twelve minutes.

Back in the living room, Conrad was still talking on his phone. He snapped it shut as he saw me. The last image I ever had of my apartment was of Marcus sitting in front of my laptop, his flying fingers logging on.

We shot down Eleanor Roosevelt Drive and reached the heliport by the river, opposite the Bellevue Free Hospital. Galla went to the office with a bunch of papers and brought back a pilot. The helicopter engine noise was deafening, and I struggled against the downdraft from the rotors. Conrad helped me on board while Maro loaded the bags. Galla sat up with the pilot; Conrad told me she was a qualified pilot herself. She gave the signal and we were airborne. Conrad squeezed my hand to reassure me, but his attention was elsewhere. He kept glancing at his watch until we left the city limits. The rotor noise obliterated any hope of talking.

An hour later, we crossed the wide expanse of Chesapeake Bay and approached Washington. We dropped down and followed the Anacostia River as it wound south-west through dense woodland. Flights of birds swirled up from the marshland by the banks. If I'd been a tourist, I would have been thrilled to see the Presidential Mansion – built before Georgetown had been renamed Washington – the heart of the country I had grown up in. I admired the view clinically, with a bitter feeling in my heart. We landed by the river near the new International Sports Park, ducked out of the helicopter and scrambled toward three waiting vehicles. As the back door of the middle one opened for me, I turned, lifted my hand half in a wave and watched the helicopter vanish up into the sky.

21

The driver navigated our car with precise, composed movements and slid through the busy streets, somehow never slowing, staying within inches of the SUV in front. The one behind was nearly in the trunk.

'Where are we going?' I asked.

'The Roma Nova legation,' Conrad said. 'You'll be safe there. It's one of the most secure buildings in Washington.'

I rubbed my forehead with the fingertips of my right hand. 'Look, I don't know why we had to run away so suddenly. Was it that necessary?'

'Yes. Steven Smith's warning was near miraculous.' He pulled his eyes away from scanning the streets left and right. 'Before he left yesterday evening, I arranged some code phrases with him, in case he couldn't speak freely or was under duress from Renschman.'

I shivered at the thought of the immaculate Mr Smith being worked over by Renschman's thugs.

'And how did you know that was a warning?'

'When he called me "captain" and mentioned the fictitious meeting, I knew something was wrong. He's an American; he would naturally say "reschedule", so we agreed "rearrange" to mean the opposition were on their way. The clincher was when he said "immediately" and he trusted we would understand.'

'Do you ever have a normal conversation?'

'Of course. I'm having one now with you.'

'I'll try and remember that.'

In a wide, tree-lined street, we approached an arched gateway framed by a high stone wall. Double gates swung open. At the end of a driveway curving through gardens and lawns stood a large building in pale gold stone, fronted by a portico of classic columns.

Two figures emerged through the building entrance as the SUV stopped. A tall, slim man arrived first. His jet-black hair contrasted with green eyes. Nature seemed to have made him thin and stretched out, but his face showed a smile.

'Welcome, Karen Brown.' He shook my hand firmly. 'I am Favonius Cotta, chief of staff to the ambassador. May I present my protocol officer, Gaia Memmia.' Beside the striking Favonius, she looked pretty normal with brown hair, brown eyes and olive skin.

Favonius greeted Conrad, eyelids half-closed and his tone cool to the point of frost. 'Well done, captain – another successful mission to notch up.'

Ouch. What was that about?

Favonius led us inside to a lobby area with dark-tinted glass walls. He ignored the impeccably groomed man and woman behind the reception counter. He placed his open hand on a small screen, glanced into an aperture above it and spoke his name. A glass panel slid back silently to reveal an enormous courtyard open to the top of the building and covered by a clear glass roof. I gasped with surprise. I had never seen anything like it.

Around the hall ran three storeys of galleries, with a tile-floored walkway on the ground floor. In the centre lay a large garden with trees, shrubs, grasses, paths and seats.

'Impressive, isn't it?' Favonius smiled down at me. 'There's an olive tree in the middle that the first ambassador planted when the legation opened in 1792.'

He led us around the side to an elevator which we took to the second floor. His office was splendid: thick green carpet, leather couches and birchwood panelling reflecting the sunlight from the tall windows.

'Miss Brown, may I extend a formal welcome to you. As an important member of one of our leading families, the legation and its facilities are naturally at your disposal. Please call on me at any time if you have a question or would like me to arrange anything.' He smiled again. I figured he was being a little too gracious, bordering on the unctuous. He definitely wanted to be my friend. 'We've arranged accommodation for you until the, er, legal and administrative issues have been resolved.'

I glanced at Conrad but he wore a poker face.

'That's very kind of you, Favonius Cotta. How long do you think that will be?'

'Your legal representative has contacted our political officer to work on this. In the meantime, we'll do our best to help you settle in.' He nodded to his colleague. 'Gaia Memmia has a few suggestions which you may care to look at tomorrow. I imagine you'll wish to settle in today. If you're not too tired, the ambassador would like you to join her for drinks at eighteen thirty.'

Panic struck me. I had nothing to wear for a diplomatic occasion. I had little to wear at all except what I stood up in and a change of shirt and underwear.

Favonius read my mind. 'She stresses it's very informal. "Come as you are" were her exact words. In the meantime, Memmia will show you to your quarters and answer any immediate queries you have.'

He continued smiling but stood. We had come to the end of the audience with him. His firm handshake gave me the impression of a strong will behind the smile.

'Oh, Captain Tellus, a word, if you please,' Favonius called as we reached the door.

Memmia ushered me out to the elevator. I wasn't sure whether to wait or not. I felt wrong-footed somehow. I absolutely had to talk to Conrad. Maybe he was giving Favonius a report. As we walked along, I half-listened to Memmia explaining the building numbering system. She handed me a wristband with a small screen and tiny keypad.

'This gets you into anywhere in the building except the personal residences. You can call anybody else in the legation, order food, drink, anything from the commissary – the store, I mean,' she said, seeing my puzzled look. 'Others can call you and find you. I've set that to very restricted: only the ambassador, Favonius and myself. You don't want each and every person in the legation tracking you.'

I needed to get that changed; I didn't want *anybody* tracking me.

At a tall, intricately carved door retro-fitted with a scanlock, she showed me how passing the wristband across the sensor opened the door. A rush of warmth and light greeted me, full of the scent of honey and vanilla. The entrance vestibule gave way to a living area with two tall picture windows overlooking a back lawn, two bedrooms, an enormous bathroom – the source of the honey and vanilla – and a kitchen. In the larger bedroom was a walk-in closet, like you only see in the movies, and another bathroom. My apartment would have fit in a quarter of it. What was I to do with all this space?

'Memmia…No, can I call you Gaia? It seems so formal to use your surname.'

'Of course, *domina*, whatever you wish.' Then she became really brave. 'It's called a *nomen* or family name, rather than a surname. Yours is Mitela, like your grandmother.'

'That's more musical than plain old Brown,' I said, laughing.

She hesitated then smiled.

'I suppose I get a new first name, do I?'

'Your mother registered you with the legation as "Carina" when you were born.' The name Conrad had called me at Gianni's. 'Perhaps that's why they called you Karen in English.'

So I was reverting to my original name. It was a cool name, but did I need to get a new personality to go with it? Pushing that thought away, I looked at my watch. 'Gaia, where's Conradus Tellus?'

She glanced away. 'I think he will have been occupied with reporting in to the military commander attached to the legation.'

'So he *is* military.'

'Of course,' She looked puzzled.

"And how long would that take?"

She didn't meet my eyes. Around the room, on the floor, anywhere but on me.

'C'mon, Gaia, would it really take an hour?'

She said nothing. She acted as guilty as a junior park volunteer caught littering.

'Okay, here's the thing,' I said. 'You either explain exactly what's going on, or I take the elevator down to that big courtyard and run around making a lot of noise to find out. Your choice.'

'I…I…'

'You have thirty seconds, starting now,' I said, looking at my watch.

I hoped I wasn't losing my first friend here. I was making my way to the door when she capitulated.

She stared at her feet, looking as if her world was falling apart. 'Favonius Cotta considers it inappropriate for you to be encumbered by any obligations you may have had before coming to the legation. He wishes to separate you from the chancellor's family,' she muttered.

An hour in and I was already plunged into political shark-infested waters.

'Thank you, Gaia. I'm grateful for what you've done – it must have been hard for you. Let's you and I go for a walk downstairs and do some exploring of our own.'

She stared at me as if I were a scary snake.

'But before we do, I want you to adjust my wristband options…'

The functional departments formed the east side of the legation, with the military office in the corner between the north and east sides. Once there, I dismissed Gaia for her own protection. By the time Favonius tracked me down the old-fashioned way, I was chatting with the legation military commander. Teasing out some arcane family connections, she had found we were related. We were calling each other 'cousin' by the time Favonius came knocking at the door.

'Ah, Miss Brown,' he said, 'I was worried about you. There must be some malfunction on your wrist unit. Do let me escort you back to your apartment.'

'Oh, please don't concern yourself. Cousin Faleria and I are discussing my father's and her own military service. I'm absolutely fine here.'

He looked as sick as a pig.

'I'm sure she'll provide me with an escort back if I need one. Please don't let me interrupt your work any longer.' I gave him a full-teeth smile and turned back to the commander. I sensed, rather than saw, Favonius leave. I also saw respect glimmer in Faleria's eyes.

Face washed, teeth brushed and hair combed, I felt marginally more prepared when Conrad pinged the scanlock half an hour later. He looked preoccupied but gave me a quick smile.

He opened his mouth but I got there first. 'It's okay. Gaia filled me in. Is it going to be a problem?'

'Just Favonius playing stupid power games.' He threw himself on the huge leather couch. 'He and Uncle Quintus are political rivals. Quintus is senior, obviously, but, as the legation's chief of staff, Favonius pulled rank on me.' He snorted. 'Damn politicos.'

'I spoke to Faleria,' I said, 'and I think I may have straightened it out.'

'You?'

'Yes, me. I told her I might need your advice and support from time to time.' I glanced at him. 'She said it was fine, anytime, you just had to sign out.'

He raised his eyebrows, gave me a puzzled look, but didn't comment.

Walking to the ambassador's residence along the tall, marble-floored hallway, Conrad told me she'd been one of my grandmother's trainees at the foreign ministry. In a deep-carpeted side passage lined with oak book cabinets and marble busts, he buzzed us through a security barrier and we stopped in front of double doors with the sign 'Domus Nunciae'. Conrad squeezed my shoulder in encouragement. I took a deep breath and knocked.

'Carina Mitela, welcome. Or would you prefer Karen Brown? Such a lot to take in.' The figure in front of me chuckled. She was shorter than me, in her fifties, I guessed, with brown hair and eyes. As she led us in, she walked with the grace of a ballet dancer.

'My name is Claudia Cornelia, and this is my husband, Ted Johansson, your "fellow American".' Her eyes were full of mischief as she introduced him. Tall, blond and spare, he looked like the stereotype Harvard professor as portrayed in the movies. He told me later that that was exactly what he'd been, except it was Yale.

'Hello, Karen.' His handshake was dry but firm. I was instantly charmed. Maybe it was the warmth of his smile, or maybe because his East Coast accent reminded me of everything I'd left behind when I'd been moved out at twelve. He poured us some chilled white wine, like the German wine Hayden drank. I later found out it was a famous Roma Novan export.

'I heard about the misunderstanding with Favonius,' Claudia said.

'He should have known better. He let his personal political sense get the better of him.'

I didn't follow her.

'This may seem alien to you but, with your grandmother's political role close to the imperatrix, you're an immediate connection with the upper layers of power.'

I exchanged glances with Conrad. My most political act to date was registering my vote. I was way out of my depth.

22

I stumbled out of bed some hours later. I was only half-awake, but I felt a whole lot better when I'd had a shower. I was lying on the bed afterward in the robe I'd found in the bathroom, watching CNN, when I heard the door ping echoed by the remote control in my hand. The remote's tiny display panel showed Conrad's face. I touched the screen which buzzed him in. One of Sextilius's inventions, I recalled.

'Are you up yet?' he called out.

'Sure. Been awake for ages,' I lied, scrambling up and heading for the living room.

My mouth fell open. He was dressed in uniform: beige pants and short-sleeved shirt with shoulder tabs and breast pockets, with a black tee underneath showing at his neck. A gold badge like an NYPD detective's ID, but with a crowned eagle, was clipped to his right pocket. His hair, his beautiful long hair, had gone. Only an inch of gold stubble remained on his head.

'Bit of a change, isn't it?' He grinned. 'I can't sit around and do nothing. I've nearly caught up on my leave, so I may as well get back on duty. I've never worked on a legation detail. It's not exactly my normal line of work, but...' He shrugged.

'What *is* your normal line of work?'

'Oh, general security stuff.'

I waited but he didn't say any more.

'But it's not likely to be for very long, is it?'

A shadow passed across his face. 'I saw the political officer this morning, very briefly. She believes there may be complications with the Americans. Sometimes, the EUS seems to think it rules the whole damn planet, and we lesser mortals all have to dance to their tune. There's a case meeting this afternoon with Steven Smith. Where will you be after lunch?'

'I don't have a clue.'

He laughed. 'Memmia is bound to be along with a full schedule soon, so I'd get dressed if I were you.'

'Before you go, give me your number on this wrist thing.'

He lifted my hand, entered his number for me then glanced up to look directly into my eyes. That woke me up.

'Why don't you have a wristband?'

'I use a different system, but the number's good.'

'How?'

'Never mind, Miss Nosey,' he said, touching my nose with the tip of his finger.

I made a face at him.

'By the way, have a look in your closet,' he said as he crossed the hallway. He was gone before I could reply.

I found a small selection of 'casual smart' clothes, maybe a little preppy for me. Two pairs of shoes looked lonely in rows of transparent boxes. I had no doubt that everything would fit.

I gazed at my reflection in the mirror. I didn't think I looked any different from twenty-four hours ago. It was my world that had been reordered.

My old world interrupted in the form of a frantic text from my friend Amanda: *Where tf r u? CM ASAP.* Sure, Amanda, I'll call, but would you believe me? I texted back that I was fine, staying with friends and would call tomorrow. Inevitably, the cell rang.

'Karen? Are you okay?'

'Hi, Amanda, I'm fine.'

'That's it? I've been really worried. The boss said you'd had some accident and your "friend" had called you in sick. So did Mr Fabulous re-materialise?'

I laughed.

'So spill. Did you get it on?'

'Amanda! No.' I heard her groan. 'Look, I'm fine. I'm staying with some of his friends in Washington for a little while.'

'Washington. Jeez! I think I'd better come down there and check it out.'

'No! I mean, no, don't worry. Everything's fine. Really.'

Who was I trying to convince?

'You be careful now. Don't get up to any shit I would. Promise you'll call me in a day or two, yeah?'

'Sure. Have to go now. Love you, 'Manda. Bye.'

I could see her sitting at her wreck of a desk, shoulders hunched, sucking on a pencil, eyes darting all over the room while she spoke. Maybe looking across at my empty chair. Or she could be pressing buttons on the drinks machine in the corridor, her brick-size cell jammed between her tilted head and raised shoulder, but now getting drinks only for one.

Gaia Memmia knocked on the door at exactly ten thirty.

'Coffee?' I waved a mug at her.

She looked horrified.

'What?'

'You can't serve me.'

'I'm not serving you. I'm making you a cup of coffee.'

'Please, let me do it.'

'Look, this is my kitchen, in my apartment. Here I'll act like a normal person. Outside, I'll go along with what you want. End of discussion.' I added a smile to soften the sting of my words.

I set the coffee on the table opposite my place and sat down. She hovered for some moments, glanced over at me, but eventually took the chair where the coffee was. She sipped and collected herself. Was it going to be this hard with everybody?

'Before we get going, I'd like to call my grandmother, but I can't find a telephone in this apartment. Or do I use my cell?'

'Oh, no, no, of course not.' She led me over to the slimline PC screen on top of the small desk in a corner of the living room. She pulled up a dining chair beside the office chair already there and gestured me to sit.

'We don't use standard telephones – they're a bit old-fashioned.'

She tapped away on the keyboard then selected n entry in a database. After a couple of seconds, a solemn male face appeared on the screen. 'Domus Mitelarum. *Salve.*'

Gaia rattled off a volley of Latin, the screen cleared and my grandmother appeared. Gaia jumped up as if the seat was suddenly too hot and fled. I heard her close the kitchen door behind her.

'Karen. How are you?'

'Bewildered.'

She forced out a short laugh. 'I'm not surprised. I've heard the whole story from Steven Smith. You've had an appalling time. I'm so sorry.'

'I feel an idiot, lecturing you and Conrad on how this type of thing didn't happen here.'

The set lines in her face softened. 'Don't upset yourself, darling. You were only standing your corner for what you believed in. It's the corner that's let you down.'

I looked down at my hands – I was embarrassed at how naive I'd been. My nails were chipped and skin rough. Despite the arnica, the red bracelets on my wrist skin hadn't faded.

'I think so much has happened that your mind hasn't processed it all yet,' she said. 'Give yourself a few days to settle down.'

A few days? I doubted I would ever get over it.

Gaia emerged from the kitchen a few minutes after I'd finished the call. She had plenty of ideas for me. Firstly, Latin coaching – that was putting it politely. She would go through social and cultural stuff herself. I hoped she would get over her deference issues, but I doubted it.

She took me on an extended tour of the legation. People seemed friendly, but nervous of me. Lunchtime, despite Gaia's protests, I insisted we eat where everybody else did – I didn't want to be stuck on my own. In the central dining room, heads turned and bodies twisted around in their seats, checking out my every move. Gaia led me to the back where my new cousin Faleria sat along with Sergia, the angry woman I'd met at Gianni's. This time, she was wearing a business suit and had black hair drawn back in a chignon, but had kept the sour face.

'I believe we're meeting this afternoon,' I said, and smiled at her. Maybe she'd be a little more relaxed on her home territory.

'I think you are correct, Carina Mitela,' she replied; no, she was still uptight. Filling the silence, Faleria asked how I was doing.

'Not too bad, but I feel uncomfortable when people stare at me. Some of them are really nervous when they talk to me.'

'How would you like to be treated, then?' Sergia interrupted

'Good question. I know I'm an interloper, a refugee. I wish they would talk to me like I was a normal visitor, not some exotic alien from outer space.'

'You *are* an exotic alien from outer space as far as most people are concerned,' Sergia shot back. 'They're unlikely to have come into contact with such a senior patrician, and they're not likely to again.'

Gaia gasped at such directness.

'So are you saying I should suck it up and sit on it?'

'I don't always follow American idiom, but it sounds as if you have summarised it well.' Even Faleria stared at that. I had the firm impression that Sergia was being rude in order to provoke me. I laughed in her face.

She looked annoyed, her face flushed. Round one to me.

'Something to fortify you.' Conrad appeared at our table out of nowhere and set a steaming cup in front of me.

Oh, was I glad to see him.

'I came to see if you wanted to take a walk through the garden before the meeting.' His tone was light but, in contrast, his eyes were intense, the brown almost obliterating the green edges.

When I'd finished my coffee and stood up to go, Gaia, Faleria and, more slowly, Sergia, rose to their feet at the same time.

'Please, don't let me disturb you,' I said.

'Ladies.' Conrad gave them his bedazzling smile as his parting shot.

'I was nearly screaming.'

'You did look pretty desperate. Have you been behaving badly?'

'Not really,' I said. 'I only lost my temper once with Gaia, had a self-indulgent whine, and laughed in Sergia's face. Does that count?'

He smiled down at me and I smiled back. My fingers touched his bare forearm. As we entered the garden, he clasped my hand. When we reached some tall shrubs, he wrapped his arm around my waist and pulled me to him so tightly that a hair would have been crushed between us. He held me as if he'd been saving the strength up for some time. I raised my face, barely opened my lips and he kissed me, lightly, as if only flirting with my mouth. A soft electric flow travelled into the centre of my body and spread through my nervous system to each cell. My fingers skimmed the side of his neck, feeling the pulse beating fast. He kissed me again; the electric flow crackled sparks. I gasped for breath as he released my lips and smiled into my eyes.

'I've wanted to do that since I walked into your office in New York.'

23

A shrill beep from Conrad's pocket interrupted us. He relaxed the intensity of his hold, but his arm still encircled my waist. He raised one eyebrow as he consulted his cell phone. My hand still gripped his other forearm.

'We have to go.' His lips spoke the words close to my ear.

I didn't want to move my arms, my legs, any part of me. I wanted to stay fixed inside this moment. His eyes looked at mine, small darting movements from one to the other. His lips brushed my forehead. I closed my eyes and was consumed by sensation.

Another beep. He smiled at me again. 'We *really* have to go. We'll talk later.'

But I saw the frustration as he pressed his lips together. I found it hard to gather my thoughts, let alone my words. We walked on for a few minutes in silence.

'So,' I said eventually, 'is this meeting we're going to a council of war or a positioning session?'

He laughed. 'And you call me cynical.'

'Hey, I've been in some pretty intense meetings myself. Do you think the only sharks are political?'

He shrugged. His face took on a serious expression. 'The trouble is the legation wants to keep its cordial relations with the government here, but is under pressure from home to give you a hundred per cent support. The last thing they want is a full-blown diplomatic incident.

We don't depend on the EUS like other countries do, but we're small, and who wants to fall out with one of the three world superpowers, however annoying they are?' He looked at me. 'More than that, I don't know until we get there.'

Favonius had marked out his territory in the conference room with his immaculate leather notecase and gold pen on the big square table, his chair angled back, facing the entrance. He was standing at the window talking to Sergia.

An expressionless Gaia was tapping notes into an electronic pad. She looked up as we entered the room and got to her feet. Right on cue, Favonius and Sergia turned as one.

'My dear Carina Mitela, please, come and sit down,' Favonius projected an intense smile. 'Can I get you a coffee?'

'I'm fine, thank you. Conradus?'

Conrad gave Favonius a cold, tight smile. I could see on his face that the temptation to have Favonius run around after him was almost overwhelming. Favonius let his diplomatic shell crack enough to shoot an angry glance back. Conrad moved half a step nearer me, keeping his eyes on Favonius's face.

Thankfully, Steven Smith was announced at that moment. He grasped the situation immediately and half-smiled, his eyes bright. A second later, he switched to solemn and greeted the others formally.

'If I may, I'll bring you up to date on events since we last met,' he said, once we were settled round the table.

I was bursting with curiosity.

'Very fortunately, my classmate at External Affairs was able to warn me that Renschman's unit was obtaining special clearance for a live operation within the metropolitan area of New York.' He turned to me. 'I concluded his intention was to remove you from your apartment, despite the legal measures we initiated. I hadn't received a reply about the action for damages. Given the sensitivity, I made my warning call to you as discreet as possible.' He glanced over at Conrad and continued.

'I hastened to your apartment and reached it twenty minutes after I put the phone down. Four of Captain Tellus's colleagues arrived five minutes later and, with the two guards already there, we were able to repel boarders, so to speak. Of course, the notice declaring your apartment to be a residential annex of the legation didn't hurt. It's of dubious legality in this context, but it added impact.' He shrugged, in a very understated way. 'Mr Renschman was somewhat put out at his lack of success and lost his dignity to the extent of outlining what he would like to do to me. I'm sure he'll reach a more mature decision when he's had time to reflect. I took the liberty of recording our conversation in case his memory becomes defective.'

I laughed out loud. 'Mr Smith, you are beautiful!'

He paused, looked down at his papers then glanced at Sergia. 'Because of the political implications, I've discussed the case with Antonia Sergia. I expect an unofficial approach will be made soon to you, Favonius, probably a lunch, a country club evening or a simple telephone call. With the greatest respect in the world, for I would not dream of teaching you your job, it would be helpful if you didn't agree to anything without consulting me. Whilst I recognise the political sensitivies, the primary interest here is that of the Mitela family heir. I understand that the imperatrix has taken a personal interest in her cousin's safety.'

Favonius glanced down at the table for a second and frowned. He came back up with a bland expression and nodded at Sergia.

'This Economy Security Unit is some kind of sub-group which we think is financed by Treasury and Security possibly with some input from Defense.' She hesitated, consulting her el-pad. 'We've confirmed that Renschman is ex-CIA, ex-military and regarded as a fixer. A very efficient one. He's had some authority problems, but that's as far as my informant went. I'm pursuing two other sources.'

'Thank you, Sergia,' said Favonius. 'Keep on it.' He aimed his full smile at the lawyer. 'So what's the next legal step, Mr Smith?.

'We file for renunciation of Miss Brown's EUS citizenship. It will be interesting to see what reaction that provokes.'

'Very well. If I may give you a suggestion in turn, counsellor, I think it would be helpful to us if you didn't pursue this too vigorously and alienate the authorities in your eagerness to get this processed.'

'Please be assured, Favonius Cotta, that I'm fully aware of your anxiety. We are not entirely without the ability to be studiously courteous and patient in our approach.'

I could only admire Steven Smith for his mastery of the polite put-down.

Favonius attempted to regain the initiative. 'I think that's all, unless anybody has anything else?'

'We're going to talk with Mr Smith for a few more minutes,' I said. 'I wouldn't dream of holding up your work, so please don't let us detain you.' I produced my best saccharine smile.

He nodded and left with his entourage.

'You do enjoy pushing it, don't you?' Conrad gave me a measured look.

'Yes, but he's so up himself, it's irresistible.'

'I agree with Miss Brown,' Steven Smith said. 'Nevertheless, it would probably be wiser not to overindulge in that particular sport. Favonius is well connected and, although not one of the Twelve, his family has influence.'

'Okay, point taken.' I looked him in the eye. 'Did I understand it right? Is this going to be a problem, this nationality thing? Will it take a long time?'

He glanced away for a few seconds. 'Well, if we file the initial documentation now, it will start the process off.'

Which wasn't any kind of answer.

He pushed a printed form with several attached documents toward me – a questionnaire and a voluntary relinquishment statement. He'd attached certified copies of both my birth certificates, with a translation of the Latin one, and my social security card. 'All I need from you now is your signature in the three places marked with a pencil cross.'

I held the pen a few inches above the form. Scarcely seventy-two hours after being terrorised by government thugs, I was signing away something that other people desperately sought from that same government. Naively, they thought it gave them protection, rights and status. But I'd discovered the hard way what an illusion it was.

I duly signed *K Brown*. Would I ever use that signature again?

24

'Bit of a Rubicon for you, wasn't it?' Conrad asked as we walked back after saying goodbye to Mr Smith.

'A what?'

'Going past a point of no return.'

'Yes, I guess it is. It's leaving something I've known all my life. You're told it's a wonderful democracy where individual rights are protected, you salute the flag, recite the oath, and so on. Teachers, Uncle Brown, everybody said so. It becomes second nature – you don't challenge it.'

'Not even you?'

I rolled my eyes at him.

'But since O'Keefe and Renschman, it means nothing. I feel as if I've been taken for a ride my whole life.' I looked at him. 'Will it be any different in Roma Nova?' I tried not to sound dejected.

'Hey.' He put his arm around me. 'Don't be so worried. I think you'll find it a lot better. Probably more direct than you're used to, perhaps more regulated. People are expected to be responsible for themselves and to make an effort to take part in things, to contribute.'

'What, even those like Favonius?'

'He may want to be king of the pile, but he's not only doing it for himself – he's doing it for his family, his tribe. And somewhere under all that oil, he's doing it for his country.'

We found a couch opposite a painting of a tough but

distinguished-looking woman, brown hair piled up and eyes looking down her nose.

'But there's this patrician group I'm supposed to belong to?' Although I hadn't given her the satisfaction that I cared, Sergia's remark about being like an alien had stung.

'Yes, you do. They're descendants of the original Twelve Families that founded Roma Nova. Many of them go into public service, the law or even the military, like me.' He paused. 'Failing or dereliction by a member of the Twelve is treated more seriously – basically, they're expected to know better.'

'But I don't know what the proper things to do are, how to talk to people, whether what I'm saying is right.' I wanted to run. 'Oh God, Conrad, what have I done?'

He grasped me by both shoulders and held me at arm's length until I stopped trembling. 'It's the way you behave, your attitude and instincts that are crucial. Yours are absolutely right. Look how you reacted to Favonius's attempt to manipulate you. I've watched you set others at their ease, like Gaia. You treat them like people, not clones or inferiors.'

I thought he was trying too hard to cheer me up, but I did feel less like I'd made a huge mistake.

'Come and sit with me in the mess bar.' He took my arm and we walked back to the military office. Inside, past the scanners, opposite the entrance to the dormitories, was a small room to the left with groups of easy chairs, low tables and a counter with bottles and bar machinery behind. Photographs and military insignia relieved the plain cream decor. About half a dozen uniformed women and men sat around talking quietly. As they started to rise, Conrad waved them back down. A uniformed steward took our order for drinks. The rest of them went straight back to their own conversations.

'They'll be looking, but they won't stare,' he said.

He was right. I caught a few covert glances but they didn't inspect me like the prize exhibit on show. I saw a movement at the door. A tall woman with black hair, uniformed and with the same type of gold badge as Conrad glanced at us, nodded to others and made her way to the bar counter. She ordered a beer, walked over to us with a confident air and sat down.

'Hello, Tellus.'

'Dexia. Finished?'

'Yes, thank the gods! *Sanitas bona.*' She took a good swallow. 'I needed that.' She put her hand out. 'Antonia Dexia.'

I took it gladly. 'Carina Mitela.'

'I thought so. Have you retreated here for some peace and quiet?'

'How did you guess?'

'I expect you're tired of the politicos crawling all over you.' She took another sip of her beer. 'We don't allow them in the mess, so if you want to escape, feel free to come here for a bit.'

'Thanks. I might take you up on that.' I grinned at her.

'Dexia is the mess president, so she can give her gracious permission,' Conrad said in a dry tone. He took my wrist, tapped some keys and invited Dexia to enter her code.

'There, now you can come in when you want and run up a bar bill like the rest of us.'

What a refreshing change. She wore an olive-green tee under her uniform, unlike Conrad's black one.

She saw my gaze and laughed. 'I'm bog standard infantry, not like Tellus who's one of the glamorous PGSF lot.'

'What's that?'

'Hasn't he told you?' She threw a mischievous glance at Conrad. 'They're the Praetorian Guard Special Forces. The easiest way to describe them is special forces and FBI rolled up in one with a touch of CIA.'

'You mean Praetorian Guard, like in *Gladiator*?'

Dexia cracked up.

'Enough, Dexia.' Conrad frowned. 'A little more advanced than that.'

'I liked the film – they were tough but cool,' I said.

'I apologise,' said Dexia. 'I meant no disrespect. I couldn't help myself.' She turned to me. 'They're an elite unit, they inspire fear in the enemy and not much less in the rest of us. But they protect the imperatrix and, ultimately, the existence of the state, so we have to cut them some slack.'

Conrad said nothing further. She changed topics. 'So how are you settling in?'

'To be honest, it's disorientating. I thought I was an average person living a normal life. Now I'm some kind of elite being, but I don't know the rules.' I smiled from one to the other. 'Shades of *The Princess Diaries.*'

They both looked at me with blank stares.

I played with the coffee cup handle to cover my embarrassment. 'Anyway, Memmia is drawing up a schedule for me, so I'll have plenty to do.'

'Do you train?'

'When I have time, I try to run each day. I play some squash and do circuit training at the gym. Or I did.'

'If you feel like it, you could join in with us,' she said, a little too casually. She radiated fitness and health on a nuclear scale. Her idea of training was probably light years ahead of mine and twice as punishing.

'I think I'll catch up first, but I might take you up on that if I get fit enough.'

'If you've got any energy left after Tellus has finished with you,' she said, smirking.

Oh God! She thought Conrad and I were lovers. The red heat crept up my neck into my face. I looked down at the table.

'Sorry, that was a bit crude,' she said. 'I didn't mean to make you uncomfortable. I forgot you were brought up as an American.'

Were they always going to throw that in my face? Perhaps we were a bit prissy on sexual matters here, or was it only me?

'Okay, Dexia, I think Carina's had enough exposure to the rude soldiery for one day.' Conrad stood up. He held his hand out and I automatically put mine in it.

'Thank you, Dexia.' I turned back to her. 'I really value your welcome – it's like a breath of fresh air.'

'Go carefully, Mitela,' she said and grinned. 'Watch out for the sharks.'

25

Still smarting from his supervisor's reprimand, Renschman trudged back to his office. Another disciplinary warning was neither here nor there. What mattered most was that his assignment was still open.

He shook with fury at the memory of the raid. His hand had tightened around the baseball bat when they'd stormed into the girl's building. Contemptuous of the elevator, he'd run up the fire stairs with two others, his heart pumping, his nerves on edge, ready for the challenge.

She'd escaped.

Five of their goons stared grimly at him. Even numbers. Plus that smarmy little lawyer. Renschman calculated he could take two, maybe three, down within minutes. O'Keefe was babbling about everybody staying calm, doing that lowering voice psych crap.

The lawyer spoke the same way, asking them to leave, like some pansy at a tennis club dance. Frustrated, Renschman launched himself on him. He clamped his hand round the lawyer's throat and jerked him back and forward, demanding to know where they'd taken her, choking the answer out of him if necessary. He would take Steven Smith apart inch by inch, starting with his eyes.

O'Keefe shouted at him to let the lawyer go, reached into her holster, swung her service pistol up to face level and threatened to take Renschman out. Her eyes blazed as Renschman tried to stare her down. After a few tense breaths, he let go of Steven Smith's neck.

O'Keefe's ineffectives were so hamstrung by their respect for pieces of legal paper.

As they left, the little shit had told them he'd made a recording. Only O'Keefe's baboons restraining him had stopped him splitting the lawyer's head open.

Renschman grunted as he read the mail from his supervisor back at the office. Clyde had compelled the External Affairs Department to cooperate on national security grounds and refuse exit documentation. But that was only a temporary holding measure. Renschman had designed a permanent solution. He reached for his keyboard and sent an email to an old friend at the ECPC. He called in to the local supermarket on his way home, adding some disposable gloves and stationery to his regular shopping.

26

That evening in the apartment, I experimented with the internal mail system. I used the translation software to wring the gist out of it, but it could only go so far. I figured out *Plica, Editio, Promere* for File, Edit, View and *Mittere* for Send, but had to give up after that. I jabbed at the screen to log out. It was ridiculous; I couldn't do the simplest thing without the language.

The next morning, right on half past eight, Gaia collected me and delivered me to Grattius Duso. He would drive and inspire me, infuriate me and make me weep with fatigue, but he would make me literate.

Gaia told me that Grattius had been an academic and teacher all his career, and had only accepted this cultural post in Washington on condition he could carry on with his research. Apparently, he was well regarded by the faculty at William & Mary, giving lectures as a visiting professor. Frankly, I was as scared as hell when I heard that.

He welcomed me gravely and gestured for me to sit at his polished table which was piled with books. He was medium height, his mousey hair swept back to form little curls at the base of his skull.

He fixed his grey eyes on me. 'Now, we're going to be working together for a little while. I'm perfectly happy to teach you; in fact, I'm looking forward to the challenge, but I expect total commitment from you.' His mild voice took some of the condescension out of his words.

After an hour, he made me get up and walk around the room five times and drink a large glass of water. Then we did it again. At the end of the third hour, I had mastered the declensions and simple verbs. I was relieved that I remembered some of it from Latin class as a kid. When my stomach rumbled audibly, Grattius looked up, surprised.

'Time for food, I see,' he said. He handed me a small book. 'Try to learn these for tomorrow. I suggest after your lunch you rest and do something different for an hour before tackling your homework.'

My brain was reduced to mush so I merely nodded.

He stood up, held out his hand and said, 'I'll see you tomorrow morning at eight thirty.' Then he went back to his own world.

I arrived at the dining room without remembering how I got there.

Gaia came and sat down opposite me. 'Has Grattius worn you out?'

'My brain will never recover. He's given me homework as well.'

'It's hard, I know. I had to learn English before I came here. I'd only done it at school.'

'Really? But you speak so well.' She hardly had any accent, either. I didn't know whether to be impressed at her ability or depressed about my own.

'You've only done one session. This time next week, you'll have made good progress.'

I looked at her in complete disbelief, but she proved to be right. Within seven days, I could speak like a four year-old and I started writing. A week after that, I'd gained enough confidence to try it out on Conrad.

'*Macte!*' he said.

'What?'

'It means "well done".'

'You're not patronising me?'

'Of course not. I wouldn't dare.'

Steven Smith came to see me again three weeks after my arrival at the legation. He'd had a reply from the External Affairs Department about my application to renounce. Once we had satisfied their conditions, they would issue a Certificate of Loss of Nationality. But they were objecting at present as they considered my application had been made under duress.

How ironic was that?

'We have to prove you've made your application of your free will. Americans can't effectively renounce their citizenship while still in the Eastern United States. Roma Nova has generally had friendly but distanced relations with the EUS. Each quietly despises the other for different reasons.' He consulted a sheet of paper he pulled out of his folder. 'Currently, the American administration is upset that Roma Nova has sided with other European countries to protest about their Middle East policies. Your grandmother's friend Senator Calavia's open letter in the American media to the president, giving her the benefit of a two thousand year perspective on handling the Middle East, didn't go down well here. They suggest we make an appointment to come along to their office to discuss the matter.' He looked at me gravely.

I was so angry, I couldn't reply. My fingers curled into claws. As soon as I noticed, I straightened them out, but Steven Smith had seen.

'There is no way I am stepping out the front door of this building until this is settled. I can't bear the thought of facing Renschman or O'Keefe again.'

'I wouldn't dream of suggesting it. I have the recording of Mr Renschman's conversation. The threat is unambiguous.'

His hand touched the base of his neck, but so briefly I wondered if I'd seen it correctly.

'So what do we do?' I said.

'I'm going to suggest they come here, but with three international and neutral witnesses. Although the legation is not in the strictest sense foreign soil, the US authorities can't enter without the ambassador's permission, so there's some notion of extraterritoriality.'

I knew he was paid well by my grandmother, but I think he genuinely empathised with me in my predicament.

I was getting there with my new culture – I guessed it was being surrounded by it all day, every day. I stopped feeling awkward with the way people treated me. In turn, they stopped staring at me. When Conrad was on duty, and I didn't have a class, I often retreated to the mess bar and talked to Dexia or some of the others. They were tough-talking but natural. When I tried out my Latin on them, they laughed sometimes, but weren't too rude about my mistakes. But I couldn't always follow the flow of the conversation, the inferences or the profanities. I needed to get beyond Grattius's formal teaching.

I was in the garden one afternoon, struggling with a homework assignment on the crucial role of Roma Nova's legions in helping defend Vienna in the 1600s – Grattius was a little too enthusiastic about history – when I heard sobbing behind me. Behind a tall shrub sat a young girl, about fifteen or sixteen, crying her insides out.

'Hey, are you all right?'

She gave me a blank look, coated with hostility.

I tried in Latin. She said something but I couldn't understand it. I tried again but she looked at me like I was an idiot.

'Look, I don't speak very well and can't understand much more, but maybe I can help or listen?'

'Go away.'

Triumph. I understood.

'No, not until you tell me what's troubling you.'

'I hate this place,' she said after a while. 'Everything. All the people.' Her green eyes boiled with anger and hurt.

I remembered when I was that age. I resented Nebraska, the small-town life, my cousins, their stupidity.

'So is your family making you unhappy?'

'Them!' She flicked her black hair back with such force that I had the impression she'd like to throw them all the same way. 'My mother's married again, and I've been parked here with my father. I didn't want to come abroad. All my friends are at home.'

After a while, she stopped crying and wiped her nose. 'Thanks for listening to me. You're the only one who's really bothered.'

'Yes? I believe there are several young people here around your age,' I said. I ground my teeth at hearing myself say the words awkwardly.

'Them! Nobody wants to know. It's my father. I wish I was dead.'

Of course, the black hair and green eyes. Her father had to be Favonius Cotta.

'What's your first name?' I said.

'Aelia.'

'Very well, Aelia, I'm trying to learn Latin – I was born here in the EUS. I need a friend who'll teach me everyday Latin words, normal life words. If you want, I can talk to you about America, teach you some English.'

At first, she hesitated. Maybe she thought I was joking, or mocking her. She had to know exactly who I was.

'Of course, you have to teach me the bad words as well.'

She grinned. 'Oh, I know a lot of those.'

27

I watched PBS to keep up with US news, and sometimes dramas and talk shows, but a little less each day. Some days, I pressed the off button and threw the remote down on the table; so much of it seemed irrelevant.

I mastered the Latin email system and contacted my boss at Bornes & Black. He was very understanding about what had happened and sent me his best wishes. Amanda and I kept to phone and text. God only knew how she would react if she saw the Latin header to an email – probably figure I'd been kidnapped by foreign terrorists.

A letter arrived for me one morning, a regular pre-stamped envelope. It was from the IRS about undisclosed income. What the hell was that about? I had filed everything on time. I only had my regular pay cheque and the Brown Industries' quarterly payment. And did it matter now?

I was fighting my way through the bureaucratic slush, trying to work out exactly what it meant, when the words started to lose their places on the page. I creased my eyes up to concentrate but couldn't anchor the letters down to the paper. I looked up to see the walls shifting in waves around me. Nausea welled up. Pain gathered fast and stabbed my head. I dropped the letter and my legs collapsed at the same time. I sweated as I crawled to the bathroom. Overcome by the sourness rising in my throat, I threw up in the pan. Impossible to stand – my legs had turned to Jell-O. I opened my mouth to shout for help. Jaw too stiff to move. Only a throat gurgle.

Nobody to hear me.

Falling.

Gone.

My head. Oh, my head hurt. Parched, I swallowed. Nettle burns in my throat. I was so cold. I gasped for breath. Tears slid out of the sides of my eyes. My hand ached so hard it was all pain. I heard a pouring noise. Someone tipped my head up, a firm hand supporting my neck. I drank a few sips of a cool, lemony fluid and went back to sleep.

When I woke later, I opened my eyes to see Faleria sitting by my bed, Sergia and Conrad standing behind her. His eyes looked enormous. A drip line was attached to my arm, and something beeped. I was in a hospital room. With a uniformed and armed guard at the door.

'Slowly,' Faleria said and took my hand. She wore disposable gloves. 'Don't try and talk. Just move your head, if you can.'

I nodded. The mush in my head wobbled in a big, slack bubble. My neck was made of concrete.

'You've been poisoned, but you're going to be all right. Gaia Memmia found you unconscious in your bathroom. She called the medics immediately.' She paused, looking for my reaction, I guessed. 'I need to ask you some questions. Are you up to it?'

I moved my head infinitesimally up and down. Everything swam in front of me. I ached from head to foot.

'If you want to stop, close your eyes and we'll go.'

I peered around and found Conrad again. My eyes refocused as he came over. His hand caressed my forehead, his thumb along my hairline. The dry plastic glove on his hand pulled on my skin, but I was so comforted by his touch.

'The letter you received was impregnated with a chemical agent. It's nearly always lethal. Any idea who would send you this?' Faleria said.

I blinked.

'Apologies for being brutal, but who inherits from you, if you die?'

I managed to shrug my shoulders an inch.

'Do you have a will?'

I moved my head an inch left then right.

Faleria looked at Sergia who replied, 'Her parents are dead, we know. No siblings.' She glanced at Conrad. 'Some of her father's relations still live, don't they?'

'Some cousins in Nebraska,' Conrad said, softly, but I still heard him. 'We'll check with Steven Smith, but they're probably her legal heirs.'

The fiercely, ignorantly, patriotic Browns.

I shut my eyes and went to sleep.

I woke in the night, the headache a shadow, but my stomach ached. I fumbled for a drink. My arm wouldn't lift my hand in the right direction. The guard slung his weapon across his back, the barrel projecting over his shoulder, and came over. Before he could get to me, Conrad appeared and waved the guard back. He lifted a plastic cup of water to my lips. I gulped it down, and another. He sat on the bed, his hand circling mine, his eyes glittering.

'I thought I'd lost you.' He bent his head, closed his eyes for a moment and then looked up. 'Only Faleria giving me a direct order to stay in the building stopped me going outside and hunting Renschman down. But if I do nothing else in my life, I'll kill that bastard next time I see him.'

When I woke next, I could turn my head enough to see blankets on the floor by my bed, crumpled, and a pillow, the centre indented where his head had been.

I insisted on seeing Gaia to thank her. She was as self-deprecating as usual, saying anybody would have done what she did.

Maybe.

The letter, printed on dime-store paper, had been impregnated with a persistent agent. Whoever touched it, or somebody affected by the poison, risked exposure. The return address on the EUSPS pre-paid envelope was fake. The inside had been coated with a thin layer of plastic. No fingerprints or DNA trace. But nobody doubted who had sent it.

The bone-chill of fear spread through me as Conrad sat by my bed telling me all this with a neutral voice, but burning eyes. Renschman had reached into the protective bubble of the legation to attack me. I shook at how vulnerable I was.

Irritation and pain followed this attack. I caught an armed guard detailed to accompany me everywhere. I knew this was well intentioned, but it annoyed me to have a permanent, if silent shadow. And I rowed with Conrad.

'There's an overt threat against you, so we'll filter your post thoroughly before it gets anywhere near you,' he said. 'We have to take precautions. I don't want to watch you nearly die again.'

'It wasn't a fun experience for me, either. But I'm not having my mail read by other people.' I raised my chin.

'Be reasonable. We can't let anything through to you without checking.'

'You're not opening my mail. It's private.'

'Look,' he said, 'you have to compromise, just this once.'

'No.'

We glared at each other; our first fight. I lay back in the bed, exhausted. But I wasn't giving in.

He stomped off, shoulders set, slamming the door as he left the room.

I moved back into my apartment the next day with a full packet of drugs, and fussed over by a worried medic and, of course, my guard. He insisted on looking around first before taking up station outside my door.

As I was being urged into bed by the medic, I saw a note in Conrad's round black writing stuck to the top of a box of surgical gloves and masks. *Wear a set of these when opening your next fan letter. Please.*

28

Gaia called next morning with a bunch of flowers. She hesitated by the door and said she didn't want to bother me if I wasn't up to it. She would reschedule and wait until I asked for her. Suppressing the urge to wrap the flowers round her head for being so self-effacing, I insisted she sit down and accept my grateful thanks again.

After the breakthrough with Aelia, I had switched to Latin by default. I was determined to master it. I stumbled, but managed most things. Aelia was ruthless, in the way only adolescents can be, but endlessly funny. Gaia, in contrast, hated correcting me and kept falling back on English. She thought she was helping. I accepted it all passively now; this nervous woman had saved my life. I would always owe her and be happy to pay.

She gave me a kids' history book that illustrated how Apulius and his four daughters had founded Roma Nova at the end of the fourth century. I laughed at the heroic little cartoon characters waving their swords around, but Gaia took it all seriously. Descended from the Julii and Flavians, both tough political families, according to Gaia, Apulius had married a Celt from Noricum. Although Romanised for several generations, women in her family made decisions, fought in battles and managed property. Her daughters had inherited her qualities in spadefuls.

When they headed north into the mountains, the founders realised that to survive they had to make radical changes. So women took over social, economic and political life, and the men fought to ensure the colony survived. In the end, both sons and daughters put on armour and picked up blades in the struggle to defend their new homeland.

'If a foreign man married into a woman's family,' Gaia said, 'he followed the practice of born Roma Novans and took her name.'

'Wait a minute. Non-Roma Novan men marrying in would have changed it, surely?'

'Not at all. It's well known that women transmit cultural values and cohesion in a society.'

'They must have figured the threat was beyond serious to have decided that,' I said.

'Grim times, according to the records.'

The Roma Novans had toughed it out through centuries guarding their values, holding it all together. I was stunned but thrilled to have ancestors like these. Hundreds of years of surviving in these conditions made frontier America look like the class beginner.

'Did the women get to choose who they married?'

She looked shocked. 'Of course.'

'So this is why I have my grandmother's name. Who was my grandfather?'

'I'm afraid I don't know. It'll be in your family record books.'

'Can't you look it up in a public register?'

'No, only if you have an appropriate access code.'

'Aren't all marriages recorded?'

'Yes, but if your grandmother didn't marry then there won't be an open access record. I'll check.' She started tapping at the keyboard.

'Hold up a minute, Gaia,' I said while she scrolled down tables of information on the screen. 'Are you saying my grandmother wasn't married?' She seemed so respectable.

Gaia stared back, uncomprehending. After a few seconds, her face cleared as if something had clicked. 'I forgot EUS laws were restrictive. The eldest daughter always inherits. Contracted fathers are optional.'

Favonius was in his element. Sitting tall at the head of the table a week later, chin jutting out, eyes scanning the assembled mortals, he presided over the meeting as if he was in charge of Great War II.

'It has become obvious that this covert unit is prepared to take desperate measures to maintain control of Brown Industries. Against all its own government's proclaimed tenets, I might add. They seem to have added in a personal element.' He looked at me, paused for a dramatic second or two, and pasted an even more serious expression onto his face. 'We are now at the beginning of July. The critical period ends on the tenth of August, Carina Mitela's birthday. Thus, we need to keep her alive and safe to that date.'

Nobody disagreed, especially me.

Favonius nodded at Sergia, one eyebrow raised in question.

'I've made some informal enquiries via my contacts in the administration,' she said, 'but I've met a blank wall. Either the External Affairs Department don't know about this group or they are pretending it doesn't exist.'

She was cool under Favonius's gaze. 'However, I've discovered that Renschman served in the EUS Army. He was recruited at seventeen from a very tough neighbourhood.' She consulted her el-pad. 'Apparently, he was a marksman, technically excellent in special forces' skills, but he failed almost all command and leadership tests which prevented him progressing beyond specialist grade. After he left, he worked on black ops for different agencies. I caught one possible reference from an FBI source, but he clammed up as soon as I asked about it.' She glanced at me. 'We know FBI personnel have been seconded to the unit. Special Agent O'Keefe is an example.'

'Thank you, Sergia. Additional security, major, at all times. Level 3.'

Not a shred of reaction crossed Faleria's face, but she nodded at Favonius and rose to her feet. The meeting broke up.

Outside, I felt dizzy, my legs wobbled and I fell into the empty secretary's chair. My guard went over to the water cooler. I didn't know whether it was the physical after-effects of the poison or the stress I was living under, but I hated these attacks of weakness. While I was taking some deep breaths, I glanced at the desk. The green commset light was on, but the volume indicator was turned down to minimum. I could hear Favonius's and Sergia's voices very faintly. The temptation was too much. I edged the volume key up.

'Well, of course you can't refuse.' Sergia.

'I won't endanger my agreement with the External Affairs Department.'

'Are you trying to sabotage your career? Old Tellus'll have your hide.'

'So we'll sit it out until August. I won't offend the American government. Not after all my hard work.'

'How much are they paying you?' Sergia's voice was cynical.

'I don't know what you're talking about,' Favonius said, sounding huffy.

'That much?' Sergia laughed. 'But what about the girl? She's had a shitty time.'

'She'll be all right. Tough stock. The gallant captain will keep her amused.'

My guard came back with the water. I laid my finger against my lips to shush her, then waved her away.

'Look, I'm not having that arrogant soldier boy and his stupid girlfriend endanger my career.' I heard paper slapped down on a surface.

'Very well, Favonius, but remember she's a Mitela. If the countess gets the slightest hint you're manipulating the situation, you'll be out before you can take your next breath.'

'Well, she won't, will she?'

'Not from me.'

I heard Sergia's clothes rustle as she moved toward the door. I stabbed at the commset key and stood up, taking two strides away from the desk. I grabbed my water from the startled guard and took a gulp. As Sergia came through the door, I wiped my hand across my forehead and handed the cup back to the guard.

'Yes, I'm much better now, thank you. Oh, Sergia? Is that you?'

She threw me a sharp look, but I smiled blandly back at her.

I called my grandmother that evening. Claudia had reported everything to her. Nonna was concerned, but didn't fuss.

'And how do you feel now?'

'Nearly there, I think. I've had some physical therapy and been swimming a few times. The doctor will discharge me at the end of the week.'

'We must get you out of there as quickly as possible. I've told Claudia to push it along, but I understand there are political complications as well. Why *are* the Americans dragging their feet? They can't possibly win.'

She looked impatient. Frustrated, I guessed, at not being able to do anything.

'It's a little tense, I have to admit,' I said. 'I suppose the legation is concerned to stay on good terms with the administration. I must be upsetting things for their everyday relationship.'

I was surprised to hear my respectable grandmother use the word she did. One of Aelia's favourites. So Sergia was right. And Nonna would not hesitate to act.

29

How the fuck had she survived?

He'd 'acquired' the active ingredient via a contact at the East Coast Poison Center. There was no known antidote. Unless those Roma Novan bastards had one and kept it secret. Their scientists weren't that advanced, were they? Renschman shivered. It was rare he experienced anything remotely related to doubt, let alone fear. Maybe he'd attacked somebody he couldn't defeat.

He slammed his hand on his desk. A pen rolled off onto the floor. No, nobody was that invulnerable. Those bloody people had ruined his childhood. Now they were doing it again.

Half an hour later, he handed the new weapon back to the range master. Curious – the lightness made it feel like a toy. But the grip was like a standard-issue grunt sidearm he used in his twenties. Perfectly adequate to terminate a life.

30

I made my way to Grattius's teaching room ten days after the attack. He gave his formal good wishes for my recovery and, a minute later, we resumed the punishing study schedule.

Two days later, he was making me sweat on a text about the treaty with the Ottomans after the fall of Constantinople when I heard boots thudding along on the tiled hallway. The door burst open and Dexia, of all people, rushed in.

'Come with me now, please, Carina Mitela.' Her face was deadly serious, almost frowning. She extended her hand as if she was going to grab my arm.

'Captain,' came Grattius's calm voice. 'Kindly explain.'

'Sir, we don't have time. Sorry.' She went to take my arm, but I stepped back.

'What's going on?' I said.

She looked impatient. 'There's an incident, downstairs, in the reception area, and I'm taking you to the safe room. Now.'

She hustled me out and two other soldiers fell in behind us as we hurried towards the elevator. Her gaze fastened on the elevator display panel flicking through the floors. I took a pace back and grasped the gallery rail.

'Okay, Dexia, I am not going one step further until you tell me – now.' A tingle passed across my shoulders like a little alarm, and my pulse speeded up. I had a really bad feeling about all this. The doors swished open.

'Please get in. We're trying to protect you.'

'No. Not until you tell me.' I searched her face for clues. She wouldn't meet my eyes.

'Where is he? What's happened to him?' I grabbed hold of her arm and shook it.

She peeled my fingers off. 'He's fine; he's got it all under control. Our orders are to take you to the safe room,' Dexia persisted.

'Screw your orders. I want to know. Now.'

'I'm sorry, I can't,' she said. She gazed into the distance. She nodded as if listening, but I didn't see what to. 'Very well,' she said to nobody in particular. She glanced at me. 'Not very. I suggest the security centre?' She focused on something over my shoulder as she listened. 'There in five. Out.' She dropped her gaze to my face. 'The situation's stabilised, but still playing out. We're going to the security centre where they're monitoring it.'

She wheeled around abruptly and we rode down to the first floor, hurrying through an optical-controlled door into a plain room manned by beige uniforms, some sitting at desks but most in front of banks of monitors. The ambassador was there, her face tense, immobile. Favonius was bent over, hands braced on the desk in front of the monitors, talking to one of the soldiers. They both looked in my direction as I entered the room.

'Carina,' said Claudia. 'Oh, my dear, come and sit down.' She took my hand and led me to a table at the back, and seated me in a chair with its back to the monitors.

'What's going on?'

She looked directly at me and took both my hands in hers. 'Two EUS Americans with FBI ID came to deliver what they said was a subpoena ordering you to appear in the district court. The receptionist alerted the security office immediately.' She relaxed her face a little. 'It's standard practice when any EUS law agency calls. We ensure we have one of ours present as a professional courtesy, if for nothing else. Captain Tellus was the duty officer. As soon as he entered the reception area and recognised Jeffrey Renschman, he sounded an immediate alert. Renschman drew a gun, but Tellus reacted very quickly and was only slightly wounded.'

The pattern of the floor tiles wobbled, swirling and merging for a few moments before it settled back into its original rigid state. I recovered my breath.

'What's...what's happening now?' I looked away from Cornelia, skewing around toward the monitors.

Faleria answered. 'We think Renschman got past the scanner with a ceramic-resin-mix weapon. I didn't know the Americans had developed them beyond the experimental stage.' She shrugged. 'If it's a prototype, it won't be too stable, so he may or may not be able to fire another shot.'

I swallowed hard. 'Where's Conrad now?'

'Behind the reception desk with the staff,' said Faleria.

I searched the monitors and saw him on the central one, crouching, poised on his toes behind the end of the counter, two other men huddling behind him. 'We've moved up a support team, including a marksman to take Renschman out if necessary,' continued Faleria.

'So what now?' I amazed myself, sounding so detached.

Before Faleria could answer, I heard Conrad's disembodied voice over the monitor speakers.

'Give it up, Renschman. There's a SWAT team just behind that door, ready to take you out. You're never going to win this one.'

'Maybe, but I'll take you with me. Your little tart will feel bad about that for the rest of her life. Serve the bitch right.'

My hand flew up to my mouth. I hunched back into my chair. Claudia squeezed my other hand in support.

Unbelievably, Conrad laughed. 'We're tougher than that, Renschman. And she's more so, more than you'll ever know. I'll take the bullet for her any day to stop you. And if I can kill you on the way, then that's a bonus.'

In the security room, heads turned in my direction, eyes fixing on me.

'Fine words.' Renschman's voice grated. 'You won't risk it.'

I heard Conrad laugh again.

What was he on?

'Now!' came his whisper.

Barely a nanosecond later, Faleria spoke into the mic and the glass panel behind the front desk flew open. Renschman's attention was momentarily diverted and Conrad leapt out at him. I heard two gunshots, a third, followed by the high-pitched explosion of breaking glass. Another, the deep crack of something heavier breaking. Armed soldiers burst into the reception area. More shots. The monitors filled with figures in combat fatigues, shouts accompanying their rapid movements. Within seconds it was over.

Faleria spoke a clipped command into the mic.

One of the soldiers trotted up to the camera and gave her report. 'Area secured. One enemy light casualty, one secured, one friendly medium casualty, two civilians unhurt but in shock. Medics on their way.'

I closed my eyes. A hand on the back of my head forced it over, something touched my chest and I threw up into a wastepaper bin.

Dexia smiled down at me, wiped my mouth and gave me a plastic cup of water. Then I started shaking.

'Calm down, Mitela, looks like a flesh wound. He's tough as hell. He'll be fine,' she said.

Claudia Cornelia looked furious at Dexia's casual tone. 'That's enough, captain.'

'No.' I looked up at Dexia, then across at Claudia. 'No, that's okay. I want to see Conradus. Now.'

Dexia took me down to the wrecked reception. The dark glass wall was intact but the reception desk gaped open in two shattered halves, surrounded by an oval patch of splintered glass. Renschman and another suit were lying face down on the floor, handcuffed and guarded by soldiers. I stepped around the glass and damaged furniture. A medic was kneeling on the floor, back to me, obscuring a beige-clothed body, one of whose legs was bent up at the knee. Another medic was setting up a collapsible gurney. She clicked the lock into place, joined the other medic side by side and lifted the body across onto the gurney. When they raised it to waist level, I nearly passed out. Conrad lay on it, desperately still. A large pad secured with a bandage was tied around his upper leg. Red stains were spreading through the fabric of his beige pants either side of the pad. His face was pale, pulled into harsh lines, a sheen of sweat on his forehead. One of the medics finished tying a second bandage around Conrad's upper arm. He half-opened his eyes, looked around and saw me.

'Why aren't you in the safe room?' he croaked, and frowned at me.

'Do you think I would go skulk there while you were in danger?'

He sighed. 'It's over. We've stopped him. Only sorry I didn't get the chance to blow his head off.'

I stared at Renschman as he was pulled to his feet by two soldiers. As they took him away, he limped and stumbled. He threw me a venomous look. I flinched like he'd struck me in the face.

The medics had put up an IV drip for Conrad and wheeled him away, pushing through the chaos. I went to follow but a stretched arm prevented me.

Dexia. 'Let them sort him out.'

Later that evening, I sat in the sick bay room I had left only a while ago, watching by his bed. Still pale, his skin sagged over his cheekbones. A plastic tube from his nose was taped above his lip, and the line from the IV drip was embedded in the back of his hand. Dark red stains under his fingernails from dried blood. The doctor had said the bullet had passed straight through his leg, avoiding bone or vital organs or veins. He would recover well because of his natural strength and acquired fitness, he said. But Conrad looked so ill and vulnerable, I didn't believe him.

He ran a light fever but it subsided after forty-eight hours. On the following day, although he looked tired, he was half-sitting up and arguing with me.

'Is it always going to be like this?' I touched his forearm. 'I mean, you getting shot, me having an anxiety attack?'

He laughed. 'Well, it's hardly likely to be the other way round, is it?'

'I guess not.'

31

I shouldn't have been surprised to see Steven Smith the next afternoon. We sat in the birchwood conference room with Favonius, Sergia and Gaia. Yesterday's attack had caused a monumental diplomatic row. It couldn't be hushed up like the poison letter. The legation had sent its strongest possible condemnation first thing that morning to the EUS Secretary Of External Affairs – Junior Hartenwyck's father. In diplomatic speak, that ranked one below declaring war. An SUV had been allowed into the legation grounds earlier in the day, under guard, to collect Renschman and his colleague from the secure basement room where they'd spent the night.

I'd been petrified of being taken by Renschman on the outside, but somehow he'd got inside, into my safety cocoon. Twice. My head swam with reaction. I took another gulp of water. The July sunshine streamed through the window glass. I was grateful for the calming effect of the air-conditioning murmuring away in the background.

'I think we'll find they're able to grant you a Certificate of Loss of Nationality immediately in return for the legation not publicising this incident.'

'I just want it over, Mr Smith.'

'I know. I do sympathise. I asked Favonius earlier today to insist they send a consular officer to hear your oath of renunciation within the next forty-eight hours. I understand this is scheduled for this afternoon.'

I looked up from my study of the table. 'Thank you so much for your support through all this.'

'My pleasure, Carina Mitela.'

I stared at him.

'I know the certificate has to be issued, but it will be backdated to today. You'll cease to be Karen Brown from this afternoon.'

The certificate arrived four days later; even the formidable Favonius was impressed. We stood by the railing on the walkway outside his office, looking down at the garden.

'I'm sorry you'll be leaving us so soon, Carina Mitela, but I'm delighted at the positive outcome.' I was astonished at Favonius's friendly tone.

'Yes, it's ended well.' I looked him straight in the eye. 'I trust all this hasn't endangered your agreement with the External Affairs Department. You must have put in a lot of hard work on it.'

He went very still.

'I've learnt one thing here that's surprised me. I seem to be able to take life-threatening events in my stride. But then I come from tough stock.'

Now he knew.

'I'll be sure to let my grandmother know all about how you've supported me.'

I had a farewell meeting with Claudia Cornelia and her husband. He gave me his private email address.

'Please don't hesitate. I know what it's like. There'll be moments when you yearn for some trivial, stupid thing, like a Hershey bar.'

He laughed when I made a face at the thought.

'No, truly.' He became serious. 'If you don't mind me saying, I think you've come through a rough time very well. I envy you the journey of discovering the pleasures of Roma Nova. I lived there for four years with Claudia before she was posted here.' He smiled. 'When we arrived in Washington, I was excited to be returning "home" to the EUS, picking up with former colleagues and friends. But you know what? I was disappointed. I found it superficial. I missed the committed sense of community, of responsibility, if you like.' He glanced over to Claudia. 'We'll be posted home to Roma Nova within the next two years, and I'll be thankful to be back there.'

Was he pushing the official line, or saying it to make me feel better? Glancing at his serious face, I believed his words came from the heart.

Conrad and I left in the same formation as we had arrived – SUVs ahead and behind us. I turned and waved to Gaia Memmia, Aelia, standing next to her father, and Grattius. Political stuff aside, they – apart from Favonius – had given me not only friendship but their unstinting support. I was still as nervous as hell about going to Roma Nova. But not as relieved as shaking off the threat from Renschman.

On the way to Sterling Dulles, I looked at the olive leather-bound book Grattius had given me as we had shaken hands under the legation portico. It was a set of Catullus's love poems. What an old romantic. Conrad considered some of them were a bit ripe, but I didn't care – it was a lovely gesture. A good way to enter my new life.

PART II

TRANSITION

32

How surreal could it be?

We boarded a Dassault private jet in the general aviation area of Sterling Dulles and were welcomed on board by a flight attendant with movie-star looks and matching charm. Conrad told me that an old friend of Aurelia's, some French business magnate, had lent her his personal plane. Did he realise how like a television mini-series that sounded?

It had everything: a sleeping area, where Conrad could lie and rest his leg on the bed, a tiny bathroom and luxurious sitting/dining area. You could do all the usual office things and probably conquer the universe in the afternoon with all the equipment on board. I spoke to my grandmother briefly; the flying palace had satellite communications, of course.

I gaped like a tourist out of the window several hours later when land came into sight: my first view of Europe. We landed early afternoon local time and thirsty for a view of my new home, I glued my face to the window. Mountains stretched up into the sky in the background, conifers clinging to them under the snow line, fields and isolated houses below them. As the tyres touched the runway, I was disappointed to see it looked like any other airport, until I saw the terminal building with the sign PORTUS – ROMA NOVA. It was true, then.

We taxied past the main glass-fronted building to a smaller single-storey one with three wide shallow steps and glass doors. A gold eagle crested the arch above the doorway. Two men in suits and a woman in a blue uniform stood waiting on the tarmac for our plane to stop. Fresh air flooded in as the door opened.

'Ready?' Conrad smiled at me and held out his hand. He stood awkwardly, leaning on a cane. His leg must have been so sore.

Nervous didn't describe it; I was extremely reluctant to leave the comfort of my leather seat.

'Yes, of course.' I was wearing a new cream designer pants suit. I checked my hair and face for the hundredth time. I thanked the French crew as I stood hesitating in the doorway. I swallowed and placed my foot on the first step.

Outside, it was warm, but not as oppressively hot as Washington had been. Above the sour smells of fuel and tyre rubber, I caught a fresh, sharp tang of pine resin. On the ground, the VIP suite manager and his assistant welcomed me with smiles and energetic handshakes. I didn't catch the blue-uniformed woman's role, but she and Conrad nodded to each other.

In the glass-walled lounge, a tall, older woman in a chic forest-green suit rose to meet me. Assured and elegant, with an indefinable air of power, her direct look intimidated me. The heavy gold antique ring on her manicured right hand was curiously out of place. I *did* look like her, especially the eyes. I didn't think I had such a defined jawline. She had the same slender build but, instead of my red-gold, her hair was all over different shades of grey.

Conrad gave me a light push in the small of my back and retreated. I took one step and stopped. My mouth dried up. She smiled and closed the gap between us in two paces.

'Hello, darling,' she said and held her hands out.

'Nonna.'

I gave a nervous laugh as she embraced me. Honey and cinnamon. It was the cookie smell from when I visited as a little girl. I took a couple of breaths to steady myself. I didn't know what to say.

She scrutinised my face. I was unsure what she was looking for but, after a flicker, a tightening of anxiety in her eyes, I only saw warmth. She looked away for a moment or two, her face confused by sadness, by longing. But, almost instantly, the smile and warmth were reinstated, her eyes liquid.

'I don't know what you like,' she said, 'what your favourite colour or food is; what you enjoy doing.' She coughed. 'Never mind, we'll get the hang of it as we go along.'

She was as nervous as I was. But I think she understood almost by instinct how awkward, how disrupted I felt. I loved her from that moment.

'You'll find things are different here; some better, some worse, some unexpected,' she said as we left the airport. 'You seem resourceful and bright, Carina, but you must ask if you don't understand something. If you're unhappy, you must tell me, however trivial. It's the small things that cause most misery.'

'Thank you, Nonna. I'm determined to do my best and learn quickly. I don't want to let anybody down.'

'Carina.' She took hold of my hand and looked straight at me. 'Don't do it for me, or for anybody else. Don't try to please everybody or you'll drive yourself insane.'

Travelling from the airport to the house, I was fascinated by the buildings – cream stone with terracotta roof tiles mixed in with tall, much grander blocks. Modern stood alongside older, but somehow it all fit together. I couldn't tell what most roads signs meant; how could they be so different? Cars looked more stylish and compact than in New York, and surrounded by clouds of bicycles. Shops with wide sidewalks in front, colourful awnings stretching over chairs and tables outside restaurants. People strolled along; some stood in groups talking animatedly; some were buying papers and small stuff from kiosks. They looked pretty much like people anywhere, but darker, neater, more self-contained.

In the centre of the city, we drove past one side of a huge open square, surrounded on the other three sides by a forest of stone columns and grand buildings. My grandmother told me this was the forum; the buildings contained various public offices, including the Senate. The smaller ones were mostly temples. My sense of unreality grew – it was like a movie set from *Gladiator* with extras going up and down the steps, but in normal twenty-first century clothes.

I shut my eyes for a few moments to attempt processing this. When I opened them, we were skirting a hill rising steeply to an old ruin perched at the top of a cliff commanding the whole river valley. Halfway up was a beautiful golden stone house, a mansion as large as on any colonial estate in the EUS. With long, single-storey wings running out from each side, it looked like a bird poised for take-off.

We rode on along a tree-lined street about five minutes from the centre, but quieter, with individual entrances spread out. As we approached a tall gateway, the arch carved with woven branches and small leaf motifs, the car slowed and the driver put his hand out against a screen set in the side post and spoke his name. The gates swung open.

A square-built four-storey house with tall arched windows rose on one side of a wide gravelled courtyard. Single-storey buildings spread along two other sides, the whole framed by tall plane trees. I wanted to touch the gold and cream stone that reflected the soft light of late afternoon; it looked like blocks of honey.

A solemn woman, around fifty, came down the steps of the house and opened my grandmother's door, bowing as she did.

'*Domina*,' she said.

Nonna turned to me as I followed her out, took my hand and said, 'Junia, this is my granddaughter.'

She bowed to me. 'Welcome, *domina*.' Her expression was deadpan, betrayed by eyes full of curiosity.

'Junia runs the household along with Galienus, the housekeeper and under-steward,' Nonna continued. 'If you need anything, mention it to one or the other. Junia will take you round tomorrow so that you know where everything is.'

Junia's serious face relaxed a few millimetres to produce a half-smile. She exchanged nods with Conrad who had ridden in the front. The vestibule (as I later learned it was called) led to a long, high-ceilinged hallway lined with statues and portraits called *imagines*. It was like walking through a museum. At the end was a marble bust of a young woman, hair tied high. The sculptor had caught an air of wistfulness: tendrils escaping from the thin ribbons around her head and curling down around the hollows of her neck, a hesitant expression, an other-worldliness. Marina Mitela, the inscription said.

My mother. I stopped and stared. The tears welled, but I didn't let them escape.

As Junia pulled open the double doors into the next room, I gasped. A huge hall, open on one side with plate glass doors slid back, marble floors and a glass roof arching overhead, was golden in the sunlight. This was the atrium, the heart of the house, the enormous room I'd seen when I was four years old.

Nonna and Conrad talked, their voices contained, sometimes rising, never loud, almost a background murmur as I detached myself and stared around. Lush green planting at the centre made it like a shopping mall but the light wood tables and easy chairs came from anybody's living room. We were interrupted by the steward murmuring that a car had arrived to take Conrad home to Domus Tellarum. He looked exhausted. As I kissed his cheek at the entrance door, I whispered he should get some rest. He just smiled and left.

Nonna led me back to the hallway and stopped in front of a wide door. She grasped the chased brass handle and beckoned me to follow her in.

'I'll leave you here to settle in,' she said. 'A lot to absorb all at once, isn't it?' The empathy in her voice was unmistakable, but I'd already started doubting if I could cope with the strangeness of it all.

Next morning, Nonna took me to the censor's office to register my presence. The censor herself came out to kiss cheeks with Nonna while her assistant fitted me with a personal tracker – a tiny chip inserted into my shoulder that gave me ID, access and protection, apparently. Better than a wallet full of plastic cards, I supposed. At least I couldn't lose it.

Conrad had been put on medical leave. I visited him several times; Domus Tellarum was the other side of the city but only twenty minutes by car. On my fourth visit, I met his Uncle Quintus who in the flesh was a darker, shorter version of Conrad, hair more silver than brown. Although my Latin was pretty fluent by now, I wasn't entirely sure about some of his jokes. We left Quintus answering the imperious ring on his cell, talking with authority and clicking fingers.

Conrad grasped my hand and led me across the wide marble terrace down into the garden, to the outdoor triclinium – a summer kitchen and dining room combined. Willows and birches shielded teak couches on the patio in front. I slipped off my sandals; the warmth radiating from the stone trickled up through the soles of my feet.

Conrad bent down and kissed me on the forehead and the palm of my hand before sitting down beside me. What a pleasure it was when such an attractive man smiled at you, intent only on you. We sat close and he put his arm around me. He looked toward the tall trees at the end of the small parkland at the end of the garden, the skin around his eyes drawn tight.

'I have something important to say to you.' He cleared his throat, but his voice wavered nonetheless. 'When I came to find you in New York, it was for Aurelia. I was curious to see whether her granddaughter would be a typical American spoiled brat.'

I rolled my eyes at him and tapped his chest with the back of my hand. He captured it and smiled back. I could see the pulse in his neck working.

'The minute I walked into your office with Sextilius, I knew I'd found the most precious thing in my life,' he said, cradling my hand in his. 'I fell in love with you. Of course, I didn't realise I had until Renschman kidnapped you.' His throat constricted as he swallowed hard. 'I'm desperately hoping it's not a cruel trick of the Fates.'

His thumbs massaged my palm, gently at first, but becoming firmer as he spoke.

'Now you're here in Roma Nova, you'll find a lot of people will want to be your friend or lover, perhaps your contracted spouse. You've only met me so far, a choice of one. I guarantee you'll be courted for your wealth, your looks, your position.' His eyes narrowed, the outside corners appearing to slant upwards. 'Perhaps even for yourself.'

'Then I'll need you with me at all times to keep the predators away.' I tried to keep it light, but my voice cracked. I didn't care how many others wanted me – I wanted only him. I raised my face, and he pulled me to him and kissed me deep and hard. Recovering my breath, I looked up and searched his eyes and traced his lower lip with my finger. Desire so intense that I didn't recognise it as desire rocketed through my body. Neither of us said a word. He pulled me up, led me indoors to a bedroom and slammed the door behind us.

· · ·

An arm came up and wound itself around my waist. I gazed at this amazing, gorgeous man who had made love with me so passionately. He left me breathless and exhausted. His head lay in the damp hollow of my shoulder, his eyelids closed, eyelashes resting on his cheeks.

'Conrad,' I murmured.

'Mm?' He opened his eyes and smiled like an idiot. He pushed up, supporting himself on his forearms. As he leaned over me, he winced, but kissed my eyelids, my mouth, the small hollow at the base of my neck. I was horrified as I remembered his wound.

He laughed. 'That's not going to stop me making you writhe and moan again for the next half-hour while we both die from pleasure.'

I gasped as his hand came up and he set out to prove it.

After dinner, we sat on a couch together in an alcove in the atrium at Domus Tellarum, and talked about small, intimate things that new lovers do. He caressed my cheek with his fingers and played with my hair. I stroked his hand as he did. We couldn't bear not to touch each other in some way. I had come home.

33

Conrad was relentless in undertaking daily physical therapy and strengthening exercises to banish the pins-and-needles pain and reduced dexterity from his wound. He returned to his unit in under five weeks.

When he wasn't working, he took me all over my new home, sometimes tearing along at fanatical speed on the back of his motorbike, me clasping his warm body and hanging on for my life, sometimes drifting along lazily in a sailboat on the river. Up in the mountains, we made love, crushing fragile summer flowers beneath us; hiked through pine woodlands; and scrambled to the foot of the harsh limestone rock faces.

I was both thrilled and repelled by gladiatorial games we attended – thankfully no longer to the death, but contests of skill and daring that robbed me of breath with their intensity. I loved the theatre, but hated the interminable poetry evenings. Whenever I threatened to fall asleep, Conrad bent down and whispered a rude story about one of the prominent people in the audience. And so, I gradually fit the jigsaw of my new life together.

Nonna told me humorous and serious stories about people, politics, and, poignantly, about my mother, when her voice became sad and puzzled. It remained a mystery to her why her daughter had run away and, even more, why she'd killed herself.

I studied with a tutor, and started reading some classical books, history as well as literature. I was drawn in by the old accounts by Tacitus, Pliny and Caesar of military and political battles, and the strategies they developed to achieve their aims, and laughed at what a shocking gossip the younger Pliny was. I was lost for hours, often only leaving the library to eat. How strange was that?

I jogged most mornings, sometimes in other parts of the city, but didn't wander too far. The first time, I had gotten up early and finding the front door time-locked, I'd gone down to the domestic hall. I hesitated in front of the big oak door. I had every right to go anywhere but, deep down, I was uncomfortable with the notion of servants. I was gathering my courage to knock, my curled hand halfway, when the door opened. Junia looked as surprised as I was.

'I didn't want to bother you, Junia, especially so early,' I gabbled like some five year-old ditching class, 'but I want to go for a jog. Could you let me out the back, please?'

'*Domina*, it's no trouble, of course, but are you sure you don't want somebody with you? It would only take a few minutes to get one of the juniors ready.' I bet it would. Junia struck me as the type that, when she said, 'Jump', they replied, 'How high, ma'am?'

As I followed her through the vestibule of the domestic hall, I noticed she limped and that as she turned, her spine from the vertebrae at the base right up her neck moved stiffly as one. But she didn't use a cane. Nonna hadn't said anything, so I figured I wouldn't pry. We passed open shelving and racks of pigeonholes hung on one wall. Two shallow but long wooden tables, one with two PCs, stood under them. A large LED panel for the domestic system occupied the wall at right angles. Our two biosignatures were displayed as blips moving along the lower corridor in the yellow zone. Further in, I could see the dining hall and the corridor that led to the sleeping areas.

Junia gave me the day's access code for the back service entrance, and then I went. After half an hour, I jogged back to the house and surprised some of the house servants as I made my way back through the hallway. Junia sprang out of nowhere, smiled and invited me to take a cup of coffee with her. I knew I'd broken down an invisible barrier.

'I'm taking advantage of nearly twenty years' service with your grandmother.' She smiled, almost to herself. 'I've seen the difference you've made to her life. She's been lonely for many years and saddened by the lack of close family. Now she's refreshed, revitalised. Please don't hesitate to ask me anything if I can help you, however unorthodox your request. These are not polite words – I mean it.'

She told me about my cousins, famous guests, events, crises and household secrets. The servants made up an integral part of the Mitela family. Roma Novans considered the whole household from top to bottom as an organic entity, each member with their own duties and responsibilities. That included my grandmother and me.

I was crushed with kindness and comfort; nothing was too much for any of the staff. I indulged myself by ordering and watching every movie I'd ever wanted. I swam every day in the mosaic-lined pool in the basement. I photographed everything in the grounds, especially in the walled garden, full of exotic, protected plants.

Nonna had asked Helena, one of my new cousins, to help me find my way about the town, to go eating and shopping. Helena air-kissed cheeks with Nonna, her immaculate red lips stretched in a smile, though not wide enough to distort the perfection of her peach-skin cheeks. With her slim figure coated in a cherry-red suit, her silver jewellery in perfect harmony, she looked like something out of *Vogue*. Helena looked me up and down out of her blue Mitela eyes as if measuring me, but she complied. She was polite if superior, especially when I stumbled on a word or didn't know something basic.

But Conrad was my anchor in the confusion of my new life. One weekend afternoon he was visiting us, I walked with him through the garden down to the parkland. I sat folded in his arms under a large linden tree one of my ancestors had planted, relishing the warmth and the light filtering through the veined leaves. I must have dozed off and only woke when Conrad stretched under me.

'Hello, sleepy,' he said, and kissed the palm of the hand he was holding. 'It's getting on, shall we go back?'

What more could I want?

34

Nonna was kept busy in her advisor role. She seemed to be at the palace half the time, the Senate the rest, whenever she wasn't having business meetings with her corporate managers. We caught up most evenings, but I didn't have a whole lot to contribute to the conversation.

The prospect of my twenty-fifth birthday had been the trigger for my terrifying flight from New York. The day itself passed quietly, Nonna raising a glass of Brancadorum champagne to me, Conrad smiling to himself as we sat on the shaded terrace, sheltering from the brutal August sun.

Steven Smith flew in with papers to sign and with Uncle Frank Kearly, from Brown Industries, a colleague of my father's whom I remembered from when I was a kid. Steven Smith's colleague at External Affairs had reported that Renschman had been dismissed from the ESD and his supervisor reassigned to the colony of Alaska. But I was still on the national watch list and would be detained if I ever returned. Three days later, I watched them cross the short distance airside from the VIP suite to their plane at Portus airport. I might have been a little bored now, but I was safe.

One day in September, Helena dragged me out shopping. Roma Nova was a beautiful city built in the loop of a wide river, and based on a standard grid. It reminded me of New York. In a way, I missed the bustle and even the stress of my life there.

We wandered around the Macellum: it was like a shopping mall, but with a large plaza inside, colonnaded around to provide shelter and encourage shoppers to linger in front of large plate glass windows designed to entice them in. An oasis of trees and benches in the middle gave shaded seating, complementing the colourful restaurant umbrellas and café tables dotted around. While it couldn't be called crowded, a lot of people were milling around. Most stores were local, but a few international names stood out, especially fashion. In the university bookstore, I was surprised to find a large English language section, with all the bestsellers as well as more intellectual stuff.

'We're not a crowd of ignoramuses, you know,' Helena said with an acid tone. 'People come from all over Europe, and beyond, to study here.'

I bought a couple of novels, handing over notes rather than use my cash card with my name all over it. The money here was pretty much like dollars, but different colours, and only coins for one and two *solidi*.

'I love these small shops – and I'm not being patronising,' I added, seeing Helena's eyebrow rise at my comment. 'You get such variety and great service.'

'Have you considered starting or investing in some shops or businesses yourself?' Helena asked. 'You're smart and have experience of the commercial world. It would give you something to do.'

Where did that come from? Helena had trained as a teacher, not a businesswoman. Was she trying to free herself from being my babysitter?

'Would it be appropriate?'

She laughed. 'Where do you think the family money comes from? Aurelia's got so many fingers in business pies all over the world, I'm surprised she hasn't grown a few extra. Multiply that over centuries, even the bad times, and you see what I mean.'

'So that's it?'

Helena laughed again. 'Yes, coupled with an instinctive political slipperiness to keep neutral in conflicts, it's kept gold in the pot.'

I hadn't got over my nervousness of her. She was so glamorous and self-assured, but I laid my hand on her forearm and gave her a big smile. 'You know what, Helena? I'm really glad you talked me into going out today. Let's go celebrate.'

She took me to a riverside café with a spectacular cantilevered terrace decked out with smart designer seats and tables. Through the crowd, she waved to a group of young men and women at a table near the river. They waved back, beckoning her over. She was outgoing, good-looking and smart – of course they liked her. She introduced me as her cousin, Cara, and winked at me. I was so surprised at her friendliness, I couldn't even smile back. They all wore the same kind of uniform as Conrad, but as I was about to say something. Helena gave me a stern look.

'C'mon, Publius, Marcus,' she said as we arrived at their table. 'Give two exhausted girls your seats like good boys.'

'Exhausted, right,' answered Marcus, tapping our designer carrier bags, but they smiled and stood up. Publius gave me a long look while Marcus ordered wine. Publius hovered with the bottle, ensuring I had a full glass. He was very dark, with almost black eyes and a sassy smile. I imagined he never had any trouble getting a date. Somehow, he found another chair and pulled it up by mine. Helena smiled and left me to it. I loved his banter but was relieved I could keep up.

'I'm trying to work out where you're from.' He smiled, raising one eyebrow. 'You have a lovely accent.'

'Do you know Castra Lucilla?'

'Oh, in the south.'

He seemed content with that.

'So, how long are you here for? If you have a free afternoon, or evening, I'd be more than happy to show you around a bit.'

'Sorry, Publius, I have a fairly full schedule, but thanks for the offer.'

He pushed it for a bit, then back to general stuff with the others. But, like any practised flirt, he came back to it. He was leaning toward me, one leg stretched out but not touching, and I was thinking about a way out when the group's attention was diverted. I followed their gaze and focused on two uniformed figures coming toward us. One was tall, dark and not particularly handsome, his intelligent eyes watching everything. The other was also tall, but blond, wore sunglasses and approached with that big-cat grace that fascinated me.

'Crap, it's the captain,' came Marcus's voice in a hiss.

'We were here first,' said another.

'I heard he had a serious girlfriend,' whispered a third.

'Like that's going to stop him,' said Publius. 'Don't worry, sweetheart, we'll protect you from the big bad wolf.' He grinned at me.

'But—' Then I stopped. I remembered Helena's look when we arrived. I was stung by their easy condemnation.

'Ladies,' Conrad drawled as he reached our table. As the younger soldiers stood up, Conrad slid into Publius's chair, much to the latter's chagrin. The other man with Conrad leaned against the parapet railing, crossed his arms and watched the pantomime unfold.

'Get me a beer organised, please, Publius,' said Conrad, not looking at Publius and still wearing his sunglasses – both impolite. Or was it deliberate?

I heard a stifled chortle from Helena. Marcus drowned a chuckle in a cough. One of the female soldiers smirked. The beer arrived and Conrad took a long sip then turned to me.

'You're Helena's cousin, I believe. Are you enjoying the city?'

Okay, let's play make-believe. I nodded.

'Have you seen the panorama from the river?'

'Er, no, not in detail.'

He stood up, held his hand out and drew me over to the far parapet out of earshot. As he pointed things out to me, our shoulders touched.

He bent over to whisper in my ear. 'This is fun.'

'You are so bad, winding those kids up.'

He took his glasses off and grinned at me. 'I know, but it was irresistible. Besides, Publius Munius was getting too familiar. You acted your part well, though. I didn't know you could do that.'

'You'd be surprised what I can do.'

'Very likely.' He shot me an appraising look then he beckoned his friend over.

'Lucius, may I present Carina Mitela? Carina, this is Lucius Punellus Niger, my comrade-in-arms.'

I extended my hand, and his dark head bowed over it. When he looked up, his face was solemn, but his eyes were laughing. I liked him instantly.

'I am honoured and intrigued to meet the woman who has managed to put the brakes on Conradus.' He winked at me.

Had I done that? I glanced at Conrad and laughed.

'Thank you, Lucius Punellus, for the compliment, but I think you overestimate me.'

The laughter in his eyes calmed as they scrutinised my face, as if searching for something.

'No. I don't think I do.'

What was that supposed to mean? I returned his look, trying to think up something clever to say, but failed. His steady gaze defeated me. I retreated into banalities.

'So how long have you known Conradus?'

'Since we were recruits, several years ago. He always took the risks, and I always covered his back.' He sent a mocking look at Conrad who mouthed something back at him.

Conrad consulted his watch. 'We have to go now. Enjoy the rest of your day – I'll see you this evening.' His eyes lingered on me and I was conscious of warmth in my face. He replaced his sunglasses. He and Lucius sauntered off, falling into step.

'Are you okay?' Publius said.

I wrenched my gaze away from following the man to look into the face of the boy.

'I don't suppose you'll look at me now,' he said.

'No, but don't worry, Publius. Not wishing to be brutal but you weren't in the running.'

Back at Helena's car, we loaded our bags into the trunk. Although she overawed me, it was a relief when the two of us went out without any chauffeur or household servant hovering around. I guessed Helena was considered sufficient escort. I was opening the passenger door when my eye caught a reflection in the baker's shop next to the car. A face with frameless glasses stared back at me. I froze. Impossible. Renschman couldn't be here. I forced myself to turn around to face the original, but nobody was there. When I looked back at the window, the reflection had vanished. I scrambled into the car, gasping for breath and my heart pumping.

'Carina? Are you okay? You're as white as ice.' She took my hand. 'And as cold.'

'I'm...I'm fine. Let's get home.'

She searched my face, then apparently satisfied, glanced up and down the street, her gaze lingering for a second on a couple by a black car. As she drove the short journey, I took deep breaths to calm myself. I tried to analyse it logically. It was ridiculous. Some innocent passer-by, around Renschman's age, with brown hair and frameless glasses, had confused me. I could mention it to Conrad and ask him to look it up on his spook databases – he would think I was crazy – or I could just put it down to a fanciful mistake. By the time I reached home, I'd decided I'd imagined the whole thing and shelved it.

I took up Helena's suggestion and, following two sessions with Nonna's accountant, started a micro-loan agency which helped a bar, a florist and a domestic decorating agency start up. I stumbled with the vocabulary for a week or two and found the regulations were stricter than in the EUS, but I persevered. By the fall, they were breaking even. Even Helena conceded I was doing well, but I had stopped seeking her approval; I was too busy. Coming up to Saturnalia (or Christmas in the Christian West), I was getting good returns. Looking through the figures on the spreadsheets, I was delighted I was making a contribution at last. Nonna was impressed, which meant a lot to me.

'Well,' she said, 'these figures are very encouraging, especially Dania's bar. You obviously have a flair for it. The florist is a little risky, I'd say, but it's not a big amount.'

'I think he'll make it, Nonna. He's a prima donna, but his designs are cutting edge and will appeal to those wanting to make a high impact on their guests or partners. I think the key is to make strategic partnerships with regular repeat orders, preferably with other businesses like hotels. That's where I'm helping him most.'

She searched my face. 'I'm very pleased you're doing so well, darling, but don't tire yourself out. You have your first Saturnalia to get through, and that's ten strenuous days.'

'It'll be fine, Nonna. Most of the businesses will be pretty nearly self-sufficient by then.'

And they were, even the florist. Maybe now I *had* found something professional, I could settle into doing something with a purpose.

35

The ATM warned Renschman in perfect English he was approaching his daily credit limit of four hundred *solidi*. The notes looked trashy, gaudy, but he stuffed them in his wallet. He had funds left for five more days. His last chance to terminate her.

He'd followed the girl to the bar with her friend, but they were surrounded by kids in uniform. But his sightline was clear. Not that he could shoot her today: he couldn't carry here. The border guard had been officious enough about his quad-band smartphone, a leaving concession until the contract ran out next month. If he was still on the government payroll, he could have drawn a weapon from the embassy. Christ, she'd wrecked everything. He had no job, no income and a medical bill which the department refused to pay.

Carrying their designer bags full of expensive crap, the girl and her friend left and made for a side street, turned left and stopped by an Audi A5. Renschman followed on the opposite side, a little way back, and stared across into the window of the baker's store where the car was parked. The girl gasped, eyes wide and unbelieving. Her hand flew up to her mouth. He smiled at her terror. All he had to do was cross the street.

Renschman took one step off the kerb. Then he caught a woman watching him. She flashed a quick glance over the shoulder of her companion who lounged against a black Golf, his arm around her waist. At the same time the man smiled down at her, he glanced in the window of the store two down from the baker's. The light bulge under the man's arm betrayed a gun. As the man turned, the holster showed under his open jacket. Oh, shit. Only cops and military carried weapons openly in this place. Renschman reversed abruptly and hurried away as they turned in his direction.

Damn her to hell.

36

I'd only met the Imperatrix Silvia Apulia once before, for just over five minutes, shortly after I arrived. She was some kind of relation; her father had been Nonna's youngest cousin. She'd been gracious and friendly. But I'd detected an undercurrent I couldn't pinpoint.

This time, the dark-leaved evergreens lining the palace driveway were covered with clusters of red and blue berries. The first snowfall had left enough traces to make it look like something out of a Christmas card.

We walked through the magnificent colonnaded atrium down some steps into a narrower, much older stone hallway with several doors off. We passed through an oak door set back in an archway at the end, into Silvia Apulia's private drawing room where she was waiting for us.

'Aurelia, Carina, welcome.'

The stone-walled room was comfortable: pale blue furnishings with dark blue and oak couches. Family photographs on a side table and a few toys cleared into one corner gave it an intimate air. Silvia had soft red-brown hair drawn back in a slide in the nape of her neck, and clear brown eyes. In a chic, olive-coloured linen dress and gold jewellery, she looked more like a model than a ruler. She was a little over fifteen years older than me, but didn't look it.

I didn't know if I was supposed to start a conversation, but I gave it a try. 'This is a beautiful room – I love the way the photos are grouped under the light.'

'Come and have a look, if you like. They're mostly of my children,' she said, and smiled. I guessed she only did it to set me at my ease. I remembered there were three, but I hadn't met any of them yet. She lifted one frame that showed a baby looking surprised, a laughing pre-schooler and a girl, about seven or eight, sullen. 'This is Stella,' she said, pointing to the oldest girl, 'and these are Darius and Hallie. And, of course, their father.'

I took the frame in my hand. Conrad's arms were around the middle one as he laughed into the camera. No. I looked again. Wild ideas like he had a twin brother flitted through my mind. Who was I kidding? Cold anger climbed up through my body and seized my heart. I held it together, responding on auto-pilot, too proud and, to be honest, too embarrassed to do anything else. A look of horror had passed across Nonna's face when she saw my shock, but she'd replaced it with her politician's smile and taken over the conversation until the end of that interminable visit. By the time we got home, she had run out of words, furious with Conrad and guilty toward me. She'd never dreamed he hadn't told me about his children.

I pleaded a headache and went into my apartment. I couldn't process it. I knew the system was different here; women like Silvia and my grandmother needed heirs. Silvia's children belonged to her family; there was no legal link with Conrad. But there was sure to be some emotional bond. How could he have not mentioned them? I was embarrassed at just how stupid I'd been. Sure, his previous relationships were his business. Fine. But I'd been under the impression that we had something important going between us. Why hadn't he told me? Didn't he trust me? Perhaps he was letting me settle in before taking the next step. Perhaps he was still involved with her.

When he called me on his cell the following day, he suggested going away for a winter sports weekend in the north. I'd loved skating in New Hampshire as a kid and could handle skis reasonably well. The memory of the hot, jagged tears running down my face the previous evening decided me. I told him I was doing something else and stabbed the end call key.

. . .

Next morning, sunny but frosty, I wrapped myself up well, including gloves, hat and scarf, before I set off. The chill air was sharp on my throat and nose. I needed to work off some of my hurt, but I would keep it quick this morning. Our first Saturnalia party was next week and I made sure I had a lot to do. I slipped out so early I didn't see Junia. For a change, I jogged along between the tall buildings on the Decumanus Maximus – Dec Max – Main Street, if you will, and crossed over to the road that led to the Palace Park. Originally part of the palace gardens, it had been landscaped as a pleasure garden for public use several centuries ago.

I jogged along the main pathway, past the picturesque ruins, the kiosk shuttered up for winter, and the old perimeter wall. As I reached the end, a tingle ran across my shoulders. I wasn't alone. Only one or two other joggers were around today, away in the distance. But I knew I was being watched. I skirted away from a group of shrubs. Their glossy, dark green leaves and berries coated with frost shone attractively, but the dense foliage made a perfect place to hide. Crime was relatively low here and attacks rare, possibly because of the public video but mainly because of the strong restorative justice system. But something unsettled me as I approached the open-air theatre where live music played in the summer. I passed it and breathed with relief.

I had barely registered a figure being there when he slammed into me. I stumbled and fell. I managed to roll back onto my knees. I didn't have time to stand up before he hit my head. I went down and lay crouched on my side, winded, my head swimming. He half-carried, half-dragged me toward the service kiosk behind the theatre. My head cleared a little and I struggled to get out of his grip. I tried to kick out but my lower legs were being trailed along the frozen ground. I couldn't get a grip with either foot. I clawed my hands and aimed for his face. He grabbed my wrists and yanked my arms hard. Tears sprang out of my eyes with the pain. He heaved open the service kiosk and flung me into the dark. I landed on a pile of heavy cable. I caught my breath, placed the soles of my feet on the floor and sprang up to make a bolt for the door, only to be thrown back to the ground, face down. His knee in my back, he pulled my arms, tied them together and stood back, his breath coming in gulps.

'Still a feisty little bitch, aren't you?'

Renschman.

Crap.

So it *had* been him I'd seen when Helena and I had been shopping.

He set a flashlight end up on the ground so the light cast upwards.

'Too bad your soldier boy's not around to rescue you. Tired of you already, has he?'

My head rang with pain. I could hardly think, but I knew I had to keep him talking. 'What do you want?'

'I needed to see you, Miss Brown. I hadn't finished my conversation with you.'

From where I was lying face down, I could only see his shoes. They were a little too near my face. One foot suddenly swung away. I flinched, but it was back, bizarrely opposite the other. He had sat down and crossed his legs.

'I had a very uncomfortable time in the emergency room after my disappointment at your so-called legation in Washington. My office declined to pay for my treatment so, after a day, I was forced into the public hospital. And, thanks to you, I lost my job. I was unhappy about that, Miss Brown. Very unhappy. I think you need to pay.'

I swallowed hard. His voice had gone quiet, almost a whisper. I shivered – and not because of the cold concrete floor.

'How much?'

'Oh, dear me, I don't want your pocket change. No, something a little more permanent. With you out of the way, the American Brown family can petition to inherit Brown Industries. My former office will be so grateful, I'm sure they'll even offer me my job back if I want it.'

Shit. He was going to kill me. I'd changed my route; nobody knew where I was. I was trussed up here in the freezing dark like a turkey with the Thanksgiving butcher.

He pulled me over to the back wall of the kiosk and secured my tied wrists to the electricity distribution box. I kicked out desperately, but he grabbed my legs and sat on them. I spat at him. He took out a Kleenex from his jacket pocket and calmly wiped his face. He pulled off my hat, gloves, scarf and shoes. Despite my wriggling to get away from the touch of his hands, he methodically removed my clothes sliding a razor-sharp knife through the fabric of my jacket and undershirt, and parting the fabric like so much mist.

Gods, it was freezing. My teeth started to chatter. He stood and looked down at me for a few moments, his pale eyes sweeping to and fro, assessing me like I was a piece of meat. I closed my eyes. I shuddered. He knelt down and bent over me.

'Keep away from me!' I screamed at him, and sobbed with fright.

I tensed, waiting for his invasion. Instead, he tied my ankles together, securing them to the heavy cable reel, and stood up again. The only movement I could make was my involuntary shivering.

He stayed silent, working as if alone. He reached back between the stacks of plastic boxes and bins, pulled out a bucket and placed it under the faucet above the janitor's sink. His face was impassive. When the bucket was three quarters full, he reached out and turned off the flow with a precise, mechanical movement. He looked at me for a long time. I knew it was going to be bad.

'Please, please, don't leave me here,' I begged. 'Take everything, but please don't leave me.'

He drew out a reel of duct tape, cut off an exact amount and stretched it across my mouth. I jerked my head around from side to side, desperately searching for any trace of a way out of this nightmare.

At last he spoke. 'There are very few people about. I see they don't start shows here for a few months, so they won't find your body any time soon.'

He opened the door, allowing the pale light in.

'It's twenty degrees now, five below. You're shivering nicely already. Your core temperature will drop steadily and you'll be unconscious soon. But not before you realise what a miserable and lonely death you're going to have.'

He lifted the bucket of cold water, poured it over every part of me and left.

37

I screamed and almost passed out with the shock of the cold drenching. Ice started to form on my body. Water dripping off me froze into miniature hard gums as they fell on the concrete. I struggled to loosen the plastic cable ties but only made my wrists sore. After a while, I couldn't feel them. Or the floor. A chill, hard lump grew inside me, pushing its cold fingers into my every cell. I became so thirsty, and my head hurt. More than anything, I wanted to sleep. My eyelids pressed down like two heavy stones. But I knew I had to stay awake.

I had been so stupid. After the kidnap in New York, I promised myself I would never be so vulnerable again. But I hadn't done anything about it. Too late now. My body was a stone. It would soon be over. I was really too tired to be angry with myself. Nonna...she would be devastated when they found my body. Conrad? Maybe...

I wanted to rest now. Sleep. My nightmare was full of arguing: ice monsters and black, swirling clouds of smoke, all wearing glasses. I wanted them to go away and leave me alone. I'd had enough now. Sleep. No, the shouting was still there. My befuddled mind pushed a thought up to the surface. My name. I heard my name. I shouted back, but my lips wouldn't move. They were glued together by the tape.

The shouters wouldn't know I was here. I panicked. They would go away and leave me. Please stay. The shouting faded. Tears seeped out of my eyes and froze on my skin. I sank back to sleep.

Footsteps. Please, not Renschman coming back to gloat. I couldn't even shudder. Heavy boots. The door lock jangled. The lock area exploded under a heavy impact. Light burst in as the door swung open. A tall blue figure shone a light in my face, knelt down and removed the tape from my mouth.

'No, I do not want counselling. I want to be able to protect myself against that maniac.'

Dressed in my thickest sweater and still not trusting ever being warm again, I sat in the atrium opposite Nonna and hugged a cup of the malt and ginger drink. Winter sunshine streamed in through the glass wall and fell on the table between us, making patterns on the pile of papers and magazines I was bored with reading.

Nonna looked up as Conrad was announced. Her cold, set face and minimal hand gesture showed me she hadn't forgiven him. Instead of throwing his jacket down first as he usually did, he held it in one hand, hesitated and lowered himself carefully into one of the easy chairs. He sat stiff and tense in the silence. He shook his head to Nonna's raised eyebrow.

Conrad blamed the *custodes* for letting Renschman get away. I thought they were wonderful, far better than the cops I'd encountered in the EUS. The tracker in my shoulder had given them my location to within fifteen metres. They'd searched centimetre by centimetre until they found me. After I'd been wrapped in foil and blue-lighted to the hospital, they treated me with courtesy, even when questioning me in some depth. They put an immediate APB out at railroad stations, the airport, the roads and on the borders, and tasked one of their special investigators to handle the case. She found no trace whatsoever. She initiated the international alert system with her colleagues in Italy and New Austria, but wasn't optimistic. Renschman had evaporated into the ether.

I studied the frost-coated conifers the other side of the atrium glass wall. I'd been both dreading and desperate to see Conrad again, but couldn't look at him. In the reflection, I saw Nonna get up. I whirled around to stop her.

'No, you stay and talk to Conradus.'

'I—'

She stared me down. I capitulated. She nodded and left.

Conrad stood by the window, his arms crossed tightly across his chest. 'Before you say anything, will you please let me explain?'

'Silvia and I were guaranteed to meet,' I interrupted. I couldn't keep my hurt in. 'How could you let me find out like that?'

'It was finished months before I came to New York. It was a families' arrangement. She needed children, heirs. Her husband was infertile from the cancer. He'd died a couple of years before and she couldn't face another marriage.' He shrugged. 'Lots of families make arrangements like that. It's normal for us. Despite Caius Tellus's treachery, the imperatrix trusted the Tellus family.' His voice dropped. 'I thought it would be so foreign to you.' He paused, his face drained. 'I thought you would be repelled.'

'How stupid was that?' I glared at him. 'Don't you think somebody would have told me or casually mentioned it? How in Hades did you think you could keep it from me? Why did you even try?'

'I don't know what to say to convince you how desperately sorry I am.' His voice cracked. 'I was scared of losing you.'

'You coward.'

He flinched and looked away.

'How can I be sure you're not going to pull any further surprises on me?' I said. 'I can accept the fact that you had a child, even the weird way that happened, but how could you not tell me you had three? One child could be an aberration. An occupational hazard for people who screw around like you used to. Or do you still?'

He took a step toward me, putting his hand out.

'Don't come any nearer – I can't bear for you to touch me.' I couldn't even say his name to his face.

'I am so sorry,' he whispered.

'You'd better go – I can't take any more. I have other things to think about now. You can't deliver on your promise never to let Renschman get near me again. I need to do something about it myself.'

He flushed and his eyes glinted. His whole face tightened and he took a half-step toward me. 'You know I'd do anything to protect you, but I can't be everywhere. Jogging alone was the height of stupidity. Why didn't you call me? I'd have come with you.'

'And who are you to say I can't go out without a nursemaid? Jeez, I jogged *by myself* regularly in the park in New York. I patrolled *by myself* when I worked there as a volunteer and never had a problem in four years; well, until Junior Hartenwyck.'

We glowered at each other like a couple of circling cats, radiating hostility and fury. He broke first. He went over to the bureau and picked up a silver-framed photo. Helena had taken it of us jumping into the lake, laughing, hand in hand at Castra Lucilla, Nonna's summer home in the country. He stared at it, replaced it carefully, looked at me and left.

38

I didn't take in much of my first Saturnalia, pleading the need to recover from my ordeal in the park. I didn't want to chit-chat with people I scarcely knew. Luckily, I didn't suffer any long-term physical effects, but breaking up with Conrad had left a hole in my mind as well as my heart. Worse was that I couldn't stop being a victim. In a weird way, every time I thought about either one of these, the other crept into my head. .

I started training, driving myself like a demon. It was true what they said – you did get a high from the adrenalin rush. I enrolled in a self-defence class and practised tai chi with a load of others in the park. I made myself go back there as soon as I recovered; it had been a tense experience. But surrounded each morning by friendly, supportive people intent on control and fitness was reassuring.

I ran into Conrad when our family met his. His Uncle Quintus and Nonna bantered together, a glass of white in their hands, neutral faces on, like the politicians and old friends they were. Conrad was polite, formal, but like a coiled-up spring. As families stood around the altar at Octavia Quirinia's wedding in the first week of January and she bent to sign the contract, I caught him gazing at me from the other side. Only the flicker and heat of the open torches brought me back. I swallowed hard. I had a sore hurt in my chest that wouldn't heal. I loved him still, but found it impossible to say anything after our fight. Once Octavia and her new husband had completed the formal exchange of fire and water, I wrenched myself away from his stare, turned and went to talk to somebody else. I couldn't remember who.

I tried to push this melancholic feeling away by concentrating on my businesses. I completed the expansion plans I started before Saturnalia to include an advertising agency, something I knew about. I scratched my head on choosing a fancy codeword name for the companies' registration site and eventually came up with *pulcheria*. In Latin, '*pulcher*' means not only beautiful but also excellent, honourable, glorious. Nothing like being aspirational. But it was all like walking through deep, sticky gravel.

Two weeks later, I was spending an afternoon expanding my less formal vocabulary with one of my original protégées: Dania, the bar owner. The white winter sunlight and the noise of boisterous tourists here for the extended Janus Agonalia new year celebrations invaded my head and I couldn't focus.

I remembered my moment of disappointment on learning that the festival was more a way of attracting the tourist *solidus* than a serious religious occasion. Helena just laughed cynically at me. Foreigners were intrigued by our culture; the fascination for all things Roman hadn't died since the old empire had fallen apart fifteen hundred years ago.

Full of bad taste and good wine, Dania ignored the noisy end of the bar and insisted on telling me the latest gossip. As I lifted the glass to my lips, I burst out laughing at one of her dirty jokes. It flew out like a released bird. That was a jolt.

I glanced toward Nic, Nonna's chauffeur, but he was out of earshot, virtuously drinking an orange juice with a friend he'd run into here in the bar. Something about his friend was familiar but I couldn't place him. I was about to ask Dania for a refill when I remembered. He was one of the house security detail.

In a rush, a load of pieces fell into their slots. People were always around me, at the house, when I was driven around, when I was at my business meetings, even when I was shopping or going for a walk. I was never alone. I probably had somebody shadowing me when I went jogging. Which member of my tai chi group was watching over me? Why hadn't I spotted that before?

Back at the house, I whined at Junia.

'What did you expect after the attack in the park?'

'But I'm doing my self-defence classes and jogging. I would be more ready now.'

She smiled to herself.

'What?'

She looked into her cup and then straight at me. 'You're only playing at it really. You haven't developed the ruthlessness or mental attitude you need for such close-quarter fighting.'

'And who are you to know this?'

'I wasn't always a household steward. I served with your grandmother in the PGSF until I was injured.'

I heard her. I looked at her. I saw a middle-aged woman, brown hair streaked with a few grey ones. She was ordinary, everyday, a million miles from anybody's idea of special forces. I played what she said in my mind again. I didn't find it any easier to absorb a second time.

I listened to her calm voice telling me how she'd been part of Aurelia Mitela's assault group that retook the city when Caius Tellus's rebellion had been put down twenty-three years ago. A serious back injury had incapacitated Junia and she'd had to leave the PGSF; she was only thirty-three. Aurelia knew her through their service together and trusted her. So, when Aurelia's steward was killed during the rebellion, she brought Junia back to the damaged Domus Mitelarum and the two women reconstructed the household between them.

I watched my seventy-year-old grandmother at dinner that evening, trying to visualise her in combat fatigues leading an assault. She would have been forty-six or seven at the time.

'You're very quiet tonight, darling. Anything wrong?'

'I...I was talking to Junia this afternoon.'

'So she said. You've certainly got a passionate champion there. She tactfully pointed out to me that we'd all been at fault in cocooning and confining you.' She put her hand out. I automatically met it with mine. 'I'm sorry you've found it limiting. I only wanted to protect you.' She squeezed my hand then let it drop.

'I know you meant it for the best, Nonna, but I can't live with a load of permanent babysitters trailing after me.'

She played with her gold signet ring, looking a little uncertain.

'When you lived in the EUS, did you ever go on an activity holiday or outward bound?' She didn't sound very hopeful.

'Sure. I had ten days in Montana one year. We camped out, did woodland skills, hiked, climbed. Tough, but wonderful. And, every weekend, I was outdoors in the park.'

'You said you wanted to learn to protect yourself. I know you've made an effort to become fit and follow some basic self-defence classes. But, if you're serious, you need to go up several levels.'

She looked into the distance and said nothing for a few minutes.

'Junia thinks you have the aptitude and the motivation for the hard training required. I suggest you try a fitness boot camp for a few months and see how you get on.'

39

Two weeks later, I stepped off the train and walked the three kilometres as set out in my joining instructions. The ground along my route sloped upwards from the station and was divided into small fields, glistening with droplets ready to change into frost in a few hours. Early green shoots sprouted in some, but most were dull with winter vegetables, bare vines and fruit trees. It was a chilly February afternoon and I was glad of my hat and gloves.

At the crest, I paused under a tree to drink now-lukewarm coffee from my flask. Below me lay a collection of red-tiled, mostly single-storey buildings, square to each other around a central courtyard. At the end of the track, a gate in the wall led to an open area in front of the two-storey main villa. Behind lay some barns and granaries, and further back what looked like square fishponds, an orchard, vegetable gardens and a small lake. I couldn't identify a round area which disappeared partly under the trees. Maybe something for training horses?

I reached the access door in the wooden gate, unlatched it and went in. A brown-haired woman in a navy sweats spotted me, identified herself as Tonia and told me to follow her into the main villa to check in.

I had been unwilling to enter Mitela as my *nomen* when I registered online at the place Nonna suggested. If I fouled up, I would be embarrassed for her. I remembered Helena had presented me as 'Cara' to the others at the riverside bar. That would be fine for a first name. Startled when the voice prompted me again, I started tapping in 'Br' for Brown. Horrified at my mistake, I panicked and added 'una'. How lame was that – Bruna the bear? Well, I was stuck with it now.

Tonia took me upstairs to a large sleeping area, partitioned off into cubicles. Plain grey, they were pretty generous in size, but the stud walls only went up about two metres, leaving the top open.

'Why don't you take a shower and get changed?' She pointed to an identical set of navy sweats on the bed. 'I'll come and get you just before six for the evening meal.'

At supper, there was plenty of food, simply cooked, but only water to drink. People moved purposefully, talking quietly as they took food or piled up their dirty dishes afterward. So far, it was no worse than a well-behaved adult version of summer camp. I learned later that many of them were cops, military or worked in the security industry. Afterward, Tonia took me to find Felix who would supervise my time there. Tall and chunky, around late forties, even sitting he had that superior assurance that athletes project, but he gave me a friendly enough welcome.

Unsurprisingly, I slept well, only waking when I heard movement around me.

'Coming for the run?' A dark head appeared in the doorway of my cubicle.

In the corridor, I found half a dozen others of various ages. The dark-haired man nodded as I joined them, and we set off. I considered myself pretty fit, but I found it a challenging course. No nice regular track or paths, more like trail running. As I went for my shower afterward, I was relieved I hadn't died out there.

Felix collected me after breakfast and took me to a room like a regular office, but minimalist with bare wood and metal furnishings. He was just as minimalist: no greeting. He handed me two sheets of paper.

'This is your schedule for this week – a fairly relaxed introduction.'

I skimmed it. The lists and tables reminded me of high school. I looked up and saw him smiling at me, but with an air of tolerating a child's simple mistake.

'Look at it properly, and tell me what you see.'

What type of lame question was that? It was two sheets of paper. 'I can see six parts to it,' I said, pushing my impatience down. 'Three group physical training, three other stuff. Run first thing, indoor exercises midday, yoga, mind-body and visualisation training in the evening.' I looked up at him. 'These sections marked in yellow, in the mornings, called "Personal programme" – what happens there?'

'You'll find it taxing, but that's where you learn to push yourself beyond the point you think possible.'

I stayed for three months. I made the stupid mistake of trying to be smart and impress during the first-day fitness assessment. Felix set that as the starting-off point. As I sweated my way through the interval training, the infinite push-ups and squat thrusts, I was determined to show I didn't care about his opinion. If only he didn't make that irritating little half-smile at me. I pushed and strained until I ached in every muscle, tumbling into bed each night almost comatose with exhaustion.

One day, I couldn't get up; I was so tired. Tonia came and fetched me and made me attend each session but sit on the ground watching. I was so embarrassed and fed up with the catcalls from the others I never made that mistake again.

Then I caught on: Felix had set me up to challenge myself. How stupid had I been not to see that? I discovered how competitive I could be during the obstacle courses and long treks. Once I'd got through the endurance barrier, I made sure I always came in the first group of trail runners. So, he gave me two others to look after. Sure, it slowed me up, but I couldn't deny the pleasure of seeing them work their way up from the back to respectable middle place on most things. We even achieved third place in one group exercise. Shivering in the cold, covered in mud and with hair plastered to our heads, we raised our faces to the sleet stinging our skin and laughed, celebrating our success.

I became fascinated by the whole process. I joined in the daily tai chi practice; my muscle coordination advanced beyond any expectation I had. Four weeks later, I was pretty pleased with myself, until Felix told me it was only preparation. Now I had to learn to give it back. At first, I was thrown on the floor over and over, but I learned to flow with an incoming attack, sticking to the force the opponent was projecting, finding the centre of that force. Then we started on the smart stuff, with palm pushes and acupressure points, graduating to using every part of my body to strike the opponent. Normally, it took years to train properly, but he ground as much into me as possible in the months I was there. And he was pitiless.

In the evenings, he led the group on mind-body discipline: persuading and influencing skills to enhance physical competency, and self-induced deep rest techniques to promote the body's natural recovery processes when injured. Physically drained after training all day, we struggled, especially at first. But he said that was when we needed it most.

The last four weeks, he developed a course for me which at first I thought was a mistake, but I followed his instructions and reported to an outdoor supervisor whom I discovered was a gladiator trainer. With attitude. The first day, I stopped counting the bruises and scratches as I lay smarting in my cubicle that evening. I couldn't drag together the energy to join the mind-body group. After some hard knocks, I got into the way of it and adapted my tai chi skills. My absolute favourite was the linked chain short sword fighting. My left wrist was bound by a leather cuff, attached to a chain approximately two metres long, at the end of which was a similar cuff around the wrist of my opponent. The discipline of the link was intense; physical strength was not enough. You had to be alert, light on your feet and fast thinking as you wielded your sword. Training with a sharp, double-edged, fifty-centimetre, carbon steel blade tended to concentrate the mind as well as honing reaction skills. It was the ultimate in mental agility and physical ferocity. I always had an adrenalin high from these fights, especially if I won. But, to my chagrin, I never managed to defeat the head trainer.

At the end of the third month, the day I left, Felix took me out to the garden where we sat in a sheltered spot by a stone wall. His fingers traced patterns in the dirt while he looked at the distant mountains. He drew his gaze back to the nearer hills and eventually to me.

'I'm sorry to see you go, Cara Bruna. You've transformed yourself from an amateur with promise into a disciplined, competent fighter. More than that, you've found inner confidence. Don't waste it.'

'C'mon, Felix, I enjoy the challenge, the coordination, but I'm not the military type.'

'Are you sure?'

'Of course. I really—' I stopped myself when I saw his sceptical look. I took a deep breath. My head whirred and thoughts fell into my mind like a meteor shower. Suddenly, I got it. It all clipped together like a kid's plastic toy, never able to be taken apart again. I shivered, but in a good way. Somehow, I had become the person I was meant to be. When I came to this camp, all I'd wanted was to learn how to protect myself against being a victim. I figured I could defeat Renschman now. And more.

But the idea of being a female soldier...

Nah.

PART III

METAMORPHOSIS

40

I slid silently into the atrium and waited unmoving by the back wall. I watched my grandmother bending over the planting in the centre, picking at the leaves, tutting at the same time. It made me smile; I had missed her. Sensing the presence of another, she looked up, caution in her eyes as she scanned the room.

'Nonna.'

She embraced me, tears threatening to ambush both of us. Pulling away, she didn't say anything but studied my face. She smiled, like she was satisfied, or she recognised something. For the first time in my life, I knew I was in the right place.

'You look wonderful, darling,' she said. 'Outstanding.'

'I've learnt a whole lot about myself, Nonna. And how to stand my ground. I'm never going to be a victim again.'

I spent the next few weeks shadowing Nonna. I was flattered she included me in her advisory work and asked for my views. I realised that I was now looking at the world in a different way. Like my mind had been re-booted along with my body.

Inevitably, we saw Imperatrix Silvia again, but what a contrast to the previous time: she was more relaxed, I was more confident. I hadn't noticed before how dry her remarks were, or her sense of gallows humour as she discussed tangled issues with Nonna. She questioned me in some depth about what I had achieved at my training camp.

'You must build on this, Carina. Have you ever considered working in one of the military or police services? You'd be ideal for the PGSF. Another Aurelia.' She smiled over at Nonna.

No way.

'I don't think I'd fit in very well. Perhaps I could be a consultant of some sort, but that sounds pretty boring as well.'

She laughed at my lame reply and bantered some more, but I saw something in her eyes that meant her brain was whirring away. Silvia projected a good sense of fun but, in the car driving back, Nonna said she never let it interfere with her duty. Or her resolve.

Felix had provided me with the name of a training gym run by an ex-champion gladiator called Mossia Antonia. With a membership ranging from the prominent and powerful to anybody who could pay the fees, they insisted on *noms de guerre* for all members. If you recognised somebody, you had to act as if you didn't know them. Weird, but that was the price of membership. I registered there under the name of Bruna. Their strenuous programmes with no quarter given left me breathless and my muscles drained, but I loved it and spent at least an hour of every day there.

I decided to visit my businesses in person; I'd left them to fend for themselves for three months. I didn't mistrust the managers, but it never hurt to do a little mystery shopping.

I wore a long, dark brown, curly wig, black skirt and leather boots, a dark red, roll-neck sweater and black leather jacket. I applied dark eye make-up and bright red lipstick. I disguised myself, not only so they didn't recognise me, but because it appealed to my sense of the dramatic. I had no idea just how dramatic it would prove to be.

In the bar just off the Via Nova, I sipped a glass of dry white and watched carefully. Nine tables toward the front of the bar by the picture window were occupied. Everybody had a drink in front of them, some were eating. I was pleased that no client was left more than a minute or two before a server approached them. Meals were brought promptly, and the place looked fresh and clean. I heard a few foreign accents; the tourist season was starting. The bar counter, cut from one piece of grey and blue veined marble, ran almost the whole length of the bar, only stopping where a door hung with a beaded curtain led through to the back. Standing at the far open end of the counter was Dania, my protégée, looking content with life. I wasn't sure about the blonde hair, but the smile on her face and in her brown eyes was genuine.

I was about to go over to her, reveal myself and crack a joke, when two men in their early twenties came in. One looked friendly enough, an open jokey face, the other quieter. Totally relaxed, they sauntered up to Dania but, when they reached her, they corralled her between them so intimately their clothes touched hers. She glanced around, looking every which way like she was searching for a way to escape. But she didn't attempt to push them away. What was going on? I concentrated on tuning out the other voices and tried to catch their conversation. I couldn't hear all of it, but I worked out they weren't collecting for the Christmas Club.

I shucked off my leather jacket, leaving it on the back of my chair, stood up and made my way to the door leading to the facilities. The jokey one moved aside for me, his eyes roving up and down my body as I passed. When his hand ran over my rear and pinched it, I reacted instantly. He was on the floor behind the counter in seconds, my boot heel on his wrist. I shifted my full weight onto that foot to prove the point. The diamond-sharp carbon fibre knife in my hand pointing at his face discouraged any further movement.

I held the flat of my other hand out to the quiet one and said, 'Don't even try.' He caught on quickly and remained still.

'Okay, Dania, you go talk to your customers. I'll take it from here.'

Her mouth opened, she hesitated and looked at me. But she didn't ask the question. She placed a hand on the counter for a few moments to steady herself; then hastened away with only one glance back.

I looked at the quiet one and pointed to a booth in the back corner. 'You go sit down at that table and stay there. No calls, no signals. Got it?'

He nodded.

The other one's face was streaming with tears; I hoped he was in agony. I stepped back and he struggled up.

'Fuck you, you little tart.' His jokey face was screwed up in anger.

'Nah, that's the point,' I said in a nasal voice. I was starting to enjoy this. 'You be a good boy and go sit with your friend. Go.'

Rocking on the balls of his feet, he hesitated for a few seconds.

'Unless you would like me to mark your pretty face.'

He sat. I joined them, but kept my blade in their sight.

'Now, gentlemen. What seems to be the problem, apart from laughing boy here's wandering fingers?'

Predictably, they exchanged glances.

Under the table, I stamped on laughing boy's instep. It wasn't fair, but the quiet one looked too self-contained. Laughing boy would give sooner.

'You little bitch!' He went to reach inside, but I already knew he had no concealed weapon from the fall of his clothes and his gait.

'Oh dear, forget your popgun, did you, dear?'

'What's it to you, anyway?' said the quiet one, trying to shift his weight. Was he thinking of attacking me?

'I'm not happy when I see my colleagues being threatened. So enlighten me.'

'We're collecting dues.'

'Yes? And what dues would they be?'

'Insurance.'

I laughed. Life was so like the movies.

'You go back to your principal and tell her, or him, that none of my businesses pay protection money to anybody. And if any kind of accident or fire occurs, or if business drops off significantly in the very near future, I'll hunt you, and them, down like the scum you are. Clear?'

They nodded.

'Now piss off out of here.' I stood up, hands on hips, and watched them as they left. I walked back to the bar, sat on a tall stool and ordered another glass of dry white wine. I was perfectly calm, but inside I glowed with satisfaction. Dania served me herself, her fingers trembling.

'Hello, Dania.' I held my hand out and smiled in my old way.

'Venus save us! Is that you, really?' Her eyes were wide and her mouth not far behind. She scoured my face with her gaze, and then relaxed. 'I'd never have recognised you.'

'I've been away. How long have they been bothering you?'

She looked down at the counter then scanned the open area. 'This is the second time. They're not violent; they don't smash anything or openly frighten the clients. But they scare me.'

'I've sent them home with a message. I expect they'll be back but, with any luck, they'll bring their boss with them.'

She looked at me as if I was insane.

'I'll stay here until they come. Can you put me up?'

She looked a little embarrassed.

'Problem?' I knew from the plan she'd submitted for the finance application that the building went back a long way, almost the whole block, so probably at least half a dozen rooms. Maybe she was letting them out as holiday accommodation.

She didn't answer my question immediately; one of the staff had an urgent query that needed her attention. I was phoning home to let them know I may not be there for a few days when I noticed a man pay at the till, but didn't get a drink. Instead, he took a receipt, some kind of token, a keycard, then walked through the opening at the end of the bar counter, toward the facilities. I saw him disappear upstairs.

'Expanding your income possibilities, Dania?' I chuckled at her confusion when she came back. 'I don't really mind, you know, as long as you have the health checks and licences. Can you find somewhere for me?'

'Of course I can, if you don't mind sharing with me.'

I spent the next day going through Dania's accounts; they looked healthy. She gave me an insight into the tax system as experienced by the sole trader, which I found illuminating. Midway through the afternoon, we were downstairs discussing inventory when the fun restarted. Laughing boy and the quiet one came in, the drape of their coats betraying concealed weapons. Dania and I watched the quiet one turn the door notice to 'Closed' and usher the two remaining customers out. Dania started getting up, but I laid my hand on her arm and shook my head. Laughing boy stood in the doorway, scanned the room and, satisfied, gave way to a tall figure, dressed in black. He strolled in, looking around to discover what problem there could possibly be in such a place. His black eyes took us in during his sweep and, flicking over Dania, fixed on me. I stared back, willing him to drop his gaze. There was no way I would. I was one of Felix's graduates and could play mind games all day.

Eventually, he broke, sat down and said, 'Wine,' in a commanding but soft voice.

Dania moved to obey, but I grabbed her arm so she couldn't.

He looked up, one eyebrow raised.

'Say "please",' I said.

He was incredulous.

I held on to Dania's arm. He and I remained locked in a staring contest.

He waved his hand in a bored, over-elaborate gesture. 'Very well. Wine, *please*.'

I nodded to Dania and she scuttled to the chiller, fetched a bottle and glass and delivered it to the table in record time. She managed to open it without spilling any, but her hand trembled as she poured. She retreated to the safety of the counter. I couldn't blame her. He was a frightening man; he sat totally relaxed, confident of his own power and ability to intimidate.

'Won't you join me?'

I took the chair opposite him, but moved it so his body shielded me from his heavies. A smile flickered over his lips.

'Do I have the honour of talking to the owner of this bar?'

'In a financial sense, yes.'

'I understand you are reluctant to take out an insurance policy with us?'

'No.'

'Oh, have I received an incorrect message?'

'I don't know.'

'Really, my dear, you are a very difficult person to hold a conversation with.'

I said nothing.

His fingers tapped arrhythmically on Dania's shiny blue table.

'Are you trying to get yourself killed? I do hope not – it would be such a waste.' He appraised me slowly, like I was a piece of prime horseflesh.

I chuckled and leaned back in my chair, my left hand relaxed, hanging by my side.

'Gods, woman, have you no sense of self-preservation?'

'Yes, plenty.'

He rose in his seat, leaned over me and found a carbon fibre knife on his jugular. I didn't scratch his skin, just pressed firmly so he couldn't misinterpret my message. Laughing boy shot forward but seconds later he clutched his hand and cried out. Another knife had flown out of my right hand, and now grew out of the back of his left.

I stared into the black eyes that were as close to me as a lover's.

'Sit down,' I commanded, 'and, you two, back to the door.'

I stood tall in front of my opponent, legs braced. I kept my voice level, but chill.

'Firstly, I am not reluctant to pay protection money. I refuse to. Secondly, my message was clear. If you didn't get it, I suggest your messenger boys need remedial training.' I sighed. 'But perhaps their knuckles dragging too near the ground indicate they're unlikely to absorb or benefit from it. Thirdly, I don't have a death wish but, on the contrary, a very strong sense of self-preservation. Try to remember that fact.'

I sheathed my knife, picked up the bottle of wine and glass and placed them on the counter. 'I think we're done here. Please consider yourselves banned from the premises. With no likelihood of any change in the future.' I strode to the street door and pulled it open, letting in the fresh air. I seized laughing boy's wrist and pulled my knife out, wiping the blade on his pale coat. He turned white. His knees buckled, and the quiet one grabbed him as he collapsed.

The black-eyed man clapped his hands together in slow applause. 'Bravo,' he said. His eyes fixed on mine as he walked the length of the bar toward the open door. As he passed me on his way out, he said, 'You play a dangerous game, my dear, but I give you my respect.'

He bowed and was gone.

I drank a generous mouthful of the wine that Dania pressed on me. 'So who is the black-eyed man? He has quite a presence, doesn't he?'

'Are you insane? That's Apollodorus. I almost died when I saw it was him.'

'Because?'

'He runs this area. They're all petrified of him.'

'Maybe so, but he doesn't run this bar.'

'No,' she said. 'Not now.' She looked at me, doubt written all over her face. 'You really think he won't come back?'

'No. I've banned him.' I smirked.

'Venus save us. You know something? You're just as scary as he is.'

I gave Dania my cell phone number and resolved to check out my other businesses. As I put my jacket on to go, I turned to her and said, 'One last thing, Dania. If they want to know my name, tell them it's Pulcheria.'

41

When I reached home that afternoon, I changed into jeans and tee and cleaned my face. Over supper with Nonna, I told her about my adventure.

'Have I gone too far, do you think?' I asked her.

'No. Not at all. I'm impressed, Carina, and proud of you for having the courage to act so firmly. Juno alone knows there are plenty of other things to bother about without adding in petty extortion.'

'What do you mean?'

She hesitated, looked down at her plate, then back at me. 'It something Silvia's worried about; Conradus also mentioned it when he came to see me yesterday.'

Those two names in the same sentence jolted me.

'Sorry to go off at an angle, but when does Conradus visit? When did this start?'

'He's been dropping by once a week or so while you've been away. I didn't say where you were or what you were doing.' She played with her ring. 'I've known him almost all of his life. I've supported and defended him when he needed somebody on his side.' She smiled, looking down at the table. 'I've paid the odd debt for him.' She brought the knife and fork together on her plate. 'Now you're back, he'll probably stop. I hope not. He made a grave error of judgement not telling you about the children, but he's desperate not to hurt you,

Carina.' She touched my cheek with the back of her fingers – his favourite gesture. I swallowed nothing in particular.

'I had hoped the two of you would form some kind of permanent attachment…'

I opened my lips to reply.

'…but I see it's not the right time.'

I ate my dessert in silence.

We sat in the atrium later, darkness taking over from the day, Nonna pensive, me swallowing my regret.

'So what's the problem that's causing everybody grief?'

'Addictive drugs. We've kept it down to what's considered an acceptable level.' She flicked the cover of her folder. 'It's never acceptable, of course, but sentences are harsh for dealing. The gods know that Health runs effective clinics and Social tries to pinch it out early, but we'll never eliminate it entirely. Every time the odd tourist gets caught smuggling in a personal supply, we maximise publicity on how severely we deal with it.' Her eyebrows pulled together in a frown. 'But, now, significant quantities, and I mean hundreds of kilograms, are coming through and getting onto the streets.'

No. That couldn't be happening here. It was too horrifying. I closed my eyes and shook my head. I had seen the despair and damage done to people through their addictions when I lived in the EUS. You only had to look at any street corner or alley. Or the rich kids, like that little jerk Hartenwyck, trying to outdo each other at parties and ending up on the morgue slab.

'But haven't the police, the *custodes*, I mean, got this?' I said. 'They have a vice squad, surely?'

'Unfortunately, they've discovered a corruption problem there. Seizures disappearing, leads being ignored. Even the PGSF is having a problem with it.'

'Why on earth have *they* been called in? They're special forces, spooks, aren't they?'

'Because it's been designated as a threat against the state, their intelligence and operations people are supporting the DJ.'

'DJ, the Department of Justice, run the police, right?'

She nodded.

'So they must have an internal affairs department?'

She sighed.

'Okay, Nonna, am I reinventing the wheel here?'

'Not at all, darling. The main problem is who to trust. These drug pushers have certainly done their research. The potential income in an underexploited market like Roma Nova makes it very worthwhile for them. The big problem for the law and security services is that all the serving personnel seem to be known to these criminals.'

'Which means, logically, they're into the database systems?'

'Precisely. Well, at least the DJ one. And they know exactly who to bribe or put pressure on.'

'This isn't a novel idea, but couldn't they use retired operatives or trainees who aren't known?'

'Two reactivated officers, one DJ and one PGSF, were found dead in the public sewer the day before yesterday.' Her voice wasn't just cold, it was despairing. 'Post-mortem examinations showed forced narcotic overdose as the cause of death for both.'

What a foul way to die – force-fed drugs and then dying helplessly in self-disgust and agony.

I didn't have anything to offer Nonna. My mind was running on. I needed information. I went to the library and started reading up on the Department of Justice, the *custodes*, the PGSF. I scanned every relevant page I could find through Quaero, my fingers aching from tapping the keyboard. After several hours, I had sore eyes, but a pretty reasonable basic knowledge. I moved, and my stiff back and shoulders protested. I glanced at the clock. Hades. It was three in the morning.

That day, I didn't get up until eight, but started again. This time, it was law enforcement, the justice system, and the drugs trade in Europe. Somebody brought me a tray of food and a jug of water at some stage.

I wasn't aiming to become an expert, just get enough background in so I could be of more help to Nonna. This was important stuff. How could I have wasted my time so stupidly before?

I put on my Pulcheria disguise again and went to check on my other businesses. None of them said they were being pressured for money; I believed them. I called into Dania's and found she'd had no further threatening visitors.

'Dania, I hope you won't be offended—'

'Try me.' She grinned.

'Do you get anybody offering or wanting to buy drugs?'

Her face puckered up like a sour lemon and her body tensed. 'I'm hurt you feel the need to ask that question. I wouldn't have anything so disgusting here. We don't even sell tobacco. If you don't want anything else, I've got some paying customers to see to.' She flounced off.

I was sipping my wine, thinking of how to mollify her, when she came back.

'I'm sorry, er, Pulcheria, I didn't mean to be rude. I don't suppose you would've asked without a good reason.'

'No problem, Dania. Really.'

'I've heard the odd rumour recently, I admit, but thought it was a joke. I mean, nobody in their right senses would mess with that stuff.'

'No, but there are some ruthless and greedy people who see Roma Nova as virgin territory and want to gang-bang her to death with their filth.'

She stared at me. 'I didn't know you felt that strongly.'

My turn to smile, but I didn't feel humorous. 'Nor did I. If you hear the tiniest whisper, a few words or anything you think is remotely connected, tell me. Ninety-nine useless things are fine if I have one good one.'

'Are you working for the law now?'

'Juno, no.'

42

The next day, Nonna had an old friend coming over for lunch. She introduced her as Aemilia Fulvia, who I guessed to be another political mover and shaker, but didn't say what she did. Although not very tall, Aemilia had an authoritative air about her; even her well-dressed grey hair seemed to fall into line.

As we ate, Aemilia asked me the usual questions about the contrast between my old life and the new, how I'd been settling in, what I'd been doing. I had the impression she was dancing around the point. Just before coffee was served, it clicked: I'd seen her face on the newscast when she was appointed minister for justice a few weeks before.

Aemilia nodded to Nonna, who asked a servant to see if the minister's assistant had arrived. A dark-haired man in a casual suit entered and nodded to Aemilia, bowed to Nonna, but said nothing. He deposited his briefcase on the table, then pulled a small velvet bag out of the leather folds and opened the drawstring to reveal a crystalline pyramid which he placed in the centre of our table. After that, he sat down at Amelia's side and studied the far wall.

'Now we can talk safely,' Aemilia said. 'The crystal will scramble our voices. Not, of course, my dear Aurelia, that there can be any doubt here, but we do have to take every precaution at the moment.' She turned to include me. 'Allow me to introduce a colleague from the Department of Justice, Inspector Cornelius Lurio.'

After greeting Nonna, Lurio turned his light blue gaze on me. His dark hair, long for a cop, was trained back behind his ears. He held himself upright and, while not overweight, had a well-developed figure. When he'd stretched his arm forward to place the pyramid, I'd seen the strong muscles of his wrist and hand. I shook hands with him, but he let go as soon as he could. He resumed his study of the back wall.

'Lurio is the only other person apart from the imperatrix who knows what I'm going to tell you,' Aemilia said. 'I believe, Carina, that Aurelia has given you some background on the difficulties we're having vis-à-vis the anti-drug operations being run by the DJ and PGSF.'

I nodded.

'Both Aurelia and the imperatrix think you may be able to help us with this.' She looked straight at me as if she were trying to pin me on a specimen board. I was stunned by her words and so wouldn't have put up much resistance.

'Um, what exactly did you have in mind?' I managed to say.

A strong masculine voice answered, irony coating everything he said. 'We need an English-speaker so wealthy they can't be bought, so moral they'll stay honest, smart yet ruthless, and unknown to the law and security forces.' Lurio looked down his nose at me. 'Oh yes, they need to be a trained fighter, have good tradecraft and nerves of ice.' He snorted.

I was getting annoyed at this cop. The way he fidgeted, looked bored and didn't hide looking at his watch made it obvious he considered this meeting a total waste of time.

'Sounds like James Bond,' I said, staring him out.

He glowered back. Aemilia made a small movement with her hand to signal restraint. 'Lurio exaggerates, but we do need a special type of person for an operation to stop the drugs trade implanting here. We've had some success, but can't make any significant headway because of the corruption. We're making good progress rooting that out, but these Western criminals are clever and experienced in their trade.'

She paused, looked down and played with the silver napkin ring. After a few moments, she looked up and studied my face, keeping her gaze full on me while she spoke.

'We see that running an operation under the radar of both services will be the only way to keep it completely clean.' She put her hand out and rested it on mine. 'If you can help us, you would have our full support, but covertly. You would also have significant input into the design of the operation, but we would need to approve it.'

She was desperate, but trying not to appear so. My mind started chasing itself around the room. What an opportunity to do something worthwhile, to use my skills and my new knowledge. What a fabulous challenge. I had to calm down and think it through. I could end up dead, disgraced, dragging my family down, be thrown in prison with the key melted down for scrap. Or just maybe I could pull it off. Three faces, one anxious, one intrigued and one contemptuous, gazed at me while I took a few minutes.

'If I agree,' I said, 'I want a watertight, hundred per cent immunity for anything I do or cause to be done. I'm not even going to think about it unless I have that, signed and sealed by the imperatrix.' Those hours of study in the library were paying off. I leaned back in my chair and waited.

Lurio looked at me as if I were something slithering along the ground. 'You must be joking. Nothing doing.'

'Fine.' I stood up, bowed to Nonna and Aemilia Fulvia and made for the door.

'Wait.'

'Yes, Aemilia Fulvia?'

'I understand your concern, Carina, but we need to have details of your design and implementation plan before such a blanket immunity can be considered.' She smiled. 'Think of it as an insurance proposal. As the underwriter, I'd want to see some kind of supporting evidence before extending unlimited cover.'

I laughed at her simile. 'Yes, but insurers always try wriggle out of things. If it's my skin, my neck and my freedom in question, I want it all covered.' I looked into her eyes. 'I wouldn't abuse it, believe me.'

'I do. I've studied you and your development here in detail.'

Great. I had a nice fat police file already. No, this was super-secret, so maybe not.

'I think the best thing would be for you and Lurio to hammer out some basics on a non-obligation basis. We're pressed for time – every day counts – so could you do this within the next week?'

Lurio looked as enthusiastic about me as I was about him.

'Of course, Aemilia. We can start now, if you wish.'

She looked surprised, but pleased. Lurio looked thunderous.

Tough.

'First things first,' I said to him. 'You don't like the look of me. I think the same about you. But I've agreed to work on this, so you might want to put our personal antipathy aside.'

We had retreated to the small back sitting room, away from most household traffic. He sat across from me, his shoulders hunched, but wouldn't meet my eyes. He said nothing.

'What, can't you even bear to speak to me?'

This was hopeless. I stood up.

'I'm sure you can find your own way out.'

Back in the vestibule, I found Nonna saying goodbye to her friend.

'Carina?'

I turned to Aemilia Fulvia. I hoped she didn't hear the anger in my voice. 'Your man isn't going to cooperate. He won't even talk to me. I'm sorry, but I think it's a lost cause.'

I bowed to them both and held it together until I reached my apartment. Once in, I leaned against the back of the door and shut my eyes. My fingers wrapped themselves into fists. I could have done this. I wanted to do it. I was so angry with Lurio; I boiled with frustration. Luckily for the integrity of my surroundings, I recalled a passage in Felix's instruction book, '*Desire thwarted is the most powerful spur to action. Always consider the consequences of actions taken shortly after the point of conflict. Sublimation is the most desirable.*'

I went to the gym.

After some warm-ups, I chose the arena. Clad in a leather protective tunic, light Kevlar helmet and wielding a traditional short sword, I found twenty minutes with one of the trainers went some way to blunt my anger.

'What happened to you today, Bruna?' he asked. 'Somebody slap your face?'

I grinned back. 'Yes, stupid bastard so far up his rear end that only his feet show.'

'Ooh! You are in a temper,' said Mossie behind me. I turned around and saw she was kitted up ready. 'Want to let some of it out on me?'

It was a privilege to train with her. A champion, the absolute top of her class, few beat her even now, but her opponents always learned something. We saluted and began circling. After fifteen minutes, I was still on my feet, which was miraculous. Mossie had only nicked me once; the dribble of blood had caked on my arm. Now my temper had gone, I pulled my mind into focus and concentrated on trying to win. A forlorn hope but, maybe, one day.

As we circled again, I noticed Mossie was favouring her left leg. Had she weakened or injured it? I lunged from the right, straight into her guard area, and my leg struck out, and she went down over it. Within seconds, the point of my sword had homed in on the hollow of her neck. I was astounded, but elated. I had joined the few.

A burst of applause from the dozen or so who had gathered to watch us surprised me. I withdrew my sword, stepped free of her and stretched my hand down. She took it, but sprang up by herself. She hugged me and whispered in my ear, 'Bloody clever move, you crafty cow.'

I laughed and we walked off the sand, arms about each other. We cleaned up and she stood me a drink at the bar.

'How are you, Bruna? You look well, but preoccupied.'

'I'm fine, just a professional disagreement.'

'You know something? If you want to change whatever it is you do, I'll always give you a job. Seriously.'

'I'm flattered.'

'Don't be. I'd work you hard for your money.'

Reliable Mossie; always thinking of the bottom line.

A message was waiting for me when I returned. '*Cornelius Lurio presents his apologies for not staying longer and will call on you tomorrow morning.*'

What in Hades was that about?

I dressed next morning in a sleek black business suit, white shirt, chunky gold necklace and earrings – a studied departure from my preferred jeans and tee. I received Lurio in Nonna's official reception room, a vast cavern decorated with murals, columns and fancy plasterwork. We only used it on formal occasions; its grandeur made you feel like an insignificant ant. As he was announced, I graciously waved him to the gilt antique chair across the low table from mine. I asked the servant to pour the coffee. Then I waited.

He cleared his throat. 'I owe you an apology.'

'Yes?'

'I misjudged the situation.'

'In what way?'

'I didn't believe what I was told about you.'

'Really?' I raised one eyebrow.

'Yes, really.'

'In particular?'

'Are you going to sit there being snotty all morning or are we going to work?'

'Not until you've told me what changed your mind.'

He sighed in exasperation. 'I got a severe dressing-down from Aemilia Fulvia yesterday. That made me all the more determined to expose you as a dabbler who'd pulled a few strings so she could play at saving the world. We don't have time for little rich-girl amateurs. I got your gym address and saw you in the arena.' He looked sideways, obviously awkward. 'You handle yourself well.'

'I am overwhelmed by your praise.'

'You've got a damned sharp tongue.'

We glowered at each other. This was going to be a fun working relationship.

'Come with me,' I said. 'We need to get started.' I took him in the direction of the small back sitting room we'd briefly used yesterday. As my heels clacked along the marble floor, I sensed his eyes watching all my moves. I stopped and turned. 'If you're going to stare at my body like that, we're going to have a problem. Deal with it.'

He flushed. I smiled to myself, pleased I had caught him unawares.

Partly driven by curiosity, partly hoping despite yesterday it could still go ahead, when I'd returned from my run that morning I'd spent the following hour drafting and redrafting a possible plan, knowing that it might never be used.

Of course, Lurio picked holes in it – out of perverseness, I thought at first. But to be fair, he was right about some of his points. When he stopped being so prickly, he was easy to work with and sharp with it. I could see why he was Fulvia's special assistant. We identified the areas I needed training in, but thankfully they were few, mostly spook stuff.

We reached a natural break when something occurred to me.

'If this operation is deep-cover then why are you here?'

'Sorry?'

'What's the reason for you coming to see me? I haven't done anything criminal yet and Aemilia Fulvia isn't here with my grandmother, so you can't have tagged along with her.'

He flushed again. Really, it was fascinating watching a tough nut like Lurio doing such a girls' thing.

'It doesn't matter.'

'Really?' I raised my eyebrow.

'Will you stop saying that in such a superior way?'

A few moments passed in silence.

'The cover story is that I'm seeing you,' he mumbled.

'What!' I burst into laughter.

He looked like thunder. His chin jutted out and deep vertical lines appeared between his brows.

'You can't be serious.'

'I wouldn't be the first man in uniform you've boffed.'

It was like a physical blow to my middle. Was that all it had been with Conrad?

'How dare you!'

He shrugged. 'As you say, deal with it.'

43

My revised plan was approved. I received my immunity document soon afterward which went straight into Nonna's safe, with a certified copy in a sealed envelope to her lawyers. Lurio arranged to pick me up in the evening as if taking me out. I'd gotten over our bruising conversation, but I didn't forgive him. Like all things that hurt, it contained some truth.

Nonna asked me for the last time if I was sure. Although she said she was fully behind me going undercover on such a dangerous operation, her tense eyes betrayed anxiety now I was at the point.

'Yes, I am. I can do this, I know I can.' As I raised my hand to stroke her cheek to comfort her, the sore flesh pulled where my ID tracker had been extracted. The gel had sealed the skin, but it didn't take the sting away. Nor the knowledge that nobody would be able to find me if I disappeared.

She kissed my cheek and we hugged.

'Be careful, Carina. Come back soon.'

'I promise, Nonna.'

It rained all the way to the training camp. As the gate barrier closed behind us, the link to everything I knew before broke. Lurio had explained how the training would run: I would become a Department of Justice *custos* – a cop – with the rank of senior justiciar, equivalent to sergeant, wear the uniform during my training period, and behave like a standard cop, albeit one on secondment. That would cover any major slips.

I wanted to know why I couldn't be an officer. In his usual blunt way, Lurio explained it was a privilege and I hadn't earned it. More practically, the upcoming course was for SJs, so I would blend in if I had that rank. He had taken me through some basic DJ stuff – ranks, saluting, uniform, powers of arrest, dos and don'ts – the week before. I took Cara Bruna as my undercover ID. At least I was used to it from my months at the training camp.

The very worst part was having to call Lurio 'sir'. I knew he would just love it, especially knowing how much I would hate it.

I had a week's general training: mud, guns, drill, oppression, then joined the specialist course on undercover work. Being from different parts of the DJ, none of the dozen or so of us knew anybody else. We learned some techniques: shadowing suspects, communications procedure, dead drops, basic disguise, but focused on developing operational tactics and information analysis. Weird that the shadow world all this belonged to coexisted with and unnoticed by the normal world.

The physical training was no challenge, nor was the technical work. My main difficulty was with the military aspect, but I tried hard, drawing on my discipline from the fitness boot camp. But I would never win a drill competition or be praised for my shiny appearance.

Lurio came back after my second week there and strutted around looking important, talking with the instructors. Sure, he looked impressive in his uniform, but he was still a pain in the fundament.

'Ah, Bruna. How are things going? Any problems?'

'Very well, sir. No problems, sir.'

'Really?' He looked at me with one raised eyebrow.

I nearly killed him for that.

'Walk with me,' he ordered.

We strode up the central thoroughfare. When we were safely out of earshot, I turned to him. 'How the Hades do you think it's going, Lurio? What sort of fatuous question is that?'

'Don't be insubordinate, Bruna.' He grinned down at me.

I said a rude expression. Even he looked shocked.

'Don't be coarse – it doesn't suit you.'

'Stick what you think suits me.'

'You know, you are the most tiresome person I've ever come across. If it weren't for the excellent scores you've been getting, I'd have you bounced.'

'Screw you, Lurio.'

'Any time, Bruna. Just say the word.'

In the final exercise at the end of the course to test our new skills, our group of four came top. We were thrilled when the trainers congratulated us, but Lurio, always the hard man, just smirked at me. Later that afternoon, he picked me up from the gatehouse in a shabby old car and, both back in civvies, we drove through the city outskirts to a tenement building in a blue-collar area. He handed me a key, an envelope and a cell phone, and fastened a new ID bracelet on my wrist. He turned in his driver's seat, shook my hand and wished me good luck. I was to check in every week and he would see me in three weeks, he said.

Not if I saw him first.

My temporary home was dingy and neglected. Painted in dull beige and furnished with a worn couch, a chipped plastic-topped table, hard chairs and a sagging bed, it was truly depressing. The kitchen was clean but very basic. The bathroom was similar, but with a bath with hand-held shower attachment – no regular shower. I discovered some provisions in an ill-fitting kitchen cabinet and fixed myself some black tea. No coffee, not even instant. Who was the joker who had organised this place? Now I was urban poor, I went and slumped on the couch and switched on the television. I opened my envelope; the contents were exactly what I'd ordered.

The next day, I collected two packets from the general delivery counter at a post office in another suburb. One packet contained a bundle of cash. I also rented a lock-box there and stowed some items for emergency. Getting there had been easy. My ID wristband was in perfect order – even the security fastener worked – and entitled me to free public transport. But all these movements would have been logged in Lurio's secure area at the DJ operations unit. I decided that now was the time to go freelance. No way was I going to dance to Lurio's tune.

I made my way into the city centre and used some of the cash to buy new clothes, cosmetics, a brown wig and leather messenger bag. In the restroom, I changed in the end cubicle, unlocked my ID wristband and taped it to the high flat top of the service wall. It couldn't be seen unless you stood on the seat; the dust testified it was rarely visited by the cleaning personnel.

Next, Dania's. I walked the length of the counter, straight through the door to the back and waited. When she came bustling into the back lobby, demanding to know who I was and what was going on, I held my finger to my lips.

'Come upstairs and I'll explain,' I whispered, and grinned at her.

Her eyes widened. 'Pulcheria?'

Her first floor living room was a shrine to frilled drapery. Every window, alcove and niche was festooned with shiny satin or strident gauze. Despite the hints during my last visit, she hadn't changed any of it. I needed sunglasses.

'Okay, here's the thing, Dania. I've decided to start my own campaign against the drugs trade.'

'How in Hades are you going to do that?'

'With the help of friends,' I said, 'and perhaps enemies. If these industrial-scale Western dealers get in here, it won't only bring shattering misery, but it could disrupt our economy. Even our local criminals will be affected,' I smiled, wryly.

'What are you saying?'

'I need your help and support. I'll protect you, and even make sure you come out with a profit, but we may find ourselves in strange company. Are you in?'

She stood up and went over to an alcove and played with the violet satin that loitered there. After a few moments, she turned, her hand gripping the fabric. 'I hate the idea of these drugs people.

Bastards. I trust you. You've been fantastic to me, believing in me, helping me get this place going. Of course I'm in.'

I figured I had around twenty-four hours maximum before Lurio found me by tracking my communications. Dania cleared a space and I set up a virtual network, organised domains, emails, secure access protocols. I checked the ultra-secure numbered account I'd set up with my own money before the DJ training course, and transferred funds so I could access them by card at any touch terminal.

I called Uncle Frank, my father's old colleague at Brown Industries in New Hampshire. I prayed the secure VoIP would protect this one call. Since inheriting the company in its entirety, I'd left the day-to-day running in the hands of the professionals, with Nonna advising me on overall business strategy. But I kept up with new product programmes, studying the confidential reports each month. So I was able to arrange for Frank to send me some of the experimental 'supermobiles' they were developing.

'You know, Karen, they're not market-tested, so I can't give you any promises. They'll work on any standard GSM, 3 or 4G network and simulate a normal call. We have around fifty – would a dozen be enough for you?'

'That's great, Uncle Frank, just beautiful. Can you send them by secure messenger, please, and treat it as extremely confidential? I'll forward you the exact address in a few days. Send the key to this email address, please.' I gave him the address of one of my new secure accounts.

I had Dania colour my hair black and curl it into corkscrews – the wigs were too hot and inconvenient. As she was brushing through after the treatments, I looked at the stranger in the mirror. I was still there but, once I started wearing my coloured contacts, Carina would vanish. Pulcheria would take over completely.

Having fallen off his automatic reporting system, I probably irritated the hell out of Lurio. Too bad. But he couldn't start a proper search or he'd blow the whole operation. I smiled at the thought of his frustration. Once my plan was launched, I would become very visible, but he wouldn't be able to do a thing about it. Where did all this aggression come from? Maybe it was the adrenalin I was living on. I only went out at night, meticulous with my disguises, ultra-careful to alter my body language each time. Avoiding the public feeds was impossible – that's what CCTV was for, spotting illegal activity. At least I realised how much of a beginner I was at this.

Next, I instructed a commercial agent to find a very specific property. I demanded total discretion and left him an escrow draft for a hundred thousand *solidi* as a mark of good faith. His cut would be ten per cent if he found the right place within a week. However, his rate would reduce by one per cent each day. The ninth day after the original week, I would find another agent.

On day five, he found exactly what I wanted. I promised him a substantial bonus if he would organise the renovations and fit-out. Within two weeks, I moved into the new property. As I wound my way between pallets of plastic-wrapped materials, groups of artisans and workpeople decorating, cabling and carpeting, the smell of sawn wood, paint and new fabrics hit me.

The agent had provided an on-site assistant, Martina, to supervise the project. I found her in the middle of the floor, directing three different conversations that she terminated with a flick of her fingers when she saw me.

'Madam, welcome! Please, sit.' She indicated a ramshackle wooden chair near the new stage. She waved her long, slender hand again and a plascard cup of instant coffee appeared within a half a minute. Not the best drink I'd ever had, but what service! Her efficiency was belied by her tall, thin, almost fragile figure; she looked under-nourished.

Right on time, Dania turned up, and we stepped over cables and stacks of panelling to reach my new office behind the performance area, at the back of the building. Instead of windows, it had a bank of CCTV screens on one wall. The furniture was futuristic, the lighting pure designer. Carefully conceived to give subliminal visual cues so that whoever sat in the chair behind the desk radiated power and could manipulate psychological responses, it appeared deceptively natural.

Dania, Martina and I worked long days over the next week. Furniture was ordered and delivered, a chef, catering and bar staff engaged, a sommelier tasked with procuring and managing the cellar, show producers and artists booked and musicians installed. The gods know how she did it, but Martina had a stellar international line-up for the opening night. Thus was Goldlights born.

The morning of our opening, I had a bad fright. Two uniformed DJ *custodes* strode in behind the musicians who had come for their final practice. Had Lurio found me despite all my efforts to hide myself? Remembering to breathe, I followed their movements from the screen in my office. The cops waved the doorman aside and marched in their studded boots across the dance floor, heading for the group around Dania. Sure, I had deviated a considerable way from the original plan, but surely Lurio wasn't going to endanger the whole operation because he was miffed at me?

The two blue-clad figures stood over Dania, throwing questions at her. They strutted around, looking at everything. One spoke into his communicator while the other looked over paperwork on the bar counter, the sommelier producing more paper from under the counter. Dania hovered, ready to answer any further questions. After half an hour, they went. I put a hand to my forehead in relief and found it coated with sweat.

That evening, I checked everything through again with Martina. She had masterminded the invitation list, focusing on the 'beautiful people' of Roma Nova, but I had added one of my own. Whether he would come or not was anybody's guess. I figured he would, if only out of curiosity. But it was crucial to my plan.

44

Renschman kicked the table leg in frustration, adding another scuff to the cheap pine. He supposed he was fortunate: he'd found this job very quickly. The pay was good, the work easy, and he was given some respect for his talent and dedication. But he was owned body and soul by Palicek, which was why he was waiting at eleven at night in this abandoned shop with rain-sodden posters curling off dirty windows.

Last December, he'd upgraded to business class on the flights back from Roma Nova to London and Washington. He'd timed his flight beautifully. Two hours after he'd left her in her concrete coffin, he was over Bavaria en route to London. The girl was dead and he was going to be rich, very rich. Overloading the credit card was no problem. The snowstorm that almost prevented him landing at Sterling Dulles had heralded a weather lockdown. He'd filed for probate as soon as he could, battling the Arctic weather to deposit the application personally. Eight weeks later, he'd nearly choked over the court letter stating they had received no notification of death.

Jerking the mouse around the pad, he'd concentrated on his screen. He'd started at the Roma Nova Washington legation site. After nearly two hours of searching and sifting, he'd found a four-line notice in the social news section in *Acta Diurna* gazette from the previous month. He'd right-clicked to get the English translation. Following an illness, Countess Mitela's granddaughter, Carina Mitela, had left the city for an extended stay at their country home at Castra Lucilla. She was not expected back until June.

The following day, he'd bought a new keyboard to replace the one he'd smashed.

His main problem was to get free of Palicek. There was no retirement or holiday plan, except a permanent one. He glanced at his watch. This pick-up was not going to happen. Too bad for the dealer – his last mistake. His ideas about the way he'd punish the defaulter were cut short by a harsh ring from his pocket.

'Pack your bag. We're flying to Europe tomorrow afternoon.'

45

The opening night at Goldlights was a success. A jaw-dropping success. Martina shrugged her blue-sequinned shoulders and said, 'It's all down to planning.' She flashed me one of her rare smiles.

'How would you like to manage the club on a permanent basis?'

She looked at me, gauging whether I was serious. 'What pay and benefits are you offering?'

'Fifteen thousand more than you're getting now plus a percentage.'

'Certainly worth considering,' she murmured.

I took that as a nearly yes. 'Let me know by tomorrow. I think we're going to be busy.'

By midnight, the maitre d' reported very healthy bookings for the following weeks. Now we had the perfect framework for the next phase. I was taking a sip from my glass, the champagne bubbles teasing my mouth and throat, when I had the sensation of being watched. I scanned around from under my eyelashes and spotted him in one of the back booths. He raised his glass to me and smiled.

Crunch time.

'Good evening, Apollodorus. Are you enjoying the show?'

'Immensely. I am most impressed. Won't you join me?'

I hesitated for a few seconds. Not a trace of hostility showed in his face from our previous meeting. I needed him and I was on home territory so I sat down, leaving a space between us. Watching the next act, he laughed at the jokes, smiling at me as if we shared a sense of humour. I smiled back, not entirely relaxed. He talked lightly and made every effort to be charming. As the room exploded in applause, he bent near and said softly, 'Mine or yours?'

'Mine. Here. Tomorrow morning at eleven.'

I stood up and held out my hand to shake on it, but he got to his feet with me, took my hand and kissed the back. I couldn't see his expression in the semi-darkness, only the light reflected from his eyes. As I walked away, I knew he was still watching me.

He arrived the next morning, the second my watch blinked eleven. I recognised one of his companions – the quiet one, from Dania's. The other one was about the same age, but with a rounded face. They were both carrying, but I signalled security to let them through.

'Good morning, Apollodorus, I trust you enjoyed last night?'

He gave me a half-smile, but said nothing.

'Your friends can stay here. I want to speak to you alone.'

The round-faced one took a step forward but Apollodorus flexed his fingers and waved him back.

'They'll be perfectly safe,' I said, 'but I would appreciate it if they didn't shoot anybody.'

In my office, I invited him to sit on the other side of my desk.

He glanced around and smiled when he looked up at the lights. Clearly this was an intelligent man with much more than average street smarts.

'Apollodorus, I have a proposal for you, but I need to ask you something first. Why did you accept my invitation last night and want to meet with me this morning?'

'Who would not want to find out more about the beautiful Pulcheria? You obviously have resources,' he waved his hand around, 'and the will to use them. That is always interesting. You don't frighten easily. You fight to protect your position and your people. That intrigues me.'

I said nothing.

'I have the feeling you may be a rising star. It's always wise to align oneself in the correct place in the firmament. But I think there's something else, a purpose to your actions.' He looked into the distance over my shoulder then drew his gaze back to my face. 'Now I have bared my soul to you, I think it's time for you to reciprocate.'

His black eyes bored into mine. I found the intensity unnerving. This was a man used to dominating. As a right.

'This club is a significant investment for me, and the projections are favourable,' I said. 'By itself, that's very satisfactory. But there's another reason for its existence.'

Could I ask him? I forced myself to slow my increasing pulse, to damp down the adrenalin rush. My instincts said he would do it. Logic said he would laugh in my face. It was one hell of a risk.

'Is it a case of crossing the Rubicon?'

I stared at him. The last man who said that to me was Conrad in the legation in Washington. I pushed back a feeling of sorrow and longing, and took a deep breath.

'Yes, so I might as well get on with it.'

'Courageous with it,' he murmured, half-laughing.

'You'll no doubt know about the attempts by Western drug dealers to bring their filthy trade here. It's very low level at present, but I'm dangling a golden goose in front of them in the hope of attracting and catching at least one big player. He or she will then be made an example of to discourage others.'

I held my breath and watched his face for any reaction. If he was already involved in narcotics, the whole mission was dead.

A flicker passed over his eyes, like he was reviewing something a long way down in his memory, and was firmly dismissed.

'I don't wish to be indelicate or even insulting, my dear Pulcheria, but is this all your own idea?'

'Of course not. But the method is, and the passion.' I got up and walked over to the bank of screens, not looking into any particular one of them. After a few moments, I turned to face him. 'You have the organisation and connections, I have the money and high-earning potential. I think there is common interest here, if we share the same goals. That's the crux of the matter.'

'Who are you?'

'Pulcheria.' I paused. 'A citizen.'

'Straight answer, please. DJ, PGSF or something else?'

'Something else is probably the nearest I can give you at present.'

'Hmm. Neither body normally has such resources. You must have some official backing.'

'I need your agreement before I can say anything else.'

'Do I need to decide now?'

'Yes.'

'And if I don't?'

'Please don't force me to answer that question.'

After a long five minutes, he rose and crossed the room. The open edge of his black coat touched my arm. He stared down at my face. 'I have to say you do nothing but surprise me, Pulcheria. Very well, I agree, subject to an indemnity for my people.'

He stepped back and we shook hands, formally, like a couple of *mafiosi* in a movie.

'So do tell me who your mystery backer is.'

'The operation is legalised directly and personally by imperial order, entirely independent and covert from other services or operations.'

'Mercury Esus!'

'Now you know why I couldn't say.'

He buttoned up his coat. 'I've just realised what a dangerous place I've put myself in. If we get it wrong, I'll have not only ruthless drug dealers after me, but an imperial hit squad as well.'

'You'll have the consolation of knowing I'll be in jail till the next millennium.'

46

I moved into his house by the river the next day. The first afternoon, Philippus collected me from the club, ushering me into a silver Mercedes with a bow verging on the ironic. We approached the exterior gate of Apollodorus's house with its graceful stone arch, negotiated the coded entry system and drove over a gravel area, through another gateway with barred gates curved to fit the archway, finials a breath away from the stone. The Venetian scrollwork disguised how solid they were. They shut with little more than a clink, as metal kissed metal.

We stopped under a portico in the courtyard where a servant led me through into the atrium. Not as large as at Domus Mitelarum, but more elegant, minimalist even. White upholstered benches ran around three sides, and alcoves placed along their length provided intimate seating areas. I looked up at the large glazed bull's eye in the roof through which late spring sunlight fell; it made artificial lighting redundant.

Through the glazed doors at the far side, trees bordering a veranda swayed in the breeze casting flickering shadows on the stonework. I glimpsed the river between Scots pines and cypress trees that obscured the house from prying eyes on the opposite bank.

Apollodorus was waiting for me in an alcove on the right wall of the atrium. His head was bowed; he was sifting paper in a file, like a public servant sorting health permits. Didn't they have computers?

But when he looked up and focused his gaze on me, I was taken aback again by the power of the man, the concentrated force in him, here, in his own lair. Would I be able to control him? Had I made a huge mistake?

'My dear Pulcheria. Welcome. Come and sit down.' He laid his papers to one side and glanced once into the distance, and a servant appeared with two glasses of white wine.

'Not quite sundown.' He glanced at his watch. 'But we can cheat a little.'

I was sure Apollodorus cheated in many ways, little and big.

'I think we'd better go through a few details together before I introduce you to my associates,' he continued.

I set my glass down on the table. 'Apollodorus, one of the most important things I need is for you to run the day-to-day business of the new organisation. Naturally, the financial split will reflect that. I wish to remain in the background as much as possible.'

'So I'm to be your front man?' He chuckled, which was disconcerting from such an intense man.

'I didn't mean it to sound like that. I want to be completely straightforward with you – I don't have the time to play games.'

He leaned forward, his head slightly tilted. 'You must never, ever worry about being truthful with me.'

At that moment, I was sure he had his own agenda for fighting the drugs trade.

Apollodorus led me to a black and white room at the back where two men and a woman sat at a dining table, talking; she was gesturing at the others with a sheet of paper from the open file in front of her, the other two looked evasive. I paused in the doorway. Faces swivelled in my direction, three gazes moving as one. A close-knit team, all criminals, yet they were to be my new best friends. Apollodorus ushered me in.

Philippus, his round face neutral, pushed his chair away from the table, stood up and extended his hand.

'Ah, Philippus you already know.'

I nodded at him as we shook hands. Apollodorus gestured toward the quiet one I'd seen with him at Dania's and Goldlights.

'Flavius here has been fortunate enough not to have served you yet for target practice, Pulcheria. I trust his good luck will continue to be unbroken.'

I didn't know whether to laugh or be furious with Apollodorus. I soon learned he spoke in this ironic way all the time. You had to be most careful when his tone softened to a whisper.

Flavius had a light but nonetheless definite handshake. His mousey brown hair and mid-brown eyes made a pleasant but not outstanding combination, which made a great asset for a criminal or a spook; nobody remembered the average. He stayed quiet as before, but nodded and gave me a half-smile.

'And lastly, for the moment, we have Hermina, who recruits our team members and looks after their security and welfare.' She nodded her blond head. I took her outstretched hand.

'You'll meet Dolcius, my technical assistant, a little later and also it seems, Justus, who handles, ah, intelligence.' He turned to Hermina. 'Dolcius is occupied with a project I set him, but I am a little disappointed that Justus is not here. Perhaps you would convey that to him, Hermina.'

The atmosphere in the room chilled by several degrees.

'Of course, Apollodorus. I'll see to it immediately.' She sprang up to carry out his request.

'One moment, Hermina. Tell him we'll meet in the atrium at eight o'clock for drinks before dinner. No exceptions.'

Apollodorus gave me a tour of the house. Quite a number of the rooms were undecorated. Three upper-storey rooms were being converted.

'It was built approximately five centuries ago, and updated twenty years ago, quite sympathetically. Sadly, they ran out of funding. I acquired it two years ago in settlement of a debt.'

'What will you use the outhouses for? Manufacturing, workshop areas, offices?'

He looked at me with an inscrutable air. 'Nothing is planned as yet, but if you have any suggestions, I should, of course, be delighted to hear about them, my dear Pulcheria.'

Was that yes, he would be interested or no, keep your nose out?

We progressed to a bedroom on the first floor looking out over the garden and river. It was pale blue, simply furnished; a vase of tiny yellow roses and rosemary stood on a small table under the window.

'I hope you'll be comfortable here. There's a bathroom through there,' he said, indicating one of two almost invisible doors to the side. 'The wardrobe cupboard next to it. I've had your things unpacked. I'll leave you to get settled in and see you in a short while.'

He nodded and was gone.

I stayed in the black leather jacket and skirt I was fast adopting as my signature outfit. I checked out the closet, washed my hands and face, and dragged a comb through my curls. With one last glance in the mirror, I took a deep breath and went out into the corridor. Closing the door behind me, I turned and saw Flavius. He hadn't changed from his casuals.

'Walk down with you?' he said.

He had a voice to suit his plain appearance but, when he smiled, his whole face was transformed.

'Sure.'

'I want to see Justus's face when we walk in together.'

'Why?'

He grinned. 'He likes to put one over on everybody, to show how superior he is. He enjoys making others feel uncomfortable and inferior. I don't know why he does it. He's good at his job – he doesn't need to prove anything.'

I looked at him. 'Are you trying to protect me?'

'Of course not. What do you take me for?'

Poor Justus. He really shouldn't have. Flavius and I crossed the atrium to where Apollodorus, Hermina and two men I hadn't seen before stood, relaxing over drinks. As we approached, Apollodorus broke off his conversation with one of the men. He watched my last few steps, and I kept my eyes locked on his. Maybe I was on probation, but no way would I let a nanoparticle of my anxiety show.

'Do allow me to present two other members of my team. Firstly, Dolcius, our technical wizard...'

I shook hands with an older man, bearded, the type that 'harrumphed' and saw the world as one big laboratory. He didn't wear a white coat, but he scrutinised my face with intent. After all of two seconds, he set his sharp eyes off darting all over the place, as if his brain cells were in hot pursuit of some idea, but he seemed friendly enough.

'...and Justus, our informer, who finds out all kinds of interesting things for us.'

In Latin, 'informer' doesn't mean ratty little sneak that American cop shows feature, but more like intelligence agent or detective. Looking at Justus, I went with the cop-show definition. A smooth, knowing half-smile glided across his lips, leaving no trace on the rest of his unremarkable face.

'I must apologise for not meeting you earlier, Pulcheria,' he said.

I bet Apollodorus had given him hell for that.

'I'm intrigued by your story and find it strange that I haven't heard of you before.'

I said nothing.

'Surely you're not from the sticks?'

I laughed in his face and carried on sipping my wine.

'So where are you from?'

'C'mon, Justus,' interrupted Flavius, 'just relax, for once. Pulcheria doesn't need the third degree.'

'Oh, I'm only on the first,' he sneered.

'Never mind, dear,' I said, looking through Justus's irises direct into his eyeballs and patting him on the back of his hand, 'we all have to start somewhere.'

I spotted the tiniest quiver on Apollodorus's lip. Justus looked furious.

'Don't think you can get round me like that. I'll find out anyway.'

I gave a tinkling laugh. 'My dear Justus, I'm sure you'll find wonderful ways to keep yourself occupied. But if you get anywhere near me or mine, I will tear you apart without a shred of compunction.'

The silence fell like a sharp January frost on a cloudless night.

I smiled sweetly at him. 'I do hope, now that's clear, we can be good friends.'

At that moment, dinner was announced and Apollodorus took my arm by the elbow and led me in.

'You do like a risk, don't you?' he murmured.

'I like to be unambiguous.'

Whatever the temper of the diners, the food was excellent. Justus continued to dart angry glances at me and Philippus kept ragging him about it. After a while, Apollodorus became bored.

'Enough. This is not a playground. Pulcheria is my honoured colleague. That is all you need to know.'

47

After dinner, I asked Hermina about access to and from the house. She planned to provide me with an ID wristband the next day.

'Oh, that's fine, but I need to go for a run first thing in the morning.'

She gave me a wary look. 'You could go with the twins.'

'The who?'

'Flav and Phil. They're always together, except when Phil was sick recently and Flav had a temporary partner.' She paused. 'Ah, of course, you met him, the temp. The doctor says that although the knife wound has closed, the wrist bruising will take ages to disappear.'

An awkward pause hung between us.

Hermina cleared her throat. 'Well, generally, they set off from the kitchen at about six thirty. Tell one of them tonight and they'll wait for you.'

Next morning, I waited in my jogging suit and sneakers at six twenty-five. By six thirty, they still weren't there. I was getting annoyed by six thirty-five. Just as I was giving up, they ambled in. I couldn't resist looking at my watch.

'Oh dear, are we late?' said Philippus, smirking.

'I am not accustomed to waiting.'

He was about to make a joke of it when he must have seen what Conrad called my 'Aurelia face'. Flavius made no comment and put his wrist to the door scanlock to release it, but I caught a half-smile breaking up his solemn expression.

We got going and, inevitably, it turned competitive. They were male, young and fit. I played along, happy to trot a step behind as they upped the pace. After four kilometres, I became irritated with the testosterone display so, about half a kilometre out from the house, I accelerated. When they joined me by the back door, I stood there, fully composed, foot tapping, looking at my watch.

'D'you know something, Pulcheria?' wheezed Philippus. 'I'm amazed nobody's strangled you yet.'

I laughed. 'You want to try?'

'No way.'

Later that morning, Apollodorus briefed his team on our operation. I sat back and studied my fingernails in detail.

'Pluto, it's a risk, isn't it, playing with these drug people?' said Philippus. 'I mean, I've heard about some of the vicious retaliation handed out if you cross them.'

'Yes, it's a bit different from what we do, isn't it?' Hermina shuddered. 'Perhaps I'm being romantic, but we don't get involved in anything so...so sordid.'

No, Hermina, I thought. You do theft, protection, gambling and financial scams flavoured with a little blackmail. All clean fun, of course.

'Two experienced DJs, no, one of them was PGSF, were dragged out of the sewer, stuffed with heroin, burst eyes and faces. Not that I'm going to cry myself to sleep over that,' commented the ever-charming Justus. 'But my information shows there's already some systematic small-time activity approaching the tipping point where it snowballs into mass application.'

I stared at Justus, jamming my lips together to stifle my laughter. Had he swallowed a 1990s management manual?

Apollodorus avoided looking at me. 'Flavius?'

'On balance, it's a risk, a big one. We could end up in a nasty war.' He looked down at the table and played with his papers. 'Strategically, we need to make a decision soon. If, on the one hand, we delay making connections and setting up partnership arrangements with these people, we could miss out on profitable deals. We risk being sidelined. Our income proportion will diminish if they succeed in getting a foothold here. We might even be forced out of business altogether. On the other hand, if we decide to stop them, we have to do it now or it'll be too difficult. At least with Pulcheria's help, we have the financial resources to do it.' He glanced around the table. 'Personally, I think it's a disgusting thing to force on people and destroy lives.'

Justus snorted. 'You're a soft fool, Flavius. Do forgive me for being obvious,' he said, fixing me in his sights, 'but how do we know it's not a sting against us?'

'You don't,' I said, looking up through my eyelashes.

They all stared at me except Apollodorus who smiled.

Justus threw his hands up in the air. 'I rest my case.' He looked at Apollodorus. 'I think it's highly likely to be a trap, so we should stop here and dump her. Preferably in the public sewer. Unless we get something much more satisfactory about her motives and the reason she's so graciously giving us the money to do this, I vote no.'

'Thank you, Justus, for your usual graphic comments,' said Apollodorus. He paused for a few seconds and locked eyes with Justus. 'I generally value your contributions very highly. You may, perhaps, have forgotten that this is not a democratic organisation – I merely invite you to comment. You have no vote. It would be a pity if you were to forget that.'

Justus's face took on a faint pink tinge. He dropped his gaze, chagrined.

'Pulcheria?'

'I respect what everybody has said, but I think Flavius has the crux of the matter. It *is* about timing. Justus was correct, also, in one aspect.'

Philippus and Hermina looked at me as if I was crazy.

'I agree the tipping point is approaching. My information is that it's gone beyond personal use and casual dealing. A dangerous moment.' I looked around at all of them. 'You question my motivation. I've discussed this with Apollodorus. He's satisfied. The subject is closed. The finance? This may come as news, but I intend using my investment to make a profit out of your organisation.'

Philippus chuckled.

'If you don't object, Apollodorus, people may like to discuss any issues one-to-one with me.' I panned around the table. 'I'll be in my room after lunch until six, so please feel free to come and talk with me.'

Apollodorus looked at me, raised an eyebrow but didn't say a word. The meeting broke up. As the others left, he gestured me to stay with him. 'An interesting invitation, Pulcheria.'

'If they're to buy into this, Apollo, then it has to be a hundred per cent.'

He looked at me with a blend of hauteur and disbelief, like I'd stepped on his cat or stubbed a cigarette out on his favourite leather couch.

'What is it, Apollo – dorus?' I added hastily.

'Nobody has ever shortened my name.'

I peeped up at him through my eyelashes. 'Probably far too scared of you.'

His lips were compressed into a grim line. Then they parted, his mouth opened and a laugh escaped. 'You are the most abominable girl.'

I joined in, mostly from nervous relief, like a reprieved court jester.

'Never in front of anybody else, please.'

Thus chastised, I excused myself, gathered up my papers and fled, although in a dignified way, to the dining room.

48

After lunch, I only had two visitors. The first was Hermina who opened her heart to me. She'd shrugged off a comfortable and happy childhood and married a complete waster. Nevertheless, she'd moved worlds to try and save the marriage. She'd given and he'd taken everything, including her confidence and self-respect. When Apollodorus turned up at her door to collect a large debt run up by her ex-husband, she'd had nothing. The house was rented; she was destitute and terrified.

'I'd been so contemptuous of my parents' warnings. Luckily, they died before it fell apart. After the divorce, I toughened up. It was brutal but effective.' Her hazel eyes were serious, but escaped being dour. 'I love this job with Apollodorus. I know he's not exactly legal, but he's very kind.' She looked at me as if expecting me to disagree.

'I think he's tough and demanding but will protect you to the extremes of his ability. That's quite an asset in an employer, Hermina.'

I would try and save her when it was finished.

Flavius surprised me. I would have put my money on Philippus.

'I'm trying to work you out, Pulcheria. You're as tough as Hades.' He looked at me, his eyes full of speculation. 'But perhaps that's only on the surface. I'm sure there's something else going on. And don't give me all that stuff about investments – that's not the reason.'

'Finished?'

'I suppose so.'

'You made some good arguments at the meeting, Flavius, and I appreciate your support.' I laid my hand on his tanned forearm. 'Do you think you can trust me?' I liked Flavius; he was balanced and steady.

'I'm probably certifiable, but yes.'

As we worked on the fine planning, Apollodorus seemed as driven as I was, but I worried that I couldn't catch a glimpse of his true motivation. Maybe profit and control were enough for him. Somehow I doubted it.

I met with Dolcius to discuss equipment. Although he had a workshop full of electronic gizmos, it was makeshift. He hinted there was little funding to spend on things. As an immediate step, I ordered IT equipment to do away with the paper mountain. Flavius and Philippus struggled for a few days with it. Justus and Hermina took to it like cats to milk. Apollodorus just did it.

Goldlights continued to be profitable – this was crucial – not least thanks to our viral marketing. I was going through figures with Martina, who had slipped efficiently into the club manager role, when a compact, baby-faced man carrying a solid-looking business case bustled into the club. He looked like a parody of a 1950s salesman, even to the trilby on his head. Philippus was right behind him, so I knew he'd been checked out. Martina went over to deal with him. I carried on with the spreadsheets but watched from under my eyelashes. Martina returned with a little card on which were printed two words: *Uncle Frank*

'It's fine, Martina, I'll deal with this.'

She gave me a curious look, shrugged and turned back to her laptop. I gestured the little man to another table out of earshot. Philippus made to follow but I waved him back.

'So how is Uncle Frank?' I asked in English.

'He sends his warmest and asks if you still have the snow goose?'

I laughed. 'Is that supposed to be a code word?' It was a plush toy Uncle Frank had given me as a sixth birthday gift. I'd clutched it to me all the way from New Hampshire to Nebraska and for months afterward until it disintegrated.

I dialled a special number Apollodorus had given me and was patched through to an encrypted channel. It could probably be broken by a specialist, he admitted, so best kept for one-time use only. This was exactly the reason why Mr Shorty was here in front of me.

'Hi, Uncle Frank. Yes, he's here. Could you describe him for me?' I watched the messenger while listening.

I turned to the man. 'Please take off your coat and shirt and turn round.' I ran my scanner over the skin on his back, seeking the chip under the teres major muscle. The display showed mark and number as Frank described. And everything else about the messenger. I stopped scrolling after line twenty. I swallowed hard. I would never look at roast pork again in the same way. How in Hades did Uncle Frank know such a creature? I nodded at the messenger to dress. He was totally deadpan throughout the whole process.

I handed him the cell and he spoke to Frank. I took my right boot off and gritted my teeth, determined not to react to his touch as he examined the birthmark on my foot. I put my boot back on; he deposited the bag on the table in front of me, nodded, and then waddled off. I released my breath.

I handed the supermobiles out before dinner.

'These are prototypes; they're super-encrypted and not known to the security services here, or anywhere for that matter. They'll run on our normal network, but appear as ordinary phones. If anybody tries to intercept, an engaged note will sound. This doesn't mean we can ignore our standard protocols, but it gives us a higher level of protection and security.'

They all looked intrigued and pleased, even Justus.

'They're governed by a key which I hold. If a unit gets lost or goes missing, for whatever reason, you must tell me. I will then bar it. If I think our group is compromised, I will pull the key and all the phones will be useless. However, I can reactivate with a new key.'

I was starting to know my colleagues, but had not reached the stage where I trusted them completely. 'A word of warning. If anybody is overwhelmed by the desire to open their unit, or otherwise tamper with it, it'll stop working. The person holding the phone at the time will get a deep burn, liable to heal slowly and with lasting damage.'

Justus pursed his lips in disappointment. Flavius half-smiled.

I looked at Apollodorus. 'I have one or two spares. Is there anybody else you think should have one?'

'Perhaps the doctor. The authorities tend to be sensitive about gunshot wounds; we need to ensure calls about such matters are kept confidential. Not, of course, that we'll need him, if all goes well.'

49

A week after Justus started sending rumours down his informant networks, we had the first undercover cops in. I was sitting in my office with Flavius when Martina put her head around the door.

'Zone 4. Table 15. DJ, I think.'

I nodded and she disappeared. I zoomed in: a man and woman, looking like two people on a date, studying the menu.

Flavius looked intently at the images for a few minutes. 'They're not right. No rapport. No eye signals. Not even trying to touch each other.'

Flavius took stills from the cameras and ran them through a database.

The Department of Justice database? I hoped not.

'Yeah, here they are – DJ. Not very good, are they.' He smiled at me. 'I'll go and say hello.'

He grabbed an earpiece, synched it with the comms kit under his tuxedo and disappeared through the door. I saw him a minute later, on camera, drifting through the floor area, greeting guests, having a word with Martina, and ending up at the couple's table.

'Good evening,' his disembodied voice said. 'Enjoying the atmosphere?'

They smiled and nodded back.

He bent closer to them. 'Always a pleasure to see our taxes are being well spent by the *custodes* taking a personal interest in supporting local business.'

The woman looked chagrined; she spoke too low for me to hear. Flavius kept a bland smile pinned on his face.

'I think it's time for you to leave.' He beckoned over one of the security staff. Within minutes, the two of them had escorted the cops out onto the rainy street. I sympathised with them; they were only doing their job.

Back in my office, I asked Flavius what we should expect next.

'Probably a more able team tomorrow or later in the week. I'm surprised they were so bad. Even DJ are usually better than that.'

'Unless, of course, it was a dry run or it was for somebody else's benefit,' I said. Had Lurio sent them in?

Flavius went back to the screens. I stood behind his chair while he scanned through. He panned around and zoomed in on a table of three men and a woman.

'What do you think of them?' he asked.

'They look pretty normal. Oh, that middle one's watching everything. Look at how he's following Martina. No, it's not just her, he's searching for something. Ah, he just checked out the service door. Yeah, he's in the frame. Apart from the trophy babe, I figure the others with him are probably—'

I stopped breathing. I grasped the back of the chair. No.

Flavius was concentrating on the screens, but swung around as I stopped my running commentary.

'What?'

My eyes were glued to the screen. It was him – the wavy brown hair and the frameless glasses. It was definitely him.

I pulled my smile back together for Flavius. 'I'm fine, Flav. Sorry about that.'

Of course, he didn't believe me.

'Okay, okay. We may have a problem. If I'm right, and I really hope I'm not, that's a very bad guy out there.'

'Isn't that what we want?'

'No, I don't mean the middle one who's watching everything; it's the one on his right.'

Flavius zoomed in and Renschman stared back at me.

'Flav,' I heard my voice say, 'why don't you take another wander and I'll watch them.'

'You okay?'

'I'm fine, but be extremely careful. Please.'

He rolled his eyes at me.

The memory of the pitiless cold of the concrete shed floor penetrated the warm room. And my helplessness, my fear of freezing to death, alone. I wanted to go out there and tear him apart. Maybe I would hand over what was left to the *custodes* for a very public trial for attempted murder. The rational part of my mind, struggling to get a toehold, told me it wasn't possible. It would blow my whole operation apart. How in Hades was I going to deal with this? I knew I had to exert iron control until we were finished. Even now, I was trembling with the effort. Afterward…afterward would be different.

Flavius was back ten minutes later.

'Anything?' he said.

'Yes, that one in the middle tracked your every move. So did the one with glasses, but much more subtly.'

Flavius did the screenshots and ran the faces.

'Nothing's come up for us, but the immigration database identified the staring one as Lev Palicek, fifty-six, born in Minnesota, EUSA, occupation – businessman.'

Apollodorus also had access to the immigration database – how worrying was that?

'And the other one?'

'Jeffrey Williams, forty-two, Baltimore, EUSA, consultant.'

He even kept his first name – the balls of the man.

'Right, Flav, send all that back to Apollodorus.'

I wasn't surprised to see Apollodorus an hour later. He came in through the service entrance, shaking rain from his umbrella.

'Show me.'

Only his eyes moved as he absorbed the footage first-hand.

'My instinct is that you go out on the floor and let yourself be seen,' I said.

'I agree. Your delightful Mr Palicek is a player of some reputation. Justus found that several agencies, including the American DEA, are interested in him, but there have been no indictments or convictions.

The other man is a mystery. "Consultant" covers a great deal, of course.'

He shrugged off his coat, which Flavius instinctively came forward to take. Underneath, Apollodorus was immaculate in classic tuxedo, with a European touch of velvet lapels. Nobody could doubt his presence; Palicek would know instantly he was the boss.

On the screens, we watched Apollodorus glide over to Martina's station, study the reservations book with her, and then set off on a circuit around the floor. She introduced him to selected clients. He spoke with those at the table next to Palicek's and moved smoothly by Palicek's table, smiling vaguely down at the group for a second, stopped, said something to Martina, left her and made his way back through the service door up to the office.

'Either he has the hots for you, Apollodorus, or he's our guy,' I said. I heard Flavius choke in the background. 'His eyes were glued to your every move.'

'Inelegant, my dear, but correct on the second count. I'm convinced we'll receive an overture shortly.'

Flaviusproduced glasses and a bottle of Brancadorum champagne. Once poured, he left the bottle with us and returned to watching the screens. I considered telling Apollodorus about Renschman, but decided I would see how things worked out first with our sting.

To pass the time, I tackled him about an idea I'd been developing.

'Apollodorus, I have something I'd like to run past you. I hope you'll consider all its merits before you decide one way or another. I'm conscious I may be stepping into a sensitive area.'

'I am unnerved with terror by your caveat, Pulcheria. You are normally so direct.'

I ignored that.

'When we first met, you were attempting to persuade Dania to pay protection money. I assume you have a number of businesses who pay you in this way.'

He nodded.

'Have you ever considered working the opposite way around?'

His eyebrows rose and he looked down his nose at me. 'Do explain.'

Despite his tight smile and neutral eyes, I continued. 'Services like insurance, facilities management, accountancy, recruitment and so on can be very profitable. Security advice and installation are always in demand. With your team, you could make a killing and be a hundred per cent legal. You, in particular, would be able to demand extortionate fees – no pun intended – as a management consultant. They would do exactly as you said – they'd be too frightened not to.'

I glanced at him. No reaction so far.

'With the infrastructure now in place from my investment, you could easily add in market intelligence, specialist security courier services and so on.'

His face showed nothing but smooth neutrality. Had I pushed too far? I wanted to protect these people that I'd come to like and respect, despite that they were criminals.

'What an interesting girl you are, with so many ideas bubbling away in your head. I'm surprised you have the time for your everyday life.'

'It was only a suggestion,' I grumped.

'I congratulate you on your originality.' He laughed. 'I'm actually annoyed with myself that I've never given much consideration to developing in that way.'

He said nothing more, but swivelled around to watch the screens. I saw that was as far as I was going to get. But I had the impression my idea had found a warm nest.

50

Around two thirty, guests began drifting off. Martina came in with a folded note which she handed to Apollodorus without a word. She gave me a meaningful look. We were on.

Apollodorus sat in my leather chair as if he were a king receiving tribute. Palicek was ushered in by Flavius. The screens had been hidden behind a retractable partition. I stood against the back wall by the door, hidden in a sea of black. I closed my eyes to gauge the atmosphere around Palicek. Greed – that was expected – blood, fear, craving for power.

'Mr Palicek. Please, sit down.' Apollodorus addressed him in English and smiled like a university professor receiving a dull student: patronising, but interested because he had to be.

'Thank you, Mr Apollodorus.'

'Now, how can I help you?'

Palicek had piggy flint eyes in a fleshy face set on top of a medium-height figure. He looked around, a hint of anxiety on his face. He was obviously uncomfortable under the targeted glare. Perhaps the outrageous fee for the lighting design was going to prove worth it.

He sat back and explained his proposition in lightly accented English. Bronck's Quarter. New York, second generation immigrant, I reckoned, despite his record showing Minnesota.

'We have a business model that we feel would work well with local partners, and are keen to contact interested and effective players. I made a few enquiries about you, Mr Apollodorus. I think we may share a number of common interests.'

He sounded like something out of corporate America. In a twisted way, I guessed he was. I stopped listening to the words and concentrated on the tone, his body language, his reactions. After fifteen minutes back and forward negotiating niceties, Palicek invited Apollodorus to his hotel in two days 'to meet associates'. Palicek stood up, shook hands with Apollodorus and let himself be escorted back to his group. We saw from the screens they were already in coats, the girl sitting, Renschman and the other man standing in the deserted club floor. We watched Flavius and one of the security team see them off the premises.

Apollo disappeared into the bathroom behind my office. He came back in, drying his hands on a linen towel.

'That is a most unpleasant man,' he commented. 'Not only unrefined, but with absolutely no sense of right and wrong.'

I gasped.

'Don't look as if you've swallowed your grandmother's pin cushion, Pulcheria. I may break the law, but I'm perfectly aware I'm doing it. He sees absolutely nothing wrong in what he is doing – therein lies the difference.'

Justus, Philippus, the doctor and I went with Apollodorus to meet Palicek and his 'associates'. Apollodorus and Justus led the negotiations; our doctor tested the 'merchandise'. Delivery of the first batch was scheduled in six days. I didn't participate, but went along to 'hold coats'. Disguised in a mousey-brown wig and bulked up with extra layers, I could observe through my tinted spectacles without being distracted. I stood behind Apollo most of the time, out of Renschman's direct view. It was nerve-racking, but I wasn't frightened. Renschman had swept his eyes over me, but passed on. As the only woman, the Americans assumed I was Apollo's assistant and ignored me.

• • •

The day after meeting with Palicek, we moved into the club on a full-time basis. Philippus and I were covering the early evening shift two days later when we caught our next official snoopers.

'There's a fit woman,' he said, his eyes tracking a tall figure with long red hair down her bare back. She moved like an athlete; her designer gown must have cost two thousand *solidi* upward. Her escort was tall, dark-haired and had a Mediterranean complexion. Typical Goldlights clientele.

'You're not supposed to stalk the customers.'

He grinned but kept his eyes on the screen. 'Yeah, but she's something else.'

He continued enjoying himself for a few minutes as she danced.

'Oh,' he said.

'What? Did she fall over drunk or something?'

'Something.' He studied the screen intently. 'Look at her dress, between her breasts.'

'What exactly?' I didn't generally look at other women's breasts.

He zoomed in and I saw a light mesh of hair-thin threads, barely visible.

'What do we have here?'

'Either the DJ *custodes* have stepped up a significant notch or they're PGSF.'

'What makes you so sure?'

'That wire mesh. It's a polymer fibre used by the Praetorians. It's ball-achingly expensive, but the arrogant bastards get all best kit. So they think they own the bloody planet. But they *are* good. These two definitely fall into that category.'

'I'll do this one,' I said.

'Sure?'

'Yeah, it's my club and I don't want these people in it.'

I walked around the tables exactly as Apollodorus had done but as we approached the two spooks, I turned to Martina and said I would take it from here.

'Good evening,' I said, emphasising the affected nasal voice I used for Pulcheria. 'I hope you've been enjoying the atmosphere.'

'Very much,' the man said and stood up. I figured he was around mid to late twenties. 'I love the lights,' he continued, tiny gold crescents in his eyes reflecting them. 'I've never seen anything like it – I guess that's why it's called Goldlights.' Then he smiled, charming and knowing it.

'They're local,' I replied, 'made in Aquae Caesaris. They spin the whole thing in one tube, inserting the gold strands; then weave them into loops. Each one is unique.'

'Fascinating. They must have cost a fortune.'

Normal clients wouldn't have mentioned the cost.

'We like them. But I'm sure you didn't come here just to admire the decor.'

'We heard it was the cool place to be.'

'Now you've seen it all, you and your colleague might want to make a move. Spooks that walk into our club wearing wires are not welcome. Please leave now, quietly.'

'What the hell do you mean by that?' He took a step toward me, his face angry. He closed the distance between us until his breath brushed my skin, a classic move supposed to intimidate me, but I held my ground. His face was hard now, tight lines around his mouth. My full-length black sequinned dress had side slits, and I had one of the carbon fibre knives from my thigh holster against his groin within seconds. He tensed.

'Your choice, soldier boy.'

'C'mon, Daniel, let's go,' came the redhead's voice.

'Yes, Daniel, run along like a good boy,' I added.

'I'll have you for this, you little cow.' His eyes blazed.

'Unlikely, sunshine, you're not my type. Now piss off.'

'Trouble, Pulcheria?'

Philippus.

'No, they're just leaving.'

The one called Daniel gave me a furious look. I gave him a smug smile back. He took his companion's arm and pulled her toward the door. Philippus signalled the security staff and they followed the two spooks to the street as we watched.

'Tell me something, Philippus. Why are attractive men always so up themselves?'

51

When Palicek had told him a week ago they were flying to Roma Nova, Renschman's eyes had shot wide open. When he asked Palicek to confirm it, his boss's face closed in and he frowned. He wasn't used to being questioned by his subordinates and snapped back a curt 'yes'.

But now Palicek was pleased with how the meeting with his new Roma Novan associates had gone and gave out bunches of dollar bills with a big smile. He even told Renschman to take off for a day, two if he wanted. Everything was in place. All he need do was be ready to go meet the courier at the landing field in five days, he said.

Renschman had been watching the girl's home for over ten hours now. None of his listening devices could penetrate the electronic shield so he reverted to traditional skills. He could wait. He'd waited long enough.

The girl had to come out sometime, for lunch or shopping or chit-chat with another pampered bitch. Where the hell was she? He stretched his fused muscles and decided to risk another walk-by. When he'd strolled along early afternoon, the CCTV cameras hadn't moved. Super having his after-lunch nap, lazy bastard, he guessed, or the cameras were static. Sloppy security for such a high-end house. He strode along, in the lee of another pedestrian, knowing he'd be out of camera range in seconds.

He was caught completely unawares when one of the cameras swivelled round and fixed on him. He reacted like an amateur and stared up at it. It zoomed in and tracked him all the way down the street. He didn't breathe out until he turned the corner. Jesus! They must have personal recognition software. His heart was pumping fast. He'd underestimated them again. He dived down the side street and went to cross into another street parallel to the main road – and ran straight into a solid wall disguised as a man. Another hand took hold of his arm and eased him back against the stonework.

Renschman shrugged, smiled, shook his head at the question in Latin and said in English he was a tourist. The woman rolled her eyes at her companion.

'What you do, walking past this house two times?' she asked in English. 'You are watching for something?'

'I'm a tourist,' he repeated. 'I was admiring the carving above the archway. Is there a problem?'

Her look could have dissolved steel, but he smiled back like the innocent he wasn't.

'Do not come here again.'

As he crossed to the second block down, he risked a glance backward. They stood, arms crossed, still watching him.

52

'How gratifying. We're getting some attention,' Apollodorus said when I reported the latest visitors. 'I expect they'll be back. I do hope not a raid.'

Justus had placed a sound jammer in the middle of the table. It was no way as effective as the crystal pyramids the security forces had, but better than nothing.

'Now, listen carefully,' Apollodorus continued, 'we're entering a critical phase. Please consider that by now we may have an agent, a mole, an observer of some kind, or even several, amongst us.' Hermina looked uncomfortable at his comment. 'I know, my dear Hermina, that you and Justus will have done everything to check every employee, but we cannot be overconfident. It would be equally naive to overlook the possibility that one or two may have been overwhelmed by the attraction of money.' He paused. 'A dangerous and unfortunate decision on their part.'

Faces were expressionless around the table. Nobody moved a millimetre as they processed these last words.

I coughed to break the silence. Apollodorus shot me a gleam of anger but said nothing. I thought he pushed it a little too far sometimes.

'Moving on,' I said. 'Apollodorus and I have worked on an exit strategy in case everything is screwed. If we get raided, they'll block the service entrance at the back. But there's another exit, from the kitchens. The back panel of the far corner cupboard leads to a passageway which runs the whole length of the block and comes out in the garage of an apartment building on the Dec Max. Hopefully, outside any security cordon they throw around. You just need to release two catches at the top of the back panel in the cupboard and push.'

I ignored the stunned looks on their faces.

'You'll find an envelope for each of you in a small alcove to the right, about five metres from the entrance.'

Justus was first. 'Is this a serious possibility?'

'Very much so, my dear Justus,' said Apollodorus. 'Don't be concerned. Pulcheria's plan is carefully thought out.'

'We've never been this threatened before.' He shot an unfriendly look in my direction.

'But we've never made such a lucrative deal before, Justus. Nor done anything quite so interesting.'

'If you say so.'

'The club and its trading offshoots are all in my name,' I continued. 'Nobody will be able to touch any of you or Apollodorus's other interests. You just need to quit the premises when I say.'

'Are you going to carry the whole can?'

'Only if it gets really messy.'

I saw a glimmer of respect in his eyes.

Nobody else had anything to say so we broke up in a sombre mood.

I was relieved to be near the crisis point of the operation. I wanted to finish and go home. And, for all her cool toughness and strong ideas about duty and service to the state, Nonna would have been worrying, especially since I'd broken all contact via Lurio.

The following afternoon, Apollodorus and I were re-reviewing the phoenix plan for the Pulcheria Foundation. The others presumed we were talking contingency last night. But we knew the break-up was inevitable.

'You know that, if Palicek doesn't bite, we'll have to start over, finding another target,' I said.

'I'm fully aware of that. I'd be delighted if we continued working together. I've never been so entertained or had such a charming colleague.'

I blushed. Despite his impressive good looks and cool strength, I didn't find Apollodorus sexually attractive, but I liked him and respected him immensely. I glanced at the screens. I saw the cleaning staff, the bar manager restocking, Martina sitting at a table with the chef, poring over menus, a maintenance woman fixing something up on a door frame. All pretty humdrum. I was about to turn away to resume with Apollo, when my heart nearly stopped.

Conrad.

He materialised in the doorway and advanced onto the main floor.

What in Hades was he doing here? I was immobilised, only my eyes moving, tracking him as he weaved between the tables. He turned and glanced at the stage then headed for the bar. The bar manager pointed toward Martina and he made his way over to her. He looked tired and strained. His hair had grown, but not so long as it had been in New York. I hadn't seen him in months. I wanted to go down there. To see him. To be with him.

Then I registered that he was in uniform and had that Daniel with him.

'Ah. Reinforcements – a PGSF major. Interesting.'

'No, he's a captain.'

'It seems he's been promoted,' Apollo said. He swung around, fixing me with the full force of his black eyes. 'Perhaps you'd care to tell me exactly how you know him, my dear Pulcheria?'

I crossed over to the side table, poured myself a tumbler of water and took a large gulp. First Renschman turns up as Palicek's sidekick, now Conrad was prowling around. If this operation ended well, it would be a miracle. I took some deep breaths, calmed myself and turned, ready to go back into battle.

'Apollo, sorry for that. Let's get back to business.'

He raised an eyebrow, but said nothing.

'Captain, no, Major Tellus is a senior, and very effective, operator. You may know of him, perhaps from one of your databases.'

'Unfortunately not. The PGSF appears to have an unbreakable encryption system. Dolcius thinks it has components imported from the EUS.'

Surely not Brown Industries? Ironic.

'Very well. I told you at the beginning that I know some of the personalities in the security forces. He's one of them.'

'Is that all? You seem to have had a strong reaction to his appearance.'

He didn't blink as he held my gaze. I refused to break first as his black eyes bored into mine. After several seconds when I forgot to breathe, he turned back to the screens.

'Very well, I accept your story. But if it compromises the security and success of our endeavours, I will take appropriate action. Is that clear?'

'Of course. I understand.' Icy fear brushed my skin.

'I'll go and see what they want. Do me the courtesy of watching their reactions.' He disappeared out of the door, pulling it shut with more force than was necessary. I was annoyed. Whatever my emotional quandary, I would still do my job properly.

The screens showed Conrad with his arms crossed, a smile painted on the surface of his face, his index finger playing up and down his shirt sleeve, watching an over-relaxed Apollo deliberately taking his time to listen and answer. Neither would face the other, but positioned themselves at right angles. A neuro-linguistic specialist could have made more technical sense of it, but I saw the signals clearly enough. I didn't know who I wanted to shake more.

Apollodorus came back after fifteen minutes. I don't think I could have stood it any longer.

'What a dangerous young man that major is. You were quite right. We must be very careful with him. Somehow, I invited them to be my guests tomorrow evening.'

'You did what?' I gasped.

'Yes, disconcerting, isn't it? It's rarely I get boxed into a corner like that.'

I couldn't believe it. I never dreamed Conrad would be able to manipulate Apollodorus.

'No. Listen. You can't.'

'I can't pull out now. Have you so little confidence in my ability to handle him?' He looked stung.

'I'm sorry, Apollodorus. Of course not.'

.   .   .

I arranged for Flavius to watch with me that evening. Conrad and Daniel arrived at half ten wearing tuxedos and sat with Apollodorus at one of the wall tables. They drank, they danced, they needled. I listened via Apollo's comms kit but, after a while, became irritated by the polite bickering. Flavius jotted down a few notes, but I was more than content to sit and listen to the lilt of Conrad's voice.

'What do you make of him?' Flavius said.

'Clever, professional and a damned nuisance.'

Flavius laughed.

A sudden change in tone alerted me. I heard Conrad say, a little too casually, 'Are we not to have the pleasure of the company of your colleague, Pulcheria?'

'I'm afraid not, major. She's not with us tonight.'

'Pity. Daniel's been telling me all about her.'

I bet he had. I wanted to wring Daniel's neck at that moment.

'Nevertheless, I'd like to meet her. Perhaps tomorrow?'

'She's not back then, but I shouldn't think she'll be doing anything special the day after.'

No, only almost getting myself killed.

53

They left at half one. I sat back, let the lids fall over my strained eyes and stretched my arms over my head. I hadn't realised how tense I was.

'Why didn't you want to go out there tonight?' Flavius asked. 'You saw the younger one off so easily the other night – wouldn't you have enjoyed a skirmish with his boss?'

'I'm feeling a little off at the moment, so I asked Apollodorus if he would do it instead.'

He gave me a 'Why do you expect me to believe that bullshit?' look. 'I don't know, Pulcheria, you can do better than that.'

'Really, Flav, I have a very good reason. Sorry.'

'Okay,' he said, but he dropped his eyes and looked away. I had disappointed him, I knew.

Apollodorus reported he'd found the major pleasant, but tricky. He was definitely on a fishing expedition. Despite keeping his guest's glass full, Apollo hadn't learned anything useful.

'He seemed to enjoy himself dancing and flirting with our best-looking young women but he declined the offer of a companion. The younger officer was pleasant, friendly, apparently on detachment from an allied service. Why did he take against you, Pulcheria?'

'A knife threatening his vital interests?'

. . .

I was at work by eight the next morning. I wrote, exported and emailed for nearly two hours at my laptop. I wiped the hard disk, trashed the laptop and threw it in the kitchen incinerator. I changed from my jeans into my black leather suit, dark red tee and, despite the warm weather, my black boots. I applied my make-up with more than usual care.

At a quarter after one, Lev Palicek arrived with Renschman and one other associate who carried a small business case. Our screens were hidden as before, but the concealed cameras were running. As before, I stayed back, hidden in the far corner. Renschman cocked his head and glanced around, searching. He sensed something, someone; his instincts must have been working overtime, every nerve straining to find it, or them. I knew he couldn't see me: the Stygian blackness in the back wall zone was complete. Nevertheless, I held my breath, straining not to attack him.

Very little was said. Our doctor bent over the case, ignoring the circle of concentration focused on him as his fingers worked deftly, sampling the contents of three baggies he selected randomly. I watched Renschman. He had positioned himself a step back from Palicek, having everybody in view and reach, but he kept his frameless glasses trained on Apollodorus.

Philippus opened our case with half the payment in EUS dollars and handed over an envelope containing the transfer ticket for the balance. Everybody looked contented as Apollodorus shook hands with Palicek. The next delivery was scheduled in two weeks.

Once they had gone, we stared in silence at the business case brimming with transparent packets of white powder. We had just committed a crime attracting twenty years' hard labour. And who in Hades expected to survive that living death in the mines?

I gathered up my brains, panned around the stunned faces and took a deep breath.

'Right, bail out, via the kitchen passageway,' I commanded. 'Regroup at the house.'

After anxious exchanges of glances and gathering murmurs of protest, Apollodorus flicked his fingers at them like he was shooing cats. They went. I hoped Apollodorus would be as compliant.

I made the call on my supermobile, spoke one word, 'Gracchus', shut it and gave it to him. 'The network will go down in fifteen minutes. Go.'

'I'll stay with you.'

'No.'

'Don't be stubborn. I'm not leaving you.'

I made a big production of looking at my watch.

'You now have just over twelve minutes. Don't forget to pick up your own envelope.'

His eyes widened.

'Did you think I would leave you out?' I stood on tiptoe and kissed his cheek. 'I'll be fine. When I get out of this, I'll contact you.'

He stood there, his face in turmoil, his eyes burning.

'Go!'

He paused by the door. 'One last thing. What *is* your real name?'

'Carina Mitela.'

'No!' He froze. Even his face refused to move.

'Will you please go? Now.'

He hesitated, rocking on the balls of his feet.

I pushed him through the door. He glanced back once then disappeared.

'Go carefully,' I whispered at his retreating figure and shut the door.

54

Five minutes later, the screens and audio burst into life. Street doors were thrust open. Boots thudded across the polished wood dance floor. Shouts and screams from the staff, orders barked out, metal jangling, smashing open of doors and cupboards. Boots pounding along the corridor, like the thud of jackhammer road drills. Hades, they were early. My office door burst open. A dozen figures in full battledress stormed in, fanned out and trained their weapons on me.

'Good afternoon, ladies and gentlemen, how may I help you?'

I sat in my leather chair behind my desk, forcing nonchalance. I played with my silver pen, not looking at the little drawings I was making on the notepad. I didn't need to look down to know my fingers were trembling. I prayed the others had made it out.

The green and brown figures stood still. The room lights thrust maximum lumens at their faces, deflected by black semi-visors hinged down from their helmets. The only sounds were their breathing, the involuntary creak of boots flexing, metal brushing cloth.

'Don't stand there like a load of dummies.'

Ah, the delightful Daniel.

One of the figures seized the business case, snapped it shut and disappeared. I was pulled out my seat, shoved up against the wall, my arms wrenched behind my back and handcuffed. I was frogmarched out, across the dance floor. Staff had been herded against the wall, a cordon of armed soldiers and DJ *custodes* guarding them. Some protested, some were crying, some comforted others. Marched outside, I was thrown in the back of a Jeep-type truck with four soldiers to guard me.

After a fifteen-minute ride bumping around on the dirty metal floor, I flinched as the vehicle jarred to a stop. Two of my captors leapt out, boots crunching on the gravel, reached in and pulled me out. I blinked against the harsh sunlight. I found myself in a vast sand-strewn courtyard, flanked by a tall block that looked like a government office. But it wasn't the *custodes* station I was expecting. All the people here wore beige uniform or fatigues.

Merda. I was in the Praetorian barracks.

Gripped by my right arm, I was marched through a basement entrance door into a corridor, through a set of barred gates into an area with narrow benches on each side. An older, grim-faced soldier was working on a keyboard on a shabby desk. A smell of disinfectant, sweat and somebody's over-strong aftershave hung around.

Lurio had warned me this stage would be 'challenging'. He had ordered me to maintain my cover whatever happened. He would be along shortly after the take-down to spring me, he'd said.

An aeon ago.

A female guard removed my handcuffs, gave me a yellow tunic, and told me to strip everything off and change into it. During an embarrassing visual body search, I just stared at the opposite wall and tried not to think about what they were doing. Afterward, I was allowed to drink a cup of water, handcuffed again and pushed into a room full of nothing. I heard the clunk of the door lock behind me. I slumped down to the floor, my back against the wall – not easy with your hands shackled behind you. I trembled, my shoulders contracting. I tried not to think of what was coming. But the good part was that Apollodorus and the others must have gotten away by now.

I'd held it together in front of my captors, but their cold, mechanical handling was unnerving. None of them looked me in the eye. They handed me from one to another like I was piece of trash. I shut my eyes and started deep breathing. I focused on forcing my aorta pump to lessen its thudding, the fluids in my arteries to slow. I willed the adrenalin coursing through me to disperse. I made my muscles relax by naming them. *Thank you, Felix,* I breathed. When they came for me, no way would I give them the satisfaction of seeing me uptight and jittery.

Or terrified.

After a few minutes of hard concentration, I had calmed my body down. The concrete floor was so cold and the ache in my arms and shoulders heavy and dull. My loose curly hair falling across my face like a black veil and getting in my mouth was beyond irritating.

Heavy footsteps in the corridor. Lurio come to bail me out. At last.

The metal door clanked open and Daniel strode into the room.

Hades.

'Not so bloody superior now, eh?'

Stripped of his helmet, vest and webbing, and down to basic fatigues, he was no less forceful.

'That supposed to be funny?' I said in Pulcheria's nasal whine. 'Or are you into pseudo-domination practices?'

His head jerked back in surprise, but he recovered and threw me an angry look. 'Look, you little tart, you're in so much shit. I'd mind my mouth if I were you.'

Then I said something extremely coarse. He frowned, his eyes blank, puzzled. So he *was* foreign-born.

I heard a laugh that almost stopped my heart.

'That wasn't a very ladylike expression. What *have* you dragged in off the street, Lieutenant?'

Daniel hauled me to my feet, clamping his fingers on my arm at the exact point where the previous guards had grabbed me. It was excruciating, but nothing to the agony I knew was coming. I bowed my head, begging Scotty to beam me up this instant. Even through the black mass of curls covering my face, I couldn't mistake that cat-like movement as the newcomer crossed the room. His hand came up and he pushed my hair to one side. I raised my face to meet Conrad's gaze.

His eyes widened and, for an instant, his mouth opened in surprise. He stared, unbelieving. I stared back.

'This is Pulcheria?' he asked Daniel. His eyes tightened but never left my face.

'Of course, sir.'

Disbelief gave way to shock. His face hardened, eyes narrowed and tilted upwards. I saw the rage flare. His hand came up and struck me hard across the cheek. I gasped, stumbled backwards and hit my head. Pain, then everything went black and I lost consciousness.

I woke, lying on a high, narrow bed. My left wrist was shackled to the frame. My sore face was throbbing. It brought Renschman and New York back. I'd been a child then.

I touched my head where it hurt. Just a bump, no skin break. I dragged myself up on one elbow. I was in a small tiled room, a bedside cabinet and a drape at the side. Like a public hospital. I twisted to reach a plascard cup, the shadow of the water showing through. Bliss.

'Oh, you're awake? Good.'

A uniformed medic approached me. I shrank back. 'Here,' she said and handed me two white pills. 'Major Tellus said to make sure you took them.'

I looked at them then back at her.

'You're in no position to query it, but for what it's worth, they're painkillers.'

With a capital P stamped into them, they looked like standard panalgesics. They could have been anything. Either I would throw up, talk myself hoarse or my head pain would go. After another minute's hesitation, I decided to take them. The good part was another cup of water.

I lay back and closed my eyes. Where in Hades was Lurio? He told me to 'go with the flow', but this was turning into an uncontrollable torrent. And Conrad. Why had he hit me so hard? I hated him for that.

The medic went away. I had to stall. My head was starting to ease, so I slowed my breathing and heart rate, straining though the last end of the headache to induce a trance. After some effort, I slid under and was gone.

I woke up exactly four hours later with a cluster of anxious faces bending over me and no head pain.

'She's coming round. Stand back.'

The same medic as before. She pushed her bioscanner up against my forehead and clamped her fingers on my wrist to confirm my pulse. When she shone a torch in my eyes, I automatically tracked the cheap plastic pen she moved in front of my face.

'Okay, you're fit.' She nodded to two uniformed figures. One came forward, undid the handcuff linking me to the bed and cuffed my hands behind me. Where was I going? Why did I have to be fit?

I was taken to a windowless room where a uniformed woman was sitting at a table. The guards pushed me down onto the empty chair on the other side of her table.

'Hmm. Pulcheria.'

She was around thirty-five, forty, and looked like a tax inspector, complete with glasses, thin lips and tight, ordered hair. Although the rest of her face didn't show any hostility, her pale grey eyes were cold. Just like O'Keefe. She waited for a full five minutes before she spoke again.

'Suppose you tell me why you think you're here.'

'No.'

'That's not going to get us anywhere, is it now?'

'No.'

She looked at me intently. 'I hope you're not going to be difficult. You're facing twenty, twenty-five years' hard labour for drug dealing, so cooperation now would probably soften our attitude.'

I laughed. 'Do you think I'm that simple?'

'Aren't you?'

'No.'

'You know, we could be here a very long time, talking together, so let's try to move on from "No".'

'You only have twenty-seven more days to question me, so I'll just stick with "No".'

'Oh, I think I might be able to change your mind within that time.'

'Oh, I doubt it.'

We continued like this for nearly two hours. She was relentless, like an automaton, pushing questions at me in that same dull voice. It was simultaneously boring and nerve-racking. I wanted to scream at her, if only to provoke a reaction. In the end, I used her monotonous tones against her, harnessing the rhythm of her voice. I detached my senses, tuned out the interrogator's repeated questions, focused my whole self on my internal core, reduced my breathing, gave a sigh, rolled my eyes up and put myself out again.

I woke in a cell, my hands free. Despite the chain attaching my left leg to the bed, I managed to use the bucket in the corner. Considerate of them to put a cover on it. A tray with a plastic cup of water and a bowl of mush had been left on the floor. After drinking half the water, I sniffed the bowl contents. They smelled like crushed vegetables, so I ate them, using my fingers. If it had some drug in and I threw up, their problem. I drank the rest of the water then lay back on the bed.

It had to be early morning. I couldn't tell; there weren't any windows. In a shitty day, the worst hadn't been the arrest, the humiliation, the being shackled. It had been Conrad. Immobile, cold, but so angry. His hand had hurt me more than physically. It would take me a long time to forgive him. But if I didn't convince him I wasn't a dealer, I guessed I would have a long time. I had my immunity certificate, but how could I get a message out? And be sure of avoiding one of the officers under suspicion? Nobody here knew who I really was, except for Conrad. And he'd presumed I was guilty. I was going to kill Lurio when I saw him. If he ever turned up.

These angry thoughts tumbling around in my head were interrupted by the door opening.

Daniel.

'Get up, you little cow. You may fake it with Somna, but you'll find me harder.'

He gestured two guards to bring me along to the same room as before. No handcuffs this time, just a compressing grip on my upper arm. The same interrogator, presumably Somna, was sitting at the side, a clipboard resting on her lap, looking like a trainer assessing a student.

The guards placed me a little way from the blank wall.

'Arms out,' Daniel shouted at me. 'Fingertips touching the wall.'

'No.'

He slapped my face. I whirled around and kicked him in the groin. As he bent over in agony, I raised my fists together, brought them down hard and body-rammed him to the floor. The guards tried to grab me, but I was too quick. Screw Lurio, screw going with the flow, and screw taking what they dished out. I leapt high, landed next to the interrogator and, within two seconds, threw her to the floor. My knee in her back pinioned her to the concrete. I neck-locked her and pressed her head forward.

'Stay completely still, interrogator, if you don't want to die,' I hissed in her ear.

I looked straight at Daniel, who had staggered to his feet but hunched in a crouch. From the pain, I hoped. 'Now, if I pull another two centimetres, I'll snap off her head. Don't be so naive to think I won't do it.'

'Let her go, you little cow,' he croaked.

'Oh, Daniel, you are such a stupid prick.' I threw Pulcheria's nasal laugh at him. 'Not even that, from what my girls tell me.'

He was boiling by now. He took a step toward me. The guards approached one from each side in a pincer movement. I flexed my arm muscle to press another few millimetres on Somna's larynx, which emitted a terrible rasp. They all froze. The only sound was Daniel breathing hard. Somna experimented with a tiny movement of her shoulders. I jammed my knee further into her back and she grunted. Daniel exchanged glances with the two guards. I was bracing for their next move when the door was thrown open.

'Stand down, Lieutenant!'

55

Conrad.

I registered him on the outer edge of my vision, but didn't unpick my eyes from the three poised to attack me.

'Everybody out. Now. Recording off.'

Daniel refused the guards' assistance with an impatient gesture as he limped out with them, but threw a vicious look back at me. When they'd closed the metal door, I switched my gaze to Conrad.

'You can let her go now,' he said in a dead voice.

'You have to be kidding. She's my ticket out of here.'

Unbelievably, he laughed. But it was a short, bitter laugh. 'I don't know where you got that illusion from. This isn't some American movie. Somna knows she'll have to take her chances.'

Juno, he was hard. Or maybe they were all like that.

'If I let her go, what guarantee do I have you won't attack me? Like you did before.'

'None. But if I have to come and get you, you'll be very sorry. I can promise that.'

His face resembled a piece of Aquae Caesaris granite. No ambiguity; he meant it. And I knew how strong he was. I released Somna. But I stepped back and stayed balanced on the balls of my feet, fingers curled, ready.

The interrogator rubbed her neck and glanced at Conrad who

raised an eyebrow. Somna turned her head left and right, slowly. She nodded and left the room.

'Sit down.'

I teetered on the edge of refusing. But the adrenalin was draining away, fatigue washing over me now, so I perched on the plastic chair Somna had used.

He stood over me, arms folded, and eyes dark and tilted upwards.

'Drug dealers can expect very little quarter from the law and none from me personally. We won't tolerate importing tainted things from the West that poison our life.'

He meant me. My heart thumped. A sour taste rose up from my stomach. I was going to throw up. But I swallowed hard to tamp it down.

'I don't know how you got to this point; there are various options to deal with it. You can cooperate with Somna or not. Your choice. But she is successful within the twenty-eight days allowed almost without exception.'

'Is that a threat?'

'No, a fact.'

I was determined to be an exception. What did I have to lose now?

'Next, if you display one more sign of threatening behaviour, I'll have you shackled twenty-four seven.'

'Then keep that moron Daniel away from me with his fucking stupid little tricks.'

'And you can keep the foul language to yourself or I'll have your mouth taped up the rest of the time you're not answering questions.'

'Proper little Renschman, aren't you?'

His body stiffened. He flexed his fingers. Was he going to hit me again, or worse? A few seconds later, his face relaxed and lost its ash-white colour. He laughed, maliciously.

'Nice try. Clever, but you don't get me like that.'

A knock at the door interrupted our tête-à-tête. A guard came in and whispered to Conrad who frowned and made the guard repeat her message.

'Very well. I'll be along in a couple of minutes. Stay here, and don't let anybody into this room except me or on my signature. No exceptions.' He turned and looked at me. 'Oh, and cuff her.'

· · ·

236

I was starting to give up on Lurio. Where in Hades was he? When I gave the codeword 'Gracchus' for the take-down of the drug dealers, he was supposed to ride in and rescue me. According to the operational plan, there should have been a clear ten-minute window. But the PGSF troops had arrived five minutes too soon. Now I was stranded here, my face and arms aching and sore, my defences running thin, amidst these tough soldiers determined to take me apart piece by piece. I didn't know how long I could stall them nor how long my nerves would hold out. Not that I was going to let any of them see that I was intimidated. But if Lurio didn't appear within the next twelve hours, I was going to scream 'lawyer' and screw the mission.

56

Shortly afterward, the door opened and two soldiers came for me. They took me upstairs where the corridor had a wood floor. Much better. My bare feet were ticked off with concrete. These were regular offices. I saw blurred figures moving behind smartglass as we walked along. We stopped at a door with the sign 'Major Tellus, ATU'.

I would have preferred Somna or even Daniel.

Inside, Conrad sat behind his desk, talking to a blue-uniformed figure half-sprawled in the chair opposite him. Both looked up as I was brought in, the DJ officer craning his neck around.

Lurio.

He didn't greet me or say anything else. He straightened up and fixed me with an intense stare. A warning. Absolutely no mistake. I stayed silent, but my thoughts were unprintable. He was so lucky my hands weren't free.

Conrad dismissed the guards. He glanced at me then turned a full-strength glare on Lurio. 'Is this really your agent, inspector?'

'It certainly is, major.' He smiled at me. 'Hello, Bruna.'

'Hello, sir.'

Conrad's eyes locked on to me. He stared at me as if I were a Martian. His disbelief was obvious. Despite feeling cold, tired and furious, a glimmer of smugness stirred in me.

Lurio beamed an extra-friendly smile at me, his shoulder turned away from Conrad. 'Have you eaten recently?' His faux concern was overdone, I thought. He was relishing getting one over the oh-so-clever PGSF.

'Only a small bowl of mush since I've been enjoying these people's hospitality, sir.'

'Some food, if you would, major?'

Conrad reached out mechanically and spoke into a unit on his desk. Lurio looked at me and touched a finger to his lips. I nodded. We waited like a set of dummies, Lurio brushing an invisible speck off his leg, or scratching his ear. Conrad got up, went over and looked down out of the window for a minute, his back hunched over. When he came back, he threw himself into his seat and stared down at his desk, pretending to look at a folder. I glared at Lurio as the minutes dragged by, but I bowed my head and slumped when a guard entered, carrying a tray with two plates of sandwiches, two glasses and a carafe of water which he set in front of Lurio and Conrad. As the guard closed the door, I rolled my eyes. Lurio grinned and placed a crystal pyramid on the desk.

'Could we have the cuffs off, please, major?'

Conrad exited his trance, looked everywhere but at my face, came around behind me and undid the handcuffs. The brief touch of his hands sent a tingle up both arms. Or maybe it was my tired nerves reacting to my wrists being released.

'Sit over there and eat,' ordered Lurio. 'Slowly.'

I grabbed a plate. I hadn't realised how hungry I was. I wolfed the lot and picked up every crumb with my fingertip. I gulped down a whole glass of water.

Lurio mock-sighed and shook his head. 'Major, may I present Senior Justiciar Cara Bruna of the Department of Justice *Custodes* Organised Crime Division? One of my most promising, if most insubordinate, operatives.'

I nearly choked on the last crumbs; Conrad didn't do much better.

This was really stupid; we all knew who I was. Why did we have to keep up the pantomime?

'Really?' Conrad said after a pause. 'And how long has this been going on?'

'Oh, quite a while now. This is a deep-cover operation, major. As you know, there've been leaks where there shouldn't have been. We've plumbed ours, but we haven't had any confirmation the PGSF have managed to do the same.' He smirked at Conrad. 'As a test, we sent a rumour down various suspect channels yesterday, each with slightly different content. The only one that failed came here, to this unit. We can't identify your traitor specifically but, perhaps with Bruna's help, we can flush her or him out.'

'And what precisely was this rumour of yours?' Conrad's tone was curt. His brows were pulled together, deep vertical lines between them.

'That you were about to take a suspected drug dealer into custody who knew the traitor's identity.'

I couldn't stop my mouth falling open.

'And you were going to tell me when?' I threw at Lurio.

'I'm telling you now.' Seeing my face, he said, 'Relax, Bruna, you've been under guard at all times.'

'Yes, but, hello, one of those guards could have been the traitor and terminated me. Perhaps that had escaped your thought processes. Sir,' I added.

'Is this why you delayed collecting your agent, inspector?'

Yeah, Lurio, was it?

'Not at all. We were trying to sort out the foul-up over the operation at the Goldlights club. Your over-keen guards went in five minutes too early, major.' He looked Conrad straight in the eye, his voice taking on an unusual chill. 'I would like to know exactly why that was.'

Conrad said nothing, but tapped something on his keyboard. He waved at Lurio to continue.

Lurio shrugged. 'Luckily, we had the real dealers already. By the time I'd found out what had happened, Bruna had disappeared until "Pulcheria" came up on the confidential part of the joint watch report this morning. To her eternal credit, she hasn't bleated.'

I almost fainted with the shock of Lurio's praise. I decided to sit there and look enigmatic. Lurio said the DJ had all the dealers. Including Renschman, I hoped.

'So what now?' Conrad asked.

'You have to flush out your traitor. We're prepared to use our agent in place, if she's prepared to do it.' Lurio turned to me. 'You don't have to if you feel you've had enough. It's their problem.'

Crafty bastard. I gave him a dirty look. Lurio would never let me forget it if I gave in now. I also wanted to have the edge over Conrad.

'You know full well I'll do it,' I grumped. 'Just don't get me killed.' Lurio laughed. I smiled back in a sour way.

Conrad looked thunderous. 'I won't have you endangering her life,' he shouted at Lurio.

'Really? You've given her the benefit of your hospitality for over thirty-six hours, not exactly a rest cure. And the danger, if I may point it out, is from one of yours. If there isn't a traitor, then everything's wonderful. If there is one then we'll have stopped the rot. Worry you, does it, owing us a favour?'

Conrad studied Lurio for several minutes. 'Tell me, inspector, do you often use amateurs to pursue experienced, hard criminals?'

Lurio laughed. 'Bruna's no amateur. Personally, I feel sorry for the criminals.' He dropped his laugh. 'Do you want our help or not? If you don't, we'll be going.' He stood up, moved his chair back and nodded at me. I stood, ready to follow.

Conrad shrugged. 'I'd be stupid to let the opportunity pass. I hold you responsible for what happens to your agent.' He looked up at Lurio. 'Entirely responsible.'

If the atmosphere had been any tenser, it would have started an electric storm.

Lurio went to the back corner of the office and spoke into his wrist set. Conrad stared at me while I devoured the second plate of sandwiches. On top of being dumbfounded at me turning out to be the DJ agent, he'd lost it when I'd agreed to be Lurio's bait. Did he still have feelings for me? He'd been so hard in the interrogation room but, on the plus side, he'd kept that idiot Daniel away from me.

57

I was lying on the bench with my eyes shut, thinking about nothing in particular. The six open-barred cells were arranged in a row, with a guards' post on the opposite wall. Apart from the CCTV camera panning, the only noise was the tip-tapping from the one PGSF and two DJs playing checkers. Lazy bastards. I suppose it was boring for them; only two of us to watch, me in the end cell and somebody else in the fifth one along.

The guards' commset buzzed and the occupant of number five was collected and taken away by two DJ guards. Who initiated that order? I watched through barely open lids. A few minutes later, a PGSF officer came in. She had red hair tightly bound and piled up on her head. Juno save me! It was the same one that had come into the club with Daniel. She nodded to the desk and the PGSF guard started to get up, but she waved him back down. She talked to him for a minute or so. He nodded and left.

She came over to me. 'Pulcheria. Not so comfortable now, are you? Getting as much rest as you can before a little trip to the mines?'

'Piss off, Ginger.'

'You won't be so perky when you've worked a ten-hour shift on prison rations for a year.'

'Yeah, well, it's not always that straightforward.'

'Oh, I think it is in your case.'

'So what's your point, Ginger?'

'There are ways to, how shall I put it, make the time go a little faster.'

'Sorry, you're not my type.'

'You'll be begging for help after three months.'

'Yeah?' I pulled myself up on my elbows. 'Don't worry about little me, Ginger. I have my own insurance.'

'Don't bet on it.'

'Oh, I'm pretty sure them upstairs will want to underwrite me when I tell them.' I swung my legs down, stood up and came over to the cell door. 'But you know that already, don't you?'

I wasn't fast enough for her hand which shot between the bars and grabbed my hair. She tugged my head viciously toward her until it hit against the bars like a squash ball against the court wall. My head exploded with pain. I blacked out for a second. I only just remembered to press the radio pressure switch between my fingers. Through the waves of pain from her grip, I dimly hoped the fricking thing would work. My head was skewed sideways against the bars. I brought my hands up to reach through and jab her eyes, or hit her nose, or anything to release the merciless grip. But she pulled her head back. I clawed at her fingers, raking her skin. I prised one hand off, but she slid the other further down my hair out of my reach and yanked downwards. The solid plate at the bottom of the cell door prevented me kicking out at her shins. Where were the damned guards?

Her right hand came back up. I saw blood dribbling from the back where I had broken her skin. I shot my hand out between the bars to grab and hopefully break it. Anything to stop the pain of my hair being torn out. But she pulled away out of my reach, flicking her wrist sharply as if shucking off a case or cover. I heard a container hit the floor. She brought a hypodermic into my view, her thumb curled over the top of the plunger. Fuck. She was going to kill me.

'Stop! Stop! You bitch,' I gasped. 'They know it's you, they know you're the traitor.'

She paused. 'How?'

'Too bloody greedy.' I gulped for air. 'Two thousand *solidi* dress on your pay? Don't think so. Ow!'

She yanked my hair hard, jamming my head against the bars again. Blood trickled down my face. I was going to black out again. I screamed for my life. Then, in an instant, the pressure vanished. Released so abruptly, I staggered back and collapsed on the floor.

'Got it.' I heard Lurio's voice. Then a smack of flesh on flesh. From my cell floor, I saw Ginger, hands forced behind her back, a blue-clad knee pinioning her to the floor. I struggled up to my hands and knees, trying to get to my feet. My legs were like rubber. The cell door slid open and a pair of strong, familiar arms lifted me up.

'It's over. It's over. You're safe now.'

The first thing I heard was an electronic beep. Next, throbbing, sending rings of pain through my head. And why did I have a hat on indoors? I raised my hand to take it off and found a sensor attached to my finger. I unclipped it and struggled up onto my elbows. Ah, the hat was a gauze bandage, like a finger bandage but for the head. I saw a cup of water on the locker, reached through the dizziness caused by sitting up and drank a cupful. The throbbing didn't pinch so much now I was partly upright. I found I was attached to a drip. What was that for? I was looking for a buzzer when Lurio arrived.

'Still damned insubordinate?' He eased me back onto the pillows with one hand, supporting my back between my shoulder blades with the other so I went down slowly. His face and upper body were centimetres from mine; it was strangely intimate.

'They spend thousands on monitoring systems, so do them the courtesy of using them,' he said lightly, clipping the sensor back on my finger.

'You're such a bully, Lurio'.

'Yes, I expect I am.'

'Is...has...oh crap, tell me everything.'

He sat on the bed, took my other hand and laughed. 'Ginger, as you call her, more properly Lieutenant Maia Robbia, had been on the take from Palicek and friends for over a year. She'd got into debt through her extravagance. Mars knows how, the money they pay Praetorian officers. They were all stunned. Apparently she's a rising star, a brilliant field officer, etc, etc.' He yawned theatrically.

I remembered how fast and determined she'd been when she attacked me.

'Palicek and associates are all in custody and will be indicted in four weeks' time. They're not going anywhere soon. Which leaves me with one very pertinent question. We can't trace any of your, ah, former associates.' He held my hand very firmly. 'Somebody tip them off?'

'It was just me in the club that day, apart from the staff. I couldn't say what's happened to them.' I became very interested in playing with the sheet folds.

'Right.'

'Don't pressure me on this, Lurio.'

'It'll all come out in the debrief.'

'The what?'

'Now you've done all the sexy stuff, the rest of us have to create mounds of paperwork to justify it and perhaps learn a few things we can teach others about how not to do it.'

'What do I have to do?'

'Write long reports, submit to interminable questioning and drink huge amounts of alcohol in the bar that your colleagues buy you in congratulation.'

'My colleagues?'

'You signed up, if you recall, as a member of the DJ. You're part of a service.'

'But that was purely for the operation?'

'You have to stay in for a while, while we do all the post-op stuff. It's not so bad, you know.'

I chewed my lip, unable to meet his gaze. 'I've been on the other side of the law far more than on this one.'

'Then you need to balance it up.'

'Why are you pushing on this?'

'Look, Bruna, I'm trying to be nice as you're not feeling well. I'm not even going to bollock you for going off-plan, but you've basically got no option. Besides, you might enjoy it, you never know.' He grinned.

'Huh!'

'At the moment, you have to concentrate on healing. Then we'll sort you out.'

'Er, Lurio, where am I?'

'In the PGSF hospital wing.'

'Oh.' I shivered.

He pressed my hand again and leaned over to give me a comforting kiss on the forehead. For some reason, I gulped, loudly. I shuddered. He pulled me to him and held me, stroking my shaking shoulders and back.

After a few minutes, I pulled back and wiped my palms over my eyes. 'I'm really sorry. I didn't mean to be so soppy. I must be tired or something.' I flapped my hand around in embarrassment.

'No problem at all. Perfectly natural reaction to the stress.' He looked at his watch. 'I have to go now, but I'll call in later tonight, if you're still awake. Try to behave.'

58

A uniformed nurse bustled in to check my vital signs again before lunch. Medics always loved being in charge. She handed me a cup of the same restorative Conrad had given me in New York when I had a hangover. The ginger and malt smell brought it all back. A tear escaped my eye.

'Are you all right? In pain?'

'No. Sorry.'

'For Mercury's sake, don't be sorry – you had a hard trauma to your head. The scan showed several impacts, and that's without the hair root damage and torn tissue.'

'Juno. Do I have any hair left?'

'Yes, of course,' she said. 'You're healing well, but you'll be here for a few days.'

After lunch, I napped. The food on this floor was an outstanding improvement on the basement menu.

I was filling time, looking through some magazines the nurse had found for me, when the door opened. Conrad. He hesitated, uncertain, but came over to my bed and pulled up a chair.

'I waited until you were settled in,' he began. 'How are you feeling?'

'Good, thanks. My head's as hard as teakwood, I'm told, and even my hair will survive.'

He turned his signet ring around and around his finger, like he wanted to polish away the pores on his skin. I had been thinking through what had happened in the past forty-eight hours. While he'd been so wrong, I'd started understanding why he'd acted as robustly as he did. Maybe after he apologised, I would forget it. I had some news that would cheer him up. The DJ would have checked out the dealers' identities, and presumably forwarded them to the PGSF liaison team, but did he know Jeffrey Williams was Renschman? Knowing Renschman was in custody would be a great moment to share, a resolution to that tense time in America, and our fight before Saturnalia. And maybe a start to healing the rift between us.

I was so busy playing out my optimistic scenario that I was completely unprepared for what he said next.

'When you're up to it, I'll take you home. Aurelia can get a specialist in to check you out and arrange your aftercare.'

'What do you mean?'

'You'll want time to recover. Perhaps a few weeks at Castra Lucilla, in the country air.'

'What are you talking about? I have a pile of stuff to do. The debrief and reports are going to take weeks.'

'No.' He did that 'face set in concrete' thing. 'If they want statements, they can come to you while you're convalescing. I'll try and get you released as soon as I can. Aurelia knows Aemilia Fulvia. She can pull a few strings.'

'Now wait a minute,' I said. 'Are you seriously proposing I sneak off home? Desert my post?'

He stretched out and took my hand in his. The pleasure of the warm, masculine touch was cancelled by his next words.

'Look, love, you've had a hard time and perhaps you're not thinking clearly—'

I liked the 'love' but screw the rest. I pulled my hand back.

'Let me explain something, Conrad. I loved this mission. I planned it and trained for it. And I damned well succeeded. I aim to carry on with the job. It's too important to give up.' My head was throbbing again. I took a couple of breaths to try and ease it. 'I'm sorry if you don't like the idea, but you'll have to find a way to deal with it.'

'You don't know what you're saying. It's a brutal life. You've only touched the edge.'

I took another deep breath. 'That's unfair and you know it. And don't you quote brutality at me. It's my decision, and I've made it.'

'You stupid girl,' he shouted at me. 'One day you'll get into something right over your head and you'll come home in a body bag. What's that going to do to Aurelia?' His eyes blazed.

'Don't pull that one on me. You don't have any right.'

I was as cross as Hades. His face began to swim along with rest of the room. The throbbing in my head was shaking my mind. I was going to pass out.

'For Asclepius's sake, will you stop shouting?' The nurse rushed in, fury all over her face. 'Major, I won't have you upsetting my patient. Please leave. Now.'

He threw me an incinerating look and stormed out.

What a mess. What was his problem? He knew I wasn't some delicate flower. Was it guilt? Or something else? I was getting worked up again when Lurio put his head around the door.

'Can I have a couple of minutes? The nurse said you were a bit tired so not to stay too long.'

I hadn't realised it was that late. I must have dozed off. Lurio would never qualify for Mr Sensitive, but he didn't try and think for me or cocoon me.

'Hi. Yes, come in.' I patted the bed. He gave me a curious look, but said nothing.

'The nurse reckons you'll be able to have the bandage off in a couple of days. They'll do some remedial treatment on your skin and probably discharge you in a few days' time.'

'Great. So I'll be starting work on the mop-up?'

'That's what would normally happen. But I talked to Aemilia Fulvia about your misgivings. She said we owed you such a debt, she'd respect your wishes if you chose to leave.'

'No, I want to stay. I want to see it all through. And afterward as well. Permanently. You'll have to be patient with me if I foul up somewhere. Just say something cutting and sarcastic and I'll get the message.'

Next time Lurio visited, the bandage was off but my scalp was still sore. I was allowed to shower, but the nurse cut my hair short and washed it with some antiseptic medical stuff that stank. My own red-gold was starting to grow through by the time I left the unit. I was strictly forbidden to colour or straighten my hair for twelve weeks, so basically I had to let it grow out. Fabulous.

I was given three days' leave, so I went home to Nonna. I had a DJ guard with me as I was a 'vital witness'. I told Lurio that Domus Mitelarum was as secure as Fort Knox, but he wouldn't listen.

Nonna fully supported my decision to stay at the DJ as a *custos*.

'I can't follow the logic in Conradus's thinking, Carina. I served in the PGSF for several years and survived. Even through the rebellion. You're as tough as I am, so I'm sure you'll be perfectly all right in the DJ. Perhaps he still loves you, and would do anything to keep you from harm.'

'You're wrong, Nonna. He treated me so badly when I was arrested.'

'Probably overreacted from the shock of discovering that you were Pulcheria.'

'Maybe.'

'He'll see the full extent of what you've done after the debrief. I know Aemilia Fulvia can't sing your praises enough.' She smiled. 'She asked if I had any more granddaughters like you.'

59

I reported to the Department of Justice headquarter building holding my posting letter and with my guard in tow. She vanished once Lurio came down to reception to greet me.

'Ah, Bruna. Follow me.'

Normal service resumed. We exited the elevator at the fifth floor and crossed a small outer office into a larger one with 'Insp. Cornelius Lurio' on the door. He told me to sit and went outside again. After a few minutes, he came back in with an el-pad which he thrust at me.

'Right, I've assigned you to one of the Organised Crime sections, but seconded to my office *pro tem*. It's best you continue using the name Cara Bruna, at least for the present. The department has a few members of the Twelve Families, but certainly no heirs. It'll save you a lot of unnecessary personal hassle.'

I glanced at Lurio. Of course – with his name he must belong to the Cornelia family who were nearly as prominent as the Mitelae. He took me to the Organised Crime Division where I was introduced to an inspector, my nominal chief. I was allocated a desk and a minder, Senior Justiciar Sentius.

'Sentius will get you kitted out and show you round, Bruna. Back in my office at seventeen hundred, please.'

Sentius turned out to be old school, so we started with a coffee. After him asking and me dodging a load of questions, we settled down to get my ID and mail account. At the quartermaster stores, I was issued sets of dark blue uniform, badges and insignia, a belt and pistol holster, and a large duffel to carry it all in. I changed from my civvies into the everyday uniform and caught my reflection in the mirror. I looked like the real thing.

After lunch, we went to the indoor range where the master-at-arms issued me my personal weapon. I shot some rounds down the range. The resulting clusters were a little loose but acceptable. I had only used a pistol occasionally in Nebraska; Uncle Brown had been a rifle man.

I knocked on Lurio's door promptly at five.

'Sit down. I'll be with you in a minute.'

I used the time to look around his office. He had two bookcases, crammed with technical books on organised crime, policing theory, law and order, a full set of the *Lex Custodum*, some general and biographical books, and business management handbooks. Certificates, commendations and a few photos hung on the walls above a small display case containing tiny artefacts that I couldn't identify.

'Had a good look?' he said, his eyes still focusing on his papers.

I chuckled.

'Right,' he said, closing the file. 'You're assigned to the PGSF for the next few weeks, as anticipated. Major Tellus advises me that Lieutenant Stern will not be in your part of the debrief team.'

'Sorry, who?'

'Work it out, Bruna – the one you call Daniel. He's Operations, and quite junior, so he won't see any of the finished reports.'

I hoped not. He really hated Pulcheria. I dreaded the idea of meeting him.

He hesitated. 'They wanted you to stay in their barracks, as an honoured colleague, of course, for the duration of the debrief. I told them nothing doing. Although it was a joint operation, DJ were leading and you'd be in my custody.'

'So I can live at home, I presume, or here?'

'Home's out – I'm not spending more budget on a twenty-four hour guard for you for goodness knows how many weeks. It's a bit basic here, so I've arranged for you to stay at my apartment.'

'And you'll be staying where?'

He gave me that tight-lipped, wide-eyed, exasperated look of somebody dealing with an idiot. 'What's the problem? It's large enough to contain both our egos for a while. I'll put locks on the doors if you're worried you may be overcome with desire for my body.'

'You're abominable.'

He grinned.

I was still fuming as I sat in his car on the way to his apartment. Just who the hell did he think he was? But, as we rode along, Lurio cursing softly as he peered through the rain, I calmed down; I was overreacting. Firstly, like it or not, he was my superior officer so I had to do as I was told; secondly, he could have left me in the utilitarian barracks dormitory for several weeks; thirdly, he'd saved me from further PGSF hospitality; and lastly, under all that smart-ass gruffness, he was funny and didn't try and smother me. Nonna would have called him 'bracing' like a sharp, but not hostile, wind.

I had called home to send a bag of things. Outside the gate to Lurio's block, Nonna's chauffeur sheltered in the Mercedes from the summer storm. He nodded to me and drove in behind us. He lifted two bags out of the boot and carried them into the lobby.

'Which floor, *domina*?'

'Inspector?' I asked.

'Leave them here. She can carry them up herself.'

The chauffeur looked shocked and pretended he hadn't heard correctly.

'That's fine, Nic,' I said, 'just leave them there. Please thank Junia for sending you.'

He bowed and left, sending a hostile glance at Lurio over his shoulder.

'How ever are you going to manage without your little band of servants at your beck and call?'

'Oh, shut up, Lurio. Whatever you think of me, you could at least have the courtesy to treat people who can't answer back with some dignity. He's only doing his job, so don't sneer.'

He said nothing, but picked up one of my bags as we stepped into the elevator. He was right: his apartment was large. The block had been built in the early 1800s, with spacious, high-ceilinged rooms with rich cornicing, double doors and large sash windows. I touched the beaded and recessed panelling as I followed him in. I was surprised; Lurio didn't strike me as the type to like such romantic architecture.

He showed me to a huge corner room with a connecting bathroom.

'Perhaps not what you're used to, but I think you'll be comfortable enough.'

'It's very nice, thank you.'

He raised a sceptical eyebrow. Maybe he didn't know much about my life before Roma Nova.

'I don't suppose you can cook so I'll do it this evening,' he said and walked out.

The food was fine, not gourmet, but perfectly acceptable. We ate in silence. I picked the plates up and offered to wash the dishes, but he waved me away.

'Zero seven hundred tomorrow morning,' he said.

'What for?' I said. 'Breakfast, leaving here, run, getting up?'

'Leaving. If you think I'm going out for a run tomorrow morning in this rain, you must be more stupid than I thought.'

60

Entering the courtyard at the PGSF headquarters wasn't a problem. Getting out of the vehicle and going into the building was. I couldn't move from the shelter of the car door. And the summer rain had stopped ten minutes ago.

'Come on, Bruna, we'll be late.'

'I...I just need a moment to balance myself.'

He looked at me sharply. 'You're going in the professionals' entrance this time, not the cells, and you're not manacled. Let's get on with it.'

He put his hand under my elbow and propelled me forward.

At the entrance, we had to surrender our sidearms. I swallowed hard as my service pistol vanished into the safe-box, leaving me vulnerable. A guard gave us a message to report to Captain Somna. No. Not the same one I had held in a neck lock, threatening to kill? I looked around, preparing to run. Lurio's hand clamped onto my elbow so hard I couldn't have escaped him without injury.

'Don't let the bastards have the satisfaction,' he whispered.

I didn't like this building, I didn't like these people. But I'd promised Lurio. *And* I'd chewed Conrad out for thinking I couldn't do it. I braced my shoulders and took a deep breath.

Captain Somna received us with neutral formality and introduced us to her staff. I didn't take it in. Her grey eyes locked on me and tracked every move I made. They were as cold and disconcerting as before.

'Your team has just arrived, inspector. Shall we go through? We're using the main conference room.'

Amidst the pack of blue and beige uniforms, I saw Sentius sitting at the main table and half-smiled at him; he winked back. At least I had one friend here. Three seats had been left for us. Lurio placed himself between Somna and me.

'Good morning, ladies and gentlemen,' said Somna, tapping a water glass to compel silence. 'This is the first plenary session of the debrief for Operation Goldlights.'

They had even stolen my club's name.

'We'll proceed as follows: each participant will write up their diary and report one day, and discuss it with appropriate DJ and PGSF specialists the next. Some of you will obviously have more to report than others. We'll have an interim plenary this time next week.' She looked around the dozen or so faces in the room. 'Support will be available from the specialists in my service and their DJ counterparts. The aim of this debrief is to draw out the most information in a neutral and technical process, not to condemn or commend anybody in particular. Lieutenant Murria has schedules and assignments which she is now distributing. Please let her know if you have any problems. Questions?'

Nobody dared.

'Then I'll let you get on with your work.'

I watched them read their schedules and sort out their teams, a low-level hum of voices replacing the cold silence. Nobody had given me anything. I was happy being unobtrusive.

'SJ Bruna?'

I looked up to see Lieutenant Murria hovering over me. I stumbled up.

'Yes, ma'am?'

'You're to come with me.'

I swallowed hard and glanced back at Lurio, but he was busy talking to Somna. I picked up my notecase and followed her to a small office. Everything was square straight and nothing superfluous.

'I expect it feels a bit strange, but you'll get used to it over the next few weeks. It'll be an easier start for you to use my office today. Back to the conference room tomorrow. One of your colleagues, Sentius, will be sitting in with us. He'll be along in a few moments.'

She was friendly enough. Slightly shorter than me, with black hair and brown eyes. She looked very fit but slouched in her chair like a normal person.

'We'll chat informally at first and record it as we go along. You can edit and amend it from the printscript. Okay for you?'

'Fine. Thanks for making it easy.'

She laughed. 'You may not thank me in a week's time when your voice is hoarse and your eyes are on stalks after reading reams of double-space printscript. Or would you prefer on-screen format?'

We talked casually for a few minutes – I'm sure it was one of their techniques. By the time Sentius knocked at the door with a tray of coffee and pastries, I was reasonably relaxed.

'Sentius, a man after my own heart. Twice welcome.'

'No problem, ma'am.' He grinned. 'I know Bruna can't start the day without coffee.'

Lurio had ordered me to tell them everything except my true identity, but I left out other things he didn't know about like the BI supermobiles, my redundancy packages for my colleagues, and the phoenix plan. I didn't consider them relevant. Sentius handed me a glass of water now and again. After a while, I noticed that neither Murria nor Sentius were taking notes; they were staring at me, listening intently. Three hours after I started, my stomach made a loud rumble. The heat flushed across my face as I looked away in embarrassment.

Murria looked at her watch. 'Jupiter's balls. We've overrun. My fault. Let's get to the mess room before it's all gone.'

Sentius and I followed her. He'd been here once before and knew where we were going, but I was wary of everything. Swing doors opened into a huge dining room; the noise was stunning. I noticed a large hatch to one side and a raised area in one corner. Everywhere was full. Murria sailed through the sea of beige-covered bodies, aiming for the far side, through more doors and into a smaller room where we found the rest of the debrief team and a buffet with plenty of food. I piled my plate high.

Sentius and I ate in silence. Murria had gone to sit with some of her colleagues.

'You know, Bruna,' Sentius said, bringing his knife and fork together after he'd finished, 'I knew you were impressive, but not that much. You're quite an operator, aren't you?'

'Am I?'

'And scary with it. In fact, you're like that lot out there.' He jerked his thumb back toward the dining room we had passed through.

'Juno, don't say that.'

'Why not?'

'I don't like them.'

'Okay, they're a bit arrogant, but they're professional and get excellent results, so not all bad.'

'You ever been on the other end of them?'

He gave me a strange look. 'Whatever have you been up to?'

'You'll find out.'

By the time we had gotten to late afternoon, I had a dry throat and a headache, and my words were coming out minced.

'Right. You've had enough,' said Murria. 'We'll get this printed up for you tomorrow and you can revise it in the conference room in the morning. If we get it circulated by lunchtime, the interrogation team can start tomorrow afternoon.'

She must have seen the anxiety in my face. I couldn't say a thing.

'Don't worry. They'll only discuss your report with you and ask a few questions. They're not going to beat you up.'

That would make a change.

She was right. The three of them mainly wanted to know why I'd made certain decisions and what my thinking was at the time. But they picked everything apart, in yawn-inducing detail, even the obvious things that I thought everybody knew. I had gotten less nervous about the people coming and going during the afternoon so, when I turned and stretched my hand out to grab another sheet of paper from the side desk, I nearly choked to find Somna roosting right behind me. I leapt to my feet.

'SJ Bruna.' She nodded. 'How is it going?'

'Very well, thank you, ma'am.' What in Hades should I say? I looked away, longing to be the other side of the double-paned window overlooking the courtyard entrance. But there was no escape, in any sense. I hesitated for a few seconds more before I gathered my courage to speak.

'May I speak with you about something?'

'Of course. Let's use my office.'

Somna's office looked fairly ordinary, furnished with standard desk, chairs and low table, with bookshelves the dominant feature. She seemed to have more books on psychology and philosophy than applied harassment. But she definitely wasn't into collecting china kittens.

She stared at me and waited.

I cleared my throat and focused on the bridge of her nose. 'Please believe me when I say I wouldn't have snapped your neck. I was anxious at the time and needed to strengthen my negotiating position.'

She didn't say a thing, so I fell into the classic trap of babbling to fill a vacuum.

'I'm sorry if your neck is sore. I hope there's no permanent injury.' Then I stopped. I really didn't have anything else I could say.

She looked at me with those cold snake eyes. 'I'm glad we've had this conversation, SJ Bruna. Thank you.' She stood and opened the door, so I was obliged to leave. I didn't have a clue whether she'd accepted my apology or not.

'You look fed up. Do you want to go out to eat this evening?' Lurio asked, as we made our way across the parking lot to his vehicle.

'Um?'

'Please yourself.'

'Sorry, I was miles away. What did you say?'

'You know, Bruna, I'm not used to people not paying attention to what I say.'

'I apologise from the bottom of my heart.'

'Don't get sarcastic with me. Do you want to go out to eat or not?'

'Yes, let's do that. My treat.'

'Don't patronise me, Miss Moneybags.'

'You know, Lurio, you might want to shed those chips on your shoulders sometime. Better sooner than later.'

He glared at me and we rode back in silence.

Once in the restaurant, he thawed out after the first beer. I told him about my conversation with Somna.

'You'd have been better leaving it.'

'Yes, I think so now, but I did feel bad. I half-choked the poor woman.'

'Don't waste your pity on her – she's a cold bitch.'

'I'm petrified of her.'

Lurio took my hand in his. 'If you get a problem with her, or any of the rest of them, refer it to me. I'm responsible for you.'

'Thanks, I appreciate it.'

'I'm not doing it because of your lovely face, Bruna. I'm your senior officer. That's what I do for my people.'

Was it the alcohol, my insecurity, the natural closeness of sharing, or nothing in particular? Back in the apartment, as I turned to say good night, he put his strong arm around my waist and kissed me in his thorough and efficient way. He carried me into my room, stripped the clothes off my body and made love to me in the same way.

The next morning, he got out of bed, went into his room, showered, dressed and started breakfast as usual. We rode to the PGSF in silence but, as we arrived in the courtyard, I turned to him and said, 'Would you care to explain last night?'

'What about it?'

'Has anybody told you that you are totally impossible?'

'Frequently.'

'Why aren't you dead?'

'If I were, I wouldn't be able to look forward to screwing the socks off you tonight.'

61

How I made it through that day, I don't know. I put the conversation aside and plunged into my work. I was getting into the routine of talking to Murria and Sentius in the conference room with other people listening in. I started writing my own notes, following their style, and discussing it in the afternoons with the full team.

I was also getting used to Lurio and his robust ways. We had a day's leave and spent it eating, making love and sleeping. He had a disconcerting habit of sitting in bed and doing his paperwork. Then he'd put it down, turn to me, take the book I was reading out of my hand and have me. It was funny, annoying and touching. I didn't love him, or really lust after him. It just seemed a natural part of life, like eating or drinking. But, inevitably, we drew closer.

I was writing up the visits to the club by Palicek one morning. I was uncomfortable and not a little guilty over what I knew about Renschman. I should have insisted on having him indicted for trying to murder me last year. But that was as Carina Mitela, formerly Karen Brown. He would have gotten life for that. But he was guaranteed to get twenty plus years' hard labour for drug dealing. And very few survived that long. I should be satisfied with that. I supposed it didn't matter he was going down as Williams. Or did it? Should I say something? Atrocious as the thought was, I had to seek advice from Somna. I knocked on her door.

'Come.'

Crap. She was in.

'Ah, SJ Bruna.'

I closed the door behind me and waited.

'Yes?'

I was here now, so I launched straight into it.

'Ma'am, I have some additional information which may or may not be relevant to this investigation.'

She gestured for me to sit and focused her unblinking gaze on me. I took a deep breath.

'I don't know where you and the DJ are with Jeffrey Williams, or even where he's in custody, but you should know I've encountered him before. He's ex-EUS military and ex-CIA. He headed up the enforcement group for an EUS government agency called the Economy Security Department. It sits somewhere within the American Security and Trade departments.'

I recovered my breath and waited.

'You seem remarkably informed, SJ Bruna.' Her grey eyes blinked once, like a lizard's.

'Has Major Tellus taken you into his confidence about me?'

'He and I frequently exchange information, and he has given me some details of your background, yes. In the strictest confidence.'

'Then you'll know I was kidnapped in New York by people from the ESD. This Williams ran the operation, but his real name is Jeffrey Renschman. He attacked me here last year, nearly killing me, as well as instigating the incident in the Washington legation.'

'I see. Please wait one moment.' She turned to her commset. 'Murria. Somna. In here, stat.'

We sat in silence. I didn't know where to put my eyes. The chair creaked under me as I fidgeted. Was she going to tell Murria everything?

Murria appeared in under a minute. She raised her eyebrows when she saw me sitting opposite Somna.

'Lieutenant, we have fresh information about Jeffrey Williams.' She gave Murria only the details about Renschman's background. The junior officer hurried off to process them.

'This is valuable intelligence, SJ Bruna. Do you have any other gems you wish to share?'

Should I push it? I wanted my five minutes with Renschman, to see him crushed, no, destroyed. To be honest, I wanted to gloat.

I cleared my throat. 'I wondered if it would be possible for me to have a few minutes with Renschman?'

She tapped her fingertips together a few times and studied a file on her desk.

Crap. She wasn't going to play.

'Your request is most unusual, you know. The best I can do is for you to be an observer at the next session with him. We're sharing the questioning with your colleagues, so the presence of another *custos* won't appear untoward. But I must ask you to be discreet and stay silent. On no account will I tolerate any ideas of retaliation at this stage.'

I figured that was it – disappointing, but it was something.

Later that afternoon I was editing a transcript when Somna came into the conference room and told me to follow her. Sentius gave me a funny look, but I scurried after her.

We went down to the custody suite. I steeled myself as I placed my foot on the first step of the stairs. Not the real descent into hell, but this wasn't going to be pleasant. I shivered as we slipped into the back of the same interview room I had left only a few days ago.

Murria was leaning against the wall, one leg bent at the knee so her foot was flat on the wall. She looked bored and was examining the nails on her left hand with intense interest. Renschman had his back to us. He wore the standard prison tunic, his hands cuffed behind him. I heard him tell the DJ interrogator to go screw himself.

Somna and I listened for around ten minutes. She must have forgotten I was there. Murria turned into bad cop now, head jutting forward, within millimetres of Renschman's face, questioning aggressively, slamming her hand on the table. But they weren't making any progress. It didn't help that they were forced to do it all in English and that he was answering in American street talk in order to confuse them.

I leaned over to Somna and whispered, 'Would you take a chance and let me have a try?'

Give Somna her due – she could make a decision. She narrowed her eyes, looked up and a little to one side then back at me then nodded.

She beckoned the two interrogators to follow us into the corridor. Once the door was closed, she gave them her reptile stare and spoke in a low voice. 'What you are going to hear next in that room is to be kept completely confidential. You are never to allude to it in any way. I will personally edit the recordings and transcript to produce an extract.'

They nodded, but I saw a flash of resentment in Murria's eyes. She gave me a cool look. 'Captain, may I ask what this is about? We're making some progress, not very rapid, I grant you, but now we know he's a professional, we can use a different approach.'

'I understand, Lieutenant. But Bruna here can cast a unique light on this. I think we could give it a try.'

Murria didn't look happy. She was senior in her branch, so I guessed she didn't like being treated like a rookie. I had the impression from her that I needed to deliver or I would be back down here myself.

Murria turned away from me and tugged on the door. As I prepared to follow her and the DJ interrogator back into the room, Somna caught me by the arm. 'Ask only one thing at a time. Repeat it until you get a reply. And remember what I said in my office.'

I took a deep breath as I went back in. But I was no longer some soft city girl terrified out of her wits. I crept up behind Renschman's chair, bent down and spoke right into his ear.

'Ain't it just the pits when something comes back and bites you in the butt?' I said in my whiniest Bronck's Quarter accent.

He jerked and his head whipped around. His face was like some kid's play mask: brows halfway up to his hairline and huge round eyes above a mouth fixed open. He stared for ten full seconds. He recovered, closed his mouth and waited. But his eyes searched around, uncertain.

'Yup, it's me.' I came round in front of him and perched myself on the edge of the table. I crossed my arms and brought my right ankle up onto my left knee. I was tense, but determined to give out an impression of total relaxation.

He attempted one of his creepy smiles, but most of his face was wary. He couldn't help but stare at me. The combination made him look like a carved Halloween pumpkin. And about the same colour.

'Lousy shock, isn't it? I've waited a long time for this.'

I signalled toward Somna, Murria and the DJ interrogator standing at the centre of the back wall behind Renschman as if dismissing them. They didn't move.

'Now we're alone, we can continue that little talk you started in New York.'

'Go screw yourself.'

I raised my hand and swung it down fast in a vicious movement.

He flinched and turned his head, attempting to avoid the blow.

I stopped one centimetre from his face. I smiled and shook my head. 'I forgot. I mustn't hit you. I'm not a trained interrogator, so I don't know the proper rules.' I bent down right into his face. 'On second thought, I wouldn't dirty myself by touching you, even if you were lying on the morgue slab.' I sat back into my relaxed stance. 'Unless, of course, I was carrying out the post-mortem and wore rubber gloves. But then, I wouldn't bother killing you first.'

He swallowed. His Adam's apple bounced hard. A few drops of sweat formed on his upper lip. 'You can't do that.'

'Really?' I kept my tone cold, utterly flat. 'You'd be surprised.' I smirked at him. 'Who are you going to complain to? The EUS government would deny all knowledge of you, so don't look there for help. You know we're not bound by international protocols. Forget the Vienna Conventions. You're out in the cold.'

He leaned back in his chair, imitating relaxation, but his shoulders were rigid with tension. 'What do you want?'

I laughed. And waited. I was enjoying this. I drew my carbon fibre knife out of the sheath strapped to my ankle. Murria took half a step forward, but Somna put her arm out and stopped her. I traced a few patterns on the table with the knife. Although my touch was light, it scored the surface.

Renschman's eyes followed the knife's circling tip.

'My colleagues would like to know why you're here and what you've been up to. I'll hand back to them in a moment – they're much more civilised. They don't have any kind of personal grudge. But then, you haven't tried to kill them twice.'

I stood up, right in front of him. 'Look at me.'

He raised his head slowly and looked up reluctantly. I was so close, he was forced to bend his head right back. I used my trick of looking straight into the back of his eyeballs. 'You need to tell them everything. I'm going to listen for a few minutes. If we don't make enough progress, I'll have Captain Tellus join me. He told me he was going to kill you the next time he saw you. He was very, very angry. Your safety and well-being would be entirely in our hands. I would think about that if I were you.'

The sweat oozing out on his forehead shone in the intense light. He looked away first, grunted and bowed his head. He slumped in the chair, making no attempt at movement.

I'd won. I'd conquered my fear and I'd conquered him. The terror he'd inflicted on me in New York and in that freezing kiosk in the park was gone. I could hardly believe how easily he gave it up. It dawned on me he was a bully, and so a coward.

I beckoned Murria and the DJ interrogator over and retired to the wall, still looking straight at Renschman and still playing with my knife. I watched him and listened as he told them about Palicek, the drug distribution, his role, payment mechanisms, their contacts to date in Roma Nova. It was sweet.

Murria forgave me. I thought. Later, back up in the general office upstairs, she gave me a coffee. 'I'm not going to speculate about how you know him, Bruna, but you certainly pulled off a hell of a trick there. My congratulations.' She smiled at me. 'Ever thought of working in the Interrogation Service?'

I couldn't find any words. How could she suggest such a horrific thing?

She laughed and walked away.

62

Three days later, Lurio and I had finished lunch early and gone to grab some air. The weather was hot and I was glad of short sleeves. The clear air was refreshing, a tonic both on my skin and in my lungs after the air-conditioning.

At the back of the main building, a few tough nuts were sweating round the sports track. We paused, half-hidden in the shade thrown by the side wall of the semi-circular grandstand. He pressed me gently against the wall, slid his arm into the gap at the back of my waist, bent down and kissed me. His kiss was thorough and surprisingly passionate. My arms around his back pulled him in, my legs instinctively folding around his. I gasped as a warmth beyond tenderness rolled through me.

He drew his head back, looked into my eyes, closed his own and gave a tiny shake of his head, as if to himself. Eventually, he released me, and pulled me into the grandstand to sit on the steps. He laid his arm across my shoulders and drew me to him.

'They want to pull it all together by the end of this week,' he said, his voice subdued. 'Trials for a week, after that it's back to normal.' He looked into the distance.

I leaned over and kissed his lips lightly.

And at that moment, Conrad came jogging past on the track.

. . .

I wasn't surprised when Murria gave me the message that Major Tellus asked me to drop by his office before I left for the night.

'I know he's been reading your reports and following the transcripts every day, so perhaps he wants to congratulate you. Or even recruit you.' She laughed. 'Don't look so worried; he won't eat you. Besides, you have your inspector to protect you,' she added with a sly look.

I wasn't going to bite on that.

I hadn't seen Conrad since our row in the hospital wing. I was careful to keep out of his way when he attended the debrief sessions. I'd accepted a while ago that what we'd had was over. I gathered myself together and knocked on the door. Nothing. I knocked again and went in.

He was sitting behind his desk, but the chair was swivelled around and he was gazing out the window.

'You wanted to see me, sir?'

'Did you think I wouldn't find out?'

'Sorry?'

'That you were screwing Lurio.'

'With the greatest respect, it's none of your business.'

He turned around, his face set and eyes cold. 'Not very professional, is it?'

'Then refer it to the DJ internal affairs people if you feel that strongly.'

I knew he couldn't. And he knew it. The DJ was a separate service; they would politely ignore him and, as long as it didn't impact on the work, or service discipline, they didn't care what relationships people had with each other. How dare he? We hadn't dated for nearly a year.

'Do you think I'm made of steel, Carina? I was bloody furious when I saw your face staring out of Pulcheria's body. How the hell did you become part of that dirty world, living with criminals? And dealing drugs?'

He slammed his hand on the desk. Everything on it rattled.

I jumped.

'Then bloody Lurio prances in and announces you're the undercover agent. Jupiter's balls! What in Hades possessed you?'

I wasn't going to say anything. I'd tried once, from my sick bed.

'And how did you learn to fight like that?'

'After Renschman tried to kill me in the park, I learned to protect myself.'

'That's it?'

We stared at each other. He looked down at the file on his desk and waved his hand over it.

'How can this be you? I'd be extremely pleased if one of my field officers did this type of work.'

'Strangely enough, people outside the PGSF are perfectly capable of producing results.'

'Don't be bloody sarcastic with me.'

'Sorry, sir. You asked.'

'Hmm. You've learned to be insolent like them, I see.'

I said nothing.

'And that business with Renschman. Why in Hades didn't you tell me?'

'Not my call.'

'You're totally impossible.'

'No, I'm not. You just can't accept it. Imagine how I felt facing up to him. But I did it. He was a dirty bully and I had my revenge. And now he's going down.'

He looked down at the file again for a minute, and glanced back up through his eyelashes. Did he realise the effect that had? I tamped it down.

'If you were anybody else, I'd apply to have you transferred immediately into the PGSF.'

Cold rushed through me. No. I couldn't be shuttled from one service to another. Could I?

'You can't do that,' I croaked.

He leaned back in his chair and smiled. Not a pleasant smile.

'Actually, I can. Then we'd find out what you're made of.'

It was one of those 'Superman, save me' moments. I couldn't find words, even in my head, to describe the dread of that prospect. And my anger.

'Contrary to the delight almost everybody else would show at such an invitation, you don't seem very happy about it,' he said. He was right. Most people would move mountains to join the elite PGSF.

'No. I like it where I am.'

He laughed. 'Not up to it?'

'Not a problem. I'd go up against anybody. No, it's…'

'Yes?' He smirked.

I wanted to slap it off his face. 'If you want the truth, I don't like the idea of being surrounded by arrogant, brutal morons so up themselves they can hardly breathe. Sir.'

His face darkened. 'Is that really what you think of us?'

'That's my experience so far.'

'You're wrong.'

'Probably. It's always me that's wrong, isn't it? You can't possibly make a mistake, can you?'

'Don't be so bloody stupid.'

'Like I said – arrogant.'

We glowered at each other.

It was at that precise moment the door opened and Lurio marched in. Thank Juno.

'Major.'

'Inspector.'

They didn't bristle or circle each other but, if they'd been a few steps down the food chain, that's exactly how I would have described it. They stared each other out for a full minute. Then Lurio walked forward, braced his hands on the desk and bent down to within centimetres of Conrad's face.

'If you want to talk to any of my people, put in a formal request. Got it?'

'Get your attitude out of my face, inspector.'

Lurio stood back and, without turning, said, 'Okay, Bruna, get going.'

I was out before I could take a full breath. I stood in the corridor trembling, looking down at the wood floor. I heard the door open and shut again.

'Take me home, Lurio. Now,' I whispered.

'Keep it together till we get out of here.'

At the apartment, we made for my bedroom, where we had the most shattering sex ever. He stroked my back and head afterward while I told him about my interview with Conrad.

'You know something, Cara Bruna?' he said, his finger touching

270

the tip of my nose. 'You are the most tremendous fuck I've ever had and I'm going to miss that.'

How coarse he could be, but it was a great compliment from him. 'What do you mean "going to miss that"?'

'After the trials next week you'll be free to go home.'

63

The evening before my first day in court, I tried on my dark navy uniform jacket and skirt; it looked smart. When I turned in front of the mirror to check the fit, Lurio said, 'Yes, yes, you look very nice. Now take it off or it's going to get creased.'

I'd been briefed on the procedure by a legal type and had her support before going in, but it was still intimidating. I had never been inside a courtroom in America. My life there had been excruciatingly ordinary, with not even a jaywalking ticket. Here, a dark oak, carved dais for the judges and the examining magistrate hovered above the rest of the mortals, dominating an elaborately decorated witness box and benches where the defendants and their lawyers sat. A scattering of uniforms broke up the overwhelming civilian presence in the audience area. Many were media, national and international, invited here to push the message of how severely the Roma Nova authorities punished drug dealers. I was screened from them, but not from the officials or defendants, in a smartplex box under the pseudonym of 'Officer B'.

My written deposition had been filed Friday and I was asked to clarify various points. The defence lawyer tried some fancy stuff, but the magistrate told him to stick to the point. They were big on making long speeches, though, but I spoke simply as advised by the legal team. Palicek, Renschman and friends sat impassive most of the time on their bench, but Palicek threw me a poison look when I said my piece about the two meetings. Renschman? If doing hard labour in a tough prison gave him an inkling of the terror and pain he'd made me endure then I wouldn't be too unhappy about it.

They went down for twenty-five years each, and I went home.

On my way, I returned to Lurio's apartment by myself to collect my things; he'd gone directly to report to Aemilia Fulvia. I hesitated before dropping the keys through his mailbox. I didn't know if I wanted to stay or go.

Junia welcomed me back to Domus Mitelarum. I breathed in the familiar smells: polished wood, honey, even the stone and marble gave out a subtle scent. Over dinner, I told Nonna everything, except for the sex with Lurio. She had it out of me eventually. Going up against Aurelia Mitela was never a smart idea.

'I don't know if I feel guilty, defiant or couldn't care less. Being with Lurio seemed the natural thing to do at the time, I was so lonely.'

She put her hand over mine. 'Carina, you don't need to be so defensive. It's always your choice.'

'I'm so ticked off with Conrad, Nonna. He can't seem to accept what I did professionally. But Lurio thinks he'll try again to transfer me into the PGSF. Can you imagine how difficult it would be, working with Conrad like that?'

'He's due here tomorrow evening. Why don't you talk to him then?'

I really didn't want to see him. I would go out tomorrow.

Later, I tapped on Helena's door.

She stared at me, her eyes widened in surprise. Then she grinned.

'Carina! Come in. Brilliant to see you back.'

She poured out a glass of wine, handed it to me, and looked me up and down.

'Nice uniform. You look fit. Having lots of sex?'

Heat flooded my face. Would I ever get used to this frankness?

'So that's a yes. Who is he? Tell me everything.'

I managed to fend off most of the personal questions and gave her a strongly edited version.

'So Goldlights is closed? Really? I'd heard it'd recently been refurbished.' She went over to her terminal and loaded the site. I looked over her shoulder. It was under new management and had reopened two days ago.

I drove into the DJ building next day in my own car and parked in the visitors' lot. No sign of Sentius in the Organised Crime Division, so I sat down at my desk and logged on to my account. Among the crowd of infomails was one message all printed in capitals. Such subtlety could only be from Lurio. I answered it then went to find some coffee. The section inspector invited me into her office and offered me a honey-coated biscuit – apparently a sign of great honour. After five minutes, I was on the point of excusing myself to check if Lurio had replied when the door opened abruptly and he strode in.

He nodded to the section inspector then said, 'You're not being paid to sit on your arse, Bruna. Come with me.'

I mouthed 'thanks' to the section inspector, and hurried after him.

'What?' I said as we walked along the corridor.

He raised an eyebrow.

I sighed. 'What, *sir*?'

'Upstairs.'

In his office, he flung himself into his chair.

'Aemilia wants to see you, but first, why did you leave so abruptly?'

'Isn't that what you wanted? You know, clean break.'

'No, it's what I feared.'

His face was rigid, the light eyes staring at mine.

Oh, gods. I'd completely misread what he'd meant.

'I'm so sorry, I didn't mean to hurt you. Do you want to talk about it?'

He shrugged, said nothing and looked away.

At home, I dropped my personal weapon in the vestibule safe-box and headed straight for the atrium for a drink. I flopped in a chair and downed it in one.

'Feel better now?'

274

My hand flew up to my chest. Where in Hades had he come from? The last person I wanted to see.

'Juno, Conrad. You want me to have a heart attack?'

'Don't be so melodramatic.' He brought the decanter over and refilled my glass. I watched him walk back to the side table, set it down on the tray and come and sit opposite me.

'You look tired. Are they working you hard?'

'Difficult day.'

'I'm sorry I lost my temper last week.' He looked down at his glass. 'It was unprofessional. You were quite right. Your personal life is no longer any of my business.'

The hollow comfort of being right pressed down on me.

'But I cannot understand how you've been able to carry out this operation. It takes years to reach this level.' He was wary, as if expecting a hostile reaction. 'You've totally confused me.'

'I'm too tired to argue with you, Conrad. Leave it.'

We sat silently, finishing our drinks.

'Shall we go and eat?' Conrad asked.

I opened my mouth to say I was going out when I realised I didn't want to. He stood up and held out his hand. I looked at it, and put mine in it as I stood up. The warmth passed up my arm into my whole body. I was jolted to see his eyes full of longing. I was so confused. I thought I'd had managed to get over him, to squash it all away in one corner and throw a blanket over it. And walk away. Minutes ago, he'd said the same. No, he'd said that it wasn't any of his business. Did he still feel strongly about me, but was containing it? Was that why he'd been so hostile when I'd turned up as Pulcheria?

I'd forgiven him for his deception about Silvia and the children, but not how easily he believed I was a criminal or the harsh words about being tainted and poisonous. More than anything, I resented him not recognising I could make something of myself and succeed in a dangerous environment. It was too raw. I let my hand drop and the moment passed.

After dinner with Aurelia and Helena, I walked alone with him to the vestibule where he collected his jacket and sidearm.

'Look, Carina, I'll see you at Robbia's hearing, but I wondered if you'd go out for some dinner one evening, somewhere quiet where nobody knows us. No obligation, no game-playing, just friends.'

Of course I would go. Maybe we could be friends. Who was I kidding? I wanted him. I wanted to rip his clothes off, get him on the floor and have him.

I cleared my throat. 'Yes, that would be good. When did you have in mind?'

'This Friday? I could pick you up about seven thirty.'

He turned and went into the cold night, and I went to my cold bed.

64

The first day on the project when Jeffrey Renschman was six, the resident kids watched him move in with his mother. They came for him and left him battered inside and out, petrified, with bruises blooming but no broken skin or bones. He paid respect for a few months and learned to fight his way up the hierarchy. When Renschman left at seventeen, he was at the top of the pile.

When the sliding metal gate of Truscium slammed shut behind him, he knew he'd have to repeat the process. They'd given him twenty-five years. He gave himself six months.

Then he'd start payback. He'd bust these people's idea of escape-proof. He'd start hunting the judges, the petty criminals who'd betrayed him but, most of all, he'd find her and cut her up into slivers of twitching, bloody flesh.

65

I arranged to pick Sentius up next morning; his car had to go to the workshop. As we cruised along the peripheral at the max speed limit minus one, setting citizens a good example, a silver Mercedes flew past us, veered across and cut sharply in front, millimetres from my red paintwork. It picked up speed and raced off into the distance. We weren't traffic cops, but I was incensed. I looked at Sentius; he pulled out the blue light, activating the roof clamp and siren. I floored the accelerator. Tyres squealing, I spun the wheel hard to the left and pulled my Giulietta out into the outside lane. A dark SUV braked to get out of the way.

Rocketing around the long curve before the river crossing, we weaved between vehicles that didn't get out the way of the blue light. We were catching up fast. The curve straightened out and we barrelled toward the Pons Apulius. The huge cable-tied bridge rushed toward us as the speedometer showed 130 kph.

Once parallel with the Mercedes, I eased the Giulietta relentlessly to the right, the rotating blue beacon reinforcing the message the front wing of my car was conveying. If they didn't stop within the next thirty seconds, I would personally make sure they would be off the road for five years. The Mercedes slowed and pulled over to the kerb right in the centre of the bridge.

Sentius hopped out and ran back to place the flashing blue road light behind the Mercedes. He took up position on the nearside kerb, nightstick ready. I peeled myself out of the Giulietta, hand on my holster. I rapped on the driver's tinted glass window with the Furies behind me.

'Open this bloody window. Now.'

Flavius.

I stared at him. He didn't recognise me. Maybe it was the sunglasses covering my eyes. Maybe it was because I no longer whined as Pulcheria.

'Get out of the car,' I said.

'Of course, officer, no problem.' He smiled his bland smile.

I twisted him round. 'Hands on the car.' Of course, he was carrying. I cuffed him, unclipped the magazine, pocketed the weapon, and nodded to Sentius to take over. He took Flavius over to the kerbside. I knocked on the tinted back window. As it slid down silently, I peered into the darkness.

'If you don't have a good reason for this, Apollodorus, I am going to throw the entire *Lex Custodum* at you.'

A lovely ironic laugh came first. 'I apologise from the bottom of my heart, but I did want a little word with you.'

'Use the telephone.'

'So abrupt. Come and sit with me.'

I stared into those black eyes. 'No, you talk to me out here or not at all.'

Sentius narrowed his eyes, but didn't say anything as Apollodorus got out of the car and walked a few metres along the bridge sidewalk with me.

'Well?'

'That's no way to greet an old friend.'

'You nearly scratched my new car.'

'Dear me,' he murmured, 'you are a cross little scarab, aren't you?'

I knew he was winding me up by using scarab, the derogatory word for the *custodes*. I might deal with a lot of shit in my job, but I was no dung-beetle.

He looked down the river toward the wharves with their grey and brown warehouses, stacks of containers and cranes. I conceded to politeness and removed my sunglasses. But I kept my back to Flavius.

'My dear, I have a bone to pick with you. When we discussed the phoenix plan, we did *not* agree you would donate the club to me via some complex Helvetian financial scheme.'

'Oh?' I shrugged. 'Must have slipped my mind at the time. We were busy with other stuff.'

'Hm.'

'Lighten up, Apollo. It's yours. If it makes you happier, give me free drinks for life.'

His black eyes shone like obsidian.

'Very well, I accept your gift. But listen to me. If you ever need help, whether for something trivial or important, you know everything I have will be at your disposal.'

He lifted my hand and kissed the back. I glanced toward the cars, anxious that Sentius might have seen, but he was still harassing Flavius.

'That's a big offer. But I won't take it. I parachuted into your lives, we fought a common threat and we achieved it.'

He threw something over the parapet and studied its trajectory as it flew through the air down toward the water. Without looking up, he said, 'I've taken your advice and set up a series of business service companies. You're quite right: the profit margin is very attractive, even after taxes and contributions.'

I laughed.

'One more thing. I would appreciate your advice on something.' Twin creases formed on his forehead – unusual for Apollodorus. 'I am concerned about Flavius.'

I stared at him. A pulse of fear for Flavius beat through me. How in Hades had he crossed Apollo?

'Since you've gone, he seems restless. His role is not important now we've become legal. I'm not sure what to do with him. He has an excellent range of weapons and planning skills, and handles teams well. But I fear he is a little bored at his new desk. And bored is dangerous.' His eyes glinted in the sunshine.

'He's a wonderful asset, Apollo, a hundred per cent loyal. He would do anything for you.'

'Yes, but Philippus can take over the remaining parts of his job with ease.'

'Has he said anything about it?'

'No, I think he's trying very hard to adapt.' He paused. 'He's been with me since he was fifteen. I can't throw him out arbitrarily, but I think we're going to come to a crisis point soon.'

I watched Apollo walk back and get in the Mercedes. I signalled Sentius to let Flavius go and watched them drive away across the bridge.

Crap. Nothing was ever straightforward. But I couldn't let Flavius be in harm's way.

PART IV

RESOLUTION

66

I finished the corrupt senator case I'd been working on for the past few weeks and filed the reports. Lurio suggested I went for the investigator's exam to qualify for promotion. I downloaded some of the modules, checked out relevant books from the library, and filed private study time.

Back home, I changed into a plain tee, jeans and a light sweater, went down to the garages, slipped on my leathers and helmet, and set off on my bike. I cruised along the Aquae Caesaris road at an exhilarating 120 kph. About fifteen kilometres out of the city, I turned off into a village and drew into the parking lot by a small inn. The heavy wood panelling in the narrow entrance lobby sucked in what little light escaped from a dirty ceiling fixture. I paused, looking into the main room where warm, yellow-orange subdued lighting bounced off polished brass and old, dark wood furniture. A folksy smell of beer, oak and cooking permeated the place. I spotted an empty corner booth.

Before my brain could detect and react to its owner's presence, a cold, hard object jabbed into my neck, pressing on my skin. I stood perfectly still as his free hand searched me. Nobody saw, not because of the dim lighting, but because nobody was there. I took a slow, deep breath to calm my body's response to a gun threatening its termination. He lifted my weapon from the holster under my arm and nudged me forward, his knee pushing on the back of mine.

'In the corner. Slowly. No sudden moves.'

I sat, laying both my hands on the small square table. The lacquered surface was greasy with spots of congealed food. He eased down onto a seat at ninety degrees to me, and gestured the server who had at last appeared. We waited in silence until the beers arrived.

'You know, Flav, you're one of the very few who can sneak up on me like that, and live.'

He said nothing, took a good swallow and replaced the glass, centring it on the paper beer mat. 'Was that really you, that scarab on the bridge?'

'Yes.'

Flavius shrugged and looked around. 'It's quiet here, safe. I suppose it won't be now, once you file your contact report.' He sounded bitter. 'I trusted you. But here you are, a DJ *custos*. I suppose you're going to arrest me now.'

'Flav, listen to me. I am *not* going arrest you or file a contact report. I'm meeting a friend for a quiet drink in the country, a friend who works for a perfectly legal business.'

'Don't be bloody naive. If you don't, somebody will report you.'

'Oh, so you think I'm stupid enough to leave a trail?'

'No, I don't suppose you would.' He looked straight at me for the first time. 'That's what I mean. I find it hard to believe you're a scarab.'

'I do special cases. I don't direct traffic or book drunks in on a Saturday night.'

He gave a sour laugh. 'I'd love to see that.'

'Don't think too badly of me. I undertook the mission to help stop a foul thing happening. The problem was that I got to like Apollodorus's team as well as knowing them, especially you, Philippus and Hermina. I wasn't supposed to do that, but it happened.'

I could see the hurt and uncertainty in his eyes. I expected Apollodorus had coerced him into meeting me. Or maybe he was intrigued. Only low-level television sound from the other end of the bar and the barman mumbling into his cell phone interrupted the silence around us. Two men came in, ordered drinks and settled at a table to play cards. After a few minutes, Flavius's hand moved over the table surface, covering the shape of my service pistol as he passed it across. I reached out and our fingers touched as I slid the weapon under my hand. He glanced at my face, then retreated to his beer.

I remembered my promise to Apollodorus. I coughed to break the uncomfortable silence.

'I hear things are changing quite a bit at the Foundation. Have you ever considered going into a different line of work?' I sipped my beer, not looking at him.

'Did Apollodorus put you up to this?'

'Of course.'

Flavius rubbed his leg with the tips of his curved fingers. 'He's all I've known since I was fifteen, when he scraped me off the street. He taught me everything: how to spot a mark, follow them, pick their pocket, hustling, thinking out your strategy, how to intimidate without force.' He looked at my surprise. 'Oh, yeah, the force bit as well, but you get far better results from terror.'

That sounded like Apollodorus.

'And then, the odd times we had to fix things more permanently, I used to leave that to Philippus or Justus.' He looked blankly at the table.

'You know, that all sounds perfect training for the military, for the special forces even.'

'The PGSF? You're raving.' He sat back in his chair, his eyes wide open in shock.

I ducked it. 'Well, it was only a thought.'

He thawed and we managed to reinstate some of our previous closeness. At about eleven, I stood up to go. I saw mischief in his expression.

'Going back to what you said earlier,' he said, 'would you be interested in a bet? Hypothetical really, so no danger of having to pay up.'

'No way. I know what your and Philippus's crafty little tricks are like.'

'All right, a bargain.'

'What?'

'Just for a laugh: if one of us goes into the PGSF, the other one has to follow.'

That was as likely as me going back to the EUS, which I knew would never happen, so I agreed. I had drunk only two small beers the whole evening, so my judgement wasn't that impaired. We shook on it.

We all have our off days.

67

When you're a new believer in something, you're very enthusiastic. When, one day, a tiny doubt creeps in, you bat it away impatiently. But it sneaks back, quietly and inconspicuously. You start to not like the thing so much, you begin to find it a duty only. Then you groan and dread it. Finally, you hate it and will do anything to get out.

I wasn't at the dread or hate stage, but I'd started to find life as a DJ *custos* tedious. Conrad kept needling me about it, softly and cleverly, describing the vivid challenges he and his unit dealt with. I saw him at least once a fortnight now for dinner or a Sunday afternoon ride. I knew what he was doing. So, when Lurio came striding up to my desk and threw a PGSF circular down on it with a grunt, I didn't automatically throw it in the bin.

The PGSF was running its annual 'fitness for task' field exercise and extended an invitation to all arms to send up to three representatives who might benefit from participating. 'Benefit' – huh! Still arrogant. A six-week preparatory training period with the PGSF to cover military skills, strategy, field tactics, intelligence gathering and fighting skills was required. Applications to be made, etc, etc.

I stared at it and ran my fingers over my cheek. It would be wonderful. What an opportunity. My training gym was good for fitness, but I missed being out in the field. My most dangerous challenge at present was negotiating the copying machine.

No – I would hate it. All that beige arrogance. I put it on the far corner of my desk and went back to my desperately unattractive book on financial crime. Half a page later, I needed a coffee. When I returned to my desk, the circular was still there. I picked it up again and held it between my thumb and forefinger. Why did those bastards have all the fun? I took an early lunch, talked a while with colleagues, watched a newscast and found myself back in my office with only forty-five minutes gone by. In the end, I knocked on Lurio's door, circular in hand.

'Come.'

'Is this supposed to be of any interest to me, sir?'

He chuckled.

I glowered at him.

'You're bored, Bruna. Your reports are getting ironic, and references to obscure research keep popping up in them. It's too clever for the average scarab, you know.'

'I'm sorry if my submissions are not appropriate, sir,' I said in the most neutral tone possible.

'Sit down and stop being a smart-arse.'

'C'mon, Lurio, you know it's a trap.'

'Sure, but one you'd die of joy to fall into,' he said, smirking.

And he'd called *me* a smart-ass. I applied. Afterward, I tried to forget I'd done it.

I met Flavius in the town this time; we liked to vary locations. He kept looking around the bar, with its plastic mouldings and pseudo-seventies atmosphere, and wouldn't meet my eyes.

'Are you okay, Flav? You seem a bit jumpy. Something happen?'

'You're going to kill me.'

'Just say it, Flav.'

'Okay. Just don't go ballistic. I thought a lot about what you said a few weeks ago. I saw an ad on the net one day, and I clicked through and applied. I did an assessment week and some interviews, tests and so on.' He looked down and rubbed his fingertips round the base of his glass. 'I've been invited to go for a trial period of six months.'

He looked up. I saw his eyes shining and his cheeks flushed with enthusiasm – not the usual unflappable Flavius.

I grasped both his hands. 'You don't know how pleased I am for you.' He looked happier than he had for weeks. 'So what's the job?'

He swallowed, then put his shoulders back and looked at me, deadly calm.

'The PGSF.'

'Sorry?'

'The Praetorian Guard Spec—'

'Yes, yes, I do know what the initials stand for.'

I studied his face, searching for any signs of insanity.

'I didn't mean it as a serious suggestion,' I said, appalled at the idea. 'Do they know who you are?'

'Hermina's made me a new identity that's mostly true. She says it'll stand up to pretty nearly every scrutiny.' He glanced at me. 'I need a character witness and I wondered if you'd do it.'

He had the nerve of a PGSF guard.

My own little confession would be simple after this. 'Have you told Apollodorus?'

'Not yet. I think he'll be okay. Under that tough exterior, he cares for his people. I think he'll be glad I've found something I want to do.'

'You know you'll need to cut all connection to him and the Foundation,' I said. 'And face the possibility of confronting him from the other side of the law.'

He nodded. We sat in silence for a few minutes.

'I have some news for you,' I shot him a glance. 'To be honest, I was dreading telling you, but now I have a completely clear path.'

He waited, eyes narrowed and wary.

'I'll probably be seeing you professionally soon. I'm taking part in their annual assessment exercise in two months' time.'

'You?'

'Yes, well, let's not make a big production out of it.'

'Jupiter! And I was shitting bricks at the thought of telling you. You little demon, letting me sweat like that.'

68

I cleared the PGSF gate security and entered the sand-strewn courtyard. I looked around a little warily at the beige figures walking across, singly or in small groups. I could have been invisible. I released my breath. Clutching my posting order, I weaved my way through the crowd of people in the lobby. Every uniform was there, even air force and customs. At the reception counter, I waved to my two DJ colleagues but, before I could go over to them, somebody touched my arm.

'Senior Justiciar Bruna?'

I turned to find a beige-uniformed girl whose cheerful face contrasted with her severely bound brown hair. One curl over her ear had made its escape, though. She had bright, intelligent eyes and a friendly smile to go with them.

'I'm Sergeant Paula Servla. I'm here to show you around, get your kit and accommodation sorted out.'

'Thanks, but shouldn't I wait for my DJ colleagues?'

'Oh, they're fine. You're the senior non-com in this batch, so you'll be in the sergeants' mess with me.'

She showed me a room that was small but adequate, then took me to the quartermaster where I was given a pile of beige uniform.

'Um, Sergeant Servla, do I actually need all this? Won't I wear my own uniform?'

'No, it makes it easier all round if everybody looks the same. You keep your unit insignia and rank badges, of course. And please call me Paula.'

'Cara,' I said, extending my hand from under the pile of beige. I liked her already.

Roll-call took all of fourteen minutes, taken by the duty officer. We ate in the large dining hall I had walked through before, with some of Servla's colleagues.

'Looking forward to a bit of rough treatment, are you?'

My hand froze halfway to my mouth, strands of pasta falling off my fork.

'What do you mean?' I stared at the woman opposite me.

'It's a bit different from dishing out traffic tickets.'

I realised she was joshing the DJ, not threatening me personally. Juno, I had to stop being so sensitive. I'd volunteered to come here, so I had to get a grip.

'It gets a little tenser than that in my unit. I'm in Organised Crime.'

'Profitable, is it?'

They all laughed and I relaxed. A little.

Next morning, Paula knocked on my door and we went for twenty minutes' run. After my shower, I put the beige on. I looked in the mirror. My DJ insignia – the blue circular cloth one I fixed on my left sleeve, the rank stripes below and the silver metal lapel badges – were almost lost. I was determined not to follow.

The twenty-three of us 'imports' were welcomed after breakfast by a Major Julia Sella and given personal IDs and schedules. We had the rest of the morning to organise ourselves. Full training would start that afternoon.

While most of our group could fire pistols, only a few were used to rifles. I had the benefit of Uncle Brown's homespun tuition over the years. He'd been granted a gun licence like most farmers; he'd insisted we all learned to shoot and practise weekly. Girls should be able to blast any vermin, he'd said, especially on an isolated farm.

On the range, I hit the target with satisfactory clusters. I was surprised I could still dismantle, clean and reassemble the weapon without having any parts left over. I started forgiving my father's cousin. The senior centurion instructing us grunted that at least she could be sure I wouldn't shoot myself. My reward was to go out on tactics practice with the regulars the following day.

I was trying not to feel too out of my depth in a forest full of armed PGSF wanting to score points when I heard a familiar voice at my side.

'I knew you'd turn up soon, Bruna.'

'Flav. Am I pleased to see you.'

'Down!' He yanked me onto my face as paint shots whistled over our heads.

'Right, let's get that bastard.'

He signalled me to circle and we advanced in a pincer movement. This was fun. Thanks to Felix, one thing I'd learned at the boot camp was to move silently. I was there first while Flavius made a tiny distraction noise. Finding no backstop behind me, I jumped on the shooter, downing him in one, twisted his arm behind his back, kicked his weapon away then ground his face into the mud.

'Yes!' I clenched my fist and jerked my forearm down in the age-old soldier's gesture without realising I was doing it.

Flavius laughed. 'Okay, you bloodthirsty little demon, let the poor man breathe. It's only practice.'

'Oh, yes, sorry.' I rocked back onto my heels and let our opponent recover. When I saw who it was, I nearly fainted.

'Thank you, Flavius,' he said, as he sat up. 'Who's your little friend?'

'Sorry about that, sir, she's a bit enthusiastic. May I present Senior Justiciar Bruna?'

'Oh, is that who—'

We all three flattened ourselves to escape another shot which passed over our bowed heads.

'I like enthusiasm, Bruna, but save it for the exercise,' he said.

'Sir.'

'If you want to learn more technique rather than rampant aggression, I'm giving a talk tonight after dinner. Flavius will bring you along.'

I stared at him and nodded, unable to say another word.

He turned, picked up his weapon and loped off into the undergrowth. I released my breath, relieved he hadn't recognised me. For that was when I met Lieutenant Daniel Stern for the third time.

69

Hard training followed for the next six weeks. We had one weekend pass, but most stayed on base, catching up on sleep. I was never so stretched, or so fit. I saw Conrad twice; once when he gave a lecture and the other time in the mess room, eating with the other senior officers. He'd cast around as if searching, stopped at my face, smiled and turned back to carry on talking with his colleagues.

Jogging around early Monday morning with Paula in week six, I noticed a few things out of place: trucks had moved, the stores cargo bay doors were slightly ajar and I glimpsed the assistant quartermaster. Now that was spooky; he was never up early. At half eleven, the alarm sounded. We had thirty minutes to get back to the parade ground with our kit, ready to move.

In the middle of the night, deep forest can be lonely. Knowing four hundred trained elite soldiers with live ammunition were out there competing with you could have made it pretty unnerving. But my team, Victis, were calm and self-confident; the training had clicked in.

I was grateful to find myself with both Flavius and Paula. A coincidence? I knew two of the others slightly: Livius, a joker, but very fit, and Atria, who could talk the fish out the water as she'd demonstrated in her lecture last week. We had to find and retrieve a series of coloured markers – traditional simulation for live targets, I learned. Each one was part of a pattern pointing to the end objective. The more markers you found, the easier and quicker you would achieve your objective and finish. Unfortunately, we were in competition with every other team, and the admin staff warned they would be throwing in 'surprises'. Fabulous.

'Okay, listen in,' Paula whispered. We hunkered down around her in a circle, sheltering in the lee of a rise in the ground. 'Bruna and Livius, you go and do a close recce around this area.' She pointed to a spot on the map. 'We'll backstop you in a square.'

'Come on, Miss Blue Dude,' Livius said, winking at me as we set off, 'try and keep up.'

'Hah!'

We found a good observation point behind the crest and waited, stretched out, for ten minutes and scanned the woodland in front of us. No sound but our breathing.

'Far too quiet,' I whispered in his ear. 'No wildlife.'

He nodded. We crawled along the crest of the rise until it tapered off into the ground. I swept the area with my hand sensor and detected a perimeter wire half a metre in front of us. A tiny noise cracked to our left. I was ahead of Livius; I signalled him to go behind while I advanced, crouching and wary. Then I saw her, standing by a large tree. Not very tactical. Too easy. Then she half-turned. Oh, crap! Major Sella. Was this one of the 'surprises'?

'Locked on to unfriendly,' I whispered into my mic. 'But no attempt at cover by subject.' I glanced through my helmet sensor. 'And no detection field up.'

'Confirmed another here. Same status. Locked on,' said Livius.

Were they so confident their wire would be sufficient?

'Good to go.' Paula's distant voice in my ear.

'On my mark,' I said. 'One, two, three. Mark.'

I brought her down in one movement. She was winded by the impact. I kicked her weapon away, rolled her onto her front and tied her hands behind her with a cable tie. I crouched, braced for attack from a backstop. I circled in a three-sixty check. Nobody. Silence.

I pulled Sella behind the tree, her face down. I extracted my carbon fibre knife from my jacket and angled it against her neck just to the side of the external jugular. I pressed lightly on her skin. 'Where's the marker?'

She said nothing.

I bent down so my mouth was millimetres from her ear and said in my softest tone, 'I don't have time for pretty please, major. After thirty seconds, I'm going to get annoyed. You don't want me annoyed, I assure you.'

No answer. I jerked down harder with my knee.

'Come on, major, or you'll have a scar on your neck for life.' I encouraged her by nicking her skin. She gasped at the sharp bite of the knife.

'Root of the tree. Behind you.'

Livius appeared at that moment with his prize, another training staff.

I retrieved the marker and tied green labels on their wrist bindings to signal they were neutralised and out of the exercise. The dribble of blood on Sella's neck had turned dull and started to clot.

Tabbing back to the rendezvous point, Livius shot me a look.

'You don't think that was a bit overdone? I mean, sticking a knife into the training major's neck is not a good career move.'

'No prob, Livius. I'm not planning on making my career here.'

His eyes widened.

'Hey,' I said, 'do we want to win or not?'

He grinned, stopped and faced me. He gripped my forearm with his and said, 'Didn't know you had it in you.'

We were only on day one of three. We crouched around, planning our next move.

'That was far too easy,' Paula said. 'Presumably meant to dull our guard.'

The others grunted in agreement.

I jabbed at the map. 'It's only a theory and I don't know the training area well,' I began, 'but here, here and here would be obvious places to drop markers, so we could sweep the sector to see if we could catch another team. The problem is they'll be double-wary.' I looked at the others. 'Or we could do the unexpected and travel into another sector; then go hunting there. In either case, we could "liberate" the other sector teams' markers.'

Three faces stared at me.

'What? Hasn't anybody ever done that?'

'Of course, but I didn't expect it from a scarab,' drawled Atria.

'Shows how spectacularly ignorant you are, then.'

Despite the warm day, the temperature chilled.

Atria said nothing, but tried to stare me down.

Flavius coughed and laid his hand on my arm. I shook it off, my eyes still locked on Atria's.

'Enough, Atria, Bruna,' snapped Paula. 'Move.'

We broke camp and travelled a little under twelve kilometres west. It was exhausting work, remaining tactical over such a distance, and we gave ourselves three hours' rest. Thanks to Felix, I could fall asleep within two breaths. I woke just over two hours later. Instantly. Somebody was in the trees nearby. Not one of our team. Flavius was crouched beside me, awake, watching as sentry. I signalled with my fingers and jerked my head to the south-west. He raised an eyebrow, nodded and set off south. I went westwards. After three minutes moving silently, I spotted two figures in a small clearing: Lieutenant Stern and a woman I recognised, but didn't know her name, were standing five metres away consulting an electronic map pad. He shifted his weight from one foot to the other and made small jabbing movements with his hands as if agitated. He kept glancing at his watch. Strange. They were quiet but not covert. Was this some kind of decoy move?

I shouldered my rifle and took out my knife. I spotted Flavius across the clearing and signalled him to wait one minute. To my surprise, Stern spoke into his commset. We were supposed to be on total radio silence. He looked around as if hoping to see something.

I gestured Flavius to approach obliquely. I burst from the undergrowth and felled Stern, my knee in his back. I knew I had to be quick; he was a very effective field operative and strong. I had him tagged within five seconds. Flavius had secured his companion and trained his rifle on both. I gathered up their weapons. Sure, it was an exercise but, with live fire, I didn't want any casualties.

'What the fuck are you playing at?' Lieutenant Stern's voice echoed unnaturally loudly around the trees. He rolled over and sat up, eyes blazing.

'You came into our defence area,' I hissed. 'What did you expect? And keep your voice down. Sir.'

'Gods, it had to be you, Bruna, didn't it?'

He sounded really pissed at me.

'Gather your team up. You're going back to base.'

Flavius and I exchanged glances.

'Why?'

'Because I'm giving you an order.'

'With respect, sir,' Flavius said, 'how do we know it's not some trick part of the exercise?'

'Reasonable point. Codeword Honoria. Convinced?'

Flavius looked puzzled and glanced at me. I didn't know either. I was on the point of arguing when I saw the others approaching.

'It's okay, Bruna. Stand down,' Paula said as she jogged toward us. 'It's a codeword to finish simulations stat.' She bent down and released Stern. 'What's the problem, sir?'

'Yours is the first team I've found, Sergeant, though Mars knows what you're doing in this sector. I need one more. Any idea where the next one is?'

'About two kilometres south of here,' she said. 'We were going to ambush them tomorrow early.'

He gave her a sour look then tapped into his el-pad. 'Transport will be here in fifteen minutes. Stay here and wait for it.' He and his companion took off in a southerly direction.

The six of us recovered our kit and squatted in the shelter of the trees at the clearing edge.

'What in Hades is going on, Paula?'

'Not a clue, but we're no longer on exercise.'

70

The exercise base camp was swarming with activity: equipment piling up ready for transport, tents coming down, kit being thrown into vehicles. The adjutant was standing in front of the main tent, el-pad in hand, throwing out orders, his assistant relaying them over the comms net. Lieutenant Stern was standing beside the adjutant and furiously entering data into his el-pad. He still looked miffed, but was now distracted.

The adjutant looked up at the sound of our vehicle approaching and summoned us with an impatient wave as we pulled up.

'Out, you lot. Grab a quick bite and back here in five. Go.'

Paula took one look at his face and herded us toward the open-air mess, now consisting of a harassed cook, a field burner and a single trestle table. The cook sloshed milk-free coffee into mugs and thrust a bacon sandwich at each of us.

Ten minutes after reporting back to the adjutant, we were bumping along in the back of a truck, heading for the local air base to be inserted into a support operation in the north. The base staff calmly handed us hot drinks, open country fatigues, fur-lined fatigue jackets, Kevlar helmets and cold rations, plus survival kit. We had twelve minutes to wait before the flight.

'Didn't reckon on this, did you, Bruna?' Livius said and thrust another mug of steaming chocolate drink at me. 'Here, get as much warm inside you as possible.'

'But why are *we* going? There must be a reserve when the unit's on exercise?'

'Yes, but we're nearer. The other tactical units are still out on the exercise ground and out of radio comms. So lucky us was the only choice.' He grinned at me, his eyes brimming with some kind of muted excitement. 'The DJ are pinned down by some maniacs and need back-up now. We can be there in under thirty minutes and inserted within another five.'

I sipped my chocolate and chewed the hard energy biscuit.

'Bruna, Livius, over here.' Lieutenant Stern beckoned us over to where the four others were waiting. He gave me a fierce look, but said, 'I'm not going to eat you, Bruna, though how a scarab took me I'll never know.' Flavius trod on my foot before I could retort.

Lieutenant Stern called the six from the other team to gather round. 'Right, the silver mine up at Truscium had a security alert and called in the local scarabs.' He looked at me. 'The *custodes*, I mean. They only have about a dozen there as the electronic security is normally iron-cast. But somehow a group of prisoners have organised themselves, broken out of the barracks and taken over the admin building. We don't know what's happened to the staff or the administrator. As of two hours ago, we understand six of the *custodes* are dead, two others injured. Their emergency centre lost comms with them twenty minutes ago.'

Silence fell. All I heard was other people's breathing and background noises. An air force clerk appeared and distributed maps and satellite photos.

'Our task is to hold the area and stop a breakout spreading until they get enough regular reinforcements up there to take it back. We need to secure and hold these points here, here and here.' He jabbed at the large-scale map he had pinned on a cargo crate. 'Then we control the site entrance and the admin centre.'

He wiped his finger across the brow of his nose. 'I must emphasise this is a containment operation, not a take-back. But timing is crucial. If they've managed to disable the internal electronic security systems at Truscium, then getting through the external barriers may not be difficult for them.'

'Livius, you lead the marksmen, three teams of two. These four, you and Bruna.' I stopped drinking and stared at him. He glared back. 'Your record says you can shoot. Problem?'

I shook my head.

I sat opposite Paula in the helicopter as it pounded its way into the mountains, fighting the early morning light. I clutched my new rifle and scope. I'd had five minutes to sight it as best I could with the help of an armoury sergeant from the air force base. If I hit anything, it would be a miracle. But none of the others was in any different place.

The cold blast hit us as we tumbled out of the helicopter. It was mild October on the plain, but up here it was Arctic winter. The rest of me was warm, but the wind stung and picked at my face. I followed Livius as we scuttled then crawled on our stomachs up to our designated point on the crest of the ridge. I lost sight of the others as they dispersed to their positions. We were no longer playing.

Livius unpacked a small bivouac, more like a large sleeping bag for two, and we eased inside it, pulling the sides together with a drawstring. He stuck bracing wires into a small flap and pulled it over our heads, giving us maximum camouflage as well as protection against the wind, but leaving our sightlines clear. 'No point freezing our butts off,' he said.

'Take a really slow sweep across an arc in front of the admin centre door. Get to know every mark on it, the handles, the rim, every detail. Don't worry, the sight glass is honeycombed. It won't reflect.'

I followed his instructions, my arms forming a triangular frame with my elbows on a support mat. I heard him muttering into his commset. I gasped as I saw a figure in bright yellow prison clothing run across the courtyard behind the admin building to the side perimeter. A crack came several hundred metres from my right and the figure fell.

After thirty seconds, the figure rolled over on its side toward the admin building. Hands reached out of the door and dragged it in.

The wind whined around us, rattling our shelter as we waited. The sun began its slow drag upwards, giving us a little warmth, but the light it projected was horizontal. I needed to squint to see anything. More movements below. I nudged Livius. He muttered into his radio.

'Stand by,' he whispered. 'I think we have some business.'

A swarm of yellow burst out of the admin centre and flowed to the entrance. I took aim for the top of the door and fired. It shut abruptly. I fired again, hitting the crossbar at the top of the main gate. I heard other shots crack out. The swarm disintegrated, figures throwing themselves on the ground, inching their way to the wall and cowering behind it.

I breathed out. Silence. Minutes later, a burst of shouting down by the entrance. Then it subsided. I peered through my sight, relating everything that I saw to Livius. When nothing had happened for ten minutes, we relaxed a notch.

'Well done, Bruna.' I heard a faint pop of an instadrink packet. 'Here, drink this.'

Malt and ginger, but synthetic. Who cared? I took a long swig then handed it back. I lay my head down and closed my eyes to rest for a few moments. I was so tired from the exercise but adrenalin had kept me going. An urgent hand on my shoulder dragged me back.

'Wake up, sleeping beauty, more happening.'

'Juno, I'm so sorry. I didn't mean to fall sleep on you.'

'I let you have a full ten minutes. I think I'd have been out myself if I hadn't woken you.' He grinned at me. How could he do that on the side of a freezing mountain in the middle of a live operation? 'Flex the muscles in your arms and legs. They've probably got stiff.'

He pointed at the armoured wire perimeter, hardly moving the tip of his finger. 'Somebody's crawling around the gate. I think we should discourage them. Want to try?'

I aimed, squeezed and missed the top bar, but hit the middle panel of the gate.

'Again.'

I hit the crossbar this time. He muttered into his radio and more fire poured on to the gate. A figure crawled away, pulling himself along on his elbows. I had a perfect view of his face. I didn't move my rifle. I blinked to clear my eye. There was no mistake. Brown wavy hair, utility glasses instead of frameless. It was him. I checked my aim again, breathed out partway and squeezed the trigger. The yellow figure collapsed on the spot. I released the other half of my breath and dropped my head onto the cold ground for a few seconds. What had I done?

71

Shots rattling down from the compound toward the two gullies below the entrance made me jerk my head back up. I glued my eye to the sight rim. We knew from the DJ recordings that the prisoners had penetrated the secure access into the armoury. We saw Paula's group return fire from several positions. They clung on to the mountain face like tough alpine plants, fighting with minimal protection and bad sightlines as hopelorn criminals tried to kill them.

Both Livius and I gave covering fire to take the pressure off them. We might have been cold and exposed up here but Paula and the other team risked far more from this direct fire. A deafening crack. A fountain of gravel exploded to our left. We threw ourselves flat, clamping the hard rock.

'Move time.'

We slithered down the back slope, gathered up our kit, crawled a hundred metres east and set up again. Lungs heaving from exerting ourselves in the cold air at the high altitude, we rested for a few minutes to steady our bodies before settling down to scan again. Livius fired off another round in front of a yellow figure approaching the main gate. I was watching through my sight and opened my mouth to whisper the result when I heard a dull thud, followed by a stifled cry.

'Fuck.' Livius was clasping his upper left arm, face contorted in pain. 'Bastard's shot me.' I dragged him back behind the crest and scavenged in his pocket for a field dressing. His eyes followed my hands as I unzipped his coat and applied the pressure pad. He winced as I pulled the bandage tight, but encouraged me with a ghostly smile. I found his drug pack and gave him a shot to ease the pain. I laid his arm across his chest and listened to the string of whispered curses.

His commset buzzed. I reached over, grabbed it and fixed it on my ear.

'One friendly casualty, upper arm. Stabilised, but need medivac as soon as possible,' I said.

I had no idea how long we were going to be there.

Organising the shooters via radio was no different from organising any other team. You needed two things: to be able to count and to stay cool. As the medics dragged him away on a sledge, Livius had pushed his digital code card into my hand with all the station IDs and freqs. The four other snipers seemed happy to take orders from me. I supposed technically I *was* the senior rank left. I had them fire in a random pattern and move every fifteen to twenty minutes.

We were dotted around the ridges of these remote mountains for nearly two hours, picking and worrying and herding the yellow-clad figures at the admin centre. As I glanced at my watch to check for the next move interval, I heard a hum begin behind us. It grew relentlessly. Screwing my eyes up in the pale but piercing sunlight, I saw what looked like a swarm of hornets. Below us, trucks were winding up the valley. I closed my eyes in relief. It was the 5th Cavalry.

Back at the airbase, my fingers were welded to a cup of hot malt and ginger. Every muscle in my body was exhausted. The buzz of mutual congratulation encircled me, but my numbness came from the feeling that I had murdered a man. Deliberately, without compunction. Sure, the official reason would be operational casualty. But when I'd seen Renschman through my telescopic sight, I'd shot to kill him. I shut my eyes to try blot it out. I couldn't process it.

'Bruna.' Livius, arm in a sling but still grinning, interrupted my wild thoughts. I was surprised to see him. He hugged what would have been my waist under the thick parka with his right arm. 'You star. Where did you learn to shoot like that? You're on my marksman programme from now.'

I looked at him in complete bewilderment as Paula handed him a cup of steaming liquid.

'You're going to stay, aren't you?'

His slim fingers grasped the base of the plascard mug he tipped toward me to emphasise his point. His light blue eyes travelled up and down, assessing me.

'I don't know. I may have upset a few people.' I glanced at Daniel Stern, busy talking into his commset. 'Depends if they want me.' I shrugged, trying to appear uncaring one way or another.

'They'd be stupid to let you go, and they're not stupid, so I reckon it's a done deal,' Paula chipped in. 'I'd hate to lose you as a comrade-in-arms.' She gave me a knowing look.

I stared into my cup, now empty. They were tough, no doubt of that, and dedicated, which meant their response to threats was robust. I could see that now. But their confidence wasn't arrogance; it was skill enhanced by continuous hard training. I saw in a sudden, clear moment how precious their comradeship was and what motivated Conrad; why it was so important to him.

The engine noise of a short wheelbase arriving echoed around the hangar. It braked abruptly and the noise cut. A tall figure jumped out. Conrad. Lieutenant Stern trotted over and talked with him for a few minutes before they both came over to us, now formed up in two ranks.

'Ladies and gentlemen, stand easy.' Conrad looked over us and paused briefly on each of our faces. 'First of all, congratulations on an excellent job. The whole mine area, including the prison barracks and the administration centre, has now been secured. The administrator is alive although injured from rough treatment. Two other staff are dead. Inevitably, an internal enquiry will follow.' Some shuffling of feet. 'Thankfully, we are not involved. Transport will be here shortly to take you back to barracks and a well-deserved rest. Again, well done. Dismissed.'

They crowded around him, Flavius producing a coffee for him, Atria evidently on good terms with him, laughing and joking, sending him flashes with her eyes. So that's how it was. But Conrad was interested in everything. Impressed by the new lightweight precision rifles, he listened intently to stories about individual actions. He wasn't only their commander, he was their comrade. I hung back. I didn't have this shared history.

Flavius came over and bent his head down toward me. 'Come on, Bruna. I'm sure he'll want to thank you.'

I shook his hand off. 'No, really. I'm fine here.'

I knew I was a hanger-on, outside the circle again, like it had been with the Browns in Nebraska.

'Tough,' he said, and gripped my arm in a merciless hold.

Livius turned from Conrad and spotted Flavius forcing me forward.

'Here she is, sir, my partner-in-crime. I want her in my marksman programme once she's been transferred over.'

Conrad's eyes widened. 'I'm not sure Senior Justiciar Bruna is as enthusiastic about joining us as you are, Livius.' He turned to me. 'What do you have to say, Bruna?'

Crap squared. Conrad, the hint of a smirk on his face, Livius and Flaviuslooking eager. I was trapped. What in Hades could I say?

'It's something I'll have to give some thought to.'

Livius rolled his eyes. 'Don't be such a wussy. You're a natural. What's the problem?'

'Back off, Livius,' came Paula's voice. 'Maybe Bruna has a few brains she'd like to consult first. Not something you'd know about.'

He made a face at her, shrugged, gave me a puzzled look and went to talk to Atria. I saw him minutes later, weary, conceding to sit at last. The transport arrived shortly afterward. I was bone tired. I wanted to crash out in the back.

As I queued to climb in, Conrad tapped me on the shoulder. 'Ride with me.'

As we drove back, he kept his face forward and concentrated his eyes on the unlit road. We soon left the heavier truck behind, the glare from their headlights and the noise of the diesel motor diminishing with every minute. He told me in an even voice that he'd been monitoring and grading at the far end of the exercise area, tens of kilometres away. He'd radioed Lucius to send up the first two teams he could find, jumped in the short wheelbase and barrelled through the exercise area and onto the airbase road.

On a long, straight piece of the road, he looked across at me. I braced myself for the usual over-protective speech.

'Thank you for going with them. You didn't have to, you know.'

'That wasn't the impression I had from Lieutenant Stern.'

'Mm, yes, he's a bit over-keen.'

'So I remember.' A minute later, I said, 'You know, he doesn't have a clue about me being Pulcheria.'

'Let's keep it that way.' His voice was hard.

We made good time and were approaching the city.

'You have to make a decision now. Either I turn right and take you home or you come back with me to the PGSF. I need to know by the time we get to the peripheral. I hope you'll say yes.' He glanced at me. 'You'd be a tremendous asset.'

I caught my breath. Juno, he was serious.

I watched, fascinated, as he slipped into official mode, his face calm, but the underlying passion seeping through in his voice. He talked about how PGSF collected intelligence, carried out counter-intelligence and unconventional operations but, above all, they protected the imperatrix and the state.

'We do what's needed.'

'Okay.'

'So you understand?'

We reached the peripheral. 'You need to take a left here,' I said.

72

I slept for a whole day. I was coming out of the waking fog when my commset peeped. Paula. She would collect me in thirty minutes for supper; then the debrief meeting. I did it in twenty-seven. A clean PGSF uniform pack had been left in my room: beige outers, black tee. I had nothing else to wear until I recovered my exercise bag from the transport room. I attached my DJ badges saved from yesterday's muddy and grubby uniform wrecks; I had no others.

I had a few nods of recognition in the mess room, but most people were absorbed in their food after days on field rations. I was nearly finished when Lieutenant Stern materialised at our table.

'Come with me, please, SJ Bruna.'

I exchanged a puzzled glance with Paula, scrambled up and followed him along the main corridor to Conrad's office. The regulation cream was broken up with three rows of bookshelves, prints and maps, and a display cupboard. Not things I'd taken in on my previous visit. But right now it was full of serious faces.

Lucius, the adjutant and Major Sella were sitting at the table with Conrad, a file in front of each. Conrad nodded. 'Thanks, Daniel. Go and get yourself some food.'

As the younger man shut the door, Conrad indicated a fourth chair. 'Sit down, Carina.'

He'd used my real name. I shot a look at the other two. Not a trace of surprise.

'First, practical details,' said Lucius, all businesslike. 'These are voluntary transfer papers. If you're sure, sign and date them. As Cara Bruna, please.'

I signed.

'Now, the more delicate part.' He glanced at Conrad, who nodded. 'If you're going to make your career in the PGSF, you need to revert to your real name. There's no reason now for keeping your pseudonym, and it makes a clean break between the two service histories.'

My hand rested on the table. Almost detached, I watched my fingers play with the pen. He was right. Karen Brown, Pulcheria, Cara Bruna – assumed identities, the first unconscious, the others deliberate, but all false. I was done with not being myself.

'Will I transfer in on a similar level?' It would be good to be with Paula.

'No,' said Conrad.

I should have expected I'd have to start at the bottom, but I was disappointed.

'You were outstanding during the exercise. But it was your willingness to take part in the live operation when you didn't need to, and the quick way you took over when the team leader was wounded, that decided us to commission you. We all think you'll be ideal for a senior leadership role in the future, so you need to get on that path straightaway.'

Juno. They were going to make me an officer.

Major Sella smiled at me. My eyes were drawn to the sticky bandage on her neck. I wouldn't have smiled at me if I'd been her.

'I'll run through your training schedule with you tomorrow,' she said. 'Stick with me for the rest of this evening.'

Conrad finished by saying, 'There may be some social awkwardness but, with your ability and track record, you'll get through it.'

I blinked. Again, no trace of anxious protection.

Surprisingly, Daniel Stern was the first one to congratulate me when the remaining officers filed in for the pre-meeting. Conrad said later that the others had hung back because of my social rank, but I didn't buy that. Unfortunately, he was right. But Daniel didn't realise or care about such things. He looked at me and shrugged. 'You've earned it. As a fellow newbie, I think we should stick together. Pax?'

Who'd have thought?

We both laughed. Mine was mostly nervous, hoping he would never connect me to Pulcheria. If he ever did…

I fingered the gold eagle ID badge hanging from my shirt pocket.

'It'll take a bit of getting used to.'

'You won't need this any longer,' said Daniel, and ripped the blue Velcro DJ badge off my sleeve. Lucius handed him a black-backed PGSF gold eagle badge to fix in its place. I rubbed my sleeve to firm it on. My latest Rubicon crossing.

I figured I survived the evening on the strength of the success of the live operation. Murmurs rose from the audience of nearly four hundred at the mop-up meeting, but it was in the bar afterward I had more direct reaction. Some tight smiles, nods, but a certain distancing.

'Any more shock revelations, Lieutenant?'

Livius.

'Not this week. No guarantee for next, though.'

He looked away.

'I have to say it's unexpected,' I said, hoping to reach him. 'I've been undercover so long, I don't know who I am sometimes.'

'I know what you can do, ma'am. Not sure it'll be the same now.'

I laid my hand on his good arm. 'I'm still Bruna. I've changed who I am, but not what I am.'

'Of course, ma'am.' His tone was so deferential it was almost an insult. Not you, Livius. Please.

'For Juno's sake, Livius, stop being such a poet,' Paula said, coming up behind him. 'She's still Bruna. The old man will let her be in your hunting pack. Sorry, ma'am, I mean the major.'

'Paula, never, ever change how you say things like that. And thank you.'

Flavius didn't say much at the time, but later told me he was so used to me changing who I was I would probably turn out to be the EUS president next.

On the fourth evening into my new life, I was in my room, puzzling over some strategy exercises I had to prepare for the next afternoon, when my door alarm beeped. Hades, my muscles were aching from the tactical practice that afternoon and I was only halfway through my assignment. All I wanted to do was finish and go to bed. I closed the file, snapped the laptop lid down and stomped to the door. This had better be important.

'Carina. May I come in?'

Conrad.

I caught my breath, but ushered him in, gesturing him to sit in the one easy chair. I'd gone jogging with his group the previous two mornings, but hadn't seen him alone since we'd driven back from the air base after the operation. I couldn't recall anything he'd said that night as I'd plodded across from the garages to the mess half-dead with tiredness. I remembered him supporting my arm as I stumbled up the stairs to my room.

Now, he shifted in his seat several times, hands clenching each other. He looked around my small room, but there was nothing to see beyond the standard furniture and cream walls. I hadn't had time or even thought to personalise it.

'I was a fool about you,' he said at last. 'I got it completely wrong after the Pulcheria operation. More than that, I lost any chance of you.' His voice was low, gruff almost. 'I don't expect you to take me back.' He looked away and I saw the deep lines of strain as the skin pulled over his cheekbones. When he turned back to me, I sensed he'd withdrawn into himself, back into his public persona.

'I hope we can stay friends as well as colleagues.'

Staggering how stupid men could be, but he was in such misery I took pity on him. I walked over to him, put my arms around his neck and kissed him. 'Stay.'

I woke first, sometime between five or six. I huddled into the warm arms around me.

'I am never, ever going to let you go again,' he said into my ear, and gently nuzzled it.

'Fine by me,' I murmured in an attempt to sound offhand.

He laughed and I giggled back. We missed the morning run.

73

I attended the Land Forces Officers' Training School, which was not without incident, but I graduated. The head of the school told me I was like almost all PGSF students: too maverick to aspire to the top of the class, however disappointed my unit commander might be.

The said unit commander did not impress the hierarchy when he arrived at the school on the back of a powerful and noisy Moto Guzzi the Friday afternoon of our one weekend leave. He sauntered into the reception area, his figure covered in leather from neck to foot and dark glasses over his eyes. Taking them off, he gave the assembled students one of his nuclear smiles and caused general havoc. I appeared, similarly clad, signed myself out, and gave him a beaming smile. We exited, his hand on my rear, obviously intent on mischief. The collective intake of breath was audible. We thought it was funny, though.

Back at the unit afterward, the ongoing training was arduous and I had little time to myself. Not only did I have responsibility for my thirty regular troops, but also for the formation of my own Active Response Team. An echo from the ancient times, this was a cross-disciplinary group, almost like a small personal staff, that each officer developed around them and took first into any emergency.

But in all this busyness, I had a frightening problem that was getting worse. I had pushed it away over Saturnalia. Last year, I was recovering from Renschman's attempt to freeze me to death. This year had been entirely different: I was too tired from partying to do anything but fall into exhausted sleep, most nights with Conrad in my bed.

This January morning, I woke alone, haunted by the recurring vision of a rifle scope framing a yellow-clad figure with brown hair and glasses as he fell to the ground. So far, I'd been able to push it away as my mind concentrated on the day's tasks. Now it started invading my head during the daytime. Images I hadn't seen for real, of blood welling out of holes in his yellow prison uniform. I couldn't stand it any longer. Like most people, I used the word 'Furies' casually, but didn't believe they existed. Until now.

I came back from close-quarter battle training in the small woods behind the barracks, Renschman's image filling my head. I tried all my visualisation and mind-body techniques to bat it away, but without success. I had to settle this nightmare. I shied away from the idea of a shrink. Maybe if I saw the death record, I could find closure.

I started an intranet search, via the DJ site, but my old access had been cancelled. My clearance hadn't been that high but I figured I could have reached the prisons' database.

I emailed Sentius to meet for a drink but he was away on leave. Nothing on this earth would force me to ask Lurio.

I put in for a day's leave, made up a persona as a university researcher, and took the high-speed train up to the district government office covering Truscium. In the curia files, they would have local death records, including the prison. But the bland-faced clerk told me access was restricted, and I would have to apply to the mine administrator. I stood in the public hallway and dithered. It was gone two. It would be dark in two and a half hours. Did I have time?

At the station, I hired a car and drove up to the front gate of the mine where I flashed my PGSF badge. I glanced up. An icy shaft of wind plunged down the neck of my jacket. Two gouges made by my rounds in the top of the main gate frame hadn't been repaired. The guards bent and crouched over my car, scanning every centimetre. I had to hand over my keys and walk in.

I shivered as the massive steel door slid shut behind me. The grey sky reflected the gravel courtyard and granite buildings. Truscium was beyond grim: a place of efficiency, order and despair. Only the most hardened and dangerous criminals were sent here. As a deterrent word, Truscium was legendary. No one had ever escaped. I believed it.

After I walked through the tunnel scanner and the security guards had frisked me again and handed me an optical badge, I was admitted into the administrator's office. His very polite assistant regretted he couldn't release the information without a signed authorisation. I ground my teeth. Nor would he take me on a tour around. Security, he said.

I signed out, returned the car to the rental depot and fumed on the train back. Was Renschman dead? Yes or no? Simple question, I thought. Apparently not.

Not unexpectedly, I was summoned to Lucius's office next morning. He left me standing and took his time finishing whatever it was he was writing. His office was traditional: eagle and flags in the corner, unit photos, plain dark wood meeting table and chairs, placed with military precision. The winter light reflected off his display cabinet containing awards and plaques, and some childish pottery pieces and a tiny ivory finger ring.

'Would you care to explain what exactly you were doing visiting the Truscium mine yesterday?'

'I wanted to look around to see it on the ground. Sir.'

'Don't bullshit me!' he growled. 'You wanted some personal information about prisoners.'

I said nothing.

'One of your ex-friends in there?'

I glared at him.

'A friendly warning. Stick to your job. No more maverick trips. Understood?'

'Sir.'

'Now get out, and go and do something useful.'

Still smarting, I went for a session in the gym. I found Flavius there and persuaded him to do a turn in the arena.

'Not if you're in a bad temper.'

'I'm perfectly under control, thank you.'

He was cautious as we circled and only made a few exploratory jabs for the first few minutes. Training with the sharp, double-edged, fifty-centimetre carbon steel blade concentrated the mind as well as honing reaction skills. In a formal session, if you were cut, you were cut; then chewed out for being careless. At this precise moment, I needed to release and ground my tension. I was the trickier fighter, but Flavius more strategic. After fifteen minutes, I was lying on the ground with a nicked arm and calf. And still jumbled nerves.

'What happened to you?' Conrad touched my skin just below the sticky bandage on my arm. We had gone out to the Onyx, a discreet restaurant with a fabulous Greek menu.

'Being careless.'

'Hmm. Any special reason?'

'I was embarrassed.'

He smiled and looked down.

'Okay, I was in a temper. I was trying to find out something really simple and getting frustrated for no good reason. Then Lucius clambered onto my case. So I made an idiot of myself practising against Flavius. Satisfied?'

He took my hand and rubbed the skin on the back of my fingers gently. It soothed me. 'Why do you want to know about the deaths during the breakout?'

'Some unfinished business.'

His fingers grasped my hand more firmly. 'Which would be?'

I looked over at the silk swathed between the onyx columns that gave the place its name and tried to pull my hand away. He didn't move but my hand stayed trapped. I brought my gaze back.

'I have to know whether I murdered Renschman.'

74

Conrad gave me a signed authorisation and a day's special leave. The administrator's assistant greeted me as smoothly as before and laid the files out on the table in a small, cold side room.. I examined every detail of the records, flicking back and forth until I knew them by heart. Even the guard watching me study the pages looked bored. At the end of an hour, I had nothing. Conrad's order entitled me to a visit. Followed closely by a guard as if I was an inmate myself, I scrutinised every male face. All I found was contempt on a few hard faces, fear on the rest. One man spat through the bars. Two block guards dragged him out and took him away, leaving me to the obscenities of the others. I insisted on visiting the sick bay: only one resident who was obviously not Renschman. But I knew he'd been sent here after the trial. And I knew it was him in my sights that day.

In the end, I cheated. I asked Nonna to fix up a meeting with Aemilia Fulvia. Unfortunately, the only slot was during office hours at the Department of Justice late next afternoon. I gave my sidearm in at the vestibule and was escorted through to the elevator like I didn't know where anything was. Strange being on the PGSF side of the antipathy barrier. I ignored the over-neutral glances as I rode upward in the car and stepped out on the fifth floor. I couldn't see light under Lurio's door which was a relief. My escort left me with Fulvia's assistant who buzzed me through.

'Carina, come in. Lovely to see you.' Fulvia had come out to greet me.

We kissed cheeks and she waved me to a chair. I outlined my request, described my research so far and watched her face close up. 'Is there a problem?'

'Unfortunately, records were lost during the re-securing of the facility,' she said, her eyes challenging me.

I couldn't call the justice minister a liar, but the records I'd seen three days before were complete.

'Please don't think me difficult, but I think you'll find there's been a mistake. Maybe you haven't been given the most recent update?'

'I'll certainly look into it. Thank you for alerting me to this. I'm only sorry I can't help you.'

Dismissed, I stood outside in the corridor, thinking through what had just happened. I'd been suckered. The hallway seemed narrower, confining, as I made my way back down.

Conrad listened in silence to my report early next morning but, when I'd finished, he frowned. 'Very well. We know Renschman was consigned to Truscium after his trial. I don't doubt it was him you had in your sights the day of the mutiny. Not a face you'd forget, is it? It's disturbing you found no trace of him when you visited. Worst of all is Fulvia's stonewalling.'

He tapped the palms of his hands together, saying nothing, his eyes unfocused as he gazed into the air. After a few minutes, his hand darted out to the desk commset, he punched some numbers and picked up the handset.

'Valeria? Conradus.' Now he played with a piece of paper as he listened. He laughed that rich, infectious, unbelievably sexy laugh at whatever it was she said. 'No, not for a while. Listen, I need your help. Could we meet for a drink, around six? Usual place?' He listened some more. 'Can't wait. You too. Bye.'

I waited, trying not to feel like an affronted librarian.

He scribbled on the small square of paper. 'Go and eat at this place at around five thirty, but take your time. You need to still be there when I meet Valeria. Wear something plain and neutral, and a commset, frequency eight.' He smiled at me. 'Don't look so worried. We'll find out.'

Most of the rest of my day passed in admin tasks. Around five, I signed out and changed into downmarket casuals. I dressed my hair back, removing most of my make-up, and walked into the bar carrying a discount-store plastic bag. My reward was to be treated with indifference by the serving staff as I ordered my food. I shrugged off my pressed wool coat but kept the scarf around my neck. The little bar was unremarkable except for the sleek zinc counter. I didn't know they existed outside French movies.

Conrad came in just before six. I studied him to see how such a remarkable-looking guy had toned himself down to look like an ordinary working man dropping in for a quick beer before going home. It wasn't the dull, worn clothes or scuffed sneakers: he'd rounded his shoulders and assumed a drawn, emotionless face. He crossed the room hesitantly, as if conscious of not being in the right place. He looked relieved to have reached his seat safely.

Five minutes later, a bottle-dyed brunette in a short skirt and leather boots paused in the doorway, spotted him and gave a knowing smile. She breezed over to his table and tipped her chin up for his kiss. I had the full sound effect over my commset.

'Hello, lover,' she said.

The mushrooms in my mouth tasted like rubber.

'Good to see you,' she added. 'What do you want?'

He told her not to be so cynical, smiled and asked the favour. From my vantage point, I saw her face lose some firmness. Her tongue skimmed her lower lip.

'Juno, that's some ask. I'll go as far as I can, but no promises.'

They talked on for a few minutes then she left. We made our separate ways back to Domus Mitelarum. In the atrium, we mulled over what we hadn't learned.

'I don't want Valeria to endanger herself, but I'm concerned we can't find a simple piece of information,' he said. 'It should be available to cleared personnel like her, so I'm optimistic she'll deliver. She owes me.'

I didn't want to know what exactly she owed him.

A horrible, impossible thought pushed itself out of my brain. 'Has anybody ever escaped from Truscium?'

'No. It's the highest security there is. Nobody has ever got out. Not until they finish their term. That's why Renschman was sent there. That's why they ordered in special forces to contain that last incident.' His eyes narrowed, but I was there ahead of him.

'Hades,' I said. 'You know something? He's escaped and they're refusing to admit it.'

75

I thought I'd shaken Renschman off when I left the EUS. I thought I'd seen the last of him when he was taken down after the trial, manacled, on his way to an escape-proof prison. I thought I'd killed him on a cold mountaintop.

But he kept coming back, just like the Furies.

Valeria had gotten nowhere. The case had been recalled and was *sub judice* with a minister's investigation underway. She was a chief information analyst with access to almost every government document that existed; it should have been simple.

So Conrad and I set off a day later from the PGSF headquarters in an official vehicle, with kit appropriate for an inspection tour of regional outposts. As they were strung out mainly near the borders, the trip was scheduled to take a week.

Twelve minutes after the PGSF vehicle gate closed behind us, we promptly disappeared into Domus Mitelarum, swapped to the hire MPV I'd had delivered there the day before and packed it with suitcases for hotel stays, backpacks, boots and camping equipment for off-piste activities, and, most important of all, scopes and hunting rifles. As well as taking my standard sidearm, I strapped on my carbon fibre knives. I asked Nonna to refuse all requests to track me, whoever wanted to know.

'Darling, the Styx at the entrance to Hades would have to dry up first. I'm annoyed that Aemilia Fulvia fobbed you off.' She looked at us in turn then gave us a brief nod. 'Good hunting.'

We made fast progress north, leaving open fields and pastures behind, and plunged into conifer woodland. As we pulled up that evening outside a folksy chalet hotel complete with carved balcony and checked drapes, something struck me.

'You know, when I went to see Fulvia, there was no sign of Lurio. His in-tray on the PA's desk was empty.' I narrowed my eyes, reconstructing the scene in my mind's eye. 'No, it was turned over as if he was on leave.'

'Why is that remarkable?'

'He's had his main vacation this year, three weeks' walking and hunting in Italy.'

'On assignment somewhere, perhaps?'

'No, he's desk-based, fixing political or strategic stuff for Aemilia that has to be done discreetly. I've never known him be away from the office like that.'

'Are you suggesting he may be hunting something on two legs?'

'Not necessarily, but Sentius in Organised Crime is supposedly on leave as well. He's one of Lurio's ball-carriers.'

We were the only guests. We booked up for a week as Charles and Patricia Miller of Bridgeport, CT. 'Please call us Chuck and Pat, Mrs Sertoria,' I chirruped to the owner in my best Connecticut accent as I pretended to struggle with filling out the police registration card. 'We're here looking into Chuck's ancestors and soak up some of the atmosphere of their home country – it's so exciting.'

I fed the same story to the curia clerk at Truscium that afternoon. It was thin, but it had to do. Conrad kept the clerk occupied in stilted Latin with a heavy American accent while I scanned the birth, marriage and death records. Flustered by his smile, she handed over the key to the whole record batch without filtering it first. Annoying how easily he'd manipulated her into it. He passed it to me almost casually without letting up the bantering, planted his elbows on the counter and continued flirting with her.

Over at the computer booths, I scanned the entries and printed out birth and death certificates of some random family. I couldn't believe it when I found a page marked '*Confidential – no disclosure*' listing the death records from the prison. That had been missing from the records I'd been shown on my second visit to Truscium. I hovered over the printer and snatched the page out and stuffed it in between the other printouts.

I returned to the desk where Conrad was laughing with the clerk, slipped the key across the counter and made a big fuss of counting out the correct amount of *solidi* and *denarii* for the paper I'd used. I gushed my gratitude and dragged Conrad out.

'Let's go get some coffee at that cute little bar over there, sugar,' I drawled.

'Sure, honey, great idea.'

Back in the car, I showed him the printout.

'So, no Renschman. Looks like you didn't kill him after all.'

I didn't know whether to be relieved I hadn't committed murder or miffed I had missed him.

The next day, we drove to the foot of the gorge leading up to the mine and parked up under trees twenty metres from the end of a track. We loaded up camping equipment and enough rations and water for three days onto our backs, even though we intended to only stay out one night. Two and a half thousand metres up a central European mountain in mid-February was not an ideal camping trip.

The mountains rose at acute angles from the narrow valley floor. After three hours, we stopped for a rest, some snack bars and water. It was a clear, sunny day with tiny puffball clouds in a luminous, deep-blue sky. Beautiful and treacherous. Within half an hour, it could be blizzarding. We bivouacked for the night among trees, two hundred metres below the alarmed and CCTV-monitored perimeter fence which ran fifty metres out from the edge of the mine complex. Mountain walkers were not encouraged.

The only route Renschman could have taken was by following the river down – milky green and glacially cold, with frequent steep drops. It was a hazardous trek for us in the cold and snow, but we had solid boots, carbon fibre poles and warm breathable coats and pants. Renschman, clad only in a yellow prison uniform and light shoes, would have found it exhausting and dangerous. Maybe he hadn't made it and his body was up there.

The next morning, I crawled up nearer the fence and was about to turn back when I found a tear of yellow cloth flapping in the cold wind, trapped under a stone.

'No working party ever comes outside the perimeter.' I remembered their routines from the files I studied on my official visit. 'It has to be him.'

'Not exactly conclusive, but, no, there shouldn't be anything like that here,' Conrad said. We crouched under the trees, drinking lukewarm coffee heated from the chemical burn packs and trying not to shiver in the bitter wind.

'Come on, we'll retrace and see if we can find anything else. It'll be a slow trek back.' We packed up, roughed up the earth and strewed pine needles over where we'd been.

I looked up at him, almost shyly. 'Thanks for coming up here with me, for believing in me.'

He stroked my cheek with the back of his hand. 'Silly. Of course I'd come with you. But it's beyond personal now. Renschman's a menace, and a damned clever one. If he can get out of Truscium, he's perfectly capable of starting all kinds of trouble. I want him dealt with permanently.'

76

That night, it was a relief to be back in the warm chalet under a feather comforter with Conrad, relaxed after a hot shower and warm cooked meal. I watched the man as he slept afterward, his muscled body covered in fine golden down, his skin warm on mine, one arm still looped around my waist. Despite our hunt, and the reason for it, I was content.

'Mrs Miller, I presume?'

I woke instantly, every nerve jangling. Conrad's body beside me tensed.

'Sheeyt! Who the hell is that?' I cried out in a broad Connecticut accent into the pitch-dark. The bedroom light snapped on and I found a gun barrel millimetres from my forehead.

'Oh, very good.'

Bloody Lurio. And Sentius, his semi-automatic trained on Conrad.

'What in Hades are you doing here?' I struggled up onto my elbows. He drew the weapon back. His knuckles were almost breaking through his skin.

'I might ask you the same,' he said.

I scanned Lurio's face, trying to figure out what was behind his intensity, when Conrad sprang out of the bed and slammed Sentius against the wood-panelled wall, neatly catching the pistol as it dropped from his hand. He lobbed it over to me, wrenched Sentius's arm up and, gripping his neck with his other hand, frogmarched the cop to the doorway and flung him through it. He advanced on Lurio who had twisted around ready to face Conrad, arm outstretched, Glock in hand.

'Try it,' Lurio said.

Conrad snorted.

After staring at each other for a full ten seconds, Lurio lowered his weapon, the anger in his face receding.

Conrad grabbed the door handle.

'Out. Wait downstairs.'

Lurio raised his chin, like he was going to say something, but turned and left without a word.

I was already scrambling into some clothes. 'I knew it, I knew it was wrong when I saw they were both gone.' I was trembling with rage.

Downstairs, Lurio stood by the hall stove, legs braced, arms folded, his face dull in the glow from the nightlight. The night porter was nowhere to be seen. I wouldn't have put it past Lurio to have thrown him out. Sentius was reading a tourist leaflet, but jammed it back in the display as we came down the wood stairs.

Before anybody could stop me, I walked over to Lurio and struck his face with the palm of my hand. 'What in Hades was the point of that dramatic little pantomime?'

'Temper, temper, Bruna.' He rubbed his cheek. 'Well, it got your attention.'

'Right. You like interrupting people's vacation, rousting them out at five in the morning?'

'Vacation? When you and Major Tough Guy are sneaking around a high-security area pretending to be American tourists? I don't think so.'

'I suppose you and Sentius here are looking for a venue for your next girls' outing, are you?'

It was so still that a mouse scampering across the guest house lobby would have sounded like a truck driving through. I took a deep breath. Conrad laid a hand on my arm and shook his head. I could see him exercising considerable effort to calm himself.

'Very well, inspector,' he said to Lurio, 'let's ditch the personal. I think we're both on the same search. Jeffrey Renschman's escaped, and you and Sentius are trying to catch him before it gets out. You've even got the minister lying.'

'You *have* been a busy boy, Tellus.' Lurio sat down on the cushioned bench. He shrugged. 'You're quite right. He went missing six days ago. His tracker tag was found in his bunk. How the Hades he extracted that, I'd like to know. No matter. If word gets out, we don't only look careless, but the whole concept of escape-proof is shot. We reckon we've got three, four days max left to find him before the shit hits the fan.'

'We found this,' I chipped in, and held out a plastic baggie with the scrap of yellow cloth. 'By the stream, around a hundred metres outside the south perimeter fence.'

He took it, turned it through his fingers and grunted.

'So what do you have?' Conrad asked.

'Next to nothing. The CCTV doesn't show anything out of the ordinary. We got zilch from interrogating the rest of his wing. They just smirked at us, the bastards. The only break was yesterday afternoon when a farmer reported lost property. The local station wasn't interested but the farmer insisted they log it. They're a new crew after the station was wiped out in the shoot-out a few months ago.' He paused, glancing at Sentius. 'Probably not used to dealing with stroppy old yokels. And it wasn't exactly crime incident of the millennium. The farmer had first noticed the stuff gone three days ago, but hadn't got around to reporting it.' He flicked his hand toward his companion. 'Sentius was making our fond farewells with the duty sergeant when the farmer came in. Turns out it was clothes and boots. So we've got a three day-old description.'

'If he's walked, he'll have got to the bus and railways by now,' Sentius said. 'We've put out the usual alerts and got the local teams questioning the train, bus and taxi staff.'

Conrad and I exchanged glances. Renschman would have ensured he left very little impression and covered that with a professional's expertise.

'Tell me,' I said to Lurio, breaking the silence that had intruded. 'How did you know we were here?' I had to know if we'd been sloppy.

'I could say solid police work, but it was a complete fluke. Sentius recognised you leaving the curia office when he sneaked out to buy a packet of cigarettes.'

We spent another twenty minutes throwing it around, but knew in our hearts we had nothing to go on.

Lurio stood up. 'Not much more we can do here. You'd better leave us to seal the border and try and contain him that way,' he concluded. 'It'll come out, but I suppose we'll live it down. Eventually.'

'No, it's not that easy, Lurio,' Conrad said. 'He kidnapped Carina and tried to seize her father's business. He nearly killed her in Washington and in the park last year. He got in with Palicek. He's a bloody dangerous black operator and a vindictive son of a bitch. Jupiter knows what else he'll do. He's likely to ramp it up. Apart from anything else, I'm sure he'll come after Carina again if you lot can't find him.'

'Then why don't we let him?'

The three men stared at me as if I'd made an indecent suggestion.

But none of them protested by return.

After a long thirty seconds, Lurio said, 'Not the stupidest suggestion you've ever made.'

I was pleased I'd smacked him as hard as I did.

77

Sweating, feet lacerated, Renschman had reached a farm on the outskirts of the town. He crawled into a goat pen and collapsed into sleep. A faint red glow on the eastern horizon provided the only light when he staggered out, filthy, thirsty, feet throbbing. He sluiced down in a cattle trough, washing sweat and goat shit off. He crept up to the farm buildings and opened the door inch by inch. The kitchen was unlit, empty. He made for the refrigerator and seized a carton of milk. It dribbled down his chin and neck as he gulped it down. Grabbing cold cuts, bread and a bottle of water, he stuffed them in a cloth bag from the back of the door. A muffled noise upstairs pulled his glance upwards. He cocked his ear like a wary cat and waited. Nothing. He took a jacket, shirt, trousers, socks and boots from the utility room, a small pile of *solidi* bills lying on the dresser and left on his trek to the city.

Watching the girl's house this time, he stayed well back from the high stone walls. Despite his thinner face with its furrowed scar across his forehead and the new beard, he couldn't risk the software cutting through to recognise him again.

The tall gates opened and a red car, Italian, paused in the entrance. The driver looked around, her red-gold hair shining in the early light. She wore a beige uniform shirt, military tabs and some kind of black arm patch with a gold design. He couldn't see what it was from this distance. She turned right and sped off toward the city centre.

He'd found her again. No longer a cop, but military. Going off to a cosy little office, pushing a few indents and travel orders around, no doubt. Poring over a computer in the *Biblioteca Publica*, he found the uniform. Special forces? He checked again. She must be some kind of office weenie. Sure, she'd been the bait for the drug bust, but that hardly needed such high-level specialist skills. Besides, she was a woman. All the same, he needed to be a little careful.

78

Back at the PGSF, I kept to a skeleton routine and spent a lot more time out in the open. Renschman had to know we were watching for him. I wanted to sit in the park reading my magazine, waiting for him to pounce; it would save us all time and effort. Nothing had happened after a week. Was our strategy too straightforward?

I was in the university bookshop, choosing a gift for Nonna's birthday, when a boy came up to me and asked if I was Lieutenant Mitela. I wasn't in uniform. He handed me an envelope. Remembering the previous letter I'd had from Renschman, I held it by the corner and dropped it into a plastic baggie as a precaution. But even Renschman wouldn't poison a letter to be carried by a child, would he?

I crouched down and thanked the boy. 'Could you help me out here a little more?'

He looked wary, but nodded. I smiled at him, took his hand and led him over to the service desk. I flashed my gold badge at the startled assistant.

'Back office, please. Now.' I glanced at the nervous face beside me, the dark eyes darting around. 'And a glass of milk and some cookies.'

The clerk had to tap in the entry code twice, he was so nervous. As we waited, I watched the boy demolish the honey cakes and milk. He laid the empty plate on a pile of papers on the desk and looked up at me expectantly.

A knock on the door. I signalled the child back to hide behind the door. He scurried into the corner and folded himself into a coat hanging on the back. I flicked out my carbon fibre knife and sheltered behind the edge of the slowly opening door.

'Bruna, it's Sentius. Your alarm went off.'

'Slowly, Sentius.'

His hand came through the gap, tobacco-stained fingernails holding his ID. I breathed in relief.

He saw the boy, now scared. Sentius pulled out a paper handkerchief from his pocket and dabbed the child's eyes. 'Hey, come on, come and sit with Uncle Manius.'

Did Sentius have children? He knew all the moves. The child sat happily with Sentius and babbled about how he'd been given two gold *solidi* and a chocolate pastry by a man to deliver the note. He was only about eight or nine, poor kid.

A patrol car brought us all to *Custodes* XI Station where I disinfected my and the boy's hands. My hands in plastic gloves and a mask covering my face, I drew the letter out carefully and unfolded the single sheet. I read the two simple sentences. Horror crept up on me as I took in each word.

Sentius snatched the note from my nerveless fingers, read it and dived for his commset. I called Conrad. 'He has Helena.'

Renschman had ensured I would come to him willingly, happily even. I would give him anything. I would sing and dance, and do handstands for him, for the safe return of my friend and cousin.

I fussed and fidgeted around the barracks for the rest of the day. I couldn't keep my eyes or my mind still. Renschman instructed me to meet him, alone, by the service kiosk behind the palace park theatre at ten. The same place as before. Helena would be frightened to her core. If he'd tied her up like I'd been, she'd freeze. The memory washed through me. Bastard. He wouldn't have killed her already. No. I couldn't let myself believe that.

A PGSF hostage psychologist briefed me on what to expect, how to act, what to say. My Active Response Team – Flavius, Paula, Livius and Atria – plus Daniel had deployed already to the park, well hidden, ready to act. I made it clear that the minute Helena was safe, their prime target was Renschman. I made a will, addressed to the censor's office as well as a copy for Nonna.

Conrad and I went back to my room. A while later, I pulled myself away from him, got up out of the bed, showered and made myself a drink. I wept quietly as I sat watching him sleep. He woke. I smiled at him. I glanced at my watch. An hour to go.

I took some high-energy tabs and a cup of the malt and ginger drink as we waited. Conrad would drive me to the park gate.

The moon was full and every leaf, branch and stone was outlined in sharp silver light. I wore warm walking pants, roll top sweater with shirt underneath and fleece and reinforced sneakers on my feet. As I walked through the park gate and along the path, I was calm and prepared. Maybe it was my time.

His silhouette emerged from behind the stone theatre semi-circle when I was around twenty metres away.

'Stop.'

His breath plumed out in the chill temperature.

'Three-sixty turn, arms stretched out.'

I complied.

'Advance. Slowly.'

I stopped five metres from him. He had a Glock semi-automatic tucked in his waistband.

'Did I tell you to stop?'

'I need to see my cousin.'

'If you disobey me, you're going to make me kill her.'

'If you kill her then you lose me.'

He half-turned and pulled a female figure into view, hands behind her. It looked like Helena.

'Carina. Don't—'

He slapped her, hard. The high pitch of the staccato contact on her skin echoed in the clear night, followed by her cry and sobbing.

I compressed the rising red flood inside me back down.

'Send her forward, Renschman. I need to see her properly and check she's unhurt.'

He pulled her round in a circle. Her right ankle was tied with a short rope to the lamp post by the theatre wall, so she couldn't run. Crap.

'She's all there. You come here and she can go on her way.'

'No, you'll have us both.'

He stooped and picked up a coil of rope, looped one end and threw the rest at me.

'Guess I'll have to reel you in. Now you do exactly as I tell you or I'll slit her throat from ear to ear, and you can watch her bleed to death. That image will haunt you for the rest of your life.'

He held a knife against her throat and nicked her skin enough to release a dribble of blood along the length of the cut.

I swallowed hard and just about resisted the urge to close my eyes.

'What do you want me to do?' I asked.

'Make a nice strong double loop, with slip knots. No cheating now. Then you're going to slide your wrists in and pull tight. I don't want you running off before we've finished.'

Shit.

'Not until you cut her loose. She has to walk free the minute I put my hand through the loops.'

'Dear me, don't you trust me, Miss Brown?'

He had totally lost it. He was completely crazy.

'No. Now let her go.'

I made the slip loops. I stared at them as if they were hangman's nooses. I put my left wrist in and tightened it. I raised it, rope falling in a slim line so he could see. He bent and cut Helena's tether and pushed her forward as I slipped in my right wrist and held both up. She came up beside me.

'Carina,' she whispered.

I smiled at her and said, 'Run like Hades.' I watched her stumble toward the gate and closed my eyes in relief. He jerked the rope and I stumbled and fell. He dragged me across the gap and stood over me.

'Now we can finish our conversation.'

79

He pulled me to my feet and secured the rope to a metal loop cemented into the back wall of the theatre. My wrists rested at the back of my waist.

'Wire?'

The hostage specialist had instructed me not to make any smart-ass remarks. She said I mustn't stir him up.

So I nodded and looked down at the ground as he pulled the wireless mesh out from under my roll top. He forced my mouth open, searching for a tooth mic. After he yanked both my ears and found nothing, he grunted, apparently satisfied. He frisked me thoroughly, professionally.

'Nice knife. I think I'll keep that.' He slashed it through the air, leaned in and drew it across my jaw and neck. The sharp sting surprised me. I gasped. Blood trickled down my neck, inside my sweater, over my collarbone.

He pulled a wood crate out of the kiosk and sat on it. He fished a small device with a screen out of a black rucksack and set it up. Next, he unfolded a small collapsed cup on the top, which started rotating when he switched the device on and inserted a wireless earpiece into his right ear.

'I'll be able to detect if any of your friends are foolish enough to think of rescuing you. I'll be very disappointed if they do because I'll have to shoot you, which will be far too quick a death. I have something much more interesting in mind for you. '

I couldn't help glancing at the listening device. It looked like something out of toy town compared with our detection field projectors.

'Ah, you're wondering where a convicted prisoner could lay his hands on this kind of technology.' He smiled. 'Your left-luggage facilities here are not time-limited. You never know when you might need a little stash of equipment in a foreign environment. What a wonderful country.'

My neck and jaw began to throb. I stretched my fingers a centimetre at a time up to the cuff of my right shirt sleeve, easing the edge flap away to release a tiny titanium cutter with lethally sharp teeth. But it wasn't the fastest technique ever.

'But we've come to the end game now.'

His urbane mask dissolved. His eyes flared like some feral creature. The corners of his mouth tightened downwards as his expression solidified into something harsher and destructive.

'You don't have a clue, do you? You don't know about your hero father and his sordid little past, do you?'

What in Hades was he talking about?

'No. You don't. Maybe I would have been a little kinder if you'd remained an innocent. But you've caused me so much trouble all by yourself, I'm going to enjoy destroying you for your own sake.'

I started sawing, shifting my weight from foot to foot to mask my movements.

He leaned back, totally relaxed, as if he were in an armchair at some country club relating his last fishing trip. He drew out a cigarette from a packet in his shirt pocket, lit it and inhaled deeply.

'William Brown, the Somalia Dawn hero, was married before he met your crazy mother. He married Donna Renschman.' He looked into the distance. 'My mother. He waited until she was six months pregnant. Nice story, huh?'

I hadn't lost enough blood to be delirious, so I must have been hearing right.

'He divorced her when I was six. I left the project we were forced to live in when I was seventeen and went into the military. I heard my

336

father had remarried – some European woman. Your mother. But he didn't want to know me when I called one day.'

My father would never have rejected his child like that. Would he? This shocking thought must have passed across my face.

Renschman looked at me and snorted. 'Oh, he was truly polite with his nice middle-class manners, but he closed me out. I was just sixteen. He gave me sixty-three dollars. Sixty-three dollars. Christ.'

His eyes were boiling now, hard and grey. I knew what it was to be poor and unloved at sixteen. But I hadn't become a vicious, amoral killer.

'I stood on the outside step in the teeming rain. I beat on the door for ten whole minutes. Nobody answered.' He spoke to the ground, scattering gravel with the tip of his foot. 'I'd heard how rich he had become. I promised myself I would have some of that. And I would have had all of it, if you'd died when you should have.'

He assessed me with a now-calm but granite-hard expression. 'I can still do that now. An American court would give me Brown Industries.' He paused. 'Once you're dead.'

He was insane. No possible doubt.

I swallowed. Juno, my neck hurt. 'You don't have to kill me, Jeffrey. I'll sign it over to you.'

'Too late, far too late, Karen.'

He stood up and came toward me with the stub of his cigarette. I smelled the acrid smoke. The heat touched my skin. I braced myself for the burn, the pain. He grazed the lobe of my ear, paused and ground it out on the wall. I closed my eyes, trying to block out the smell of my singed flesh.

A tiny scrape on the gravel. Renschman's head jerked up. He braced himself, balancing his weight evenly on his feet. The semi-automatic was already there, with scope. He paused, listening. A black figure ran straight across in front of him, left to right, and vanished. Another diagonally. Another, opposite diagonal. He fired at that one. Another ran across behind.

'Think you can get me like that?' he shouted to the air. He moved over and grabbed hold of my hair, the Glock on my temple. 'One more and she's dead.'

Total silence.

He waited for a few minutes, glued to my side, his breath crawling over my face and neck. I struggled not to shiver. When he moved away from me, he bent down to retrieve something from his bag. A shot rang out, only missing him because he rose quickly. He rolled, fired and jumped back to the wall next to me. He stamped on my instep with the force of his body weight. I lost my breath. My foot went numb. Then rolls of pain pulsed through the crushed flesh. I fought it, but couldn't help shrieking out at the agony.

'One more and I'll throw a body part out.'

I forced myself to take even breaths. The tiny saw was nearly through the rope holding my wrists. I had to keep going. Warm liquid, my blood, seeped down over my fingers. I prayed the saw wouldn't slip through my fingers.

'This time, I'm going to make sure you're really dead before I leave.' His warm breath on my face repelled me. 'Your toy knife will be perfect. They won't recognise the corpse. Ever heard of the death by a thousand cuts? I have a modern version all worked out for you, starting with your face.'

He was so intent on me that he didn't sense them. By the time he heard them, they were on us. He swung and fired. One figure dropped; he advanced to meet the next. He fired, turned and ran back to me, murder in his eyes. His hand swung the Glock up to kill me.

I tensed my arms and jerked my wrists free of the last threads of the rope, tearing more flesh. I brought my fists together in front and slammed them upward against the underside of his right arm. The Glock flew through the air. I kneed him in the groin. He doubled forward in pain. I chopped the back of his neck with vicious strength. He should have collapsed. He shook his head and charged at me, but his feet were slow. As he staggered, I twisted sideways and kicked his right kneecap with my steel-capped sneaker. Eye-watering pain raced up my leg as my damaged back foot took the recoil and my full weight.

The crunch of bone was echoed by his scream as his shattered knee landed on the concrete. He pushed up on his left side, but I slammed him down on the ground. I straddled him and struck his face with my fist, the jagged saw round my left wrist ripping his and my skin. He caught it and punched me in the base of my ribcage. Pain seared through my chest and I bit through my lip. My eyes blurred for a few seconds as my breath was suspended. He bucked and pushed me off.

He rolled over, crouched in an attempt to stand. The moonlight reflected the shine of sweat on his face. His balled fist swung around wildly near me, but I was faster. I pulled away and struggled up, gasping for breath. My foot was pure agony from Tartarus, but I kicked him hard in the ribs with my good one. He fell, grunting, hitting his head with a heavy thud. I dropped on him. I hit him. And hit him. I would have pulped him but somebody seized my hands and held them.

'Stop. Stop it. Now.'

My lungs were heaving and sore, my head throbbing, I trembled with fury and adrenalin. My nose and eyes ran.

'Stop, Carina. You've won. You've defeated him. He's finished.'

80

I limped to the bathroom. No way was I going through the humiliation of a bedpan. My whole middle ached, and my neck and wrists were engulfed in bandages. Above my stitched and swollen lip, a large purple bruise bloomed on my face, matching the one showing each side of the strapping on my left foot. Only the reinforced upper of my sneaker had stopped my foot being broken. I looked like a cross between an Egyptian mummy and a suicider.

A medic found me truanting and put me back to bed, where I regained my breath and the throbbing receded. I couldn't put myself under, I couldn't focus enough, but drugged up with painkillers, I managed to nap for an hour. The medical director breezed in after lunch when my grandmother was visiting with me. Inevitably, they knew each other. The senior doctor with her gave me my report, none of which I didn't know already.

'But I'm very pleased to confirm the pregnancy is still intact.'

Nonna looked at me, eyebrow raised. I flushed, which made my face hurt like Hades. I'd only missed by ten days. It could have been stress.

I woke later to find Conrad holding my hand and smiling at me. He tucked an errant curl falling across my face back into the paper hat.

'Rested?'

I nodded. 'Helena?'

'She's fine. Shocked, some scrapes and bruises, face just like yours.'

Renschman had been hospitalised in the secure wing. The knee injury alone would immobilise him for some time, but the blow on his head when he fell had put him into a coma. If he recovered, he would live out the rest of his life in a high-security wing of a mental hospital, not at Truscium. Lurio said the minister was humbly grateful for our help. I would really have liked to hear her say that. Flavius had a flesh wound from his run-past.

After a few minor details, Conrad clammed up. The first two fingers of his right hand rubbed at the hairline at his temple.

'Tell me.'

He looked down. 'Sentius. He—'

But I knew.

'He insisted on being in the runners-by. It's a risky tactic. Perhaps I should have barred him. But whoever it was would have been a casualty.' He gently rubbed the back of my hand. 'I'm so sorry.'

I wept for Sentius: my supporter during the Goldlights debrief, my colleague in the DJ, my friend. Dressed in my formal PGSF uniform, leaning on a cane, I stood ten days later by his funeral pyre and threw on my libation through the smoke. It didn't really help.

Renschman's revelations were true. Stephen Smith called me from New York after he'd investigated further. Renschman's original birth records had been buried when he'd started black operations. But the DNA tests proved we were half-brother and sister. Further digging showed my father had made good provision for Jeffrey and his mother, including a house and a monthly allowance, but she'd drunk it. Still, I wish I'd known.

I wondered whether I should feel something. Anything. But I didn't. Not now. Maybe in time, when I'd processed it.

The day I left hospital and told Conrad about the baby, he gave me his mother's gold ring. I knew I would always love him. I asked him to join my family formally, and we married the day after I left work on maternity leave. We followed the traditional form: clasping hands, exchanging vows, and he signed away his own family name and took mine. But when Helena handed me the open torch and crystal cup of water to exchange with Conrad, the flickering, intense heat of the flame and the iciness of the water reminded me of everything we had endured together.

I returned to work four months after our daughter, Allegra, was born. A week after I settled back in, Conrad strolled into the bullring, officially called the PGSF duty room, a report sheet in his hand, and made his way over to my shabby desk. I glimpsed flickers of interest in the faces of the other juniors. Nobody had really figured out how to handle the dynamic of our new formal relationship.

'Lieutenant,' he said, his face neutral. He handed me the sheet. 'Customs report some suspicious activity in the mountains north of Aquae Caesaris. They think somebody's using the old smuggler routes. Take your team up there for a few days and discourage them, please.'

'Sir.' I stood up, bending down to pick my jacket off the back of the chair. Faces swivelled back to their screens.

'Good hunting.'

I nodded, gave him a brief smile and left.

The story continues in PERFIDITAS...

WOULD YOU LEAVE A REVIEW?

I hope you enjoyed INCEPTIO, the beginning of Carina's
Roma Nova adventure.

If you did, I'd really appreciate it if you would write a few words of
review on the site where you purchased this book.

Reviews help INCEPTIO feature more prominently on retailer sites
and introduce more people to the world of Roma Nova.

Very many thanks!

HISTORICAL NOTE

What if King Harold had won the Battle of Hastings in 1066? Or if Julius Caesar had taken notice of the warning that assassins wanted to murder him on the Ides of March? Or the Spanish Armada had defeated and conquered England in 1588? Suppose Christianity had remained a Middle East minor cult?

Alternative history stories, which allow us to explore the 'what if', are underpinned by three things: the point of divergence when the alternate timeline split from our timeline; how that world looks and works; and how things changed after the split.

INCEPTIO focuses on one main character, Karen/Carina, and her struggle to overcome her personal and professional challenges in a baffling environment as well as to stay alive. I have dropped background history about Roma Nova into the novel only where she (and the reader) needs to know it as part of the story. Nobody likes a straight history lesson in the middle of a thriller! But if you are interested in a little more information about this mysterious country, read on...

What happened in our timeline

Of course, our timeline may turn out to be somebody else's alternate as shown in Philip K Dick's *The Grasshopper Lies Heavy*, the story within the story in *The Man in the High Castle*. Nothing is fixed. But for the sake of convenience I will take ours as the default.

The Western Roman Empire didn't 'fall' in a cataclysmic event as often portrayed in film and television; it localised and eventually dissolved like chain mail fragmenting into separate links, giving way to rump provinces, local city states and petty kingdoms. The Eastern Roman Empire survived until the Fall of Constantinople in 1453 to the Muslim Ottoman Empire.

Some scholars think that Christianity fatally weakened the traditional Roman way of life and was a significant factor in the collapse of the Empire. Emperor Constantine's personal conversion to Christianity in AD 313 was a turning point for the new religion. By AD 394, his several times successor, Theodosius, banned all traditional Roman religious practice, closed and destroyed temples and dismissed all priests.

The sacred flame that had burned for over a thousand years in the College of Vestals was extinguished and the Vestal Virgins expelled. The Altar of Victory, said to guard the fortune of Rome, was hauled away from the Senate building and disappeared from history.

The Roman senatorial families pleaded for religious tolerance, but Theodosius made any pagan practice, even dropping a pinch of incense on a family altar in a private home, into a capital offence. And his 'religious police' driven by the austere and ambitious bishop Ambrosius of Milan, became increasingly active in pursuing pagans...

The alternate Roma Nova timeline

In AD 395, three months after the final blow of Theodosius' last decree banning all pagan religions, over four hundred Romans loyal to the old gods, and so in danger of execution, trekked north out of Italy to a semi-mountainous area similar to modern Slovenia. Led by Senator Apulius at the head of twelve senatorial families, they established a colony based initially on land owned by Apulius' Celtic father-in-law. By purchase, alliance and conquest, this grew into Roma Nova.

Norman Davies in *Vanished Kingdoms: The History of Half-Forgotten Europe* reminds us that:

...in order to survive, newborn states need to possess a set of viable internal organs, including a functioning executive, a defence force, a

revenue system and a diplomatic force. If they possess none of these things, they lack the means to sustain an autonomous existence and they perish before they can breathe and flourish.

I would add history and willpower as essential factors. Roma Nova survived by changing its social structure; as men constantly fought to defend the new colony, women took over the social, political and economic roles, weaving new power and influence networks based on family structures. Eventually, the daughters as well as sons had to put on armour and carry weapons to defend their homeland and their way of life. Service to the state was valued higher than personal advantage, echoing Roman Republican virtues, and the women heading the families guarded and enhanced these values to provide a core philosophy throughout the centuries.

Roma Nova's continued existence has been favoured by three factors: the discovery and exploitation of high-grade silver in their mountains, their efficient technology, and their robust response to any threat. Remembering their Byzantine cousins' defeat in the Fall of Constantinople, Roma Novan troops assisted the western nations at the Battle of Vienna in 1683 to halt the Ottoman advance into Europe. Nearly two hundred years later, they used their diplomatic skills to help forge an alliance to push Napoleon IV back across the Rhine as he attempted to expand his grandfather's empire.

Prioritising survival, Roma Nova remained neutral in the Great War of the 20th century which lasted from 1925 to 1935. The Greater German Empire, stretching from Jutland in the north, Alsace in the west, Tyrol in the south and Bulgaria in the east, was broken up afterwards into its former small kingdoms, duchies and counties. Some became republics. There was no sign of an Austrian-born corporal with a short, square moustache.

The time of INCEPTIO

Twenty-three years before the action of INCEPTIO in the early 21st century, Roma Nova was nearly destroyed by a coup, a brutal male-dominated consulship and civil war. A weak leader, sclerotic and outmoded systems that had not developed since the last great reform in the 1700s and a neglected economy let in a clever and ruthless tyrant. But with characteristic resilience, the families' structures fought back and reconstructed their society, re-learning the basic principles of Republican virtue, while subtly changing it to a more representational model for modern times. Today, the tiny country has become one of the highest per capita income states in the world.

THE ROMA NOVA THRILLER SERIES

The Carina Mitela adventures

INCEPTIO

Early 21st century. Terrified after a kidnap attempt, New Yorker Karen Brown, has a harsh choice – being terminated by government enforcer Renschman or fleeing to Roma Nova, her dead mother's homeland in Europe. Founded sixteen hundred years ago by Roman exiles and ruled by women, it gives Karen safety – at a price. But Renschman follows and sets a trap she has no option but to enter.

CARINA – A novella

Carina Mitela is a new officer in the Praetorian Guard Special Forces. Disgraced for a disciplinary offence, she is sent out of everybody's way to bring back a traitor from the Republic of Quebec. But the conspiracy reaches into the highest levels of Roma Nova…

PERFIDITAS

Falsely accused of conspiracy, 21st century Praetorian Carina Mitela flees into the criminal underworld. Hunted by both security services and traitors she struggles to save her beloved Roma Nova as well as her own life. Who is her ally and who her enemy? But the ultimate betrayal is waiting for her.

SUCCESSIO

21st century Praetorian Carina Mitela's attempt to resolve a past family indiscretion is spiralling into a nightmare of blackmail and terror. Convinced her beloved husband has deserted her and her children, and with her enemy holding a gun to the imperial heir's head, Carina has to make the hardest decision of her life.

The Aurelia Mitela adventures

AURELIA

Late 1960s. Sent to Berlin to investigate silver smuggling, former Praetorian Aurelia Mitela barely escapes a near-lethal trap. Her old enemy is at the heart of all her troubles and she pursues him back home to Roma Nova but he strikes at her most vulnerable point – her young daughter.

NEXUS – A novella

Mid 1970s. Aurelia Mitela is serving as ambassador in London. Helping a British colleague to find his missing son, Aurelia is sure he'll turn up.

But a spate of high-level killings pulls Aurelia away into a pan-European investigation and the killers threaten to terminate her life companion.

But Aurelia is a Roma Novan – they never give up…

INSURRECTIO

Early 1980s. Caius Tellus, the charismatic leader of a rising nationalist movement, threatens to destroy Roma Nova.

Aurelia Mitela, ex-Praetorian and imperial councillor, attempts to counter the growing fear and instability. But it may be too late to save Roma Nova from meltdown and herself from destruction by her lifelong enemy….

RETALIO

1980s Vienna. Aurelia Mitela chafes at enforced exile. She barely escaped from her nemesis, Caius Tellus, who grabbed power in Roma Nova.

Aurelia is determined to liberate her homeland. But Caius's manipulations have ensured that she is ostracised by her fellow exiles.

Powerless and vulnerable, she fears she will never see Roma Nova again.

ROMA NOVA EXTRA

A collection of short stories

Four historical and four present day and a little beyond

A young tribune is sent to a backwater in 370 AD for practising the wrong religion – his lonely sixty-fifth descendant labours in the 1980s to reconstruct her country. A Roma Novan imperial councillor attempting to stop the Norman invasion of England in 1066 – her 21st century Praetorian descendant flounders as she searches for her own happiness.

Some are love stories, some lessons learned, some resolve tensions or unrealistic visions, some are adventures. Above all, they tell of people with dilemmas and in conflict, and of their courage and effort to resolve them.